THE CASE
OF
THE
PERSIAN
PLAGUE

Also Available From This Author

The MacMaster Chronicles
Honorable Assassin
Killer To Die For
Fallen Star

THE CASE
OF
THE
PERSIAN
PLAGUE

BOOK FOUR OF
THE MACMASTER CHRONICLES

a novel by

Jason Lord Case

NEW YORK

ISBN: 978-0-9825616-0-7

Published by Red Petal Press, New York.

Book and Cover Design by Red Petal Press
Cover photograph courtesy of PhotoXpress

For Gordon Douglas.

Chapter One
Deputy Rothchild

Deputy Rothchild checked his tie in the reflection afforded by the glass over an advertisement for a popular play. His tie was silk but not gaudy; a reserved color with a thin diagonal stripe. It was newer and sharper than his off-the-rack suit. He checked his impeccable shave and his perfectly professional haircut.

The Director had not summoned Deputy Rothchild for some time, but it never paid to look shabby when the call did come. There was also no excuse for not showing up post-haste. His day-to-day activities were immediately suspended by the summons. Few people would miss him at his mundane, paper-pushing, government job. It was just a front for his real activities, though he was strictly required to show up on time daily unless otherwise engaged.

The last time the call had come, it was regarding that Syrian terrorist threat. The assignment had not gone as well as had been hoped, "But," the deputy mused with pursed lips "at least we only lost one citizen and one agent." The scar across his chest itched, reminding him how close he had come to being decommissioned on that job.

Rothchild squinted against the rare sunshine as he exited from the darkness of the railway tunnel. He stood out like a single blood cell in the arteries of the city. This district of clerks, jurists and bankers led to standard clothing. The quality and age of the suits differed but those who stuck out were those not thus attired. The lack of available parking had even the most prosperous riding the underground and eating their lunches in the dozens of small, exclusive local restaurants when they did not bring bagged lunches.

The internet café that Deputy Rothchild entered had redeeming features that drew a great deal of business, including many couples. The booths had highly polished hardwood walls from the floor to the ceiling that had been sound-deadened with insulation. The booths also had solid wooden doors with stout locks. There were no terminals in the café, but each booth had high-speed cable connections sprouting from rich, walnut tables and supported wireless connections as well. The soft leather seats were cleaned constantly along with the walls and floors. It was not unusual for customers to arrive in the morning and not leave until late. The front doors were never locked though business was negligible at night. The owner was comfortably and constantly reaping a small fortune from his innovative business; he did not need the additional contribution provided by the one booth in the back, which was almost never available to the usual customers. This was the booth to which Deputy Rothchild was guided. He was provided with a cup of tea as he waited a short time, with the door closed but not locked.

The deputy fidgeted a bit, wishing he had been in closer proximity to his laptop computer when he had gotten the call. It was not the data on the hard drive he was missing, which was statistical data for the London Census Bureau. For one thing, nobody entered the internet cafés without a computer of some sort. For another thing, he could not open the other door without computing power of some sort, and he was loathe to borrow the owner's private machine even though it was available to him. The owner was not currently on hand, and though he had been directed to the private booth without question, Rothchild still preferred to wait. He picked a bit of lint off his suit and reviewed what he had seen as he entered. There had been nothing to alarm him in the slightest, but old habits die hard.

The door opened and another man entered, looking almost exactly the same as the deputy. Both men had pasty skin from not enough sunlight and blonde hair cut in the same current style. Neither of them wore any facial hair, and their suits were the same color though the newcomer's tie was polyester. He also carried both a laptop computer and an umbrella. The two men greeted each other tersely, each simply nodding slightly and saying "Deputy." The umbrella went into the ornate cast iron stand by the door, and the laptop was plugged into the access cable and power outlet without ceremony.

A knock on the door announced a cup of tea and a couple of biscuits for the newcomer. Before the door was closed behind the waiter, a third man arrived dressed in the same nondescript suit. He had a walking stick with a contoured handle and a laptop computer, though he did not plug in his equipment nor park his stick in the stand. The third man declined a cup of tea. The two already inhabiting the cubicle exchanged the same terse greetings, and the third man locked the door. Then they got down to business.

The web site accessed from this room was the only one accessible here, and without a password no page could be opened here at all. The cable in this booth was dedicated and needed to be turned on from the counter where the coffee, tea and biscuits were ordered. Since the door was usually locked, there was seldom comment about the dead line. In this case, there were three people so each entered a different password and with the final press of the enter key, a door opened in the back of the booth. Hydraulic pistons slid back the polished wooden wall and exposed a set of dusty narrow stairs heading downward. The door closed automatically behind the last man as they began to descend. The second deputy to enter grumbled about the lack of illumination and opined that he was going to fall down the stairs and break a leg one of these days.

The stairs ended with a dimly lit underground passageway, several hundred meters long, terminating at a steel security door. The peeling paint attested to the age of the door, evidence that the internet café was not the first business to be used as access to this facility. The door had been updated with a keypad for access at some time in the past. It had not received the retina scan or fingerprint recognition systems so commonly in use elsewhere in the government, nor had it gotten a fresh coat of paint.

Once again, all three men entered their passwords and gained access. When the door opened, one inadvertently made a brief sneer over the smell that issued. Deputy Rothchild had been here enough times to expect it and the third man simply had enough self-control to ignore it.

The circular underground chamber was redolent with stale tobacco and the musty smell of mold. The ventilation systems were as old as the chamber itself and in need of replacement, but the government funding was difficult to procure due to the secretive nature of its very existence. Any renovations to the area would possibly expose its existence to tradesmen or the general public. This was undesirable enough to forestall upgrades to the system, possibly forever.

A small, wizened gnome of a man whose pallor made his visitors pale skin seem healthy by comparison sat at the head of a large table that dominated much of the room. The walls were covered by computer screens displaying images from secret cameras at the entrance, feeds from spy satellites, reams of data, wanted posters, maps and constantly changing images from CNN, USPN, BBC and a hundred other networks not so easily identifiable or understandable. The circular wall of screens was broken by a couple of closed doors, in addition to the entrance the deputies had negotiated.

The man at the head of the table did not stand, though it was not immediately apparent that he could not. The huge pipe he clenched between his teeth was fuming furiously, the smoke slowly drawn into a vent in the ceiling. He was dressed in the flowing robes of a Persian in contrast with his stark white skin. The robes hid the hump of his back and flowed over his useless legs. His thick glasses magnified his eyes, quick and sharp, somehow belying his physical faults. His hair was wild and unkempt, mixing with the smoke from his pipe in a seemingly symbiotic manner.

"Please be seated." His voice brooked no argument, telling of long years of responsibility and command.

There were more chairs than deputies, but the portfolios spread on the table were at the near end. The three deputies seated themselves and began to examine the documents and photographic reproductions that had been laid out for them.

"James, please bring water for our guests." The Director's voice had barely ceased when one of the doors opened and an ancient man in a butler's uniform entered pushing a cart with a pitcher of water and eight glasses on top. On the middle shelf of the cart was a collection of bottles, none of which contained a less potent fluid than 80-proof liquor. On the bottom shelf was a collection of ale, stout and porter. The invitation was obvious but none of the three deputies elected to take advantage of it. They did accept a glass of water each. The piercing eyes of their host noted the reactions of each as if they were lab animals presented with an experimental choice.

"As you can see from your portfolios, we have a situation. I feared this sort of thing would happen after Turkey annexed Northern Iraq. Truthfully, that section of Turkey should never have been given to the Persians. I fully expected it would be retaken when the Americans invaded Iraq from the South. If I remember, the Turkish government made that offer at the beginning of that ill-fated invasion. That, however, is not our concern. The Crown gave up all rights to that area almost a century ago."

"This will be a next to impossible task unless there is more information than this," quipped Deputy Forster.

"Next to impossible and impossible are two different

things, Mr. Forster. Do you mean that we cannot assist our Turkish allies in retrieving a British subject?"

"It will be difficult. Not fully impossible. We need native allies and money to determine where the victim has been taken. Not Turkish contacts, but original Kurdish inhabitants or we will never succeed. We will end up in an information vacuum with a target on our foreheads."

"Mr. Forster, I had no intention of sending any of the three of you into that region. Not only is it too politically volatile but the Crown cannot be implicated in dealings with terrorists. It is bad enough that we are in communication with the enemy by e-mail. They are not as primitive as they once were. These communications are not secure; scrambled, yes, but still not secure. We must use an independent on this; one without dedicated ties to the Commonwealth."

Deputy Rothchild made a studied effort not to appear as relieved as he was, in truth. He resisted the urge to scratch his chest where the scar itched suddenly. "Who then, Director, will spearhead this operation?"

"I was thinking MacMaster."

The steely self control that the three deputies had exhibited when the news was given that they would not be assigned to the Middle East operation all but gave way with the new bit of information: Deputy Forster's eyes closed, Deputy Rothchild examined his tie and Deputy Phillips chewed the inside of his lip and knocked the tip of his cane three times on the hard cement floor. The Director's lips took on a small, twisted smile as he saw their reactions. "Is there a problem with that, Gentlemen?" he asked.

"Director, um…" Deputy Forster began but fell into an uncomfortable silence.

"Director," Deputy Rothchild took over. "Gordon MacMaster is a mad Scottish bull. I am sure you have not forgotten the Peruvian affair?"

"Yes, I remember. A highly efficient ending to a sloppy

affair. A bit extreme but efficient."

"A bit extreme? Director, he brought down a mountain on a small village. If efficiency means killing everyone in the area then, yes, it was efficient but hardly subtle." Deputy Phillips was on the verge of scolding his superior.

The Director was unfazed. "No one died that was not engaged in cocaine production. Nobody but the drug syndicate missed them and they were replaced within days. Agent MacMaster completed his mission and when he was done, nobody knew he had been there. He was extricated without further incident, and the entire affair was written off as a natural circumstance. If every mission went off that well at the end I would consider my life's work fulfilled." The steel in The Director's voice preempted any further argument.

"I don't like it." Phillips looked at the two who were dressed as he was and got silent confirmation. They did not like Gordon MacMaster's work though he had never been accused of not being thorough.

"Perhaps we should review that bit of work to clarify just what did happen according to the press."

The Director scooted his wheelchair over to a terminal at the wall and accessed the Peruvian newspaper, La Industria from Chimbote. "This is the only newspaper that actually printed the story. It was squashed by, of all things, the weather. El Niño hit rather hard that year and the earthquake that accompanied it was much more dramatic news. As a fishing town, Chimbote is much more interested in the affairs of the sea than some. Ah, here it is. Give me a second... There!"

A picture popped up on the screen along with the headline *El Castigo de Dios?* The picture was of the remains of a fortified mansion, built abutting a cliff. Access was restricted from the front by the walls of a narrow canyon. It looked to be as secure a location as a Swiss bank until one focused on the carnage wreaked by the avalanche that had wiped it out.

The Director smiled sarcastically at the three men visiting his stronghold. "You see, gentlemen, the rumor mill has once again churned out unpalatable grist that sits not well in the stomach, but rises again and again in ever changing form. When I said efficient, I meant efficient. Humberto Juancarlo de Humacao thought he was above national and international law. It seems he was not above the natural law of gravity however. The most local newspaper reported it as the Wrath of God and the international press never even picked up the story until weeks later. Then, with the area clear of our agents, we turned it into front-page news to overshadow a different event and blamed it on the seismic instability of the area. There was no slaughter of innocents, as you believed."

"Gentlemen, I rely on field agents for my information, not newspapers. If you cannot give me more reliable information than this then I need a different set of agents. I cannot believe you swallowed the story of the village being buried without some research. It is not as though you do not have resources. A simple search would have revealed the extent of the assault, and yet, you allowed your own prejudices to let you believe what you wanted to believe." The Director's voice was getting rough and he called for James to bring him a porter. The Deputies were relieved to accept two stouts and a porter. They drank in silence, embarrassed by their lack of knowledge.

After a few minutes The Director began again. "There is some information I cannot access from here. For instance, where is Gordon MacMaster? He effectively disappeared after his last official assignment. Is he available for service? Can he be contacted? Is he living with the South American woman he was reported to have taken under his wing? I expect you to answer these questions for me within 24 hours."

"Yes, Director," answered Deputy Forster, "he is

available."

"You know this?"

"Yes, sir, our intelligence is only weeks old. He has taken his Argentine woman to the American State of Colorado where he has taken up residence in the woods. Costilla County, I think, in the mountains."

"Well, you've almost redeemed yourself."

"I'm not sure of that, sir. The wilds of Colorado may be a daunting area to locate a man in."

"Mr. Phillips, you will go to Colorado and locate Gordon MacMaster, retain him and apprise him of the Arab situation. I do not expect to see you again until you have completed this simple mission. If you find you cannot accomplish this mission, I never expect to see you again.

Mr. Forster, you will provide Mr. Phillips with all the information in your possession and then proceed to Greece. Mr. Particka has the physical end of our bargain sealed up there.

Mr. Rothchild, you will move the liquid assets to Athens."

"That's a large load of cash to transport on a commercial airline, sir."

"Yes, Mr. Rothchild that is a large liquid load. That is why you have been given the assignment and that is why you will be accompanied by Agent Sylvan. The two of you are to be a couple from Surrey vacationing in Greece. Agent Sylvan speaks a passable Greek and has been cleared by Internal Security. She knows very little of the nature of the operation and has no need to know more. The two of you will not leave sight of each other or the payload for a second."

"I'm sure I can accomplish that." Deputy Rothchild's demeanor relaxed and he smiled widely. He took a final draught of his stout and sat back.

"Yes," The Director's sneer was a mix of disgust and appreciation, "I'm sure you can. Are there any questions at this point?"

Deputy Rothchild was the first to ask the question that was hanging in the air. "What makes this man worth the expense and potential scandal of our involvement?"

The Director fixed him with a cold stare. "That, sir, is none of your concern. You have been given an assignment and you will carry it out. The larger picture is nothing you have the political or mental resources to appreciate. You will perform your duties as described and reap the benefits thereof. If, at some point in the future, I deign to apprise you of the Service's motivations in this matter then you will have been so informed. Until that point, you will act as though God himself has spoken to you. Is every one in agreement?"

When nobody said a word, James was summoned back with a bottle of Canadian whiskey and four large glasses. The deputies were less appreciative of the whiskey than the beer, though the whiskey was a good blend. After a couple of rounds their tongues loosened and the questions started to flow more openly. The Director did not allow them to become soused and it was unlikely that they would have done so, but once they were a bit looser planning actually improved.

Chapter Two
San Luis Valley

Under the guise of an astronomer/geologist looking
for asteroid fragments, Deputy Phillips learned that the San
Luis Valley of Colorado is the largest high-mountain valley in
the world. At 7500 feet above sea level and ringed by the
Sangre de Cristo and San Juan Mountains, it encompasses
8000 square miles, roughly a twelfth of the size of the Island
of Great Britain. This was daunting until he subsequently
learned that the population of Castillo County was less than
4000 inhabitants and 800 of them lived in the county seat.

When he arrived in the town of San Luis he went
immediately to the Hall of Records, somewhat of a misnomer
for the basement of the Castillo County Courthouse. There,
under the dim light of a 40-watt bulb, he went through the
records of recent real estate purchases. Nothing was listed
under Gordon MacMaster, but there had been a large
purchase credited to an Anastasia Viuda. The name did not
ring a bell but evoked a crooked smile nonetheless. It was the
only Hispanic female on the register of recent transactions
but there was more to it. Phillips repeated the name to
himself three times then broke into his crooked smile again.

Most of the lots for sale were 5 to 20 acres of land.
Most lots had no buildings but had been developed for cattle
ranches. The upside for ranchers was they did not need to be
cleared; the downside of this was they had no trees on the flat
valley floor. Anastasia Viuda had bought several consecutive
parcels of land leading from the town of Los Fuertes, south
and east of the Sangre de Cristo Range. Deputy Phillips was
certain he would find his quarry there.

Phillips' next stop was the motel on Main Street, the
only lodging in town. He was also the only customer of the
motel. The owner was quite pleasant and obviously lived on
premises. After securing a room, he left his rented Ford in the

parking lot and walked to a restaurant for some lunch.

The local sheriff was sitting at the counter having a cup of coffee and chatting with the middle-aged waitress. Deputy Phillips sat beside him deliberately and ordered from the menu. His accent elicited stares and comments. It was quickly evident that they had very few international visitors in this quaint little town. Since Interstate 25 was almost 70 miles to the east, the town was spared the truck traffic. Without an interstate any closer than that, though, they got very few visitors of any kind. A man in a business suit, speaking with a British accent stuck out like a lone tree in a wheat field.

"Good Morning, sir," he began with a smile. "This is a lovely town you have here."

The overweight sheriff looked at him warily, not sure whether or not he was being facetious. "It's the oldest town in Colorado," he said with a voice reminiscent of a gravel pit conveyor.

"Fascinating; to have such a long history and yet remain so appealing. Most older towns are subject to decay but this one has been maintained beautifully.

"People here like to see things kept in order. We don't have much but we like what we have." The sheriff began warming to the newcomer's presence.

"Well, I for one am charmed."

The waitress refilled the sheriff's coffee cup unbidden and turned to get Phillips' order from the slide-through to the kitchen.

The sandwich was palatable but the deputy was more interested in the conversation. "There must not be an awful lot of crime in these parts, then," he began and noted that the sheriff's jaw tightened slightly.

"Most of the problems come from outsiders." The sheriff's voice became less cordial, as if his handling of the office were being brought into question. His seamed and sun-browned face turned toward his new acquaintance and asked,

"What is it that brings you to San Luis anyway? You don't look like a rock climber in that suit; you look like an insurance salesman. If you're here to sell vacuum cleaners you've come to the wrong town."

"Heavens no, I don't scale rocks, I collect them." Phillips held out his hand and said, "John Farmer, Archeologist. I'm here to scout up some asteroids if I can. It seems there have been some chondrites found in the valley and I thought I might scout around a bit." His crooked smile and sparkling blue eyes seemed open and honest. His accent lent him an air of refinement and his announcement that he was an educated professional went a long way to smoothing his reception.

"Just call me Johnny, or Sheriff." The sun-browned face broke into a smile for the first time that day. "Pleased to meet you but I think you might be a little out of place. There was a group of you guys a few years back in the Colorado Springs area. Found all kinds of dinosaur bones. That's what they said, anyway. I don't believe in that stuff, but I can't stop anybody else from believing in it."

Broaching the eternal science versus religion debate with local law enforcement was the last thing Deputy Phillips wanted. He quietly bent to the task of chewing up his unusually, for him, large sandwich.

"Where was it you wanted to look for these chondarts?"

"Oh, it will need to be closer to the edges of the mountains since anything falling on the valley floor would have been covered by the eroding ranges years ago. I was thinking near Los Fuertes."

"Take 152 to 242. Los Fuertes is about six miles down the road. There's no sign for the town but follow 242 and it'll take you there. There's no lodging there but we have a nice motel here in town."

"Thank you so much, Sheriff. You've been a great help

to me. Please let me pay for your coffee." Phillips reached into his inside pocket for his wallet.

"I get my coffee free, here. Leave it as a tip for Janice. Have a nice day and stay out of trouble."

"Of course, sir, I never cause trouble. I hope you have a nice day as well."

"I always have a nice day, Mr. Farmer."

As the deputy left he heard Janice saying "Wasn't he pleasant?" He did not hear the sheriff's reply and did not think much about the man after that.

Deputy Phillips was aware of the eyes on him as he walked back to the motel. He realized at that point that the suit he was wearing was the wrong attire for a high mountain desert valley and changed into blue jeans and a flannel shirt when he got back to his room. He also recognized that he was breathing heavily in the thin mountain air.

With a small pack of implements in the back seat, to enhance his disguise, he headed out for Los Fuertes. The terrain was alien to him and seemed desolate. There was very little traffic and those vehicles he did see were mostly pickup trucks. In a short time he was in the next to last town on the road. It didn't actually deserve to be called a town.

Los Fuertes was more like a junkyard with a couple of buildings thrown in. Recycling was not something that happened in this area, and cars and pickup trucks that no longer ran ended up here. It was like a mechanical elephants' graveyard full of the carcasses of modern times with a few scavengers scratching at the picked over carcasses. So different was it from the city of Denver that had seen his incoming flight, or even the county seat, that Phillips was taken aback. He had traveled extensively and had seen mountains and deserts, plains and cities, but the high mountain desert was new to him. The post apocalyptic aspect of Los Fuertes made him feel he had been transported to the set for a second-rate science fiction movie.

He pulled into the only gas station in town and filled his tank, though it was still half full. It was, of course, a Petroleo brand station, as were almost all of them. He bought a Coca Cola from the attendant who may have been fourteen years old and found him eager and hungry for conversation. The boy joined him when Phillips took a seat outside the station. They sat on rickety chairs, and the boy began asking questions about where he was from and what he was doing in "the asshole of the world." Phillips answered, giving his new occupation as an explanation for his interest in the area.

"Well, we got rocks," the boy said. "We got cows, rocks, rabbits and wrecks, as my grampaw used to say. Hey, if you need a guide, I been here my whole life. I know every gulley, spring, stream and arroyo around here. I work cheap too."

"That may be an option." The deputy was cautious about involving locals though he knew they were his best resource. He had no intelligence on what cover MacMaster was using and did not want to compromise his potential allies.

"I can take you wherever you want to go. Just give me a couple of minutes and my dad can watch the station while we find whatever you're looking for."

"You don't get many visitors here, do you?"

"Shit. People don't even come here to die, just send their dead trucks here."

"So nobody has moved in recently."

"Not for a couple of years. Last people to move in was a couple of years back, but they didn't really move into town."

Phillips didn't want to seem too interested in the new additions to the town but needed to prompt the boy. "I should think this would be a nice area to retire to. Were they retirees?"

"No, they didn't look old enough for that. I only see

'em when they stop for gas. A big guy and his Mamasita. Boy, she looks good though. Tall, long black hair. Not that I like Mexicans, ya know, but she looks like a handful and a half in the sack. I wouldn't mess with it. Her old man looks like lumberjack. Hey, you want something a little stronger than that soda pop?"

"Certainly." Phillips contained his further interest. He knew he was on the right track now.

The boy came back out of the service station with a half-full liter bottle of Black Velvet and a clean rag. He unscrewed the cap and wiped off the top with the rag, then he took a generous pull off the bottle before handing it to his new friend.

If the foreigner was surprised by that he did not show it, simply took a swig off the bottle himself and handed it back. The boy took it back inside and brought out a fresh pack of cigarettes. The deputy did not ordinarily smoke due to his lungs having been scarred by a poisoned gas incident, but he accepted one anyway. He was pleased by the texture of the smoke, much smoother than European cigarettes. He smoked in silence while his young benefactor went on about how he was going to get out of the valley and move to Denver or Las Vegas. The whiskey was warm in his stomach and the unaccustomed nicotine made his head swim slightly. Finally he realized that the boy had fallen silent.

"So, your parents don't mind if you smoke?"

"What's to mind? I make my own money and pay for what I drink and smoke. He couldn't care less about me or we wouldn't be here. Mom was smart, she left."

"By the way, my name's John Farmer."

"Oh, hey, I'm sorry. Frank."

"Pleased to meet you, Frank. Have you got a last name?"

"Spring Elk."

"A Native American name?"

"Yeah. Not being from around here, you probably can't tell but I'm a quarter Pawnee. I don't want to hear any bullshit about drunken Indians either"

"I assure you I had no intention of saying any such thing. I am no expert on American history but I do know that the American Indian got the worst of the deal."

"Well, a quarter Indian don't make me an Indian. So you need a guide or what?"

The newcomer had not intended to hire any locals but was impressed by the candid way Frank Spring Elk carried himself. "Yes," he said "I would be happy to have you show me some of the area."

"Great, I'll get my truck. You can't drive that car off road and you can't get to where you want to go otherwise. I'll open the garage. You'll want to park the car in there or it might get stolen."

Phillips doubted the car would be stolen in such a remote area but acquiesced regardless. Putting the car in the repair bay would hide his presence somewhat.

"You got a pair of boots? Those shoes won't last long in these parts."

"Yes, I have a pair of boots in the trunk." The boots were new, purchased at an outfitters shop near the airport. Phillips had taken pains to make them look as though they had seen some use.

When the Ford was safely ensconced in the garage and a deal had been struck for the boy's services, Frank Spring Elk pulled his pickup truck out from behind the building. It was an amalgam of vehicles blended together from an unknown number of trucks. Deputy Phillips caught himself staring and realized his mouth was hanging open. He had never seen anything like what the boy drove. It stood almost four foot off the ground on what looked like tractor tires and was painted blood red, obviously with a brush.

"What on Earth is this?"

"Like it? It's a 1944 military jeep cab on a one-ton GMC frame, modified with a home made lift kit. I got the bed off an F250 an' it's got a big block Chevy engine in it. Me an' dad made it. It's a little heavy but you can't stop it. Don't worry, she don't break down."

The deputy could not stop looking at the truck in awe and with more than a little trepidation. The front bumper was 6-inch angle iron. A slide plate was welded to one side where the power steering pump was mounted, backwards, so the pulley sat under the hood. The grill was half inch rebar as were the steps welded to the side of the frame. The rear bumper was a piece of I-beam. Under a fabricated sheet metal cover in the bed was a generator set on studs driven up through the frame. An old fashioned hoist took up most of the bed, the kind used before everything was converted to front wheel drive. An adapter for front wheel drive vehicles was welded to the back bumper, but the device itself was not installed.

"C'mon Boss, let's go."

Phillips tossed his bag in the back and climbed into the cab. A half mile down the road they pulled down a long driveway and stopped at a trailer. A thin man with the ruddy skin and sharp features of an American Indian came out at the sound of the engine. Frank introduced his new fare to his father, Steven, who said little and quickly took off toward the service station in a powerful sounding El Camino.

The track that Frank took Phillips down did not warrant the name of a road. It was, in fact, not on any map. Running with a barbed wire fence on one side and an irrigation ditch on the other it was a rutted, rocky mess. It would have ripped the oil pan off any passenger car attempting to traverse this way. It could not stop Frank's truck, however; she was built for this sort of terrain.

The deputy began to be very glad he had thought to purchase the boots.

Evergreen trees came into view as they approached the edge of the valley floor. There were almost none on the flatter land but they abounded on the sloped surfaces leading to the cliff-like mountains that ringed it. Nearer to the edge Frank was actually running over small trees. When questioned he simply mentioned there was a half inch thick skid plate under the oil pan.

They drove relatively close to the boundary between land and cliff. The cutoff point was remarkably sharp. They dismounted near the edge of the strip of trees at the base of the cliff. Mostly pine and spruce grew here but at the deputy's prompting Frank pointed out Gambel Oak and Mountain Mahogany. He knew a lot about the flora of the area.

"What is the winter like up here?" was the foreigner's next question.

Frank snorted. "Brutal. It gets so cold the air can't move, let alone the animals. Coldest spot in the country, pretty regular. This and Fargo, North Dakota make the news all the time. I don't think they report this area back east, though. You may have noticed nobody drives cars up here. In the winter you gotta have a four by four and a block heater or you might not survive. We got a good road crew though. The roads stay clear and sanded but if you ain't got a good truck or some good friends we'll be burying you up here. The snow they scooped up off the roads in San Luis will still be there, under a layer of sand, when the first snow falls this winter."

"You mean to tell me that the snow hasn't melted from the year before when the first snow falls?"

"Like I said, the sand keeps the cold in so there's still snow, well, mostly dirty ice from the year before, when it starts snowing again."

They came upon a rock fall and the pseudo archeologist made a show of examining the scree but found nothing. They went a little farther and examined the rocks in a streambed. The water was clear and just above freezing, even though it was May. After a few more spots, it was decided that there was nothing of interest in this particular spot and they should move south. Frank was game but explained that a mile further south was the land that was recently purchased and they might not like trespassers.

"That's all right. I think I might like a look at this Mexican woman." A lascivious leer completed the statement.

"Mr. Farmer, the last thing you want to do is try messing with that woman. I can't say what you should do but I'm telling you that's one thing you should not do. Her old man is a monster: Six-foot-four, flaming red hair, hands like a gorilla. I ain't never seen him get mad but I'm gonna say, right now, there ain't a man in this valley could take him in a fair fight. I'll tell you what, I'll take you to their cabin and you can knock on the front door but I won't run down the side to get there. We gotta go back to the road an approach it like civilized men."

The deputy was impressed by this show of respect but then reminded himself that, despite his maturity, this was just a boy. He mused on differences between his guide and the children he had known in London. Somehow the children of the city seemed to be lacking something.

"That reminds me, do you have a license to drive this war wagon?"

"Not exactly."

"What do you mean, exactly?"

"The sheriff's my uncle. As long as I don't get stupid on the road he don't care. I used this truck to pull his cruiser out of a snowdrift when I was twelve. Uncle Johnny don't care."

"Oh. Well then, take me back to the garage and let me salvage my rental. I need to go back to the motel and shower and get some dinner."

"Okay. You want me to bring you back here tomorrow?"

"Not here. I need to look at the maps I've left in the motel room and decide where to look next."

"But you still need a guide, right?"

"Yes, of course I'll need a guide. I'll look you up in the morning."

Frank Spring Elk seemed satisfied but when they got back to the garage he once again showed business savvy and maturity. He insisted that he be paid for the day's work and the following day's work as well. "After all, if I sit around waiting for you instead of taking towing calls and watching the station, and you don't show up, then I lose both ways. I'm guaranteed to be at home tomorrow if I've been paid for it."

Deputy Phillips liked the boy's reasoning, beyond the fact that the rental car was locked in the repair section of the garage. Just to get a feel for the relationship the boy had with his father, he joined Steven Spring Elk on the chairs outside the station. The Native American ancestry was much stronger in the father's features.

"Your son acts as an excellent guide."

"Thank you. He's a bright boy."

"Is he your only son?"

"The only one I know of." The twinkle in his eye made the most mundane of jokes seem sharper.

Frank came out of the station with the bottle of Black Velvet and a card table. He handed the bottle to his father, set up the card table and went back into the station, emerging seconds later with three battered but clean coffee cups and a pack of cigarettes. They were engaged in having a drink and a smoke when the police cruiser pulled up to fill the tank. Frank went inside and got a folding chair and a fourth cup. When the cruiser's tank had been filled Sheriff Johnny joined them for a drink.

"Did ya find what you were lookin' for?" Johnny began after greeting his relatives.

"Not yet, but I'm sure I'll find something. This whole trip has been more than worthwhile, just for the scenery and the company."

"I'm guiding him, Uncle Johnny."

"I see. You got lucky, Mr. Farmer. Frank, here, is the best guide you could ask for. He got the first deer of the season last year."

"Impressive. Was it a large one?" Deputy Phillips was feeling his way through now, looking for a way to get out of the conversation and get back to his true business as subtly as he could.

"It was no trophy but a good sized doe. The real prize was Gary McCormic's buck. He just moved here a couple of years back. A little strange but a hell of a hunter."

That was the last bit of information Phillips needed. He refused another drink and insisted it was time he got back to the motel for a shower. He also needed food a lot more than he needed whiskey. He left the trio at the station and drove back to San Luis satisfied that he was halfway to tying up the first part of the mission. He also found himself enjoying the camaraderie of the area. Born and bred in a huge metropolitan area, he was unused to the laid back culture he had found here. It was restful and addictive. He began to understand why Gordon MacMaster AKA Gary McCormic had retired to this all but inaccessible area. Once established, the residents of an area like this would protect you if they could and ignore you if you wanted them to.

The sun was going down as he took his shower in the motel room. Phillips debated leaving the job for the following day but decided against it.

The telephone book actually listed Gary McCormic and gave an address but the deputy decided against calling ahead. After a meal of brown trout that he found quite satisfying, he headed out toward the address. He was forced to drive past the Petroleo station but it was closed at this hour. The Spring

Elk residence was far enough from the road that he was confident he would not be marked as he drove past. As he suspected the McCormic mailbox had no name, just a number. The driveway was long and set on both sides with young trees that could not be identified in the darkness except that they were not evergreens. The cabin was not what he had expected. It was a large two-story wooden structure. All the lights were on and a television could be heard through the open windows. Since he had driven the last 100 meters with the lights off, he was sure of being unannounced. He shut off the engine and opened the door. The interior light had already been disabled by a piece of tape. Creeping onto the large wraparound porch he raised his hand to knock on the door when he heard the distinctive Scottish brogue from behind him.

"State your business."

"I'm here to speak with an old friend."

"Bless me! Piccadilly Paul Phillips. Are ye here to drink some scotch and while away the hours with stories of past heroics?"

"Something like that." Deputy Phillips turned around slowly, making sure his hands were well away from his body.

"Then for the love of God stop sneaking around. I almost had ye fertilizing the heather."

"That would have been unfortunate. You would have missed a very lucrative opportunity."

"Well come inside then. We have some catching up to do. This attire is not issued by the Service, and where's the cane?"

"I fear they would not allow it on the airplane. I feel quite naked without it"

"Ah, yes. Can't have you hijacking the plane with it. The Service wouldn't give ye leave on that one?"

"You must have forgotten, sir, I am but a humble accountant oiling the wheels of bureaucracy. One must maintain appearances, and it would not do for accountants to get special dispensation."

"Yer not armed then?"

"I have a belt knife; it goes with the outfit."

"Give it to me."

"Of course." The lock-back skinning knife had a four and a half-inch blade with a gut hook. MacMaster did not even open it.

"Cheap Chinese trash. I should have known. Sharp when you buy it but worthless a week later. Why did ye bother?"

"It went with the outfit."

"A toy. Turn around and let's see what other toys ye have."

Paul Phillips was once again aware of the physical presence projected by Gordon MacMaster. It had nothing to do with the large bore pistol he had stuffed in his waistband; it was an elemental aura that surrounded him. His stance projected confidence, strength, control and command. More than his physical size, though that was always a consideration, was the feeling of power that wreathed him.

Having found no further weapons, and throwing the skinning knife into the trees, the master of the house motioned his visitor to enter.

As the pair entered the living room, a door opened on the right and a tall, slim woman with jet black hair and loose clothing stepped in holding a short twelve-gauge shotgun with a pistol grip and a five-round clip.

"Annie, this is an old acquaintance of mine. Paul Phillips, Anastasia Viuda.

"Charmed, I'm sure."

"Paul, I'm pleased to meet you." The barrel of the shotgun went down to the floor and a smile that could make men hunt dragons split her splendid lips. She held out her hand and Paul took it gently and kissed the back lightly.

"Annie, draw us a couple of scotch rocks. Paul and I have business to discuss."

Chapter Three
Liquid Load

Deputy Rothchild was sitting at a table in The King's Head Pub, facing the door and having a Guinness. Three men were shooting darts and another was sitting at the bar by himself. The air was redolent of wood polish and tobacco smoke; the floor was stained with many generations' worth of spilled drinks. There were no internet plugs, no video games and no women. The King's Head was not the sort of pub that attracted the young. They did not play loud, current music and there was no dance floor.

When the door opened and the fashionable young blonde entered, every eye in the place was upon her. They expected a young man to follow her in but none did. She sat at the bar and ordered a gin and tonic but when she reached into her purse to pay for it she was preempted by the man in the suit. He was not a regular, though he had been in a few times. He insisted on paying for her drink and took the stool next to her at the bar.

"Good afternoon. I had no idea that this pub attracted such dangerous clientele. I shall need to put this on my preferred list of spots." Rothchild's suit was in contrast to the tweed hunting jackets the rest of the customers wore.

"I seldom frequent this part of town and will do so less now. I had a brief fling with an artist and then found out he was wag."

"A terrible consequence. Victor Rothchild."

"Katherine Sylvan."

"Enchanted. Look, I am scheduled for an appointment with my banker. Perhaps I could convince you to join me. A simple transaction and then we could visit a more enticing spot; someplace downtown perhaps."

"Certainly. I have nothing more pressing."

Deputy Rothchild slapped a five pound note on the bar

to cover expenses, and the two of them left together. They did not hear the comments that were directed at their retreating backs but would have appreciated the effectiveness of the subterfuge if they had.

The sky was overcast when they reached Credit Suisse. The inevitable rains would not be long in coming. Agent Sylvan's compact frame and brightly colored clothes complemented Deputy Rothchild's slim build and classic grey suit well. They looked like an upper-middle-class couple coming in for an auto loan or financial advice.

The metal detectors were passed and their identification allowed them access to the Bank President's office. In the office, a retina scan verified their identities. They waited in silence while the President opened his private vault and removed a large aluminum case, the type that stands upright and flips over on the top. The case contained British Pound Notes, still more stable than the Euro and sought after by those whose business gains were not so easily banked.

"Would you care to count it?"

"Yes. Please bring us a counter and a recorder. If we were to leave with this case light it would be unfortunate for all of us."

At Deputy Rothchild's insistence, a bill counter and recorder were brought in. While the deputy was counting, Agent Sylvan was flirting shamelessly with the Bank President who was able to keep from responding overtly but was not completely capable of disinterest. The case did not come up short.

The couple signed for receipt and took their leave with the case handcuffed to Victor Rothchild's wrist. The rain had not yet begun but it was less of a concern. While they had taken a bus to the bank, they left in a limousine.

Sitting in the back seat, Victor found it necessary to question Katherine Sylvan on her actions at the bank. It had seemed terribly unprofessional to him at the time. After all they were there for highly important business, not playtime.

"My Dear Mr. Rothchild, maintaining the interest of powerful men is always important business. A girl never knows when she will need protection from the ravages of time and circumstance. That man has a wife at home he is most certainly bored with and possibly a girlfriend of some sort he keeps somewhere. The possibility of a classy fling with an attractive woman thirty years his junior will be irresistible, if presented correctly."

"That doesn't seem sordid to you?"

"Of course it is, by my grandmother's moral code. Honestly, you were an agent before you were a deputy. Tell me with a straight face you never boffed an old woman to further your chances of success. If you do, I'll know you're lying and I'll never be able to trust you again, so loosen your tie a little and remember what it's like to be in the field. Our lives are on the line and I refuse to be sacrificed to the altar of some tight-assed old prune."

Rothchild relaxed his face and smiled widely. It had been a long time since he had been with a candid young woman, especially one with Katherine's physical charms. It had also been a long time since he had been spearheading part of an operation. He had directed a lot of work from behind the scenes, but it had been years since he had gotten his hands wet. He was looking forward to some excitement but reminded himself that excitement often came with a high price in this business.

"I think I'm going to like you," he said.

"Yes, of course. Just don't get your hopes too high. I'm like a coral snake."

"Ah, pretty to look at but dangerous to touch."

"Deadly." Now she was smiling. "And what was the idea of counting the cash. You don't trust Credit Suisse?"

"I trust nobody without experience. I was, truthfully, more interested in the case than the cash. I had no doubt that the money was there."

"Was there anything else there? I should have thought to look."

"No. Your part in distracting the President was performed perfectly. I apologize for questioning your moral fiber."

"Feel free to question at any time after the fact, but kindly wait until afterward. I seldom do things without reason."

They spent the rest of the trip to Heathrow in silence, watching the rain on the windows.

"Permission to come aboard?"

"Of course, please, Roger, come aboard."

Roger Forster climbed the gangplank of the Cerberus confidently. There was nothing to be gained by assaulting him. He felt that, of the three assignments, he had pulled the best. Hyperion Particka was known as the most gracious of hosts as long as things were going his way.

Hyperion Particka was not a tall man, though his girth was considerable. He habitually wore expensive jewelry and well-tailored silk suits. His appetites were as broad as his girth but generally did not run to the unusual. As he stood on the deck this early afternoon, he was flanked by a pair of bodyguards, bulging with muscle. At his command they patted Deputy Forster down but found nothing untoward. Lounging on deck chairs were three spectacularly tanned women in bikinis and sunglasses.

Roger Forster refused his host's offer of a drink with a promise to partake later in the evening. He refused the offer of a woman in the same way.

"Ladies, I have business. Go buy yourselves some shoes." The wad of cash he handed them could have bought a lot of shoes and they wasted little time throwing on shawls and tee-shirts and scampering down the plank.

"Have you secured the product?"

"Of course. Have you brought the payment?"

"It is on its way, separately. We do not wish to cast aspersions on your honor but in this sort of business we must all be cautious."

"The times are such. There will be no deceptions on our part. We have history together and it has always been mutually advantageous. Are you sure you would not like to sample some Ouzo?"

"Thank you, no. I will remain with you until the transfer has been completed; an assurance of sorts that all will go well. My associate has the agreed upon payment."

"What associate would that be? You arrived alone."

"That information will be forthcoming when there is a need to reveal it. We merely err on the side of caution. I will place a call when I have seen what we are purchasing and then I must call again with the drop-off location for the payment."

"Are you sure you would not like to have a drink? All work and no play makes a dull boy of Jack."

"Perhaps we can play when the work is done."

"Good. A man who cannot control himself cannot be trusted." Pulling a cell phone from his pocket, Particka dialed a set of numbers and spoke briefly into it. "A car will be here soon. We will view your purchase."

The two businessmen and the two bodyguards walked down the gangplank to the roof of the three-story pier. The road was a quarter mile away and 40 feet down. The car that waited was a Mercedes. With the driver, there was barely enough room for the five of them, but Particka did not get in. He walked around and spoke with the driver, in Greek, then held the door for Forster. When Forster, Particka and the bodyguards had entered the car, the doors were closed and locked. They drove into the warehouse district and stopped on Fortune St. From inside a small warehouse, the deputy made a call to say he had viewed the catch of the day and would relay further information on where the fish were biting.

Victor Rothchild and Katherine Sylvan flew into Araxos Airport, were met by a local contact and driven to Athens. They were certain they had not been followed by the time the reached their hotel. It was not in the heart of the city but away from the popular night spots. In the reserved suite, they picked up some tools of the trade, ordered some room service and waited for the expected call. They passed the time with small talk and did not discuss business. The sun had been down for two hours and the traffic outside the hotel had virtually disappeared.

Victor's cell phone rang. He answered it without a word. It was the expected call. "Courier, we have the expected payload. Twenty-four cases of shrimp. The party will be at 2200 Fortune St."

"I got hung up and I'm still two hours out. You'll need to keep the women hot and the champagne cold."

The code word was to be 'beach.' This had been worked out between Forster and Rothchild. The official code word was shrimp. Something had gone wrong and Forster was in trouble. The address given for the drop-off was in the warehouse district, perhaps half an hour away in the Citroën that waited in the parking garage under the hotel. Rothchild pointedly said he was still two hours out and could not make it any quicker. The call was ended. Another quick call got them the location of the first call. It was a hotel 10 minutes away. There were 45 rooms in the hotel.

"How are we supposed to know what room he'll be in? We can't search 45 rooms." Katherine's beautiful young face looked pained.

"We won't need to. He told us."

"He did?"

"What did he say?"

"He said 2200 Fortune St."

"No, that was the address for the payment. What else did he say?"

"Something about shrimp. I couldn't hear it very well."

"He said 24 cases of shrimp. We are here to pick up 50 cases of munitions, not 24. We must move quickly and expect no help from him. He may be dead already."

"What about the munitions?"

"They may not even exist. We worry about them later. First we take care of our own." His face was as cold and blank as a brick wall. There was no anger showing, no fear, no nerves. He had gone from a stiff but amicable gentleman to a robotic crusader.

The aluminum case was unhooked from the Deputy's arm and locked in the hotel safe on the way out.

It took them 15 minutes to get to the hotel. In the alley in back was a man dressed in rags, clutching a bottle of wine and mumbling in his sleep. Rothchild nipped the bottle out of his arms and as he opened his mouth to protest, knocked him unconscious with the butt end of it to the head.

"Here, use this to get in the room."

Katherine did not so much smile as grimace and what came out of her throat was not a word but a growl.

The night was pleasant and it was easy to find an open window. Once the screen was cut away, they climbed inside the room, into the hall and to the stairwell. There was no one posted in the second floor hall. Room 24 was about halfway down. Rothchild pulled his 9mm Ruger with a silencer and flattened himself against the right side of the doorway.

Agent Sylvan smeared her lipstick and with a sigh, tore her blouse open. She banged on the door with the wine bottle and in a slurred voice exclaimed, "okay Brian, let me in." There was no reply. She made her voice screech as she repeated herself.

"Stupid bitch, this is not your room," came from behind the locked door in accented English.

"Brian, you son-of-a-bitch, open the door and let me in, God dammit. I gotta pee."

"Go away, you drunken cunt. This is not your room."

"Let me in, Brian or I'll scream till the police show up and say you tried to rape me. You asshole."

The door opened just a crack, but it was enough for Katherine to shove the neck of the wine bottle in and force it open a couple more inches then stumble against the door. The man's foot was behind the door, so she could not get it to open all the way, but she was able to get her arm inside and push him enough to see the bound figure in the chair with the pillowcase over his head. She let go of the wine bottle which effectively jammed the door open and dropped to her knees. "Victor, aim high," was all she had to say.

The kidnapper did not stand a chance. His eyes were on the woman who had ostensibly collapsed at the door. He never even saw the barrel of the gun that blew a hole through the door and his head. The second man was leaping off the couch when Agent Katherine Sylvan put three bullets in his chest.

A quick check down the hall confirmed that nobody had bothered to investigate the disturbance.

Inside the room, Victor pulled out two pairs of rubber surgical gloves, wiped off the wine bottle with a rag and left it on a bedside table while Katherine moved to the man in the chair.

Under the pillowcase, Roger Forster was battered and bruised. He had a sock stuffed in his mouth and covered with duct tape. One eye was swollen shut but they had not abused his nose or lips, presumably to prevent changing his voice.

"That bastard Particka, how did he expect to get away with this?" Even though he was furious, Roger Forster's voice was controlled and quiet. "We've been dealing off and on for years. He knows there will be repercussions. His reputation is his stock in trade. Why would he ruin that for less than a million Euros?"

"Don't worry about that, Dear. Let's concentrate on getting you out of here first." Sylvan's voice was conciliatory as if she were calming the fears of a child.

"The check-in man was in on the deal. I heard them talking when they brought me in."

Deputy Rothchild was stripping the bodies of weapons, cash and ID. He wiped his own gun down and left it in the hand of the driver, who had caught three to the chest. He took Katherine's weapon and left it in the hand of his victim. It would not hold up to a modern forensic investigation but might cause some initial confusion. The blood spray patterns and footprints in the gore would expose the lie, if anyone really looked at the scene. If the police were lazy, it would give them a plausible story to blow off the death of two less than desirable members of society.

Neither of the deceased had silencers on their pistols. Agent Sylvan stuffed one in the pocket of her jacket. Deputy Forster picked up his jacket from the bed and found it had been sprayed with blood and brains. He folded it over his arm anyway with the pistol in his hand underneath. They locked the door behind them, and the three left the hotel by the back door. Several blocks away, they discarded the blood-spattered jacket with the rubber gloves in the pocket.

At their hotel they parked in the underground garage and took the rickety old elevator to their fourth floor suite. Katherine was engaged in cleaning Roger's wounds while Victor dialed an international number.

"Message for The Director. Flaw in the plan. Call in a strike on 2200 Fortune Street, Athens." He then tapped in an identification number and pulled the battery out of the cell phone. "If we don't move now, we will never find that Greek bastard. The warehouse on Fortune Street might still have the munitions but I doubt it highly. Most likely it was just an ambush."

"I'm getting too old for this sort of thing." Roger Forster complained as he pulled on a bulletproof vest. "The payload was at 2200 Fortune St. though they may have moved it. What do we have to work with?"

Agent Sylvan pulled the weapons cache out from under the bed and opened it. Open, the case covered the double-sized mattress. "Sniper rifle," she said. "Two muffled Uzis, two smoke grenades, three fragmentation grenades, a long barrel 45, a pair of wrist lock Derringers and a Ghurka fighting knife."

"Can you handle the sniper rifle?"

"Please, I was first in my class in marksmanship." She almost looked insulted.

"All right then. Fix your makeup and we'll see what you can do." Forster was smiling despite his bruised face.

As soon as The Director got the call he knew Hyperion Particka had lost his edge. For one reason or another, things had not been taken care of the way it had been decided, and the plan had crumbled. The Director's demeanor did not betray him. He maintained his usual attitude and made a telephone call. Within 20 minutes, a plane was in the air and heading toward Athens.

The Director plotted the small plane's course by satellite as he filled and lit the bowl of his huge well-seasoned pipe. Calculations raced through his head looking for a conclusion, but there was no reasonable explanation. Of all the times, of all the loads, why did this one go sour? Particka had been a stable source of ordnance for years; sometimes slow, or worse yet, uninformed, but he was always stable.

The flat roof of the building was black tar and still warm. It was not right on the waterfront but only one building away. The building in front of it had a slanting tile roof, unsuited to the task. This one was perfect. A two-foot wall ringed the edge with a solid tile top but not slick tile, the unglazed, rough type. The tripod sat perfectly with the rifle aimed at a very slight angle downward.

The upper deck of the 250-foot yacht was lit by half a dozen spotlights but it was deserted. On most nights there was a party going on here, but tonight was different. The owner and captain might have been alerted already. He might have gone out to a club or a casino, which would be perfect for a good shot when he returned.

Katherine Sylvan wiped her telescopic sight with an alcohol swab. She was dressed in nothing but a skirt and a bra, having removed the shirt she had replaced the ripped blouse with. She had also removed her shoes. Her blond hair was pulled into a ponytail.

Her partners had waited until the police patrol had passed and then hastened down the middle level of the pier. The smaller yachts used the lower level and only the truly huge ones used the upper level; the middle level was almost unused. She had not seen them since they headed out.

She kept her nerves in check by reflecting on some of her past successes. Columbia had been an easy in. Hector had seen her in the market and little more was necessary. The real success was turning down his offer of cocaine. If she had accepted that offer she would have been relegated to the ranks of the trollops. Getting out had been harder than getting in. She had been invited in, but had to leave in the middle of the night, a mile in the air and in the middle of the jungle. A smile split her face at the memory of the jungle chase. She had been terrified that she would blow out the clutch on the jeep. All her work had not had the desired effect on the drug smuggling business pouring off that mountain. Hector's second-in-command was in charge the next day, and not a single shipment was missed. But her assignment was completed, and she returned without a mark.

She grabbed her shirt from the deck and wiped her face off. The night was warm and sultry. She had conditioned herself to ignore the insects that buzzed around her ears and crawled on her naked skin. Perhaps, she speculated, the men had found an open porthole and crawled inside through that. The gangplank was drawn up so there must be somebody on the ship.

Germany had not been as easy as Columbia because she did not speak German. She had vowed never to return to Germany. Still, the job had gotten done even though it was in an unorthodox manner. She had still not learned how to speak German and would not. She shook her head to clear it of the visions of gang rape that still haunted her.

Portugal had been fun. She spoke Portuguese, Spanish, Italian and a passable Greek. Her French was rusty, but she could bring that back if pressed. The men in Portugal and Spain were different from the Italian men. They were more respectful and less cocksure. She had killed a woman in Portugal, though she never knew why she had killed her. The mark had been the lover of a high-level diplomat and Sylvan supposed there was some undue political influence involved, but she could not figure out why that was worth assassination. Her partner in Portugal had been an indefatigable lover, and the smile came back to her lips when she thought of him.

She thought of Victor Rothchild's comments in the limousine and wondered if he were really so prudish or if he was just provoking a reaction.

She thought of the adoring gaze cast upon her by Roger Forster's one undamaged eye. She might have some fun with Roger.

A slight movement on the upper deck roused her from her reverie. It was a man, large in stature and broad of chest. He had the dark hair and strong features of Southern

Mediterranean men. He was also staying to the shadows. They had somehow been warned. It was probably the check-in man from the hotel who had warned them. She had thought it would be a good idea to take him out as well, but that had been vetoed by both senior partners.

The lights went out on deck and the only illumination remaining was the streetlights on the dock. Katherine shifted her sights to the stairwell enclosure that jutted above the upper level of the pier. The door was closed, but she felt confident one or the other of her accomplices was secured there. Returning her attention to the deck, she saw the gangplank being set down, 80 feet closer to the shore. It was attached to a hoist that set it and simultaneously raised the rails and ropes on the sides. Two more men appeared in the shadows, too dark to distinguish one from another.

"Patience," she told herself. "They will reveal themselves in short order. They are afraid and nervous. They are targets and they know it." It was not a smile that split her lips at that thought; it was a full wolfish grin. "They are mine and nothing they can do will save them."

The trio moved down the gangplank into the lights of the pier. None of them was Hyperion Particka. All three had automatic weapons in their hands. Two of them stood back to back, out of the corona of the streetlight; the third went to check out the stairwell. When he had confirmed it was empty, he returned to the others and all three went back on board.

"Patience," she reminded herself. "To strike before the iron is hot leaves an insufficient brand. Hmm, I wonder where I learned that phrase?"

Four men reappeared on the gangplank. Three of them surrounded one in the middle.

Agent Katherine Sylvan chose the one on the right, slightly ahead of the protected man. It would not do to have the slug go through her target and kill the only one they wanted alive. The man was halfway to the stairwell when his head exploded like a water balloon. The bodyguards reacted predictably. They had no target to shoot back at and never even heard the report of the muffled rifle. The rifle was reloaded by the time they reached the stairwell and found the door had been tied to the rail from the inside and would not open. The bigger of the two bodyguards was outlined against that door and under the light that graced it. His chest sprouted a small hole while his back blossomed a huge crimson flower.

The other two men dashed around the concrete enclosure to get out of the strike zone, and a burst of light from behind it signaled the end of the third bodyguard's life. In the brief flare, Katherine saw his body thrown upward, like he had been plucked from the ground by a mythological God. He hit the rail and crumpled. The fourth man, their true objective, backed away with his hands in the air.

The door to the stairwell opened halfway but jammed against the body lying in front of it; it closed a little then forcefully shoved the corpse out of the way. A slim man in a grey suit, and sporting a black eye, stepped through the portal.

After checking her two targets for movement, Agent Sylvan put on her shoes and shirt and proceeded to break down her weapon. She put the component parts in a small canvas bag, ensuring the lens caps were fastened tightly. She pulled on a pair of gloves, fastened the bag to her belt and threw the rope she had used to gain access to the roof over the side and slid down it into the alley. By the time she had gained the Citroën and driven to the end of the pier, she was sweating profusely. She saw the police making their rounds again, but they did not stop. They had not gotten the call yet. The doors of the Citroën opened and three men entered the car.

All four heard the airplane coming in low. It was a

fighter plane. They paid no attention to it; their minds were focused on the job at hand. Nobody knew they were on that dock. There should have been nothing to fear.

No one saw the torpedo drop from the plane in the darkness. The explosion that tore the Cerberus in half was not so easily ignored. It lit the sky and ripped away half the pier as well. Within seconds, the yacht had sunk to the bottom with only the antenna showing above the water line.

With a curse Katherine jammed the transmission in gear and tore away from the scene as fast as she could get the underpowered French vehicle to move.

Chapter Four
Recruitment

"You must be mad." Gordon MacMaster's voice was low but did not fail to convey his emotions. "First you sneak up on me like some kind of... well, like what you are. An assassin. Then you try to get me to do a job in the Middle East. Do I look like an Arab? I don't speak Arabic or Turkish or Persian. I'll stick out like a pecker in a convent."

"Believe me, sir, you were not my first choice. Ahmed is already in the area: a local, competent, and on the payroll. I think the real reason for the choice was your thoroughness. It was not that you headed the list, sir, you are the list."

"Dead men keep secrets well and drop the 'sir'. I've not been knighted yet."

"Precisely. The end product, as I see it, is not so much to free the hostage as to eliminate the captors." Unbidden, a tic appeared in Piccadilly Paul Phillips' right eye. He covered it by rubbing both his eyes with thumb and forefinger. His steely reserve was not what it had once been, and he had begun to think of a retirement in just such a place as he found himself in. He loved London but sometimes he longed for a more secluded life. He closed his eyes briefly to concentrate on the job at hand. What he had to say to his host was as applicable to his own situation as any other. When the Service called, it was his duty to the Crown, above and beyond his own life.

"What is the cargo?"

"Fifty crates of ammunition to be traded for a living captive."

"Fifty ten-thousand-round crates at wartime prices, that's half a million dollars."

Deputy Phillips looked at the ceiling and sucked his teeth for a second. "Slightly more than that in Euros, but I don't think the cost was the issue either. I think they expected to retrieve the munitions, or perhaps it was the Turks who paid for them. They are to be transported from Athens to the Turkish coast and to the Kurdish region by truck. The mission has been authorized and the paperwork drawn up. Not counterfeit paperwork, real paperwork with the Department of the Interior's seal. Did you know the Turks still use red wax for the seal? I thought that had been done away with in the dark ages."

"How many go with me?"

"Ah, yes. There are three Kurds waiting for the word in Istanbul. They have been checked out and come up as clean as one can expect for savages."

"So. Four of us are going to drive across Turkey and into the desert with a truck full of bullets to trade for some British hostage."

"I think that was the plan."

"You can go back to your penny-pinching Director and tell him to… No. Dial the number and I'll tell him."

"I'm sorry, old man, I can't do that. First of all, the number reaches an answering machine; second, you are no longer an authorized contact; third, if I report your refusal, I will find myself working for a Pakistani in a petrol station."

"Then you'll be Pakistani Paul Phillips."

Phillips exploded in laughter despite himself. The tension was broken but the issue was nowhere near resolved.

MacMaster poured them each another glass of scotch. "As a Scotsman, I fully appreciate frugality but I'm not going on a suicide mission. Inform the gnome in charge that I refuse to be a part of it. There will be no Charge of the Light Brigade for me. You'll spend the night here and I'll show you around in the morning."

"No, one must keep up appearances and not compromise one's cover. Falling out of character for me would bring attention to you. I have a room back in San Luis and I've retained a guide with a huge red truck. I will be spending some time with him tomorrow to allow you to say goodbye."

"Steve Spring Elk?"

"No, his son, Frank."

"Yea. Frank's a bit young still. I think he started high school last fall. Good hunter though. Good welder too. I had him repair the cage on my bobcat after a tree fell the wrong way. He would have made a good agent if he hadn't been raised up here. Something about the high desert changes people. You get a respect for the land and for life. You get to know what it means to rely on others. There are few fights up here and nobody has shot anybody else since the gold rush. Not a breeding ground for killers. Once in a while somebody gets too drunk, and Sheriff Johnny locks him up for the night."

"Perhaps, if you do not like the plan you can come up with another, more suitable course of action."

"Aye, maybe. Give me a day. Go out with your guide and shoot some rabbits or something. I'll review what ye have and then I'll tell ye no."

"Name your price. I'll make the call."

"It's not the price. I need nothing. I burn wood off the land and plant more trees. I need nothing up here and what's more, until your scruffy head popped into me view, there was no one seeking to harm me. Do you think I'll willingly leave my life and my woman for some fools' errand in the sands of Iraq? It won't happen today and it won't happen tomorrow."

"Sir," Deputy Phillips's demeanor changed from amicable negotiation to colder than the mountain peaks. "You will accept this assignment because you cannot refuse. You cannot get out and you know that. You've always known that."

"You're threatening me?" The Scotsman's eyes went wide and his jaw clenched.

"No, Gordon MacMaster, I'm not."

"I'm Gary McCormic here."

Paul Phillips drew himself to that frozen place in his core, the unreachable, unyielding place. "Gordon MacMaster, we have known each other a long time and you know I never threaten anyone. You have had some sort of conversion. You have lost your taste for the life you chose, but there is no getting out. There is no leaving it behind. There is no retirement on a pension or jumping ship for another career. What you have done in the service of our leaders has not been forgotten by those it injured. I found you relatively easily with the resources at my command. A note to some of the few you left alive would send squads swarming this valley, and even if you survived the moment, there would be others who would not. Your beautiful paramour is doubtless not the trained killer you are. Would she survive the assault? At best, you would need to disappear again. At worst, you would fertilize the freshly planted trees with your blood and filth and vomit as your sworn enemies danced on your body and raped your woman."

As Piccadilly Paul Phillips got wound up verbally, Gordon MacMaster became wound up internally. "Ye filthy English slug. Ye'd send a man to his doom smiling all the way. Call yer Director and tell him I've died or that I couldn't be found, that I flew the coop. Give me that professional courtesy. We be known to each other. I paid my dues and heaped payment on that. Canna ya let me be?" As a last ditch effort it was a weak and futile one. The Crown had called and there would be no evading that. The only action to take was the high road or to be actively hunted down; to live for the moment the sniper's bullet shatters his spine.

The redder MacMaster's face got, the calmer Deputy Phillips got. He knew the expatriate Scotsman would accede to his demands or make good on his implied threat to disappear. The second possibility would probably include Phillips disappearing as well.

Paul began to feel more and more naked before the storm, despite his calm and sure knowledge that his current opponent never acted in anger. The Scotsman was one to bluster and rage in an attempt to intimidate his enemies but when it came down to action, it was never done without planning.

If MacMaster escaped, Phillips might not be held accountable for it by The Director, although his words rang loudly. "I do not expect to see you again until you have completed this simple mission. If you find you cannot accomplish this mission, I never expect to see you again." The Director was not one to act in anger either and he seldom went back on his word. More importantly was the real meaning behind the statement, the one that hit home now.

How long can a man of immense stature, with flaming red hair, hide? One would not think long, but it had been over two years the British had been on the lookout for him with the most sophisticated equipment and had not located him. Spending the next few years to perhaps the rest of his life looking for this one man whom he admired but did not really like was more than the Englishman was ready to commit to. The immutable block within his soul protected Phillips from guilt and shame and conscience. There would be no retreat; there would be no deal. His job was to recruit and he would do so or he would eliminate his subject with extreme prejudice. The tic was gone from his eye and his nerves were once again stainless steel filaments.

"I will be back tomorrow. I know you will do what is right for all of us."

Phillips walked out the door past Anastasia Viuda who was leaning against the railing. She had lost both the smile and the shotgun, but something about her seemed more dangerous without the firearm. The deputy began a quick reevaluation of this dark haired woman. The British had no pictures of her and had been unaware of her pseudonym let alone her given name.

"I think," she began "that there is much I do not like going on here."

"My dear, your lover has obligations that he cannot avoid. I cannot expect you to understand, nor am I able to explain. He has hidden in this wilderness as an attempt to deny his duties, but they are undeniable. He will be coming with me on the morrow and when his debt is expunged, he will doubtless return to you." His words projected a certainty he did not feel but could not back down from.

"You play a game with much danger."

"Danger is our stock in trade. It is our breakfast. Perhaps he will explain and perhaps not, but it is not for me to tell you. I will see you again, tomorrow." With that the Englishman turned and headed to his car. This was as tense a moment as he had faced in years and half expected to take a bullet to the back any second. His sharp eyes had detected the bulge of a pistol under the woman's loose clothing and he continued to reevaluate the danger she presented. The bullet he feared was not fired, and he mused as he drove away that if she had been a professional, she would not have exposed herself on the porch.

The next day, in the guise of John Farmer, Phillips returned to Los Fuertes and toured another area of the canyon with his young guide. They found no interesting rocks in the morning but had a good lunch packed by the main street restaurant, and they saw more wildlife than the foreigner had seen in years. At the end of the day, he announced his intention to drive south into New Mexico and investigate another report from north of Taos. He paid Frank the agreed upon price and threw in an extra 60 bucks out of respect. He would never see the young man again but he would not soon forget him. They shook hands and he headed south. He did not drive over the border into New Mexico, however. He pulled back into the same driveway he had negotiated the night before.

It would be one of three things: the house would be empty, he would catch a bullet on the way in, or Gordon MacMaster would be packed and ready to go. As it turned out, the man was on the porch kissing his delectable woman goodbye. She turned and hurled epithets in Spanish at his back as he left and at the newcomer as well. Tears were rolling down her cheeks as she did her best to let the anger overshadow the sorrow and fear.

They headed south, out of the San Luis Valley.

"I must congratulate you," Phillips said as they pulled onto the road. "She is a truly impressive catch."

"Pfaugh. A man cannot hook a woman like that as he would a fish. He needs to hunt her with respect as he would a mountain lion. If anything were to happen to her in my absence, I would find you to blame."

After that, neither man said a word for some time. Finally, it was the Scotsman who broke the silence. "Trying to negotiate that path by truck is untenable. The load would never make it to the destination. I'm going to need a plane and at least 10 good men. I'm going to need the kind of plane I can land in the desert. I'll negotiate the hostage release and, if possible, I'll kill the kidnappers. I have heard nothing on the news about the abduction, so I'm thinking that this man cannot be important enough to warrant this kind of mission. There is something going on that I do not know about; something more than buying off the rebels. Civilized countries do not deal with terrorists, and they do not give them ammunition. I want to know what I am walking into because it stinks to high heaven."

"You know as much as I do. We fly out of Taos with a stopover in Newark, New Jersey. We are going to Athens to pick up the payload. We have secured that already."

"Are you certain? That's a lot of bullets. A lot of things might have happened."

The Newark, New Jersey airport had been remodeled at the turn of the century and still looked considerably better than before, but it was already getting ragged at the edges. The two co-conspirators sat together as far from the other passengers as they could, discussing the upcoming mission. MacMaster was making demands and changing plans, Phillips was taking mental notes and hoping there would be no conflict from above. The mad Scottish bull was adamant in his stand that he would not, under any circumstances, drive a truckload of munitions across Turkey regardless of whose official seal was presented for safe passage.

"This whole thing stinks. It has too many holes in it. The Turkish government would never have given permission to London to deal with terrorists. Like them or not, the Turks are some of the most uncompromising negotiators in the world. London does not deal with terrorists in the first place; it's terribly bad policy. So tell me, who this is we are going to rescue, and why he is worth so bloody much money and breach of protocol."

"I'm sorry, I've been sworn to secrecy on that count. I am allowed to tell you the truck is supposed to be filled with cans of soup. The boxes in the back would be camouflage for the munitions in the front. You are to broker the deal at that end, and get out by whatever means you can. For this you are to be paid your usual fee plus 50% bonus. If you bring back proof of having dispatched certain of the insurgents, you will be paid accordingly. Some of these men have high prices on their heads."

"If I needed the blood money, I'd have killed them already."

"Of course."

"How much time do we have?"

"As much as is expedient."

"I'll draw a team. You get me a cargo plane, and get it

loaded. Have you brought me paperwork?"

"Passports, different names, English and American."

Athens was hot and humid, not unusually so but still uncomfortable to a man used to the high deserts of Colorado. Gordon was sitting outside a coffee shop making calls on a cell phone he had bought cheaply and would discard when he was done. He was not unduly surprised to find that almost all the numbers were out of service. He did manage to contact two of his old associates: one was getting ready for another assignment, the other had quit the business but was willing to work with Gordon out of respect. He agreed to meet in Athens as soon as he could get a flight out of Madrid. He was an Australian living close to Barcelona.

Having secured a reliable lieutenant, Gordon dialed a number in Germany and asked the receptionist for Colonel Richter. There was a lot of noise on the line as transfers were made and some sort of scrambling went into effect.

"Colonel," he began. "It is the Scotsman."

"Scotsman! It is so good to be hearing from you. I believed you were retired or perhaps, ahh... decommissioned. Is it work you are looking for? I can be of service."

"No, Colonel, I was looking for men. I was conscripted."

"Ah, yes, that can occur from time to time."

"I need nine men. At least one must be a Turk who speaks at least some English, French, Russian, German or Spanish. The rest must be low profile, dependable men who will not jump the gun or hesitate. Remuneration will be slightly better than usual, but no cowboys and no high profile."

"Nine men? I will see what I can do but the labor market is tight, and we have lost a number of recruits to bad investments. Where will be the base of operations?"

"Athens."

"Ah, Athens. Is there anything else they will need to know?"

" No. Remember, no cowboys."

"There is no need to insult me, Scotsman. I will call you back at this number?"

"This number will be inoperative. I will call you from a pay phone."

"*Bitte.* And when you are done, you will come to Berlin and sample some schnapps with me. We can remember the times before I was behind this desk."

"I'd be delighted."

"Call me in 36 hours."

Gordon MacMaster hung up the phone and removed its battery.

Terry Kingston stepped through the doors of the airport into the sultry air of Greece. He had not been here in years and had forgotten much of the Greek language. A small boy with a sign that read Tarrytown was standing by a row of taxis. Kingston smiled widely and pointed to himself. The boy grinned back and grabbed for the bag the Australian was holding.

"You come with me, Mr. Tarrytown," he chirped. "We go hotel."

"Okay, *Niño.* We go hotel."

The boy held the door for him as he entered the cab and then jumped into the front seat chattering at the driver in Greek. The driver nodded without a word and they drove into traffic.

The hotel was a middle-class establishment still trying to hold on to some of its past glory in a neighborhood that had passed its prime. The boy negotiated the check-in desk for him and he signed in as "Tarrytown." In the room he gave the boy a generous tip and thanked him. The boy said he would be available for tours and knew the best places to eat.

He said his name was Anieli and all Mr. Tarrytown needed to do was to call the desk and ask for him.

After the boy had left, Terry opened his checked baggage and took out the lead-lined bag with the steel pieces of two mostly carbon fiber Smith and Wesson 38s. The nylon shoulder holsters were rolled up in a spare pair of shoes. He dressed in a conservative but expensive Italian suit that did little to disguise his physique. His broad shoulders and powerful arms did not bulge the tailored clothing, but to give him enough room to move, it was cut wide. Before he left the room, he brushed his teeth.

In the hotel bar, he found a huge red-headed Scotsman who bought him a beer. They had been through a lot together. They spoke in low voices with no concern for the other's loyalty or honor. They began with small talk, not feeling comfortable in the small bar. After a couple of drinks they took a walk to a small park and began to talk business.

"I brought a couple of pistols with me, but I don't have any ammo. It's a good thing, mate; they had dogs at the airport."

"Aye, things have become tight, but the nature of the commission should provide more than enough support. I left my guns in America. Too much trouble flying and if they catch you, it's up to five years in prison."

"I assume we're on a dedicated flight out." Terry Kingston lit a Spanish cigarette as he spoke.

"Yes. There's a British diplomat we're supposed to be rescuing in the Kurdish region the Turks recently took from Iraq."

"A simple swap?"

"No. Wet work. They want the kidnappers dead and anyone with a price on their head will be extra."

"Do we get paid if the Englishman is dead? I mean he might be dead already."

"We get paid regardless. I wouldn't have it any other

way."

"Who's paying?"

"The English. Piccadilly Paul Phillips showed up at my house of all places. I thought I was hidden but they knew right where I was. Too much trouble with everything these days."

"It's getting so a man can't get any peace and quiet." Terry threw his cigarette on the ground. "So, how do you read it?"

"It looks as though we fly into the desert, make the swap, 50 cases of ammunition for the Englishman, then take off again. We follow the tracking device in the cases, and go in for the kill when it stops moving."

"Can we just bomb the location the way the Americans did Zarqawi?"

"I don't think so. That would make too much noise."

"You know these people usually move a stash to a place with women and children. That's going to make a lot more noise."

"True. Maybe we should bomb them before they leave the desert."

"I like that better."

"That's why I called you. You have a clear head and a feel for the enemy. Let's lie low for a while. I'll be calling Colonel Richter in 12 hours to see what sort of troops he scared up for us. We also need to see where the plane is leaving from."

"So, how's the widow maker?"

MacMaster grinned. "She's wonderful. Just about filled Piccadilly Paul Phillips full of buck shot."

"Yeah? World might be a better place if she had."

Back at the hotel, they were enjoying some lamb with mint jelly when the news came on the television that the night before, Cerberus, the yacht owned by financier and international playboy Hyperion Particka, had exploded. Three bodies had been found, but they were still looking for Particka's body. There was no mention of the fact that the men were dead before the yacht exploded, and no explanation was given for the explosion, but it was under investigation.

"Hyperion... isn't he an arms dealer? Is this going to impact our little arrangement? Was it our payload that just went up in flames?" Terry seemed to think Gordon MacMaster knew more than he actually did.

"Oh, I doubt it. A man doesn't get as old and as rich as he is, or was I suppose, by being stupid. A long-term dealer would never keep a large cache of arms with him on his private yacht. I don't know if it has anything to do with us or not. Seems like too much of a coincidence not to. I'm going to call Piccadilly Paul and find out if we just lost our reason for being in Athens." MacMaster slid the battery into his cell phone and dialed a number. He was surprised when Phillips answered the phone.

"I saw the news, yes. No, it does not impact our operation. It has nothing to do with us. A leaky fuel tank or something. Our end is going well, how is your end?"

"I'll know more later tonight. I'll fulfill my end of the bargain."

"Good. Do we have an ETD?"

"Departure to be determined by manpower and circumstance. I'm assuming your end is sewed up, then."

"You just worry about your end and I'll worry about mine." Paul Phillips seemed a bit testy about being questioned, but he did not seem to object to the contact in and of itself.

Gordon hung up the phone and pulled the battery out again. He was not entirely convinced that the explosion did not impact him somehow but was in no position to look into it further.

Later that night, Gordon took a walk while Terry slept.

The cheap cell phone went into a dumpster a couple of blocks away, and the call was made to Berlin from the pay phone in a tavern.

"Colonel Richter."

"Scotsman! Punctual as always. Are you on a random line?"

"Yes, a payphone in a tavern, having a scotch."

"I have most of your crew: three Germans, two Greeks, two Turks, and an Italian. They will all be traveling clean so they will need to be outfitted when they arrive. The Greeks are setting up a safe house in The Hellenic Republic. The Germans are already on their way. One of those is a former drill instructor from the German Army, so I assume he will take the lead role among them. The Turks will fly in tomorrow and the Italian is driving. I will get you one more and you will wire me the funds."

"Agreed. I will need the address of the house and I assume your office is still on Wendigo."

"Ja, I am still on Wendigo. I do not remember the address of the house, but call me and I will transmit the message. Do not forget I expect you to stop by when the job is done."

"I'll try. You know how things are."

"Indeed I do. The house is in the hills north of Athens, a small town, very friendly, no distractions and no diversions. The Greeks will hire a cook and housekeeper. The only problem I foresee is boredom."

"We will make sure to provide some excitement."

"*Gute.* Wire me the funds and good luck."

Gordon MacMaster hung up the phone. It felt good to deal with a man he knew he could trust. He was not as sure about the English organization. He did not take it personally that Colonel Richter had not transmitted the address of the safe house. He would not have done so himself.

Chapter Five
Munitions

Hyperion Particka was understandably nervous. He muttered to himself in Greek and Bulgarian as the Citroën drove north. The fact that he was alive was only attributable to the fact that the English did not have the munitions yet. His mind was feverish with plans to keep himself alive and get free of his captors, but it all came down to the fact that he had already double-crossed them once. He cursed himself and his addiction and the casinos and women in general and incompetent bodyguards and a host of other things that had led to his current situation. Victor Rothchild was in the back seat with him pointing a very large revolver at him. He had no doubt that any misstep at this point would be his last. Visions of heads and chests exploding were seared on his retinas and his years of dealing arms from armchair comfort were eclipsed by the reality of live fire.

Several kilometers from the docks Katherine pulled off the main street and into the parking lot of a strip mall. She took a deep breath and rested her head on the seat back with her eyes closed. Roger Forster got out of the car and walked a few feet to the pay phone. He dialed the number and spoke briefly into the receiver and then hung up.

"Where to now?" Katherine asked.

"I know a spot," Roger responded. "It is a deserted factory north of here. Not very accommodating but relatively secluded. It's far enough from the city that the bums don't sleep there and the kids don't drink there."

As they drove off Particka whined, "None of this is what I wanted. It was the Russians"

Victor punched him in the side of the face, causing his head to bounce off the side window and temporarily shutting him up.

Vasilii Ivanov Scarkovich had watched through a similar feed as his crippled British counterpart. He took a sip of his drink and pulled out a Russian Marlboro. "I knew they would take the Greek. His actions demanded it. So predictable," he chuckled.

"Stephan." Seconds later a man in a business suit opened the lavishly decorated door. "Stephan, find out what they are saying on the streets about the explosion on the Cerberus. Get me word from Athens, London, Moscow and New York. Find out who is being blamed. Also, call this Ukrainian you set up to replace him. I don't want our business compromised."

2200 Fortune Street was a warehouse like any other on the street. An old building made of stone with evidence of some repairs done within the last decade. One large overhead door on a truck dock capable of holding two trailers fronted the building and a side door built to contain a hurricane were the only means of entrance.

The truck backing down into the one open bay of the loading dock was not local. The driver got out to open the rear doors and was confronted by a man yelling at him in Greek. He responded haltingly, apparently not speaking the language very well. The man from the warehouse was telling him to go away that he had the wrong address; the driver was arguing back that he was in the right place. The two moved toward the cab of the truck ostensibly to view the manifest. The driver pulled out some paperwork, apologized that he had no interior light and moved to the front of the cab so he could use the headlights. In front of the truck, the driver handed the papers to the other and as the man was engaged in looking for the address, he spun around, covered the man's mouth with his hand and stuck a foot-long ice pick in his ear. The man from the warehouse shuddered and slumped to the ground. The driver pulled his victim's body to the far side of the vehicle and down into the truck bay. Then he opened the trailer doors and finished backing the truck up to the loading dock.

The men in the warehouse were not professionals or they would never have fallen for such a ploy. They had set an outside guard to alert them of an arrival. Professionals would have waited for the guard. As it was, they had been drinking and playing cards and did not know if there was a delivery expected or not. When the truck bumped the dock, one of them opened the overhead door. Inside the truck was impossibly dark until it was lit up by the strobe effect of automatic weapons cutting down everyone in the warehouse.

Roger Forster's message pager buzzed as they reached the deserted factory. The message read "Payload acquired."

Victor Rothchild looked at it and rubbed his chin. "I think this needs confirmation but I will not chance cell phones out here. Interference and concentration make a pinpoint strike difficult in the cities but out here we are vulnerable."

Agent Sylvan looked up from where she was tying Particka's hands around an I-beam lit by the headlights of the Citroën. "Who is it we are vulnerable to? Aside from the Hellenic Police, who is looking for us?"

"I don't know, but things have gotten so far out of range I could rule out nothing at this point."

Particka looked up sorrowfully, trying to think of something that would save his life. "If you hadn't blown up my yacht I would have given it to you."

The silence that followed hung like a blanket. None of his captors knew what to say for a few seconds. Roger stepped up to the bound and kneeling man and punched him very hard in the mouth. "That's for the black eye."

Particka groaned and spat out a tooth.

"Why on Earth did you double-cross us that way?"

Victor asked as Roger held Hyperion's head back by his hair and raised his fist again.

"How did you know?"

"Know what?"

"How did you know I was not going on with it?"

"When we got to the hotel room, you were not planning to stay. You insisted we were to bring the money to the warehouse where the arms were. That was something we never did and would not do. You kept your gloves on."

"Roger, I kept my gloves on?"

"You take me to a shitty hotel in a run-down district. You were not going to stay there, with me. You did not take your gloves off. I smelled it. I could not see it, I could not hear it, but something smelled and I have a sensitive nose. Had I been wrong, no damage, but I was not. You were sloppy and I am still alive."

Katherine Sylvan caught herself staring at Roger Forster and looked away. She had some experience in the field and counted herself as observant and efficient but the clues that Roger had acted on would have slipped right past her. *"This is the one,"* she thought to herself. *"Of these two, this is the professional."* Then she spoke out loud. "Why did they blacken your eye? If you had done what they wanted, and they suspected nothing, why not simply wait?"

"When this fat poof said he was stepping out for a bottle, I tried to go with him. I knew then that I had been set up and I wanted out. Hyperion Particka never stepped out to get anything. One of his men sapped me and then knocked me about a bit when I didn't go out. I think he expected me to fall over unconscious like they do in the movies."

"So, why was all this necessary? We had an amicable arrangement and you were on the right side of a lucrative deal," Victor pressed their captive, obviously still confused.

"I lost all my money gambling. I got addicted to it. I started playing in high stakes games with people even more dangerous than I knew. I fell into a losing streak and lost it all. I was going to sell the yacht and… everything else when the call came for this job. I still owe the Russians for the armaments they sent this time and they are insisting on payment for the two loads that were lost at border crossings. It was the Russians who came to me and said I must let them handle this thing their way and that I must give you up. If I did not they would do to me what they would do to you."

"So you are not just broke, but deeply in debt to the bloody Soviets, and you are still throwing money around on parties and women." Roger punched him again, this time in the eye.

"Please, stop hitting me."

"Give me a good reason."

"Roger, we have known each other for a long time and have many dealings together. We have trusted each other. I have something I can give you that will make up for it. Something not even the Russians know about."

"I have something for you as well." Forster was almost whispering as he pulled the huge fighting knife out of its sheath. "Something very convincing. You try talking to me about trust? You fat sack of putrescence. I was the one tied to the chair. They were intending on cutting off my privates. How does that sound to you?"

Particka was staring at Forster and the huge knife in his hand, he could not see Rothchild shaking his head.

"Please, I have one treasure remaining. It was smuggled out of France as the German army invaded in World War Two. I have never been able to find anyone who will give me what it is worth. It is worth my life."

Forster picked up a piece of brick and pretended to be sharpening the blade on it. "Keep talking," he said nonchalantly. In truth, he was very interested.

"It is a collection of three works by Van Gogh that were long considered lost. I have had them authenticated but aside from a very few men, no one knows I have them. They were lost to history but I have them. They are worth millions of pounds. They are self-portraits believed to have been destroyed, but in reality they are mine. I have them in a vault in Switzerland. I will give them to you. This will make you become rich men... and woman. There are collectors who will pay millions for them. I would have sold them before but due to their undocumented ownership I was never offered more than a million pounds Sterling for them, for each of them, but I knew they were worth more than that. You should easily get three million euros apiece for the three. That would be three million euros apiece for you."

"I say we just split his head now and save us the trouble later." Forster was enjoying playing bad cop. The difference was that he would readily kill his captive.

"Let's talk about this," was Agent Sylvan's answer.

"First we need to verify that the munitions were indeed acquired. I am having trouble believing he would have set an ambush in the warehouse where he actually kept the ordnance so they may have moved it." Victor Rothchild was the least emotional of the three at this point.

"The police saw the Citroën at the dock just before the explosion. We need to get a different vehicle. Something with a bit more power." The men nodded as Katherine spoke. "They couldn't possibly identify us, no matter what they say. So, if we are stopped, deny everything. The three of us were in the hotel suite together all night."

"What do we do about Hyperion Particka and his Van Gogh collection? I think he's lying and I still want to split his head open."

Victor was still more rational. He gathered his allies close. "We need to verify that the payload was secured and retrieve the payment for it. Since we had to call in a security strike to acquire it, The Director is going to want that money back in the bank. Roger, you and I have been retired behind a desk for years. It's only fortuitous that we did not let our skills languish. Why are we back in the field? Was this set-up designed to eliminate the two of us? The Director is always well informed. I think he knew of the danger involved with this one. I am angry and somewhat afraid."

"Victor, you're suggesting he deliberately hung us out to dry?"

"I can't prove that. I can't prove anything. We have neither the skills nor the education of the younger generation and I shudder at the very thought of delving into the convolutions of The Director's mind. I think we have become expendable. Under no circumstances can we allow The Director to know we secured our associate before the explosion."

"Gentlemen, I suggest we stick to the matters at hand. I will get the sniper rifle from the auto. One of us should stay here with him. It causes less comment if a man and a woman are together. We will need a different car and we need to consider the artworks in Switzerland."

"A very capable woman," commented Roger. He watched her form from behind with admiration as she walked to the car. "A coral snake by her own admission," Victor countered.

The news was having quite a time trumpeting about the murders in the hotel. There were not a lot of handguns in Athens so any bodies that show up with bullets in them were real news. They still had not gotten the news that the three bodies found on the pier had been filled with bullet holes. They had found another body at the site of the explosion but it had been the full-time chef, not the owner and captain of the vessel or any of his bodyguards.

Paul Phillips was wrapping up the occupation of the warehouse at 2200 Fortune St. Phillips had not been present at the attack but had showed up afterward to direct the disposition of the building's contents. In addition to the 50 cases of ammunition, there were American rocket launchers, cases of German hand grenades, Russian and Israeli automatic rifles, Italian Shotguns, Spanish pistols and Mexican land mines. There were also various partial loads of ammunition of various makes and ages, and a variety of rocket-propelled grenades. Phillips cursed the fact that the Cerberus had been blown to bits. It would have been as good a place as any to hide all these arms and better than most. He called in another truck and empty trailer to haul away the additional munitions

The trailer already docked in the loading door had more munitions in it, Chinese and Korean in the rear with cases of American pistols visible behind them. They did not unload the trailer to determine its complete inventory, simply packed more in, used the truck to pull it forward far enough to close and seal the doors, and then eased it back into the dock.

What could be was loaded onto the trailer that the team had driven in. There was too much remaining to be loaded on one truck, but the two skids of shells, wrapped in plastic, were the last loaded since they would be the first removed. For efficiency, they loaded those two skids on the fork truck, backed it onto the truck, and took the fork truck with them as well.

North of Tripoli, on the Peloponnesian peninsula, in the town of Perthon, a C17 transport plane was waiting on an unused cold-war era military airport. The runway had been cleaned up to the point where it was useable. The locals were eager to see the base open again. They had lost a lot of local revenue when it had been replaced by the new military airport in Tripoli. They would be happy to provide the goods and services they had to the military, for a premium price. It was a bit of a disappointment for them to see an American airplane land, but then they remembered the stories of the prices the

four of them first.

It was early afternoon and they had all added anything they knew, so they were all fully aware of circumstances. Paul Phillips pulled a liter of single malt scotch out of the Nissan, and they all had a couple of drinks.

Roger Forster still wanted to split Hyperion Particka's skull but agreed not to do anything rash until he had slept a bit.

Paul Phillips agreed that a man might say anything when his life is on the line.

Victor Rothchild wanted to investigate the possibility that there was money to be gained.

Katherine Sylvan reminded them that even if it were true, the art was in Switzerland and it would be impossible for them to retrieve it with Hyperion as a captive. But, if they had the numbers and the key to the box in the vault, then they did not need Particka at all.

24 Timppanni Street in Giannouli was filling up with more strangers than the town had seen in quite some time. First were the two Athenians who had hired local women as cook and housekeeper. Then the three Germans arrived. The local grocery would need additional stores of beer if they stayed much longer. The two Turks did not drink but were constantly attempting to engage the local ladies in conversation. They spoke a bit of Greek where the Germans spoke almost none. The Italian man who showed up with Italian plates on his Ferrari spoke a very good Greek, but the Moroccan spoke almost none. All nine men spoke a bit of English: the Germans were quite accomplished as were the Moroccan and the Turks. The Greeks and the Italian were less fluent.

They spent a week engaged in drinking beer, playing cards, eating heavily and trying to get lucky with the local women. There were no prostitutes in the small town and while the local ladies were very attractive, most were married. Of the single women, there was none who was not watched closely by the matriarchs of the community.

The two Greeks each had Volvos and had been acting as taxi service from the rail station in Larissa. The Germans had come in by rail all the way. The Turks had flown into Athens and gotten the train from there. The Moroccan had flown into Kalamata and traveled by rail to Athens. Neither he nor the Turks knew they were heading to the same destination but had inadvertently struck up a conversation with each other. The three traveled north together to Larissa.

Of the entire group, the Moroccan was the only one sporting a full beard. The Italian had a thin, black mustache while one of the Germans wore a WWI flying ace style handlebar mustache.

The villa they stayed in was well equipped for an extended stay. The groundskeeper and his burly son had effectively kept the place in order and prevented any break-ins. There was a large dining room that had been converted into a lounge of sorts with a pool table, dart board, an old pinball machine and a large television with satellite reception. There was a video game hooked to the television screen but none of the men utilized it.

Some of these strangers were constantly arguing about what to watch, but none of their arguments broke into any sort of serious action. Neither the Turks nor the lone Moroccan wanted anything to do with the western broadcasts, but they did not object to the television being on.

None of the soldiers had brought guns except the Greeks. They were assured that weapons would be provided and it was not worth trying to smuggle them across the borders. A registered fowling piece with a prepaid hunting permit would have been allowed, but such a weapon was useless for their purposes.

One of the Turks dragged a split log into the side yard

where the building provided shade in the afternoon, and the team used it as a practice target. The log had dried and hardened in the sun so only a direct strike would stick a knife. A range of knives was displayed, differing in shape and utility depending on the environment they sprang from. One of the Germans had bought some Chinese throwing stars and sharpened the edges on a grinder. The steel was poor and had almost no temper so the grinding and subsequent quenching actually increased the hardness. While they all recognized the lack of utility in conflict, they did make for a good competition, since anyone could throw them.

The two Greek fighters preferred diving knives with carbon fiber handles. They were very good with these, though the knives were slightly blade heavy and did not suit the usual throwing knife profile. The Italian gentleman used a stiletto, of which he had a supply and never seemed to be without one. He defended his choice by saying "Small enough to palm, long enough to stab, sharp enough to cut a throat." It turned out the stiletto was also a well balanced throwing weapon once the owner had located its flipping point. The Roman's contention was voiced in response to one of the Germans saying that it was sufficient to cut a pear, but that in a fight one needed a fighting knife. All three of the Germans wore Solingen combat knives with wrapped cord handles. They were proficient with these and displayed an artistry that came of training and much practice.

The Turks used knives with a curved blade that did not lend itself to throwing. They both stoically insisted that throwing a knife was giving it to your enemy or throwing it away when you needed it most. Their blades were not stainless and required oiling to prevent rust but took an edge that could not be matched.

With the variety of cultures represented by this small group of proud young men, it was inevitable that violence would break out among them eventually. There was no accepted leader present and it is the nature of human males to assert themselves, especially when the consumption of alcohol is added to the mix. Of the three Germans, Hans Frendt was the senior and used a mix of comedy and personal charisma to keep his countrymen in check. The Moroccan kept to himself for the most part and was deferential and reserved, causing no ripples in the social fabric of the group.

The worst tension was, predictably, between the Greeks and the Turks. There was simply too much history between them. Throw in an Italian to prod both sides and the eventual conclusion could be disastrous. Discussions of politics and religion raged without any conclusion since there cannot be. It was when history was discussed that debates grew the most heated.

Hans Frendt stepped into the game room on the fifth day and was confronted by two irate Turkish fighters with drawn knives on one side of the room and the two Greeks on the other, one of whom held a handgun. A lesser man would have turned and left the situation to its logical end, but Hans, a former drill sergeant, was no such man. At six foot, he stood taller than any of the four and his bull chest produced a roar that shouted them all down.

"Stand away. All of you. I will not allow you to be at odds. Have you come here to settle the wars a thousand years old? Stand away. Sheathe your weapons, now!"

The verbal assault that replied was a mix of languages that the most accomplished of interpreters could not have deciphered. He asserted in English, "No. I will not listen. There will be no more discussion of this. We are here to be together, not to kill each other. I will not go into a zone with men that will not support one another."

Hans pulled his own knife and threw it on the floor. "If you are so eager to die, then turn your weapons on yourselves." His words silenced both sides. "Are you children in the schoolyard? Na na na. Your mother is a donkey. No!

You are all warriors, allied against a common enemy. You are premier examples of killing machines. If you kill each other, what will the song sound like? They were fools who let the past consume them. They were so stubborn they could not do the job. Blinded by hate for nothing, they died for no reason."

Drawn by the shouting, the other Germans entered and stood behind Hans.

"If you want history, stand away and listen. Nazi Germany conquered Europe because the other countries did not stand together. The American Indian was too busy hating his fellow tribesman to band together and fight off the European invasion. The Roman Empire fell when it became fragmented. The British Empire fell to fragments. If we are to fight, then let us fight as one or we will die as many. When the job is done, you will never again see the other. Do not expect you will be friends, but expect you will be allies."

The men were cowed in the face of reason and put their weapons away.

"Now you must apologize to each other. This is not what I expect from soldiers."

The Greeks and the Turks would never become friends but they did apologize to each other and there were no further incidents. Thomas Contini, the sole Italian member of the group, kept to himself after this incident. It was no secret that he had been playing the two sides against each other, but nothing was said of it. He was secretly proud of the condition he had stirred up but vowed to remain in the shadows in consideration of the integrity of his skin.

Gunter Krauss was having a beer and looking out over the olive groves that ringed the town. He was joined by Ambrose Anatolios, the Greek who had not drawn his pistol in the earlier confrontation. Ambrose had a bottle of red wine he was sipping conservatively from. The two of them sat on a flat rock that jutted out from the side of a long sloping hill.

They had not spoken in private before.

"Wine sits better in my belly than beer," began the Greek. "I say nothing bad about beer but wine suits me more."

"I drink wine from time to time, with food. When eating, wine is better. When drinking, beer is best."

"Why do you do this?"

"Watch the farmers? I guess I have a romantic thought about what it means to work in the dirt."

"Non. I ask why you do this for working."

"Ah. I…" The German pursed his thin lips and stared at his well polished boots. "I am of no good at working with people, other people."

"Mmm. I worked in vineyards and olive, uh… trees as a boy. It pays to keep you poor and the work is hard."

"Ya. I said a romantic thought. I have never worked as a farmer. I was waiter on tables in Bremen as a child. I gave the wrong soup to the public. I drove a truck and kept putting the trailer in holes, ah… in ditches. You know, turning corners. I worked in factory but my brain was working on other things and I could not continue. Why do you?"

"Not much good money in country and no education for city job. I work in a sheep house. I kill sheep and think I could do this to a man and make money. The sheep not good money. Good money for the man."

"Ja. It is for me, the only thing I do good. I do not like to stay in one place. My brain keeps saying you must go, you must run away again."

"If we fight, you not run away?" Ambrose looked concerned.

"No. Never. If we fight, I run to the fight. I only fight good. So I must fight. I try army but not good as soldier. Good to kill but not to shine officers' boots. I shine my own boots."

"I try fishing. Lots of good fishing in Aegean, and we fish for living forever to eat a lot of fish. All we get is fish, lots of fish. I want more than fish." Anatolios took a long pull on the wine bottle as if to punctuate the statement.

Krauss hoisted his half empty mug in appreciation and drained it. Wiping a drip off his chin he said, "Ja. I too want more."

After two more days, the call came in. They loaded themselves into the Volvos with what few items they had with them and headed for Athens.

Chapter Six
Transfer

Piccadilly Paul Phillips looked comfortable and satisfied with his lot in life. At 10 in the morning he was practically alone in the café. His cup of coffee was half empty and half cold. The door opened and the doorway was filled with two massive forms, one after another. They moved toward him, their grace belying their size.

"Glasgow Gordon MacMaster," he said softly as he stood and extended his hand. "And your associate…"

"Tarrytown Terry Kingston," the Australian said as he thrust his hand forward almost crushing Paul's hand in his bear-like grip. Though he did not show it in any way, Terry took personal pleasure in the almost imperceptible wince that crossed the Londoner's face. Though the two had never been introduced, they were familiar with each other's reputations.

"How are you enjoying Athens, gentlemen?"

"With all the gusto we can manage. Aye, Athens is a city of verve and life. I love it. It's wonderful to be touring Greece." The volume and words were for the benefit of the café staff. MacMaster actually was having a good time. It was his nature to have a good time, and having Terry Kingston with him to watch his back allowed him to loosen up a little. Loosening up a little did not preclude instant response to a threat, however. The nature of the business kept those so employed keyed to a constant humming vibration. It made for poor interpersonal relations for many couples.

"I'm glad to hear you're having a good time." Paul's sarcastic inflection and sardonic tone reflected that the truth was far from what he had said.

"Bring me a Turkish coffee, please," Gordon asked the waiter.

"Beer, mate," said Terry.

"Mythos?"

"Yeah, that'll be fine. Thanks."

As they drank their choices, they spoke in low tones. Piccadilly Paul told his associates about the plane, its location and the fact that the payload was aboard.

"I'll be flying the plane, Terry here is my co-pilot. So you can get rid of whatever pilot you planned on saddling us with. It looks like west of Irbil might be the best spot for the transfer. It's out of the mountains and there's not much anywhere near there. It should be flat enough there since it isn't full blown sand dune desert. We're looking at 20 miles west of Irbil, just south of the road from Mosul. I don't know how you're contacting these Mujahedeen but we need to set it up there."

"We are in e-mail contact with them. I will put forth the suggestion. It is unlikely they will acquiesce to any requests on our part. We may get something more suitable if we suggest the desert southwest of Mosul. There is no way we can get them to trust us. They will probably show up without the hostage to ensure that the goods are indeed where they should be before bringing out the Englishman."

"This sort of operation must be played by ear. Do you have arms for the team secured?"

"Yes. We got them as an unexpected bonus from our contact."

"Good, now this is what I want fabricated."

The Ferrari was left in Giannouli under the care of a middle-aged local couple who stayed in the Timppanni Street address until their return.

Nine men stuffed into two vehicles was uncomfortable at the least. Four of the nine smoked so they got in one car and five men were stuffed into the other. It took longer than they wanted to reach Fortune Street in Athens and the whole team was testy as they entered the warehouse.

Inside the warehouse they found their contacts relaxing

on couches. Introductions were begun but the big redhead cut it off immediately.

"I don't wish to know your names. You have been sent here for a job and that is why you are here. We are not here to make friends we may need to mourn later, or give up under torture. You will refer to me as Glasgow. This is Tarrytown. He is my second-in-command. You will obey him, as you would me, in my absence."

"Ah, it is partly revealing," one of the Germans began. "You may refer to me as Bremen. This is Berlin and finally, ah, Stuttgart."

"Ya, Stuttgart," confirmed the third.

"You may call me Tangiers," the Moroccan said softly with a bow.

"I am Konya. This is Van," the larger of the two Turks said.

"The Italian will be Roma and proud to be Roman."

"Only one of us can be Athens, so I will be Troy."

"And I will be Sparta." The other Greek was grinning.

"Good," roared Gordon MacMaster. "We have names, we have guns, we have a plane and we have a job. It is too late for the banks to be open but I have, here, a partial payment for each of you." He handed out packets of British pounds to each of the newcomers. "Troy and Sparta, the Volvos are yours?"

"Yes, uh, Glazgo, they are ours."

"We have a couple of associates removing them to a secure location. Roma, you did not bring your auto?"

"No. It was left. I did not know it secure here."

"Okay. Well, shall we eat, drink, and be merry, for tomorrow we die?"

Some of the crew understood the reference some did not. Gordon could tell from the expressions on some of the faces that he had made a mistake and stumbled to correct it. "What I mean is eat, drink, and be merry, for tomorrow we kill." This brought a more robust response.

There was a smorgasbord under a tarp. It would have been difficult to accommodate all the different tastes assembled here, but there was a wide array of cold foods. Given the nature of the loads in the warehouse, it was seen as prudent to have only cold foods, even though much had been transferred to the trailers. There was a variety of beers, liquors and a chunk of hashish. The crew made a feast and a party of it. After a couple of hours of reveling, the sun had gone down, the warehouse district was deserted. The overhead door was opened, and the furniture was loaded onto a new truck that was parked in the dock. Some of the nine newcomers, the Scotsman and the Aussie filled the back of the truck with their weapons and themselves and closed the door behind them. The Greeks were in the cab of the truck. None of the crew had gotten too impaired, but they were all feeling good as the truck pulled out of the dock.

The truck pulled onto the runway before morning. Gordon MacMaster pulled out his brand new cell phone and dialed a pager number then keyed in a predetermined seven number code. The back of the plane unlocked and descended. The three men in the plane walked out with their automatic weapons at ready.

"Nice night for a flight?" Gordon asked.

"It's about time you got here. We finished up the mods two days ago."

"It's all part of the job. Sparta, give them the keys so they can get this truck out of here. Everybody get your weapons and get on board. Now comes the really fun part."

The flight had a legitimate number and flight plan. It was supposed to be going to Dharbin, Saudi Arabia. Departure time from Tripoli was in four hours, and they were not going to move until then. They inspected the false wall and door, went over the plans for the transfer, talked about how long it would take and whether or not the diplomat was still alive and how best to secure the largest payoff. They decided if anyone with a price on their head was to be killed by the team then, if possible, the head should be brought with them.

After securing their gear, they locked up the hatches and started the four Pratt and Whitney PW2040 turbofan engines. By departure time, they would be nice and warm.

"Satisfied, mate?" asked Terry Kingston.

"Aye, Colonel Richter came through for me this time. I told him I didn't want any cowboys and it doesn't look like he sent me any. Every man here seems old enough to know what to do and when, but young enough to be able to move if the need arises. I'm not sure about Tangiers though. He doesn't seem the type, he looks as though he may hesitate."

"Glasgow, you're worried about nothing. Perhaps you didn't notice how that man broke down the Uzi when you handed it to him. He had it apart, inspected and reassembled before I could guzzle a beer. He's not going to be the sticker. I'd say the Roman is more likely to flinch."

"Could be. Say, did you notice what Phillips said about our supplies? Unexpected bonus."

"What bonus, the dead-or-alives?"

"No. When I asked if munitions had been secured for the men, he said they had come as an unexpected bonus from their contact. Why, or I should ask how, would there be an 'unexpected bonus' in the arms business? There is only one way that happens; when the delivering party is not insisting on payment."

"I follow. The only way the transport faction doesn't insist on payment is when they no longer have a voice." Terry began to see where this line of questioning was going and tried to run through his mental soundtrack of the conversation they had been in days earlier.

"And who would that fit at this point in time?"

"Well, they didn't find the body yet, did they? Particka's

no doubt feeding the fish. So the British blew up that huge yacht to kill their contact and seize a couple of lousy guns? It doesn't read. Your plot lacks verisimilitude. Even those tight asses need motivation and it's not there." Terry lit a cigarette and exhaled the smoke through his nose. "Hippy-on Particka was a victim of his own system. He pissed somebody off real bad and they killed him for it. Sold guns to the wrong side one time too many, probably. On the other hand, it may have been a fuel leak like the telly said."

The two looked at each other with smiles on their faces. Network news was as clueless about what really made things happen as a chicken in a henhouse. They were protected from reality by a thin veil, when, if damaged, would let the fox in.

"It's time." Gordon MacMaster grabbed the microphone and asked the tower in Tripoli for permission to take off. It seems that the proper palms had been greased because permission was granted. They were just clearing land when the sun rose in the east.

When they landed on the dry Persian plain, the sun was pounding down like a hammer. They brought the plane down close to the north-south road that runs through the eastern part of the desert, west of Irbil and east of Mosul. This was the predetermined spot for the transfer, within a few miles. The call was made to the English deputies and an e-mail was returned to the kidnappers. From there, the waiting game resumed.

After all the planning and all the trouble this operation had seen, it came down to waiting for an implacable enemy that had out-waited empires, despots and every major world power. Waiting in stressful and perilous situations is bad enough in a comfortable environment; waiting in the desert is enough to drive men mad.

It was fortunate that the men in the plane were professionals. Amateurs would never have been able to understand the need for silence and subterfuge. They would not have understood that the desert itself was as great an enemy as those they were waiting for. The psychological toll of waiting in the burning heat of the day would wear down those unprepared for it and precipitate mistakes. It would cause them to become overanxious and flinch. This crew was not easily overtaxed, though. No census had been taken among them, but it was plain that between the members of this expedition there had been enough wet work to depopulate a small city. So they waited without complaint in the blinding light of day.

After a couple of hours, the inside of the plane heated up like a furnace. It became necessary to drop the cargo door. Another hour and the men inside the false wall were unable to remain there. They stayed within the body of the plane or under the wings to keep from sun stroke. The day had that feeling of never coming to an end when waiting endlessly. Finally, the sun went down with no sight of their contacts.

Six men slept while five stood watch, then five men slept. The Greeks and the Turks were assigned opposite shifts. MacMaster had the good sense to listen when that was suggested.

The sun had not peered over the horizon when they first heard the truck zigzagging across the desert sands. The crew took up positions on the inside and outside of the plane. The military-style truck had two men in the front and four men in the back. All six men had Kalashnikov rifles in their hands and cloths wrapped around their faces. They stopped within headlight range of the plane. The man in the passenger seat got out and was surrounded by the others.

Gordon MacMaster was standing under the wing of the plane, flanked by two Turks and fronted by Tangiers, the Moroccan. All four men wore long flowing robes, not only traditional to Arabic desert dwellers but practical in terms of concealing weapons.

The arrivals were wearing Desert Storm-style camouflage gear. Two of them had the floppy Aussie hats. The obvious leader began in a loud and abrasive voice. Van, the man from closest to the region they were in, translated.

"He says they are here for the ammunition."

"Ask him where is the English diplomat."

"He says they are holding him till they get the ammunition."

"Tell him, making sure he understands, that we will not wait another day in this hell. Tell him that if we do not have the diplomat by 10 o'clock this morning, we will fly this plane out of here and they will get nothing. Tell him that we have bargained in good faith and we expect them to do the same, and tell him if he tries to take our cargo he will be blown to bits by the man on top of the wing who has them in the sights of a rocket-propelled fragmentation grenade."

The translation was made and when Van was done talking, the entire group looked up at the wing of the plane where they saw only the business end of a rocket launcher in the first dim rays of sunlight. None of the men reacted to this introduction. They were obviously members of a society that saw death as a necessary function of life. They did not seem to value their own lives much.

"He says he must see the cargo," Van translated. "He knows he cannot bully us, now."

"Tell him that he and I will move to the back of the plane and inspect the load. The others will remain where they are."

There was some noisy discussion about this. The leader would not step out of the human shield ring about him. Finally another man stepped forward to inspect the load. He and Gordon MacMaster moved to the dropped tail of the plane and went inside. The two pallets of ordnance seemed insignificant compared to the size of the plane. By the light of a pair of flashlights, the man in fatigues cut open some of the plastic and pried open one of the wooden cases. Inside the bullets were also wrapped in clear plastic. He reached out with his knife blade to cut the plastic but he was cut short by MacMaster's hand. He began to protest in Arabic but was no match for the Scotsman who all but threw him out the back of the plane. He might have used his weapon at that point, but the muzzle of an Uzi was pointed directly at him from underneath his opponent's robes.

The leader of the group took a conciliatory tone, urging his bodyguard to calm down and stand down. He was obviously aware that he was at a disadvantage, and that there was nothing to be gained with going to war with this group of infidels.

When they had returned to their standoff positions, the leader again addressed MacMaster. "He says," translated Van, "that you should come with them and he will leave a man here to ensure your safe return."

"Tell him the only way I go is if he stays here, not one of his men."

"No, he says that is impossible."

"Ask him why we are playing foolish games. No, strike that. Tell him we are both accomplished men who have seen a lot of life and a lot of death, and it will benefit us both to simply deal honorably."

"He says American infidels have no honor, but he can see that you have had many dealings with many men."

"Tell him we can both have many more dealings with men if we both act with honor today. Tell him there are no Americans here, only an American plane." After the translation, he continued. "Tell him also that he can end up with 50 cases of ammunition or 100 kilos of dead English meat. The choice is his."

That elicited a laugh from the leader. He then barked orders and the six men returned to the truck. The truck drove in a straight line, crossing the zigzagging tracks it had made on the way in. The sun was rising, outlining the dust cloud it left behind it.

"Well, mate, it looks as though that one may have been Ahmed al-Hamidi. He is worth about 80,000 pounds by himself." Tarrytown was walking into the rising sun, out from behind a patch of grass.

"Chicken feed in the long run, but worth it as a bonus. Did you mark the truck?"

"Magnetic tracker inside the bumper. Should be good for about three weeks or more.

"Good. All right crew, now is when the real danger begins. They know where we are and they are as likely to come back with an assault team as anything else. Sparta, join Troy on the wing; take a couple more rocket launchers with you. They only saw four of us so if they come back we have the element of surprise. Stuttgart, Bremen, Berlin and Rome, I need you flanking their approach. Conceal yourselves on the west side of those dunes. Two with sniper rifles, four automatics. If action begins, take out the trucks first, before you take out the personnel. A single shot to the radiator will disable a vehicle in this heat. If you can't get the radiator, take two tires. Van, you will stay here with me to translate. Tangiers and Konya, inside the body, behind the wall and Tarrytown in the cockpit. Everybody remember, if they disable the plane, we have no way out of here. We make the swap first. We need to be in the air before we initiate anything, but if they attack us, we need to make sure they are put out of business fast. Any questions?"

"I wish to carry a sniper rifle on the wing," opened Sparta.

"No, I want you holding the rocket launchers. The RPGs are heat seeking so they go straight for the engine block. Take a sniper scope with you so you can spot first and remember that they might use a different angle of approach."

"They will not attack us," said Tangiers quietly.

"What is it that makes you think this way?" asked Roma.

"They need to make a precedent. They need to set a policy. They want this to go smoothly so they can do it again and again. Recall that the civilized man does not deal with terrorists. We are dealing with them, giving them what they want. They will want this to happen very badly. They want this to happen smooth."

"Aye, that's a nice theory," said Glasgow "but we cannot allow our expectations to cause us to hesitate. If they step out of line, wipe them out."

The crew moved to their positions and the Scotsman pulled out his cell phone. His fears of having the phone pinpoint him had become irrelevant once they were in the air over the Mediterranean. He reached Paul Phillips and told him that first contact had been made and asked about the tracking signal.

"The signal is still moving away from your location. We have the plane on satellite image. It's a bit blurry but I'm sure it's you. We could see some disturbance but we don't have the resolution to make out the truck.

"Don't worry about the plane. Follow the truck. Give us the coordinates when it stops and let us know if it is returning to us."

"Roger that. We have been issued orders for you that you make sure the transfer is completed before hostilities can be initiated. Do you copy?"

"Transfer to be completed." Glasgow Gordon closed the connection. Hostilities were not to be initiated until afterward anyway.

In 20 minutes, the cell phone rang again. Piccadilly Paul gave the coordinates and some other, disturbing news. There were three trucks heading their way. MacMaster alerted the team.

It was 10 minutes before the trucks' dust plumes were

visible. A couple of minutes later the three trucks pulled into view. The middle truck had a man bound in a sheet, standing and tied around the back window. They pulled up to the back of the plane and turned so they faced away from it. Eight men got out with cloths wrapped around their heads and faces. It did not appear that Ahmed al-Hamidi was with them, but it was difficult to tell.

Gordon MacMaster met them with his hands behind his back. Van was on his side holding his Uzi at the ready.

"Here is your English pig," said one of them in English. "He is your problem now."

"Cut him free, please," Gordon said in a calm and even tone.

"Cut him free yourself!" was the answer.

"No. You are to deliver him to us. Cut him free."

"We make the rules here. We are in charge. If you were Americans, we would kill you already."

Gordon smiled a sarcastic smile and asked if he could borrow one man's hat for a minute. The English speaker translated the request, the man with the hat glanced at one of the other men who nodded his head, marking him as the leader of this little band.

MacMaster took the hat and held it above his head while pointing to the northwest. The shot was never heard but the hat was torn from his hand and thrown a dozen feet away. When he picked it back up it had a hole the size of a shilling through the top. He handed the hat back to its owner with his finger sticking through the hole. He turned to Van and said, "Translate. Make no mistake, we are not Americans and if you kill me, you will never leave the desert."

The men in fatigues did not look at ease and were staring in the direction the shot came from. Some were muttering in Arabic. One of the men, the one that had been looked to for guidance earlier, took the lead role and spoke loudly. The men looked at him but no one moved. He raised his voice further and pointed out two of the men. They jumped onto the back of the truck and took out knives. The man then spoke to the Scotsman and was translated by Van. "You will get the Englishman when we have loaded the shells."

"How do we know that is the man we are here for and that he is alive?"

The leader said something untranslatable and then ordered his men to free the Englishman's head. The knives sliced through the sheet and a man's head was brought into view. He had white hair and had not shaved in a couple of weeks. He did not look as though he was in the best of shape but he was breathing as was evinced by the torrent of words that tumbled from his mouth after the duct tape had been removed. The tape took some white beard hair with it and its removal was no doubt painful.

"Very well, load the shells."

One man stayed on the truck with the white-haired English diplomat. Six men entered the airplane and began hauling out the crates, a man at each end. It did not take long to move both skids of product that way and all three trucks got some. The one man left on the truck with a knife almost resignedly cut the diplomat loose and the man threw off the sheet and jumped out of the bed to embrace Gordon MacMaster while babbling wild thanks in English.

Even with the deal done neither side trusted the other. They backed away slowly and cautiously took their leaves of each other.

Tarrytown Terry was firing up the engines when Gordon's cell phone went off again. "Glasgow," he answered.

"The trucks are moving away. Three different directions. Was the transfer successful?"

"Transfer complete."

"Good. Listen closely. There are to be no further acts of aggression on your part. You will be paid your agreed-upon fee, including your team. No further engagement is that clear?"

"Not completely. Let me get out of the range of these engines. I'm not sure I heard you properly." Once inside the cockpit with Terry and the diplomat, Glasgow Gordon reiterated his question.

"That is correct. There is to be no further engagement of the enemy. This came last minute from above. The deal is done. You will be paid full measure. Take the plane to Dharbin and land it. You will be met by a delegation there. Do you copy?"

"Roger, copy that."

"Congratulations on a mission well done."

"Thank you." Gordon MacMaster was truly troubled when he hung up the phone. It was not that he didn't get to eliminate terrorists, that was irrelevant, and it was not the extra money to be potentially gained by securing wanted men, though extra money is always an incentive; it was the last minute orders. Last minute orders in the field usually spelled disaster; some micromanaging suit sending men into a meat grinder. In this case there was no such indication, but the second change of plans this morning left him uneasy and questioning what was actually going on.

"Are we secure for take-off?" Terry asked.

"Hang on. There has been a change of plans," answered Gordon, "I'm sorry, is there something I should get you?" He addressed the diplomat.

"Please, call me John. John Marshall."

"John John Marshall, call me Glasgow. This is Tarrytown. In the back of the plane we have a collection of murderers, mercenaries, assassins and slaughterhouse butchers. We're here to get you out of here."

"And don't think I don't appreciate it. I thought for sure I'd end up like Danny Pearl, with my head nailed to the wall. You have my greatest appreciation. I was just wondering if any of you had a cigarette I might have and some water?"

Terry fished out a cigarette for him and they left him smoking it.

In the back of the plane, Gordon explained what he had been told and why it concerned him. He asked if anybody had any idea why the mission would be truncated this way.

"One of the Iraqis has a good friend in Parliament?"

"They want to ensure that the hostage gets home safe?"

"The Turks have decided to give up their claim?" Roma's comment drew him a dirty look from Konya.

"The Turks are going to take down the group by themselves?"

"The Syrians want a piece of the pie?"

After all the other theories had been put forth, Tangiers spoke in his quiet way. "Somebody wants the insurgents to have these bullets. Perhaps they are defective in some way. Perhaps every third one explodes rather than firing. Perhaps there is a burr on the jackets that jams the rifle."

Gordon MacMaster looked at the Moroccan with growing respect. "Regardless of the reason, we have been spared the bloodshed. We have been asked to proceed to Saudi Arabia to deliver our present load. Does anyone have a problem with Saudi Arabia?"

"Yes, it's too hot, it smells like oil and it's full of Arabs." Berlin's comment broke a tension that had tightened up the crew since they arrived on the desert sands, and they all laughed explosively except the Turks who were only mildly amused.

The Director was perplexed. This is not a condition he was used to nor was he comfortable with it. His budget was slim at the best of times due to the clandestine nature of his operations, so he had learned it expedient to take outside contracts when deemed lucrative and in the best interests of the Crown. The present contract had made sense when it had been taken up, the win-win situation, but now it did not make sense. Initially, the mercenary team, untraceable to any of the major interests, was to rescue a British diplomat and remove a set of insurgents from the equation; a perfect solution. The suggestion that their Turkish allies end up with the munitions was acceptable though not optimal. The optimal solution would have been to have the deputies retrieve the rounds and eliminate the mercenaries as well. His superiors had strictly forbidden this since it might have allowed the trail to lead back to England. Once terrorists get the message that a major power will deal with them, all hell breaks loose. None of this perplexed The Director.

The confounding thing was the eleventh hour call from the financiers of the project indicating that the terrorists were to be left unmolested. He had transmitted the message. It had gotten to the mercenaries with no time to spare. Effective, efficient and thorough, Gordon MacMaster had already secured John Marshall and was about to eliminate the kidnappers. From what The Director gathered, the plan would have eliminated the ransom as well; not optimal but certainly better than allowing terrorist insurgents to retain possession of it. This move could cost thousands of lives.

The Director glanced up at the satellite image and saw three dust clouds moving away from the C17. A mile away from the plane, they split off in three different directions. The north truck had a tracker on it so there would be no doubt about where it went. It looked as though the middle truck was going back to the spot where the tagged truck had stopped to pick up the hostage. The south truck was heading to an unknown destination. The Director relit his pipe and puffed on it slowly. He turned and checked a wider-angle screen that gave him no intelligence. Then he tried a different screen, one that tracked planned flights and actual locations of airplanes. It did not show the C17, despite the plane's five onboard computers, because the satellite positioning system had been disabled. It did show one commercial flight at 30,000 feet leaving Syria, headed for Istanbul, but there was another plane detected that did not have a flight plan listed. It was a fighter plane coming in from Iran, in the direction of the C17 and suddenly, it disappeared.

The Director saw it all playing out in his head. The fighter plane was heading for the drop point and it could not be on a peaceful mission. The plane that had blown Particka's mega-yacht out of the water had shown no satellite positioning signal. He switched to a ground-based radar screen and there it was, heading in and dropping altitude.

Ordinarily, The Director would not have taken action on something like this. It was unusual that he even considered it. He shrugged and took a sip of water. He might not have gotten the munitions back for resale, but the mission had been completed as far as his American backers were concerned. They had made it clear that the diplomat was of no concern to them. Their primary concern, it seems, had been to provide the Iraqi patriots with munitions. The bottom line was the remainder of remunerations would be forthcoming and the cost of the mercenaries would be all but eliminated. With Particka's death, the cost of the arms merchant's services was eliminated and any questions about the C17 were beyond answers since it was registered as Particka's plane. Some of the munitions payment had been diverted to a down payment for the fighters. The remainder of it should be returning soon. He refilled his pipe and lit it up. There was no doubt in his mind that the incoming fighter plane had been commissioned to shoot down the huge American transport, eliminating the remaining cost of the operation. This was actually quite satisfactory to him since he would lose no men. The operation could not be traced to any British organization at this point and the C17 was of no loss to any living man. Suddenly he felt so pleased with himself he called James and asked for a porter.

Paul Phillips was watching the satellite feed closely on his laptop computer. He was in a coffee house on the west bank of the Danube in Budapest. As was his custom, he sat with his face to the door and his back to the wall. He was disappointed that there were no power outlets here, but had found that there are very few cafés in this part of the world that have internet connection and power outlets. He was running the program from the laptop's battery and with a satellite feed. He saw the dust begin to fly from behind the plane as the engines were started. He was satisfied that the trucks had not turned around and there were no other vehicles heading out.

Victor Rothchild was flying back to London with the remainder of the cash that had not been paid for the ordnance. Agent Sylvan did not accompany him. She and Deputy Forster had purchased rail tickets to Geneva. All four of them had taken advantage of Hyperion Particka's generosity. He had been carrying a large store of cash on him when he was taken. He had obviously planned on staying out of sight for a while. Roger and Katherine would call Paul when they were in Geneva. He would join them in Bern.

Roger had caught Katherine's eye somehow. Paul had pretended not to notice and Victor had not but it was enough for a sharp observer. Paul sighed and felt a jealous tug. Katherine was a beautiful woman and her dangerous side just made her more appealing.

The charge bar on the screen started flashing to indicate that the charge was getting low. Thinking that it looked like mission accomplished, he was just about to shut his laptop down when he thought of another man who had announced "Mission accomplished" in Iraq and had gotten burned for years for it. He continued watching until the dust cloud from the C17 transport plane had died down. The trade had been made and the team was off the ground. He would have some lunch and then take the computer back to the room for a recharge.

Chapter Seven
Escape

So often their line of work was just like prison. The challenge was not so much getting in or doing the job but getting out alive.

The on-board systems picked up the attacker on radar long before they saw it.

"We've got a problem, Terry," Gordon said, forgetting for the moment that they were not using real names. "It's an old fighter jet coming in from the north."

"Old is right, mate. It looks like a MiG-21. Cold war tech. It's still faster than we are."

"Almost three times as fast. If I remember, they carry two K-13s. Very much like American Sidewinders. Ready the countermeasures. I might be wrong, but I think somebody is about to try blowing us out of the sky." Switching on the intercom he said, "This is Captain Glasgow. Tie yourselves off. We are in for a very bumpy ride."

The antiquated Soviet-era fighter came in at almost mach two; the pilot pressing its systems for all it had. The crew of the C17 lost any doubt of its intentions. Pilot and co-pilot were fully aware that the top speed for the transport was only mach 0.74, leaving no way to outrun or outmaneuver the fighter. With a greater fuel payload, they could outlast it but would be blasted out of the air long before then.

Both Gordon MacMaster and Terry Kingston knew their situation was desperate. When John Marshall stood up in the cockpit and started asking questions, Terry almost got upset. He told the diplomat that he would either be seated or he would be tied to the chair. Marshall sat back down without a word and Terry threw him the remainder of his pack of cigarettes.

Almost on cue the air-to-air missiles launched. At mach 2.5 they came in unbelievably fast, but with his hand above the launch button, Gordon MacMaster would not be rushed. He waited until they were just out of final homing range and then launched the flares and the POET jamming decoys. With the radar jammed, the rockets reverted to infrared detection. The flares captured the infrared tracking system with their much hotter signature and the rockets veered off from the real target and exploded well to the rear of the transport.

"Bloody well right, mate. Both of 'em."

"That old dog still has an NR-30. We're not out of the woods yet.

Knowing that the rockets had not accomplished the objective and that the element of surprise had been lost, the fighter pilot bored in quickly with his 30 mm machine gun.

On the first pass, the transport pilot dropped his flaps, killing his speed and moving the nose of the plane up. The fighter did not score a single hit but would not be fooled by the same maneuver twice. The reality was that the transport plane was no match for even this ancient fighter when it came to agility.

On its second pass, even though the C17 rolled violently to starboard, it peppered the side with shells. The fighter was shooting for the engines and Gordon MacMaster was doing everything he could to prevent that.

The third pass came from behind. Nothing he could do would save the engines from a rear attack. Terry Kingston jumped out of the co-pilots seat yelling "Drop the loading gate," and ran for the back of the plane. The gate was already coming down when he got past the false wall. The interior of the plane was exploding with tracer rounds and short-circuits as the fighter strafed them from behind. Terry saw Troy and Sparta both thrown against the false wall with huge gaping holes blown in their chests. He also saw Tangiers, roped off in the middle of the gate as it came down, holding a shoulder-fired rocket launcher. Outlined on the gate, he was a perfect target, though not what the MiG-21 pilot was shooting for. The fighter came into range and Tangiers launched the heat-seeking missile. It was not a matter of seconds between the time the pilot saw the rocket, tried to roll out of the way, and the fighter's turbojet engine sucked it in. The proximity was such that the explosion temporarily blinded those still able to see. When sight returned, the fighter was already halfway to the ground and the C17 was climbing. There was another explosion when the Soviet fighter struck the desert floor. Everyone else in the back of the transport was roped off but Terry had no support. He began to fly toward the open bay as the floor moved toward vertical. Only Stuttgart's arm, linking with his, prevented him from joining the MiG on the desert floor. He was thrown against the dead body he had known only as Berlin, and desperately grabbed the strap that held the body to the wall.

The transport began to level off and the loading door was closing. Terry clambered toward the cockpit, his feet slipping on the blood-slick deck.

"Glasgow, we've got casualties and the skin is compromised. We need to drop altitude. I suggest we find another air field and decide how we are going to explain the dead men."

"Take over. Drop altitude and air speed and keep us over the desert. Turn us around if need be. I need to be over unpopulated land."

"You got it, mate."

Gordon moved to the cargo area to assess the damage. The port side of the plane was peppered with holes. The fake wall built twelve feet back from the actual front wall had at least a dozen holes in it, but it had slowed the rounds enough that they had not penetrated the cockpit. The showers of sparks from short-circuited wires had stopped before he stepped onto the bloody floor; their breakers had tripped.

The casualties were testimony to the devastating effect

of a 30 mm machine gun. Troy and Sparta were hanging by the fake wall, their chests blown open. Berlin was hanging on the port side, a ghastly pit where his stomach had been. Bremen hung next to him, all but blown in half at the hips. Stuttgart had escaped only because of the brace he stood in front of. Van was alive but his Turkish partner Konya had taken one in the head. Roma was standing untied in the middle of the deck wiping Konya's brains off his face and swearing in Italian. Tangiers was unclamping himself from the loading dock.

"What in the name of all holies is this?" Roma wanted to know holding out his shirt, covered with blood, brains and bits of skull.

"There's nothing holy about this. Is anyone injured?" MacMaster stood tall and spoke loud. He did not give in to the urge to stare at the dead; he had seen enough dead. "Stuttgart, are you injured?"

"No, but I fear my countrymen are dead."

"Roma?"

"I am unharmed."

"Van?"

Van was wailing wildly in Arabic and did not even hear the question. He had dropped to his knees and was crying and shaking Konya's corpse.

Gordon turned away from the Turk to the Moroccan. A blood stain was growing on his white robes. "Get in the cockpit and see if that Englishman can do something besides smoke cigarettes. Stuttgart, Roma, help me move these bodies to the back of the plane."

"Are we going to land and bury them properly?"

"No. I don't know what is going on or who else is coming after us. We cannot land anywhere with dead bodies. They go out the back. Take their ID's and any money they have on them and give it to me." It did not take them long to move the two dead Germans and the Greeks to the back, but when they approached Van, he howled at them in a language no one else could follow.

The loading deck began to drop again. MacMaster turned to the two who had been helping him and told them both to tie off. He turned back to Van, surprised to find he was standing silently, facing him. "We do it this way, but I will do the honors and I will suffer the consequences." He then turned, unsnapped the carabineer holding his countryman to the wall of the plane and threw the headless body over his shoulder. Standing tall he walked to the back of the plane and threw the body onto the now close-to-horizontal loading deck. The deck continued dropping while Glasgow and Van threw the bodies of their erstwhile partners out.

"Take some of the drinking water and clean up this blood before it dries," Gordon MacMaster barked. "We need to find a safe place to land."

"Who can we turn to now?" asked the sole remaining German. "We have been betrayed and compromised."

"I need to talk to our captive first. There is much to discuss."

Back in the cabin, Tangiers had been bandaged. A bullet had plowed a furrow in his right shoulder but had not struck a bone. He thanked the English diplomat for the bandage and proceeded to the body of the plane to do what he could to help.

Gordon began grilling John Marshall. Not much of what he had to say seemed out of line from what he already knew. The men who had kidnapped him had kept him in a dark room, blindfolded half the time and relatively unmolested as far as physical abuse went. Marshall had found it odd that the men spoke what seemed more a southern Turkish dialect than northern Iraqi.

Marshall was nothing more than Second Secretary of the British Consul in Baghdad. Given the temper of the times, he was to be congratulated for the courage it required to even stay in Baghdad. Once the United States had left, the years of sectarian violence ran their course. The lawless gangs stopped attacking every person not of their clan or sect. President Aahmed il Anahtirik had clamped down on both the Sunnis and the Shi'ites with an iron hand. He may have been democratically elected but he employed the same methods of control that Saddam Hussein had used. Then, of course, the Turks had invaded from the north and annexed everything north of the 35th parallel. The entire region was thrown into turmoil again. There was an exodus of Shi'ite Muslims from the North into the Baghdad area. The Iraqi government had pleaded for aid, but the international community was tired of the terrorist wars and even the United States refused to get involved. The Middle East news was still concerned with the recurring war between Israel and its neighbors, so the almost bloodless annexation of northern Iraq by Turkey was practically a non-event. The Turks protected the Sunni/Kurdish population better than any of the preceding governments and there were no longer any large concentrations of Shi'ites in the North. With the religious divisions dampened, they had little to fight over. The Shi'ites however saw things differently, and while they had no official government approval, the southern border violence was considerable. The PKK (Kurdistan Workers Party) a communist-based group operating out of Iran also objected strongly to the arrangement. They had long fought for an independent Kurdish state and continually caused trouble from the Mountains in the East, but they had lost much support because of the humane treatment of the population by the Turks. The Iraqi government was surprisingly poor for such an oil-rich nation and had been devastated by decades of war with Iran, Kuwait, America and Britain. In an unusually resigned manner, they complained to the United Nations but did not declare war on Turkey. They did, however, continue their program of civil rights restrictions because Aahmed il Anahtirik could not afford to be seen as weak in such a volatile nation. The United Nations condemned the actions but did not even apply sanctions to Turkey. It was accepted more readily than any invasion in history in an area that had repelled all invaders for centuries. It had historians scratching their heads and reporters baffled.

John Marshall was the first kidnapping victim in recent history that had been ransomed and released. This was incredibly lucky for him, but from a diplomatic standpoint, it was a disaster and he seemed to know that. He did not, however, know who had ordered that they be blown out of the sky afterward. It made no sense to him. His rescuers pressed him to wrack his brain to figure out what he had heard or seen while he was captive, but nothing came to mind. He claimed to have no enemies of that power or magnitude that would order him assassinated by such extreme means.

Terry Kingston summarized his thoughts as succinctly as he could. "It had to be the Turkish government. The fragmented Iraqis had nothing to gain. Those rat-vomit terrorists don't have access to fighter planes, even old ones. She came in from the mountains so takeoff was probably from Iran. Iran has nothing to gain from shooting us down. We were supplying the enemy with shells so it was the Turks. It had to be."

"It wasn't the Turks," Gordon MacMaster cut in. "We already had official sanctions from them for ground transport. If they were responsible then their first target was the kidnappers. We may have been supplying them but they were the real enemy."

"Perhaps it was the Israelis?" John Marshall was grasping at straws now.

"Now you're not even thinking. Look, Iran might be ready to invade Iraq, but they are not ready for war with

Turkey. Even they are not that stupid. It was not the Turks, either. The Turks allowed us to be here; they were complicit allies. If it were anyone, it was the English. They sent us here. They have their own resources but used outside personnel. They wanted to cover their tracks." MacMaster was looking very grim as he worked this out.

"It still doesn't read. If the English wanted Sheriff here dead, they would just leave him where he was and let the wogs do it for 'em."

"Marshall."

"What?"

"My name is Marshall and nobody in London wants me dead. Except my ex-wife."

"That's what I said, mate."

"Enough. I'm not flying us into an ambush. We'll turn west, get over the Ninawa Desert then turn north and head back toward Turkey." MacMaster told Kingston, "Keep the global disabled and fly low."

"Be off...you know this flying bathtub can't fly under the radar. Well, maybe in the desert, but as soon as we hit Turkey we'll have to climb."

"That's fine. As long as we can disappear into the desert," MacMaster said, "we may live to tell about it."

"We could fly over Kuwait," said John Marshall.

"Might be, but where from there? Qatar, UAE, Somalia? I cannot trust that Saudi Arabia is not part of the trap and we cannot land in Iran. If we fly over Syria, Jordan or God help us, Israel, we will be blown out of the sky without a second's warning."

"Turkey it is then. I'll check for bugs. What about that cell phone?" asked Kingston.

"I'll pull the battery. I have one call to make. We need to go through the plane for a tracker."

"I'll set the men to working but it's a big plane, a lot of ground to cover."

After checking to see if John Marshall had any electronic devices, Terry Kingston went into the back of the plane, where the crew was still cleaning up the blood. The two mops were in use so Terry grabbed a cloth and assisted with the walls. When a satisfactory job had been done with the clean up, the water, mops and rags all went out the back hatch as well. The bloody water was sucked down by the thirsty desert sands of northern Salah ad Din. There was nothing they could do about the bullet holes peppering the side.

Gordon MacMaster made his last call on the cell phone. "*Mi amor*," he said, "there has been a glitch. I need you to go through the procedure now. Do not wait another minute." He did not wait for a reply but hung up the phone and pulled the battery.

In the body of the airplane, Terry was asking, "Has anyone seen anything out of the ordinary on this plane? There may be a tracking device of some sort that will compromise our position and leave us open to more attacks. Have a look around and pull anything that looks wrong." Terry went back into the cockpit then. A thorough search of the cockpit followed but nothing was found. Terry retrieved the last cigarette from the pack he had given John Marshall and smoked it in pensive silence.

Before long Van stuck his head in the cabin door and announced that they had found no tracking devices in the body of the plane. If there was a tracker on this plane, they could not find it.

The C17 dropped altitude first then turned gracefully and headed north. They had not used the radio since just after they lifted off from the sands. They had claimed engine trouble as a cause for landing and had announced it was repaired when they were back on the radar. They would not be using the radio at all now. It would be a long tense flight back. Everybody on board the flight knew that even if there was no tracking device and they were below the radar, they were not immune to satellite imaging. There was no way to hide something as large as a C17.

The Director was concerned again. It had seemed things were going his way when the undocumented fighter plane attacked the transfer team. Even after the attacking jet had been blown from the sky, things could have proceeded according to plan. Since they had never dipped below the 35th parallel, Baghdad had not been alerted.

The plan had been for the plane to proceed to Saudi Arabia's Dharbin airport. They had been on the radar, heading in that direction until that cell phone call to America had come from the plane. The whole affair could still have been handled quietly in Saudi Arabia; there was a team in place in Dharbin. They would have been transported out, protected and paid. If The Director could get in touch with them somehow he would tell them that, but they had committed themselves to being incommunicado. When they changed direction, it changed everything.

The Director stared at the satellite image of the C17 flying north and chewed on his lower lip. He knew the plane was not a bomber, technically. He also knew that they had installed four laser-guided bombs behind the false wall. Crude in their initial deployment, they were nonetheless incredibly accurate once they had been thrown out the back of the airplane. Reviewing his data he saw that the plane had a range of 2400 nautical miles. It could return to Greece, but without refueling did not have the range to go much further than that.

The Director called his American backers, telling them about the fighter plane attack and its demise. The Americans had denied all knowledge of the attack. Not trusting them to tell the truth on this, he had contacted his agents in Iran who had researched the flight plans of the airports and found that no MiG-21 had taken off from any approved runway. He already had access to that information and got nothing further from his contacts. He contacted Paul Phillips in Budapest, but Paul knew nothing about it, claiming to have run out of battery power on his laptop and stopped watching the affair after the plane took off. The Director attempted to contact the Turkish Governor of the area to inform him that there had been a plane crash in the desert but never got to speak with him. The secretary he did speak with did not seem to care in the least. "It crashed in the desert?" he said. "Then it belongs to the desert."

The Director's worst concern was that he now had a team gone rogue. All attempts to contact them had gone unanswered. The cell phone had gone dead after the last call and there was no response to radio transmissions. He knew he was left no other course of action but to declare the team enemy combatants and have them eliminated. The sticking point was the Secretary that was still aboard the plane. He did not wish to see any high profile collateral damage. The mercenaries on board were completely unknown to him; the only ones he was certain of were Gordon MacMaster and Terry Kingston, and they had already been classified as expendable.

The decision having been made, the call went out to the Turkish government. They were told that the plane had been highjacked in the desert and was headed to Istanbul on a suicide mission. The information was questioned but not until the Turkish Air Force scrambled jets to intercept the terrorists.

The plane was flying low to escape radar detection. The satellite positioning system was disabled and repeated attempts to contact it were ignored. The Air Force followed protocol and gave them every chance to change course. The plane flew directly over the city of Van on a direct west-north-west course toward Istanbul. They gave it a last warning to turn around and land at the airport in Van. The pilot of the bullet-riddled plane ignored them. When the invading terrorists' plane had cleared the city of Van and was over Lake Van, the lead jet released a rocket and blew it out of the sky. The rocket ignited the fuel tanks and the explosion was cataclysmic. The titanic transport folded over like a wounded albatross and plummeted into the water.

Chapter Eight
Van Gogh

Deputy Forster and Agent Sylvan were eating dinner together in an out of the way restaurant in Geneva when the call came in. The action and possibility of a real payoff had given Katherine an appetite that could not be slaked in a restaurant. Ordinarily she did not consort with professional associates, but this time she made an exception. Originally they intended to wait for the rest of the team so there would be no questions, but when the call came in, things changed.

The Director was perturbed. He had recorded the flight of the C17 digitally and enhanced it for playback. He knew Gordon MacMaster would not have allowed himself to be blasted into a lake by the Turkish Air Force. He knew somewhere along the line they had bailed out. He played it back from the last directional change the plane had made before turning 90 degrees and heading for Istanbul. He played it in fast motion and did not find the bail out and then he played it at regular speed. He still did not find anyone leaving the plane. There was a brief moment when the plane took its final turn where the satellite lost tracking. That had to have been when they bailed. So The Director had a general location but no way of knowing how many or what the team was now composed of. He played that one track again and right as rain the flap was closing in the back of the plane as the satellite reoriented itself.

Katherine had suggested they get the paintings from the vault and move them to another secure location as soon as the others joined them. The idea was rolling through Roger's head when the call came in. The message was short and Katherine watched Roger's jaw tighten and then twitch. It could not be good news.

"We've been ordered to go to Turkey, find the Mad Scottish Bull and take out his whole team. Number of assailants unknown, precise location unknown, weapons possessed unknown. Why doesn't he just order me to cut off my own balls and eat them?"

"Roger, why so upset? The Russians didn't cut them off and the Greeks haven't buggered you, besides, I have plans for those. If we can't find MacMaster, we can't. We can spend a week looking and then come back for the goods. We have the account number, Paul has the pin number and Victor has the recording. We could wait here or there, it really doesn't matter. The important thing is that we do not raise any flags. You've been in the business long enough to know the game." Agent Sylvan's voice was soothing and her words marked her as more worldly than he expected.

"My dear, we are to be accompanied by a team of Royal Marines. There is no way we can sit out the week in the company of those hard-core bloodthirsty bastards. We rendezvous with them and the Turkish police in two days. If I know the Turks, they are already searching for outsiders and stopping all suspicious foreigners. The Anatolian Peninsula has been invaded more times than Poland. Istanbul is right on the Strait of Dardanelles between the Black Sea and the Mediterranean. A very strategic location for naval warfare. I think that's where Troy was located. Anyway, pack your bags. We're going to Turkey."

Katherine had allowed Roger to chatter a little without interrupting. Now that he had said all he wanted to say, she had nothing to follow up with. The idea of a large payoff was more than appealing but at the same time, if they were not discreet, The Director could turn his pitiless eye on them and have them individually eliminated. A life of luxury is impossible if you need to spend your entire life hiding in the Amazon rain forest. So, she picked her purse up from the chair beside her and smiled. "Istanbul, then. But not before we dirty the sheets."

Roger Forster felt his heart jump in his chest. If he was not careful he would fall deeply in love with this blonde nymph. It was not a feeling he was accustomed to, and it made him uncomfortable. He was not used to trusting anyone, let alone loving them.

Anastasia Viuda drove to town in the one ton GMC pickup. She stopped at the Petroleo station in Los Fuertes to fill the tank on the way. In town she bought some granola bars and some apples; she bought a chunk of cheese from under the glass dome on the butcher's counter and some crackers. She bought some soda pop and chatted with the woman behind the counter about it getting late to plant and how she was planning on getting a horse next week. When she left the store, she said she would probably be back tomorrow for some chicken and steak. Then she drove directly south to Taos, New Mexico. It did not escape her notice that a dark, late model domestic car pulled out of a side road behind her as she pulled into Taos, and followed her all the way to the airport. She marked the man behind the wheel as the same sort of cheap-suited government man who had shown up and taken her man away.

The airport was not as crowded as she would have liked and her height made her stick out as much as her long dark hair and classic Hispanic beauty. She went directly to the ticket line and bought a round-trip ticket to Athens and a one-way ticket back. Then she went to the restroom. Inside a stall in the restroom, she took a pair of scissors out of her oversized purse and cut the midnight waterfall off her head and threw it in the commode. She took a light brown curly wig out and fitted it to the stubble left on her head. A quick application of contact lenses turned her dark brown eyes the purple of a thistle flower and she turned her blouse inside out, revealing the other side that had been sown into it. Then she pulled off the long skirt and stockings she was wearing and straightened the Daisy Dukes she had slid on underneath. The sensible shoes she had on went into the bag and high heels went on her feet. The last thing taken from the oversized handbag was a small denim purse. The larger bag went into the trash.

When she left the restroom, she did not look much like the woman who had entered. She kept her fingers in front of her mouth and looked about, searching for someone. She found him moving through the terminal in shirtsleeves with his tie undone and the red face of a man who had stopped in the airport bar.

The man with the dark, late model domestic car had seen her come out of the restroom and had noted that she was the same size as his mark but the look was so different that he spent only a second looking at her face. His attention was drawn to the long slim legs and the tight posterior barely hidden by the cutoff jeans. When she threw her arms around the traveling businessman, the government man stuck his head behind the newspaper again.

The salesman from Sioux City, Iowa did not know what to do when this voluptuous, tall and obviously mistaken woman threw her arms around him and gave him a kiss. "Well," he said, "New Mexico really is a friendly place."

"Oh, you have no idea," she said in a husky voice. "I need to get to a hotel room right away." She stuck her tongue in his ear. "I mean right now."

Men dream about this sort of thing and it just never happens so the hydraulic valve salesman, who had been thinking about having another drink and going to bed, lost no time in hustling his unexpected prize out of the airport.

There was a hotel close enough to walk to and when Anastasia looked back, the man who had been following her had not yet stepped out of the building. She pressed her amorous advances as the man checked in as Mr. and Mrs.

Carter. The young man behind the counter did not question and the salesman paid cash for the room.

When they reached the room Anastasia said she had to freshen up. She went into the bathroom, turned on the shower and fixed her disguise more thoroughly. She quickly shaved her head bald in the shower and touched up her makeup. She had very little storage space in the little denim bag, barely enough for the different identification, makeup and a wad of cash. She wished she had brought a gun but had, realistically, no place to hide it and airports were notoriously unfriendly to handgun owners.

Stepping out of the bathroom she found the salesman naked, aroused and lying on the bed. "I need a drink, sweetheart," she told him. "I'm going downstairs to buy a bottle of rum. I'm so much better when I'm a little tipsy."

"Oh, hell no. You're going to be just fine right now. Get over here and give me some of that stuff."

She moved quickly and was out the door before he could get close enough to stop her. Downstairs, she was out the back door quickly. The only thing outside was a parking lot and the large fields one finds around an airport. There was one car pulling into the lot; it had an older couple in it. She ran up to the window on the driver's side and told the man behind the wheel, "My boyfriend's trying to kill me. Can you please just me give a ride out of the airport. Please?" She got lucky in that the couple were sympathetic and kind. The man looked at his wife and she told Anastasia to get in the back seat.

The back door to the hotel opened as the back door to the car closed and a disheveled, half-dressed hydraulic valve salesman stared into the parking lot. The middle-aged couple in the car gave him a very dirty look and drove off.

Anastasia Viuda lay down on the back seat whimpering. The couple took her out of the airport lot and onto the expressway. The first exit had a Petroleo station and a deli right at the exit. The couple dropped her off there. She thanked them effusively and went inside. It was a matter of minutes before she had hooked up a ride to the nearest truck stop, and from there she was on the road with a long haul trucker. They headed east across the Sangre de Christos mountain range and into the plains beyond. After a few hours they had left New Mexico behind and were heading east across the Texas Panhandle on Route 40.

George, the man behind the wheel, was large. Driving truck had given him little opportunity for exercise so his once muscular physique had turned to fat. He was a relatively good conversationalist, telling her stories about losing his brakes coming down out of the mountains, seeing accidents, pile-ups, families broken down on desert roads. He told her about his Corvette and his house in Tennessee. He talked about his brother, the mayor of some fly speck town in Arkansas and his mother, retired in Florida. He railed against Petroleo Corporation and the price of fuel. He had less than kind comments about the inhabitants of the Middle East and their incessant wars that kept the price of gasoline and diesel in a range that made it almost impossible for a driver to make a living.

Anastasia was polite and a good listener. She encouraged him as long as he was talking about himself and where he had been and what he had done. Inevitably the talk turned to his ex-wife and how she had done him wrong. He had no kids, no dogs or cats to divert the conversation to so his conversation eventually turned to where he would stop for the night. It was not so much where he wanted to stop, it was the sleeping arrangements that concerned him, and he was not shy about his expectations.

"Look, George, first of all, I have the HIV so if I sleep with a man he will probably die within a year. I do not look for a man to take care of me and I am not looking for a one night stand in a truck. I need a ride to the Amarillo and I will pay you 200 American dollars for that ride but I do not need or want any other kind of ride."

"I'm willing to take my chances on the AIDS. You look healthy enough, Linda. You could save yourself $200 if you would just be nice. Or I could leave your Mexican ass in the desert to fry like a tamale. That's right, you can call yourself Linda or Louise or Larry if you want. I know you're just an illegal alien lot lizard. Maybe you'd like me to drop you off at the Office of Homeland Security."

"Okay, George, you have me. I am an illegal Mexican woman but it is true that I have the HIV. I will need you to get some protective things if you want me."

Reaching out with her long slender hand she laid it on the man's leg. His speed increased 10 miles per hour. The first town they hit after this was Bushland, 14 miles west of Amarillo. George couldn't get off the expressway fast enough. Bushland was a little fly speck on the northern Texas plains and was not really set up to deal with tractor trailers. They had no police force of their own, relying on the police force out of Amarillo when they had their infrequent problems. There was one store open in the town and the truck skidded to a dusty stop outside. The driver left the diesel running and went inside. He picked out a package of pre-lubricated, ribbed condoms and practically ran back out to the truck. When he climbed inside he got an eyeful as his passenger had opened her blouse and exposed her breasts. Hurriedly he jammed the transmission into third gear and raced back to the expressway.

"Let us find a motel," she suggested. "It would be nice to get a shower and get clean for you."

"Sure," he stammered, "we can do that."

"I want tequila."

"Sure, I can get us some tequila."

"I want good tequila, do not you dare come with some cheap stuff. A liter."

"Sure."

It was only a few more minutes until they reached Amarillo. Anastasia buttoned her blouse back up. They pulled into a motel parking lot and once they had checked in she told him to go and get a bottle of Tequila, but he had no intention of leaving without her. He dropped the trailer and pulled the tractor out. If she wanted the tequila, she would be going with him. So she did. He came out of the liquor store with the liter bottle in his hand, half expecting to find she had run off, but she was right there in the truck.

They went back to the motel and shared a couple of drinks together. He made the mistake of turning his back on her and she smashed the tequila bottle across the back of his head. It did not knock him out but sent him to his knees. She took the table lamp from the bedside table and finished the job. Then she calmly tied his hands behind his back with a length of torn sheet and tied his feet together, and then she gagged him. He was in no real danger since housekeeping would check on him in the afternoon.

Looking at the smashed bottle, Anastasia Viuda let out a long sigh and then pulled his keys and wallet out of his pocket. A couple thousand dollars in cash joined the wad already in her purse.

The truck was an aging Freightliner with an eight-speed transmission. The clutch was well worn and it up-shifted seamlessly at 1500 RPM. Bobtailing the tractor allowed her to pull in the parking lot of the department store without obstructing traffic. The floppy clothes she bought disguised her figure, and another pair of cheap shoes was more comfortable than the high heels. Another shade of lipstick, some sunglasses and a different wig completed her new persona.

When she was done, she called a taxi to take her from the store to the airport.

George never told the authorities about being beaten

and tied, but he did report his truck stolen. The recovery was without incident, and the police were alerted to the fact that an illegal Mexican woman was working the truck stops. They acted as if it were news to them, promised to keep an eye out and filled out their reports. Nothing more was heard of the incident.

It was two days after receiving the call when Roger Forster and Katherine Sylvan finally reached the city of Van. The trail was cold and the Royal Marines were frustrated. They did not work well with the Turkish police, having some old animosities and a great deal of distrust between them.

The British agents met with Beylik Kamal, the Sergeant of the local police force, and asked for a rundown of what had been done. It seemed that the roadblocks had not weeded out any suspicious individuals. They had been looking for the huge redhead and his blond lieutenant everywhere in town, but nobody had seen them. Roger began to outline a plan in his head. Since he had no love for Gordon MacMaster and had no contact with Terry Kingston over the years, it caused him no remorse to ponder killing them.

"Sergeant, I find it likely that he would dye his hair black to avoid detection and blend in. We need to be looking for anyone over six feet tall. Both the men we know are with this team are over six feet."

"Two meters," the Sergeant said, dryly.

"Yes, two meters."

"We have many men two meters tall in this country, but a pale-skinned Irishman will stand out like a jackal among lions."

"He is a Scotsman, not Irish and he lives in America now."

"There is no difference to me. It is possible he never entered the city or he would have been seen. To buy anything in this town is to go to the markets. Nobody at the markets has seen any such man. We promised a reward."

"He could have sent a local to the market. But, yes, you are correct, he will stick out like a sore thumb. The Australian as well, he is almost as tall, and blond. In Istanbul maybe they could hide in the tourist areas, but not here."

"They have sent color pictures. We know what they look like. The airports and borders have their pictures. These men will not leave this country."

"I must warn you, they are quite accomplished agents, freelance now, but Gordon MacMaster was raised by a member of the Royal Scots Dragoons and was himself stationed in Fallingbostel, Germany as part of the 7th Armored Brigade."

"He was a Desert Rat?" The Sergeant's eyes opened further.

"Aye. He was a Lady from Hell. In the Georgian Wars he had so many kills, he stopped even reporting them. I'm getting thirsty, may we have some tea?"

"My apologies, I have been remiss as a host. Tracker, bring tea." The Sergeant was not even sweating in the increasing heat of the day, his starched light brown uniform was crisp and the seams were straight.

"As I was saying, MacMaster is not to be taken lightly. He went into Special Services after the fall of Lebanon and trained himself to be incredibly dangerous. He is not sadistic and does not seem to enjoy killing, but at the same time he doesn't seem to mind slitting throats. He has been known to kill many to get to his target. I don't know why he went rogue. It makes him even more dangerous because he is no longer predictable."

"If he was predictable before, he will be predictable now. You spoke of coloring his hair black. What other things can be predictable?"

"When I said predictable, I meant he could be counted

on to return after he was done. His tactics are not conventional and I'm afraid he may have some local help. In the past, he would be returning to London as a course of action. Now we do not know where he is planning to go."

During this conversation, Katherine Sylvan had not said a word. She had been warned of the prejudices she would meet in Turkey and had dressed herself appropriately.

The tea arrived and the Sergeant served Roger Forster and himself but did not serve Katherine. There was not even a cup for her. She seethed inside but held her tongue.

Roger ignored the fact that his partner had not been served. Sipping the hot, strong beverage cleared his throat. "After he went freelance, he was always selective about his assignments. He could have made a lot more money if he had not been so picky, but his effectiveness was never in question. I do not know how many men he has with him. All I know is he was not in the plane when it was shot down."

"Does he have a woman? You say he lives in America. Is this a soft spot? I know you Europeans have a weakness for women."

"Yes, he has a woman. She is Argentine. I do not know much about her, but she was sharp enough to elude the American agents we sent to track her."

"Americans are soft and romantic. Do we have a picture of her?"

"No, no picture but we have a good description. She is tall, 175 or 180 centimeters. She is thin but strong and has long black hair. She could pass as a Middle Eastern woman, but her nose is too thin and her features too sharp. I doubt she can speak Arabic."

"And the Australian, does he have a woman?"

"Not as far as we can tell. We cannot tell where he is living, only that he flew out of Madrid. We only got lucky locating the Scot. He sent money to an overseas acquaintance who had fallen on hard times and we managed to see the postmark. The Australian dropped out of sight some time back, but had worked with MacMaster before and resurfaced for this job."

"Ah. The job. What is the job? Why is this man here and why are we hunting him. The truth now, not more of your government stories."

"The mission is confidential. All you need to know is that he has gone rogue and we need your help to stop him. We do not know who hired him or what he is to do, but he has already killed a respected Greek financier by exploding his yacht. He is dangerous and we need to stop him."

"Pfaugh. You speak as though he were a superman. He will be captured or killed. He is just a man. What we need to concentrate on is not his strength but his weaknesses. All men have them: women, drugs, gamblers, some men like boys, alcohol, there is a multitude of sins that betray a man to his doom. I want to know them. I mean to find this man for you."

"He has his woman and does not dally with local trollops when on the job. He drinks almost daily but in moderation. As you can see from the picture, he is not a young man prone to the spur-of-the-moment excesses of the young. He gambles seldom but is very successful at it when he does. He does not like little boys or little girls or sheep. He will eat almost anything that isn't rotten and while he prefers scotch is capable of drinking swamp water if need be. He has been a huge asset in the past, but now he is rogue and must be dealt with accordingly. It would be a huge feather in your cap to kill him."

"Hmm. You want him dead in preference to captured alive?"

"I cannot officially say that." The sweat was literally running down Rogers back as he spoke. The Turk was still unmoved though he was beginning to show some dampness on his forehead. Katherine was the most uncomfortable of all. Ignored and scorned, she was about to explode into feminist invective. The heat was fueling the fire. Before she tipped over, Roger suggested that they had not had much rest and that it would be best to get to the hotel and begin a report.

Katherine managed to remain reserved until they had actually checked in and were in one of the two rooms they had rented.

"You son-of-a-bitch," she began. "How could you sit there and let him treat me like I was some kind of a dog whining at his table?"

"Katherine, you knew coming into this country that, as a woman, you were a second class citizen. I did not want you in that room and he didn't either. He respected our customs by even allowing you in there. It was also a test. I reminded you that it would be this way. Thank you for not saying anything in there. These men control their women ruthlessly. You will find more and more of this as you stay in this business; if you stay in this business."

"But you just sat there drinking your tea and allowing him to degrade me that way. He didn't even look at me all the time I was there."

"Look, if you want people to look at you, put on a bikini and walk out to the lake. You might make it there without getting arrested for indecency. We have been a good team so far. Don't fall apart on me because you don't understand the culture. We're not in Paris, here. Turkey is officially secular but these people are Muslims. Muslims don't think the same as Anglos. Get used to it."

"I have never been so insulted."

"Oh please shut up. You knew it would be this way. You worked in South America, right?"

"Yes, Columbia."

"So, none of this is new to you. It went well. Let's just accept that."

Katherine said nothing further but turned away with a new resolve.

Roger put his hand on her shoulder, but her ire would not be so easily pacified. He silently cursed the instability of women while simultaneously ached for the kind of internal fire she represented to him.

The Director perked up at the alarm. The cell phone that had been used from the doomed flight was making a call. It had not been in use long enough to pinpoint its positional chip, but its number had been recorded. As soon as it was used again, the alarm went off and the satellites began triangulating and homing in. In a matter of seconds, he had it. By the time the position came up on satellite image, he had already dialed the pager number. The satellite took a little longer to give him an address, but as soon as it did, that address went out over the wire.

Alimenijad was called Ali by all his friends. He had quite a story to tell his friends tomorrow but he had to stop shaking first. He had found a cell phone with a battery taped to it while he was walking home from school. When he put the battery in and dialed a friend's number, it worked. Fifteen minutes later he had finished walking home, and opened the case to try it again when the door to the house was pounded in, and all these policemen and foreigners came in with guns. They grabbed him and jacked him up against the wall and searched the whole house. Then they started asking him all sorts of questions that he couldn't answer about whoever was supposed to own the phone. He thought the foreigners were going to kill him they were so mad. They kept asking him the same questions over and over again, and showing him this picture of a foreigner he had never seen before. He was so scared he was shaking. Then they decided he didn't know anything and left. They took the cell phone with them.

Chapter Nine
Plague

The World Heath Organization was mobilized when news of the plague was released. Their volunteer workers were sent to three areas that appeared to be the epicenters of the disease. Mosul, Irbil and Kirkuk were suffering in the throes of a mysterious and devastating pestilence. It had struck all three cities simultaneously and since it was caused by a new virus, there was no known cure. The victims of this virus died painfully and horribly with their glands swollen to the bursting point. Highly contagious, the virus was spread through any casual contact with an infected host.

Foreign companies began pulling employees out of the area. The first to leave were employees of the Petroleo Corporation. Later, there would be a mass exodus from the area, but foreigners included in the second wave of evacuees were quarantined. Very few of the first wave were infected.

There were some complaints from the Petroleo Corporation employees about the circuitous route they were forced to take to get home. First, they were flown to Arlanda Airport in Stockholm, Sweden, then to Kangerlussuak, Greenland. They were put up in hotels in Greenland and provided with open air tours that were made virtually mandatory. Since the entire group was moving out of the Middle East, their systems were shocked by the temperature in Greenland. Year-round cold was not something they were accustomed to and after spending a week in this environment many of them had colds, a couple actually had fevers, but none of them had the plague.

Outside of the Middle East, there were a limited number of incidents; people who had flown out of Mosul, mostly on one particular flight to Rome. Hundreds died in Rome before the infection was isolated, including everybody that had been on the flight from Mosul. The stewardesses and the pilots were not spared either. Fortunately they were not sent out on other flights before becoming ill, or there might have been a worldwide epidemic.

They had never learned Van's real name, but he would have been easy enough to find if they ever needed to contact him again. It seemed as though he was an important man in his home town. He had a house set up that he did not live in, isolated from the general population by a high wall.

The team entered the compound during the night and Van saw to their needs. The next morning he was out at first light and had returned by noon with hair dye, razors and soap, food, clothing and a carton of Turkish cigarettes. It was a bit of a quick joke, but he had brought burqas for both the Italian member of the team and the British diplomat. They were the smallest of the group and would have the easiest time passing as women.

"I say, there is nobody after me. You can simply drop me off at the embassy. I'll be fine from there." The Second Secretary was hopeful that this could all end in an expedient manner. Of the group he had had the worst of it the night before. He had hesitated on the lip of the tail and Terry Kingston had run into him, knocking him over the edge. The descent had been thrilling, but he was unfamiliar with directing the parachute shrouds and had landed in an olive tree. His wounds were not serious but had required dressing. The rest of the group landed within a half kilometer of each other but the Englishman needed to be located in the dark. It had been an annoyance to the team and a little embarrassing but it made for a story the diplomat would tell over and over to his grandchildren.

"Nobody is going anywhere right now. I do not think they want you dead; I think they want me dead." Gordon MacMaster was insistent. "Your death could have been arranged much easier than blowing a million dollar airplane out of the sky."

The Turk had his piece to say on that subject. "I am home. My part of this operation is almost over. I am not the target unless it was the German Colonel who tried to kill us, and I do not think that is so. I was promised money and I would like to be paid." Van knew when he was dealing from a position of power.

"Get us out of this country and I will pay you all you are owed."

"Give me half of what is still owed to me and I will take the rest when you are safely out of the country."

"You are a man of honor and I will treat you as such. I will give you all that is owed you."

"This is not all mine. I will also take care of Mikara's family. You knew him as Konya but his real name was Mikara. I promised to take care of his family and I will."

"That is very noble of you. Here is the remainder of what you were promised." Gordon handed him a packet of money representing full payment for Van's services.

"Honor be upon you."

"And you as well."

"I go now to arrange passage. It may take a while. I must be discreet."

When Van had gone, Stuttgart said, "I question your payment of our ally before we have seen the last of Anatolia. He offered a reasonable deal and you did him one better. Why have you done this?"

"If our Turkish friend wanted all the money I have, he would have no trouble setting us up for an ambush and taking it all. He will hold his end of the bargain, even though his financial motivation has been diminished, because his honor will not allow him to do it any other way."

The German chewed on this for a moment and though not fully convinced, accepted the logic with a shrug. Then he said, "My name is Hans Frendt. I see no reason to continue using ahh… pseudonyms." He rotated his hand in front of him as he sought for the proper word, almost as if he was genuflecting. "We will all live this one out or we will all die. I see no other ends."

"Tarrytown Terry Kingston. Pleased to meet you, mate."

"I am Thomas Contini," said the Italian.

"Gordon MacMaster."

"There was no need for you to introduce yourself. We all knew you," said the German.

"I'm… I'm curious."

"Word of you dropping boulders on cities and ahh… killing three or four men at a time with your bare hands have been going around."

"Exaggerations, as all stories are, but how did my name get out?"

"Just happens, mate. What about you?" Terry asked the Moroccan.

"Me? I am curious how the rest of us will be paid. I know it was necessary to pay Van. We must, after all, secure transportation out of this country."

"I have money and if need be, I will pay you from my private funds." Gordon's voice was casual. He knew not to even hint at shorting men in his profession. The pool of applicants and agents for them in this field was very small, and slights were never forgotten.

"Honor be upon you. I am Ahmed de Ketama el Bali."

"I thought so. When Terry told me about the stunt on the back of the plane, I thought there can only be one Moroccan who could have attempted that. Honor be upon you and your children."

"And yours as well."

Van returned the following day with good news. He brought with him a forger of some skill who would make them up some passports that would pass a casual inspection.

The man would accept no money from the team. It seems that he owed Van a favor that would be paid back with this service and there was no way he would consider a financial payment.

In addition to securing the documents, Van had persuaded the captain of a freighter to take on some additional passengers. The freighter Pride of Bosporus was sailing out of Hopa on the Black Sea, but the city itself was active with policemen looking for foreigners. They would leave the coast in a boat and rendezvous with the ship at sea.

"I will return with a truck as soon as I have a time of departure. If luck prevails, you will not need the passports. Tarrytown, you will need to dye your eyebrows better before the pictures are taken. I will not return until it is time to leave. We need to give our man time to finish his work."

The head of Petroleo Corporation was lounging in his rosewood-paneled office in New York City. He had just gotten done exercising and spending some time in his private steam room. He lit a Cuban cigar and savored the smoke while sipping some very old bourbon. Life was good for Albert Epstein and he knew it. When he had joined Petroleo as an account manager 40 years prior, they thought he would be able to benefit the company. They had not counted on the most ruthless business man they had ever seen. Through mergers and acquisitions, undercutting the competition, busting unions and a thousand dirty tricks, he had turned Petroleo into the largest conglomerate in the world. He had paid enough money to members of the House and Senate that he was above the monopoly laws and had friends in all the right places. After consolidating most of the world's oil reserves under his banner, in one form or another, he systematically raised the price of oil again and again. He was in charge of the kind of empire men dream of and had the kind of power that made him virtually untouchable.

Epstein was not the front man for Petroleo. That would have made the situation even more tenuous than it already was. Epstein was behind a front wall of European names that hid his true place in the corporation. He had given himself the title Economic Advisor, but the truth was no man held more power and sway at the largest corporation in the world. Indeed, few men in the world held the kind of power Albert exercised.

The only problems that could touch Albert Epstein were the men whom actually ran the countries he exploited for their oil. Albert's justification for his actions was circular and twisted, but worked in his mind. "The wars in the Middle East are never ending and even Muslims don't like Muslims. So, since they want to kill each other why don't we give them what they want?"

The Middle East had proven to be a tough nut to crack. In the beginning of the 21st century, the sheiks of the Arabian nations grew much more savvy and businesslike. Instead of giving their children traditional Muslim educations that taught them nothing but survival skills, they sent them to Harvard, Yale and Oxford. Now having exceptionally good educations, the rulers of many of the Arab nations understood the planet with a new perspective and began to squeeze the rest of the world with their oil.

As Albert Epstein smoked, he mused on the nature of his crimes. He smiled as he thought of the brazenness and sheer gall his plan had entailed. He had seen it as an opportunity when the genetic engineering of viruses had begun, and he had worked on it from that point. He chuckled when he thought about how they would make a hero of him in the end.

It felt good to finally be moving again. The Turkish safe house had sparse accommodations. The bare essentials were provided but boredom was setting in, and the longer the team stayed, the greater their chances of being exposed.

The truck had a canvas-covered frame over the bed, with planks on each side to sit on. Careful attempts were made to disguise the people in the back, although one could not see inside once the back flaps were closed. A Turkish driver who did not speak a stitch of English was behind the wheel. Van rode in the front of the truck with the driver, two of his wives and another man rode in the back with the team and their rescued diplomat.

Thomas Contini and John Marshall were wearing burqas as were Van's two wives who kept their eyes on the floor of the truck the entire way. Ahmed de Ketama el Bali had suggested that Gordon, Terry and Hans wear djellabas, a full-length woolen garment shaped like a sack with arms and a huge hood that could cover the wearer's entire face to the middle of his chest. Designed for survival in a sandstorm, the djellaba's one failing was a lack of eye slots in the hood. The one nod to modernity that these djellabas had was slots on each side to access their interiors. Though they were a good disguise, they were very prickly and hot. Ahmed and the additional man that rode with them both wore kaftans.

Two situations happened on the trip. The first occurred on the outskirts of the town where there was a roadblock set up by the local police. This was not really an impediment once they knew who owned the truck and recognized that he was riding in it. While notoriety can make you a target, it can also be a good thing. The police took a look in the back of the truck and waved it on. Their families received generous, anonymous gifts later that week.

The second incident was not so friendly. The road was blocked by a truck with the hood open and six men were standing around it. It looked like a legitimate break-down until the men turned with weapons and started yelling for everybody to get out of the truck. Three of the men had rifles, the other three had machetes.

The unlucky bandits were disappointed that there was no cargo on board. Their perplexed reaction when they pulled back Hans Frendt's hood never left their faces. He had pinned the right arm of his djellaba to its shoulder as though he were missing an arm. Shooting through the material of the outfit with an automatic, he cut down two of them. Before the others could react, Terry Kingston had reached inside and pulled his two .38s and shot two more.

Thomas Contini stepped forward pulling a wire from the sleeve of his burqa. The attackers had dismissed the women as being no threat and were not actively covering them. The Italian looped the wire around his victim's neck, spun around and hauled the duped Turk from the ground over his back. The wire cut through the flesh of the man's throat all the way to his spine. The blood that poured from the gash soaked Contini from head to toe.

Gordon MacMaster did not even use a weapon. The man facing him swung his rifle toward Terry, and the Scotsman punched him so hard it crushed the side of his face, popped his eyeball from its socket and knocked him to the ground unconscious. Terry stepped forward and systematically put a bullet in the heads of all six men.

Contini was forced to discard the burqa and don clothing taken from the corpses. After that, though uncomfortable, the ride was uneventful.

The boat was waiting for them on the shores of the Black Sea as they left the Pontic Mountains behind them. It was piloted by the man who had ridden with them. He and Ahmed had talked quite a lot in Arabic, after the incident with the bandits. That is, Ehmet, as he was called, did a lot of talking and Ahmed did a lot of listening.

The team said their goodbyes to Van and headed out into the darkness toward a light on the horizon. The light began to differentiate into several lights and then individual lights. The freighter had accommodations for all of them.

The crew was friendly and respectful. They had been working this route for a long time and knew the way. There was nothing for the team to do but eat and sleep.

They were secreted as the aged ship made its way through the Bosporus without incident and into the Sea of Marmara. They were boarded by Turkish customs officials as they navigated the Dardanelles. The Captain was familiar with the procedure and the payoff was made without further questions.

John Marshall was really quite knowledgeable about the strait. He chattered about how it used to be called the Hellespont and how water flows in both directions along the strait simultaneously. He explained how it moves from the Sea of Marmara to the Aegean via a surface current and in the opposite direction via an undercurrent. Then he went on about how Troy was on the southwest end of the 61 kilometer strait and all the wars that had been fought over control of this channel over the centuries. He was more in his element now that he was leaving some of the distressing situations he had found himself in behind.

The freighter was on its way to London with ports of call in Palermo, Barcelona and Lisbon. The trip was smooth going through the Greek Islands. It was rough in the Straits of Messina between the tip of Italy's boot and Sicily. But soon enough they were in Palermo. John Marshall had by this time thrown the burqa overboard and adopted the clothing of a Turkish sailor.

Thomas was, of course, home. He still had to return to Greece to retrieve his Ferrari but that was secondary. Thomas, Hans and Gordon all went ashore dressed as Turkish sailors. They had their passports though none of them ever traveled under their real names. They stopped in the currency exchange and converted a few paper pounds to euros so they could make calls on a pay phone. The first call Gordon made was to Colonel Richter.

"Colonel, do you drink your schnapps warm or cold?"

"Ahh! I knew they could not kill you. Reports came in of your demise; I see they were somewhat premature."

"Colonel, you are the only man in Germany who quotes Mark Twain."

"But you are not the first Scot to piss on the British Crown."

"I think the phrase is to piss them off," Gordon said, smiling.

"Irrelevant. I get my reports. The Director of the Service does not know me and does not call me, but there are those who do. You have become an interested person."

"What I am interested in is a problem I have with flow."

"Cash flow?"

"Da. I paid off our Lira but lost 50% of the interest. I lost all our Drachmae and two thirds of the Deutsche Marks. I cannot cover the remaining third of the Deutsche Marks with what was cut for me, and of course the Dirhams."

There was a heavy sigh from the German end of the line. "How is it you propose to pay your gambling wagers?"

"I can cover the Dirhams. I need some temporary help with the Euros and the Deutsche Marks."

"I will cover you on this wager since it is fewer currencies than I expected, but you must understand. We are both men of honor and there is no disputing this. If you do not return the cover price to me with interest, I will have you. How is this best done?"

"Call your numbers in a week."

"Very well, my gambling-addicted friend. When do we drink schnapps together?"

"Soon, Colonel, as soon as we can. Here are two other gamblers you will need to talk to. Explain the arrangement and all will be well."

He dropped another euro in the body of the telephone

and handed the receiver to Hans Frendt. After a short conversation in German, the receiver was handed to Thomas Contini. Another short conversation ensued, this time in Italian; then the phone was hung up.

A hand shake and wishes for luck in the future was all that was remaining. The men took their leaves of each other.

Having some time left, the Scot turned to a tavern to have some scotch and soda. Then he stopped by an open air market for some fresh vegetables and a couple of bottles of wine. Fruit was not yet in season, but he bought a half kilo of a lighter roast of coffee. He had imbibed in just about all the Turkish coffee he wanted for a while. The next phone call was to Barcelona. An old woman answered the phone and the conversation, while brief, was satisfactory.

He returned to the ship with his bounty and they waited to embark. It would be two days before they could leave and John Marshall was dying to go ashore but Gordon MacMaster forbade it. The Englishman spent the second day with Gordon, while Ahmed and Terry went ashore. Marshall regaled him with historic facts about the Straits of Messina, Sicily, Napoleon, The Spanish Armada, The Ottoman Empire and a host of other subjects. He should have been a European History teacher, not a diplomat. He was suited to it and it would have been less hazardous.

After listening to the old stories for much of the day, Gordon started telling the Englishman stories about the Georgian wars. Iran was committed to annexing Armenia, Georgia, Azerbaijan and Abkhazia; essentially everything on the south side of the Greater Caucasus. They had invaded Azerbaijan and headed up the Kura River toward Tbilisi. The armed resistance was considerable but the ultimate goal was not Azerbaijan but Georgia, and the Georgian Republic was split between those in the north having allegiance to Mother Russia and those who welcomed the Muslim onslaught. The entire economy of the region had been destabilized by years of corruption and both internal and external conflicts. The Iranian economy on the other hand was booming. They had welcomed investment for years and, when the time was right, had nationalized the oil industry and confiscated all the hardware and oil wells that had been built. They had been building caches of arms for decades, and once their economy was under their own control, they invaded to the north.

None of this history was what Gordon MacMaster told his captive audience; it was all known to him. Gordon talked about the beheadings and the battles and the men he had killed. He talked about foiling ambushes and torturing the enemy for information. He talked about the stink of battle when men's bowels deserted them and the air reeked of vomit and feces and blood. When he got to cleaving men's heads in half with a machete, John Marshall had had enough. From any other acquaintance the stories might have been deemed fabrication, but after seeing the massacre of the Turkish bandits, there was no skepticism in the diplomat's mind. He told no more stories about historic battles or mythology. He did not speak to Gordon MacMaster at all for a couple of days, and he did not eat for three. His romantic vision of history had been given a taste of reality and he found it indigestible.

When Terry Kingston returned, he was more than half drunk. Ahmed de Ketama el Bali had not been gone long, but Terry had spent most of the day drinking beer. He had a story to tell as well, and this may have had as much to do with John Marshall's lack of appetite.

"Look mate," Terry began in a bleary voice. "I fear we didn't know what we were really up to. We've really done it now. We let the fires of 'ell out on the desert."

"To what do you refer?" asked Ahmed.

"The bloody plague, man!"

"Get some sleep, Terry. You've had too much to drink." The Scotsman thought his friend was having an unexpected attack of drunken conscience.

"That's why I drank so much, you big oaf. I was a part of it and I didn't know."

"You didn't know what?"

"The bullets! The bullets we gave those wogs were poisoned with the plague."

"Plague?" asked both men at the table simultaneously.

"I saw the news. I went to a hotel bar to have a beer and maybe have a go at one of the local women. The telly was on and the news 'ad a story on the plague. It centered in Irbil, Kirkuk and Mosul. They got thousands of 'em dying. The planes won' fly in. They got no idea what the disease is. But, God 'elp me, I do. There was somfin on those bullets. Tha's why they was wrapped in plastic. Shrink wrapped. Vacuum packed, I think, is more like it. It was to keep the bloody plague inside. Mate, we just delivered the box to Pandora."

Chapter Ten
Cursed

The freighter cruised out of Sicilian waters a little behind schedule. The crane operator had a touch of the flu and swore it was the plague, so a replacement was brought in. Rome was showing cases of the disease and panic was erupting in the capital. Israel had shut her borders. Syria and Iraq were making pronouncements that the epidemic was Allah's wrath upon the Turks, the Kurds and the West. But the virus spread in unusual ways and cropped up where it was not expected. An epicenter of it began to fell people like trees in Samarra, completely bypassing Tikrit and every smaller town on the way. Fanatics began to claim that it was because Saddam Hussein had been born in Tikrit. Many of them thirsted for the quiet times that had dominated his rule.

Although they were anxious to get off the ship, Terry and Gordon did not disembark in Barcelona. Terry had lived near there and could not chance being seen. Anastasia had left the city before they arrived. She had traveled to Lisbon. The dockworkers were leery of unloading a Turkish ship and some of them refused to do so. It took a bit longer than usual to unload, but the loading with Valencia oranges and lemons progressed at twice the speed it might have otherwise.

Ahmed de Ketama el Bali was to have left the crew in Barcelona but the quiet Moroccan refused. There was work to be done he said, and he was not going to allow this breach of faith to go unpunished. His quiet and solemn manner belied the resolve he felt. He spent a lot of time meditating and praying, something he had not done previously, and refused all food for two days after Sicily had been left behind. He stopped communicating much as well. Worried, MacMaster plied him with questions about what he thought he might do. Ahmed replied that there were men responsible for this abomination and those men needed to die. As part of what he saw as penance, he returned the money that had been given him as a down payment. It was evil money, covered with the blood of innocents, and he could not accept it. MacMaster could have it and use it in any way he saw fit, but Ahmed de Ketama el Bali would not accept it.

After leaving Barcelona, Terry Kingston and Gordon MacMaster spent some time on deck exercising and sparring. Terry was good, but he could not overcome the size and speed of his opponent. Gordon's precision and control were superhuman, stopping full speed punches millimeters from Terry's face. Ahmed watched from the shade of the packing crates on deck, judging his associates' skill. When he was asked to join in the exercise, he acquiesced. Gordon underestimated him.

At 5' 10", he had nowhere near the reach of the Scot. His tactics reflected a fighting style that neither of the Anglos had seen before. To begin with, the Arab was dressed in long flowing robes which, instead of hampering him, disguised his movements and created a visual distraction. Instead of blocking the strikes of the other, he misdirected them so that time and again Gordon MacMaster punched empty cloth. Sliding under a downward angled chop, Ahmed scored the first point, a slash to the midsection. If it had been a knife fight, it would have been a serious wound.

The second point went to the Scotsman when he reversed a swing in mid-air and tapped his opponent on the head.

The third and fourth points went to Ahmed as he came in creating a flurry of white cloth that disguised his movements so well he got through Gordon's attack. Once he even flipped over a sweeping kick and jabbed his partner in the side.

The fifth point belonged to the greater size and reach of the Scot. Tired of swinging and finding nothing there, he rushed forward and threw his arms around the dervish, squeezing him into submission in a bear hug.

"Understand, in true combat," the Arab asserted, catching his breath, "such an attack would have cost you your gizzards."

"Indeed," bellowed MacMaster in the best of humor. "I pity your enemies. Friends of yours are friends of mine. Honor be upon you."

"And you as well." Ahmed de Ketama el Bali smiled for the first time since before they had met those long days ago in Greece. "Now, you have burst my wound open and I must bandage it again."

Gordon insisted on bandaging the man's shoulder himself.

Terry Kingston spent the rest of the day attempting to learn how to create the whirling sandstorm effect.

Lisbon was as beautiful as ever. The mix of the ancient and the new was conducive to reflection and introspection. The castles were as magnificent as they had been for centuries. The narrow winding cobblestone streets ending at modern blacktop highways drew one across the ages.

Gordon was the only one of the four that knew Anastasia Viuda was meeting them there. He left his companions in a café having what they wanted to drink while he went two blocks away to a hotel. He asked for Rubella Contagia and called her room. She told the clerk he was a friend of hers, and he was ushered to the elevator.

When he entered the room, he was smothered by the slippery, naked, bald and shaved body of his Argentine lover. She kissed him until he couldn't breathe and then they got to the more serious matter of making love like wild animals.

Ahmed and James took the train north from Portugal through Spain and into France. They hardly needed to step off the train at Paris and they were off for London. The whole trip took less than eleven hours.

Anastasia Viuda flew out of Lisbon and landed in Heathrow as a Swedish blonde. She rented a car at the airport and took four rooms in a bed and breakfast on Earls Court Square between Earls Court Road and Warwick Road. It was in a large second floor flat accessible by a rickety elevator or a wide hardwood staircase. The proprietor was an expatriate American married to an English wife. They were wonderfully charming and discreet with no embarrassing questions. After a couple of hours, she took the auto into town and picked up the duo who had come in by rail.

The Pride of Bosporus docked at Victoria Deep Water Terminal in Greenwich. Nobody questioned the missing life boat, and it was replaced before the ship left the dock.

Anastasia's cell phone rang and she spoke into it briefly before leaving to pick up Gordon down by the river. When they returned, their parking spot had been taken, and they needed to park a half mile down the road. They walked in the dying light, arm in arm, murmuring and smiling at each other. The street was empty except for the parked cars and another couple walking down the other side of the street.

Inside the flat, Gordon greeted his host and slid him a few extra pounds to ensure his discretion. He greeted Ahmed de Ketama el Bali solemnly and John Marshall enthusiastically. Terry had acquired a different room, in a hotel near the financial district. He had planned out a sequence of events that required them to pick up cell phones. The secret was to never use the cell for calls to any number that might be monitored. If they only call each other at the new numbers, no flags will be raised.

The plan also required the assistance of an old friend of Terry's. He was enjoying a pint of ale and a Turkish cigarette when she walked through the door of the nightspot. She was not tall, but her compact form was well proportioned and she carried herself with confidence. She had never visited this tavern before but did not cause a stir in the young crowd that frequented the place. Terry stood and she glided into his arms with a long sensual kiss, then she took a long draught of his ale. After she wiped her mouth on the back of her hand, she grabbed his crotch and asked if the equipment still worked. When he had assured her that the equipment was still in fine working order, she sat down and asked in a sweet tone if he would get her a Bloody Mary and not to let the bartender make it too weak.

Her real name was Beatrice Ward, but nobody had called her Beatrice for many years. Most people who knew her did not know her name was Beatrice. Everybody called her Warden. She was a strong take-no-prisoners type of woman who knew what she wanted and went out and took it. She was unmarried because she considered that tying herself down, and she could not have remained constant to one man anyway. She did not allow herself to be dominated by most men; it was not in her make up. When Terry Kingston called, however, she melted. He was the sort of alpha male she went after, one that did not allow his women to dominate him but did not need to resort to trickery or brutality. If an attractive woman wanted to be with him for a while he would service her in fine style, but she shouldn't expect him to stay.

After a couple of drinks they returned to Terry's hotel room. There was business to be discussed but there was other business to be taken care of first. Anything not connected with raw visceral pleasure was going to have to wait until the morning.

Paul Phillips received two disturbing e-mails on his laptop that morning. One of the things that disturbed him was that he had never known Gordon MacMaster to use internet communications, despite the inherent anonymity it afforded. He was also disturbed by the fact that Roger Forster had returned to Switzerland with his now inseparable woman Katherine Sylvan. Neither of these subjects bothered him as badly as the fact that Gordon MacMaster had returned to London. He was not surprised to learn that the Scotsman had eluded both the Turks and the Royal Marines. He had been in the business a long time and was still alive. Only those exceptionally good lasted long in this business.

Paul determined that Gordon was subject to that human frailty, greed. He wanted to be paid for the job he had done; the job that was becoming increasingly devastating in the deserts and mountains of Old Persia. The news had reported this morning that the plague was beginning to appear across the border in Iran. The only way it could cross that border is with men. The mountain ranges are an effective barrier from many problems, but man had conquered them. The disease was also infecting Baghdad.

The e-mail was addressed to Paul with directions to forward it to The Director. It included instructions for payment and precise explanations of how the world news will be alerted that the English had financed the plague in Iraq, if such payment were not forthcoming. The names and dates were precise, some of them down to the time, not just the date. This was not really blackmail; all the Scotsman was asking for was payment for himself and a team of 10 others. It had been impossible to tell how many men were on the plane. The definition was not good enough from the satellite feed. Ten would not be an unreasonable figure, though.

The instructions directed The Director to place the payment in a briefcase and have a deputy bring it to the Natural History Museum off Cromwell and Exhibition Streets. He was to sit with it at the Tyrannosaurus skeleton until Gordon MacMaster showed up to take it from him. The time would be eleven o'clock on a Tuesday morning; the museum might well be filled with tourists. It promised to be a crowded venue, one safer for the pickup man.

Paul was enjoying himself in Budapest. The beer was

cheap, the rooms were cheap, the shows were cheap and there was nobody stalking him. He had found a lovely young exchange student from America who was charmed with his British accent and stories of exotic lands. He told her he was a purveyor of motherboards and that explained his lifestyle. She was uninhibited and a lot of fun to be with. It would be a pity to bid her adieu.

He sent the e-mail to The Director. There was a little lapse in time as it got filtered and scanned for viruses, and then The Director scanned it for content. When the reply came, it was no more than the word "Confirmed."

"What's confirmed?" Paul jumped as his young friend startled him from behind.

"It's the fact that your ass is nice and clean out of the shower and my mind is dirty and can't be cleaned. Come here, you little tart. You're getting too big for your britches. It's time for a spanking for you."

The young American squealed and headed for the bedroom in mock horror, Paul Phillips on her tail.

Tuesday morning was overcast, not unusual for London in the late spring. The museum is a huge and magnificent structure of stone blocks with spires and columns ornamented with terracotta animals extant and extinct. Victor Rothchild stepped off the bus in front of the steps and looked around. He did not see anyone he knew, but suspected that more than one of the crowd was aware of him. A crowd of children was milling around their teacher. A trio of businessmen from some Asian country was following a young man in a suit. A familiar-looking woman was making her way through the crowd with a German Shepherd on a leash. Four sanitation workers were sweeping down the sidewalk. Suddenly, the German Shepherd was up against him, sniffing the briefcase he was holding, and then the dog sat right there, looking at it.

"C'mon, Slug, get away from that man. His lunch is not for you," she told the dog in a cockney accent. "Get up and let's go home. I'm sorry, sir. He probably smelled your food."

"I haven't got any... Do I know you?"

"I don't think so, sir. But if you'd like, we can 'ave some fun together."

"No. I'm sorry, I'm meeting somebody."

"Oh well, maybe some other time."

"I highly doubt it." Victor sniffed and moved away from the woman and her dog with a nagging feeling that he had met her elsewhere. She was a short, powerful woman with a good set of breasts and as she turned, Victor confirmed that she had a nice, tight bottom inside those tight jeans.

Inside the museum, Victor sat on the marble bench near the fossilized dinosaur bones. His eyes were on the crowd and his ears were perked up. His connection at this point was playing the game from a position of power, with nothing to lose and on the wanted lists of all the major countries of the European Union and America. A wanted listing was not something that was done to old worn-out agents; they had way too many secrets. They were put out to pasture or killed.

The guards came out of nowhere with clubs and restraints. The loop on a pole that surrounded Victor's arms was suited to handling tigers. The club that contacted the side of his head was not so skillfully wielded. He slipped his head away from the blow and it slid off his hair. He turned to the side and kicked the guard with the heel of his left foot directly in the stomach. The man dropped like a deflated balloon. Victor turned again and dropped himself. The force of his weight on the edge of the marble bench broke the animal pole in half. When he was on his feet again, he folded the pole and charged the holder, supplying him with a flying head butt. With two men down, he tried to free his arms but the rope was jammed inside the broken pole, and he never saw the nightstick of the third man descending on his skull. Blackness exploded in his skull and enfolded him in its inextricable blankets.

The remaining guard locked Victor's hands and feet immediately and then checked his two companions. The one was still emptying his stomach on the floor, the other was unconscious. The guard kicked Victor in the stomach for good measure, then, he took out his police radio and called the local office.

The police were clearing the street and ordering the buses to move along. The bomb disposal truck pulled up. Four men, two women and three dogs poured out of the back and hustled into the museum. The dogs confirmed that the briefcase had a bomb inside it. They put it inside a special box on wheels and took it away. They also took Victor Rothchild away. Attempting to bomb a British museum full of school kids was not to be taken lightly. The police promised it would be quite a while before he would see the outside of a jail cell.

The explosives experts had a time with the briefcase. It had a triple fuse and device configuration: one set to blow when it opened, one set with a remote trigger and one designed to blow on a timer. The first device was a shaped charge designed to cut whoever was standing in front of the case in half when it went off. The timed one would have gone off sixty seconds later. The remote was wired to a bomb inside a packet of money that had been hollowed out and filled with a metal case and plastic explosive. It was easy to tell that the case was designed to kill somebody in specific, not to bring down the museum. This made no difference to the police and prosecutors. As far as they were concerned, he was a terrorist and was to be isolated, prosecuted, condemned and killed.

The Director had been foiled again and he was furious. There was no target present for the snipers assigned to the job, and there was no victim for the explosives. The target was alive and hiding somewhere. If he could be trusted to any sort of pattern, he was probably in London, but such a call was impossible to make. All the Director could do was set up for tracking a call and hope his quarry blundered into his web somehow.

The camera on Victor's lapel showed the action that ensued at the museum, and the camera on the briefcase showed the bomb squad disarming it. While he was watching this, The Director may have been better served watching the cameras mounted in secure locations around the outside of his own perimeter.

The Director cursed volubly and called for a glass of Canadian whiskey. James brought it to him and turned around. He paid no attention to the machinations of his employer; they were not his concern. His concern was the huge box of supplies that had just been delivered via the freight elevator. He took a crowbar and pried the wooden top off it and was terribly surprised to find a man with a pair of .38 caliber pistols staring him in the eye.

Terry Kingston stepped out of the box stiffly. He had not been in it long, but it was smaller than was comfortable. He hadn't been all that sure he could gain access to the inside of The Director's underground stronghold this way, but the team had reasoned that the food and beer gets delivered somehow and not through the internet café. He was grinning savagely as he stared down the barrels of his twin pistols.

"Say one word and I'll line your coffin," he whispered.

James had nothing to say but held onto his crowbar until Terry motioned that he was to set it down. The two of them walked into the circular room. The Director turned around in his wheelchair and immediately began hyperventilating. He pulled a nebulizer from his pocket, under the direct cover of a pistol, and took a pair of puffs from it.

"Both of you, into the kitchen. Do not think for a second that I will not shoot you. Nobody will hear it down here." Terry holstered one of his pistols and was putting earplugs in his ears. "You, butler, send the freight elevator back up."

James sent the elevator up, but when he turned around from pushing the button, he had a gun in his hand. It was impossible to tell where the gun had come from, only that he turned around with it. The only thing that saved Terry Kingston was that he had moved to the side. The millisecond that it took James to reorient his aim was all it took for Terry to put a bullet into the side of his chest. Cool as a cucumber, he kept one eye on The Director as he put a bullet in the butler's head.

The elevator had no internal controls and like all freight elevators, it would not move unless both doors were closed. Of course the safety devices could be fooled easily enough, but there may have been additional safeguards built in if that had been attempted. When the elevator came down, it had three men in it. Two of them were dead; the third was wearing the flowing robes of a desert nomad.

"My apologies. They attempted to block my passage. I thought it would be better to bring them down here than to leave them in plain sight."

"Quite so, mate."

The Director had regained his breath and some of his composure. Knowing he could not bluff his way out of this one, he decided to take a sweet tone until he could get to an alarm. "Gentlemen, none of this was needed. I welcome you to my cave. Make yourselves at home. Have a drink. I have some good whiskies and even some hashish if you wish."

"Shut up, you TROLL!" Terry was showing a ragged edge to his demeanor. "So far you have tried to poison us, shoot us out of the sky...twice, have the Turkish police shoot us, and blow us up in the museum. We will make ourselves comfortable after we tie your hands together. We will accept explanations after we get comfortable, out of sight of these corpses. Get in the other room. If you say something I don't like, I'm going to have my desert-dwelling associate pull your fingernails out one at a time."

Ahmed de Ketama el Bali was as quiet and reserved as a man can be despite the fact that he had just killed two men with his bare hands. He made the butler's pistol disappear into his robes and then sat cross-legged on the table, completely motionless.

Terry Kingston accepted the offer to pour himself a drink. It was a short glass and he sipped it sparingly while he smoked an English Oval.

When he had finished his smoke, he asked the question that had been eating at the remaining members of the team. "Why? Why did we start a plague in the Middle East?"

"In my own defense, I did not know anything about a plague, and do not think we had anything to do with that. It was simply coincidence."

Silence covered the room; the background hum of the circulation fans was the only sound.

"There are no coincidences of that magnitude. The payload we delivered was somehow poisoned and spread the plague. You made us responsible for the deaths of thousands and then you tried to cover your tracks by killing us. If we had opened the bags those bullets came in, we would be dead now. Then you tried to kill us on no less than four different occasions."

"Not true. Everything was set to welcome you in Saudi Arabia. You would have been back home by now enjoying your ill-gotten gains instead of being hunted all over the world. You made the decision to go rogue." The Director began smoothly but practically spat the final words.

"We were attacked by a fighter plane that made no secret of its intentions. Nobody knew we were there except those you contacted, ergo you sent the fighter after us."

"Not true," The Director said, regaining his smooth composure "I do not know who sent the fighter. I did not wish to kill any of you. I was compensated well for a job that went horribly wrong. I am perfectly willing to take care of you financially."

This was more than Terry was willing to take. He stepped forward and punched The Director in the mouth.

The paraplegic spit out a mouthful of blood and said, "I hope that made you feel manly, punching a bound cripple."

"There was a bomb in that briefcase. You intended to take care of us all right, but not the way we wanted. Is there a good reason I shouldn't beat you to death right now?"

"Money."

"Money might work for me, but my desert-dwelling associate has eschewed all payment for this service. He is working for free because you have compromised his honor. He is not the venal sort of man to be bought off so easily, and if you do not supply a more viable alternative, he is quite likely to rend you limb from limb."

The Director looked at him but there was no expression on the Moroccan's face. He might have been a sculpture for all the movement there was. A chill went up The Director's spine as he realized how tenuous his position really was.

"I reiterate my previous denial. I had nothing to do with the plague and do not believe you did either. And what is the difference between bullets and bombs and bugs. They all kill indiscriminately. All you did was supply arms to combatants who would have gotten bullets from somewhere anyway. You did not have anything to do with the plague."

"I think you are wrong and I think you lie," Ahmed

finally spoke. "We loaded bullets onto three different trucks. There are three centers of plague. The bullets caused the plague. You caused the plague."

"That may be, but I had no knowledge. I did not send you to do this thing. Had I wanted you dead, I would have arranged for you to have the plague as well. You would never have made it back here. The disease, whatever it is, matures in two days, kills in two days and dies in a two-day-old body. It cannot survive in the colder climes; it needs the heat. This is public information. This is what they have discovered so far. I cannot tell you any more than that."

"Oh yes you can. You can and will tell us who paid for this operation. You will tell us who provided the shells and who created the plague."

"My sources are confidential, but you know the shells were purchased from Particka the Greek. I say this because the man is dead." The Director said in an accusatory tone.

"I heard his boat was blown from the water," Terry said, equally accusing.

"That did not kill him, I do not think, but I feel sure he is indeed dead."

"What makes you so sure?" Terry inquired, his suspicions aroused further.

"He has not been to any of the casinos or gambling houses in Athens. He lives to gamble and he wagers large. Nobody has seen him for a week and there is no ransom note. I am sure someone paid off an old score. Once again, his boat was blown from the water by a fighter plane. It was not ours and we did not authorize it. We have another player in this game that you do not have in your sights."

"Our sights? You verminous little ogre, we were in your sights for the past week. You would have been happy to see us open the packet and die writhing in the sand or sunk in Lake Van. You are the one in our sights now, and you have told us nothing to prevent our killing you in some inventive and extremely painful way."

"There is no need to threaten. I am obviously your prisoner. Strip me naked and give me a beer."

"The thought of you naked is horrifying, but I think a beer is available. I'll leave your hands bound however."

"So kind."

"Where did the Romanian get the poisoned bullets?"

"I thought he was Greek."

"Romanian, Bulgarian, Greek, whatever he is, was... I don't care about him. I don't care if he is alive or dead. I want to know where the bullets came from."

"You sound Australian."

"So?"

"That marks you. I can help you, but I must have an assurance I will not be killed."

"Oh, I think you will be killed. I think you will be killed in a particularly horrible way."

"I bargain for my life," The Director was visibly sweating now despite the coolness of the underground lair. "I can tell you some of what you want to know and I can find out the rest of it. I have a complete network here. I can find out anything. I will provide you with names and addresses. Everything you want and everything you need."

"I do not trust him to touch any of these devices." Ahmed was as reserved as ever and did not move a muscle as he spoke.

"Nor do I," agreed Terry.

One of the phones rang and The Director was obviously itching to answer it, but nobody moved. It stopped ringing and Terry's cell phone started ringing. The reception was abominable, but he was able to discern who was calling. A couple of minutes later, Terry pushed the button and the freight elevator came down again.

Inside the elevator, Gordon MacMaster was crouched with an automatic rifle on the left and Anastasia Viuda was on the right holding a pair of 9mm pistols. In the center, looking exceedingly uncomfortable was the unarmed John Marshall.

Stepping out, the trio breathed a collective sigh of relief. "Leave the doors open and let's block the other door." Gordon began. "I want a shot of scotch and a cigar. We just entered the dragon's lair and we are about to plunder his treasure.

Anastasia rummaged around in the kitchen until she found the tobacco drawer and lit her man a cigar. While he was savoring the smoke, she poured him a shot of scotch, licked her lips and drank it, then poured him another.

Chapter Eleven
Unchained

"How did the disease get across the mountain ranges into Iran? It was not supposed to be able to survive the temperature of the high mountain passes."

"No, sir, Mr. Epstein. I do not think it can, however, the virus must be brought to life first. Only after it has been activated by moisture will the temperature bother it. I think some members of the PPK must have gotten a bag of the product and not opened them until they got back over the mountains."

"I feared this was going to get out of hand. I had not wanted genocide. Lord knows I am not a monster."

"Of course not, sir."

"Is the cure secured?"

"Of course, sir."

"If the virus reaches Syria or Jordan, announce that a cure has been found and release it in Israel. Charge a fortune for it and make it available to the Arabs only after the Israelis are taken care of. Charge them twice the fortune. I want 700% profits from this first batch and 1000% from the second. The second batch is being produced, isn't it, Michael?"

"Of course, sir."

"After a proven first batch, people will pay anything for it." Albert Epstein spoke of the plague and the cure as if he was discussing the price of cheese at the local corner grocery.

"Sir, the United Arab Emirates and the Saudis will pay almost anything for the cure, now, before they are infected." Michael Galliardo knew this to be true. The corporation had been in contact with some of the desperate and fabulously rich sultans of the Middle East. Epstein did not reveal his involvement in this 'unfortunate episode,' but he was quick to pledge large sums of money to certain agencies for developing a cure. As donations, this money would be tax-deductible to the corporation, and if nobody looked too closely, they wouldn't find out that the corporations working on a cure were all created by Albert Epstein within the past two years. The buildings were all but empty and the donations were washed and filed right back into Epstein's bank accounts

"Sir, the Sheiks of Kuwait would probably provide us with more than luxury for a guaranteed cure, just enough for themselves and their wives."

"The time is not right. We must convince them we needed time to work on the cure. We cannot allow them to know it was the Russians, not yet. Petroleo must be seen as the savior of the Middle East, not the Great Satan."

"Of course, sir."

"Has the virus proven to die in a corpse after death?"

"Yes, sir, in about 48 hours."

"What about the ones that go to colder climates, are they cured by the cold?"

"Only if there are no visible symptoms yet. If the glands have already begun to swell, there is no saving them without the cure. They are not contagious in the cooler climates though. Once activated, the virus doesn't survive well under 90 or 95 degrees Fahrenheit. There was an outbreak in Rome but once the people got into air conditioned situations, the spread of the contagion was stopped. Apparently the air conditioning on the flight out of Mosul was broken or there would have been no transfer at all."

"Good. Then it has ceased in Rome."

"The last of the infected have passed away. They are investigating the virus at the Roman hospitals. They have discovered that the cold is the best defense against infection. I think cold air in the lungs kills the virus but I can't imagine why. When the Arabs get that news, it may cause riots at the hotels and government buildings. To get air conditioning will become vital."

"Does it look like there is an exodus to the north? Are people moving out of the warmer climes?"

"Not yet, but it looks like it may happen."

"Well, Michael, the Russians came through this time."

"It certainly seems so, sir."

"Oh, speaking of the Russians, they failed to bring down the transport plane. That distinction was left to the Turkish government. I want to be certain there is nothing linking us to the plane."

"There is no paper trail on that one, sir. Cash transactions were handled through the Hercules Bank. Hercules is both discreet and understanding. We have used him for a few different things that require, ah... delicacy. The transport plane was bought and registered by Hyperion Particka and though he has not been confirmed dead, he has disappeared."

"Good. He was set up with more style than I would have expected. We are off to the races then."

Paul Phillips and Roger Forster were having a cocktail after dinner. Katherine had gone back to the Swiss hotel room to change clothes. They were discussing what the next move should be regarding Victor Rothchild.

"I don't think the recording is as vital as we once thought it might be. After all, Hyperion Particka had disappeared and nobody knows where. For him to call out of the blue and tell the bank that we are coming in might be a bit unusual and damning if they ever do find him."

Paul sipped on his drink. "They'll never find him. That shaft is a 100 meters deep. Nobody is going to even smell him. I think you're listening to your woman too much. Is she talking about cutting your partners out of the deal?"

"Don't be ridiculous. I'm just saying with all the

numbers, we might not need the recording." Roger was full and happy and did not seem to realize he was losing the edge that had kept him alive all these years. "What's to prevent us from walking into that bank with the numbers and cleaning out that vault?"

"Maybe nothing, but something is wrong. Victor has been expecting our calls, yet he is constantly out of touch. With such a nice and simple payoff in the works, it does not make any sense not to respond to your partners. I fear he may be dead. I wish you could have found the Mad Scottish Bull in Turkey."

Roger got defensive at the mention. "That was an impossible job. I'm convinced he was gone before we even got there. He was not even sighted in that town by anyone. Large rewards were posted and he never showed up. I'm calling The Director. I don't know why the communication lines went down but we need to know what has transpired there." After dialing the number and leaving a second message, Roger made sure he had a full charge on his cell phone. It always took The Director some time to return calls but never more than a couple of hours.

"You know, the epidemic is showing up in Turkey now? I mean the old Turkey, not the new section. If we had stayed in Van, we may have contracted it ourselves."

Katherine came back in a shimmering short dress with her hair piled on top of her head and high heels on. She was looking better than either of them had seen her look previously. Paul complimented her on the dress and ordered another round of drinks.

A few rounds of drinks and some light chatter, Paul began to be concerned that The Director had not called back. Roger knew there was often a delay and was not worried about it. Katherine began to press for the bank again.

"Look, dear, it might be different if we had a market for the paintings, but right now we have no market for them either. All we have is the word of a dead man that they even exist and that they are genuine lost Van Gogh. He was, after all, bargaining for his life and might have said anything. This whole ordeal is delicate and must be handled that way." Even Roger understood that just getting the paintings did not represent much of anything.

"What we need is a broker," Paul asserted. "We need a discreet professional who can deal with this sort of high-end art without causing a stir. If we show up with these paintings there will be questions, but if a broker shows up with art from an 'unnamed collector' nobody thinks twice about it. They could turn around and auction it at Sotheby's without causing a stir."

Victor had been looking for a discreet art dealer, but Victor had either gone on assignment or was otherwise occupied. It would not be long before any claim he had to the money was null and void in the eyes of his partners.

"Sotheby's might be a stretch. There have been a lot of people lately contesting the sale of art because it was stolen from their families by the Germans." Katherine had a good point. "What is important is that we get the money in cash and split it up immediately. No large purchases in cash but slowly make small deposits and even better, take out loans and make the payments in cash. That way the bank launders the money for you. Any large deposits must be made in offshore accounts or flags go up with the taxman. He will be our worst enemy. Large cash deposits or purchases will send up signals in any country."

"Except Switzerland."

"Yes, dear. Except Switzerland."

Nothing that was being said had not been discussed before. They were just making plans like people certain they would be winning the lottery any day now. They were also getting quite drunk. The Director had not called them back. They continued drinking, expecting the call, but the call never came. It was late when they finally returned to the hotel and passed out.

The next day they smelled trouble. With no call back from either party, they deduced that trouble had invaded the homeland. They quickly decided that it would be best if they retrieved the artifacts from the vault and secreted them elsewhere. The best place they could think of was a long-term storage facility. The ones in Bern were a bit expensive, but they represented a very secure environment. They also deduced, correctly, if nobody knew what was there or what it was worth nobody would try to steal it. Crime was not one of the great concerns in Bern because there was a very professional metropolitan police force.

Surprisingly, the operation went as smooth as silk. There was no need for the recording of Hyperion Particka's voice authorizing them to collect the contents of his corner of the vault. The twelve-digit account number and the nine-digit access code was all that was required aside from the box key itself. The box was brought to Paul, the only member of the team inside the building, and he was left in a secure room. Inside the box, wrapped in desiccant paper were three paintings, all of the same man, Van Gogh. There was also about 10,000 Swiss Francs. Quick calculations told him it was about 4,000 British Pounds. Not enough to make a difference. He folded it and put it in his pocket.

The only other thing in the box was the authentication certificate from a French art dealer that, in his opinion, the self-portraits were the genuine article and Van Gogh was the artist. Paul folded that and stuck it in a different pocket. He called for a cart and wheeled the paintings into the lobby. The box stayed behind. The paintings were tenderly transported to a rented box van and taken from there to the storage facility. The next order of business would be to contact the French art dealer who had certified their authenticity.

Anastasia Viuda was a magician on a computer system, compared to her lover. She was not a hacker exactly, but she knew enough about programming to know how to get around things, and knew enough about users to know what to look for. Once she had determined what the Agency's general bank account number was, it was not difficult to persuade The Director to supply her with the access codes. Most of the money from that account was transferred to a numbered Swiss account. The other accounts were somewhat dedicated to certain payments so to tamper with them would alert some government clerk to the discrepancy. The account labeled 'Arms and Munitions' had a large sum of money withdrawn from it recently and then a large sum of cash deposited 10 days later. What Gordon MacMaster was most interested in determining was where the original transfer had come from. A search of the transferring account number yielded the name of a private New York City bank, The Hercules Investment Corporation and Finance Bank. The money had been transferred in a lump sum over 90 days prior to the recent withdrawal. There was no note and no invoice but it was the only transfer from that particular bank and the only private transfer into that account all year. Every other deposit into the Arms and Munitions account was directly from MI6, Department Six of Military Intelligence.

Gordon had Anastasia transfer a specific amount of money to a bank account in Germany. He dialed a number from The Director's personal phone and read a list of numbers. Then he said, "Transfer with interest and laundry fees. Traceable funds. " Then he hung up the phone. Then they transferred a large amount to a Swiss bank account and a smaller though still substantial amount to a local bank in the name of Father McTavish.

"You know we cannot stay down here long. With the phone not being answered and nobody being authorized to come below, there is going to be questions. It will not take long before they send in the troops. I refuse to be here when they do. Ah, what was that?"

Anastasia Viuda backed up one screen at her man's question. The previous screen was a block of live squares, one of which said Official Uniforms but instead of bringing up pictures of troops, it brought up another bank account. The contents of this one were transferred to a bank in New Zealand and locked into a Certificate of Deposit for the next 20 years. If Terry lived that long it would make a very nice retirement; if not it would be donated to a charitable organization for the preservation of wildlife. The bank's policy would not allow any other form of transfer or withdrawal unless authorized by Terry Kingston in person.

The final financial transaction was to buy four plane tickets to Sydney, Australia on the flight leaving out of Heathrow in the morning.

"We have what we need and everyone else has been paid. The only thing left is to remove the reward on our heads and move along. Can you do that for us here, darling?"

"I can do one better than this. Give me a minute. Terry, may I have one of your cigarettes?"

"I didn't think you smoked."

"Hah. Only in celebration and crying, uh… mourning."

"What are you celebrating?"

Anastasia laughed, "No, I am mourning the death of my lover." She was working furiously at the keyboard. The cigarette was dangling from her pouting lips, her wig was sitting on the chair beside her, and despite the cooler temperature there was sweat on her bald head. When she was done the cigarette was long finished along with a half a bottle of scotch. Her full lips held a triumphant yet crooked smile and her eyes were glazed over. "There, my love, you're dead. I've killed you."

Ahmed de Ketama el Bali had not moved a muscle. It was as though he had turned to stone. The others were enjoying themselves, however.

The story was sent on the priority channel of MI6. It was sent to the BBC, the London Times, the local bobbies and the Office of Island Security. It showed the dead body of a man in the Museum of Natural History. He had flaming red hair and the florid skin of a true red head. The story read that a man had attempted to bomb the museum and had been shot dead by security forces. The expatriate Scotsman as he was described was the wanted terrorist Gordon MacMaster accompanied by Terry Kingston an associate and fellow terrorist. Kingston's body was not pictured due to the extent of the injuries he had suffered. Because it was broadcast on the official Ministry of Intelligence channel, the BBC and the Times ran the story that night without question. The local police stopped looking for the redheaded Scotsman and the Office of Island Security took down its transport alert. MI6 did not, however. They got the broadcast second-hand and hours late. When they checked with the police and found out that Victor Rothchild had been arrested instead they were infuriated.

The Director had fallen silent. He had been little help to his captors and felt there were few options left for him. He counted himself among the dead already until the half-soused Second Secretary spoke up in his defense. "Gentlemen, we have secrets galore. There is no need for further death. The man before us has no more interest in our deaths. Personally he may feel we robbed him but you were simply getting payment for your services. I say we spare the poor man's life and gain ourselves some Karmic relief."

The only fully sober member of the team looked around him and saw no support for the plan. He looked at Gordon MacMaster who nodded his head. A large leaf shaped blade flew out of one of Ahmed's sleeves and ended up in The Director's throat. The disabled man choked and reached for the blade with his bound hands, his eyes bugging out of his head. He actually pulled the blade out of his throat but would issue no further statements, proclamations or requests. He died choking on the fountain of blood that spouted from the wound.

"Oh dear! Was that absolutely necessary?"

"I'm afraid it was," Gordon affirmed. "Consider that he had an opportunity to pay us and part in good standing all around. Instead he sent us a bomb in a briefcase. There was no chance he would have allowed us to live after invading his lair and tying him to his chair. If he were allowed to live, we would not be, that includes yourself. I will not burden us with a crippled hostage of no real value. Now, I'm afraid we must cover you. We were paid to rescue you and we did so but we cannot have you rescued from us until the time is right."

"What are you planning for me?" he asked warily.

"Nothing special. I feel you would not betray us given the option but we need to ensure our survival and there will be those who have other ideas. I need you to finish this bottle of scotch with me."

"Of course."

"And I need you to deny seeing any of us for 48 hours."

"Of course."

"And I need you to take these pills."

"Uh... of course. What are they?"

"Just some of The Director's pain killers. Don't worry, they won't kill you. Now remember, we are going to fly to Australia and disappear into the outback for a while so if you need to be rescued, we will not be available to do it."

John Marshall took the pain killers and drank the scotch and submitted to being tied to a chair. He would not see another living soul for a day and a half. He would leave The Director's lair soiled and sore from being tied to a chair but none the worse for wear. The stories he had to tell sounded like a fantasy to MI6 and he was forced to tell them over and over again and they jumped on every discrepancy they thought they found. John Marshall did not see the light of day for another week after being "liberated." He was never told that the four plane tickets to Sydney had been bought but never used.

There is no way MacMaster and Kingston could fly out of Heathrow Airport without being spotted, even though they were both more or less officially dead. The British had a way of understanding things that could not be understood, and covering things they could not explain in public ways. The evacuation of the Museum of Natural History and the subsequent news of the bombers' death had naturally caused the press to swarm, but nothing was revealed by MI6.

The bed and breakfast had been accommodating, though old. The guests paid well and their business was not inquired about. They did raise their eyebrows when the guests left on their final day dressed as priests and the outfit the 'Spanish' woman wore could not be classified as anything but modern. She had shorts so short you could see the bottom of her moons and a shirt that revealed her midriff to the bottom of her breasts. The proprietor stared at her until his wife bashed him with her purse, then she stared too. It would provide fodder for conversation for years to come and endless speculation around the table. The Arab had shaved his beard and the big Scotsman had pasted on a fake one and shaved his head.

Father McTavish all but emptied his account in the London Bank. The money had just been transferred in yesterday and he took it out in cash today. It required a brief case to carry and the officer suggested that the Father might require a professional escort with all that money. Father McTavish answered that the Lord watched over him day and night, and took his leave with his briefcase full of money.

There was a pair of men waiting on the platform of the

train station. They had polyester suits and black shoes. They both wore bowlers and carried bumbershoots and tried to be as inconspicuous as they could while passing on train after train.

They paid little attention to the three Catholic Priests, one in a wheelchair, who entered the platform. They were not far behind the Spanish woman with the outfit that belonged on the beach. She was walking in front of them when she dropped a coin. Bending over in those high-heeled shoes and that pair of shorts with almost no crotch fueled the men's fantasies for weeks. She got on the Eurostar for the mainland, the same as the Catholic Priests did, but sat in a different car.

The train station in Paris was predictably dirty and muddled. The Government Inspectors were bored and awaiting the shift change. They eyed the Priests suspiciously but stamped them through once they learned that Paris was not their objective. Romania was distant enough and in need of a good religious revival. Father McTavish spoke a good French and his three partners said nothing at all. The tall thin nun had apparently taken a vow of silence for past sins of the mouth which the Inspectors found increasingly humorous.

They took hotel rooms in Paris; they were small and cramped and smelled of moldy bread and urine. They could have taken upscale rooms but that would have led to attention that was not wanted. In a restaurant on the West Bank of the Seine they discussed their options. The Hercules Investment Corporation and Finance Bank was small and private, despite its ostentatious name. It was not the sort of place anyone could walk into and open a savings account. There would be very little cash and consequently little need for security. The bank president's name was James Scott, one of a large and powerful family that had made a New York name for itself in the twentieth century.

When their dinners arrived they ate in silence, each consumed with thoughts of their own. The wine was sweet and sparkling and led to consuming much of it. The river smelled after being heated by the sun all day. After dinner they had coffee outside, under an awning. The coffee was very tasty and the cigars from The Director's drawer were excellent.

The Catholic disguises would be discarded after their arrival in America. Ahmed de Ketama el Bali was to keep his face bare and Gordon MacMaster his head and face shaved. Terry Kingston's hair was kept dyed black and Anastasia Viuda was having increasing fun buying wigs and changing her disguises. By mutual assent they agreed that Paris would be a good place to relax for a couple of days before embarking on their final mission.

The art dealer was very accommodating. He knew exactly what masterpieces the team was referring to, and would be happy to represent them for a healthy chunk of the proceeds. He knew also they had been in the hands of Hyperion Particka who had been rumored to have disappeared. There were a few men who knew about these works, mostly dealers and collectors in the fine art trade. Hyperion had wanted less than the paintings were worth but nobody was about to tell him that. Typical of the trade, they all wanted to give him half of what he was asking and resell them for twice what they were worth.

The Greek arms merchant had wanted a quiet and personal sale; the current possessors of the art wanted to auction it off at Sotheby's. Sotheby's represented nothing but the finest products sold to the richest clientele.

Francois de LeMarque attempted to be discreet as he explained that there might be some question as to the ownership and authenticity of the work, that there may be some claims and lawsuits instituted against anyone who did not have perfectly legal ownership of anything auctioned off. The real question they wanted answered was the payoff and how quickly it could be facilitated.

The Van Goghs would be left with the dealer to auction separately. He was a respected art dealer and would be making a substantial profit from merely handling the art. The auction was to be a closed and private affair, involving only extremely wealthy collectors with personal invitations. Inquiries as to the actual ownership of this artwork could be directed to Francois de LeMarque and would be forwarded from there to the respective parties involved. Those parties would be unavailable and will have been paid in cash.

Confident and satisfied with the answer, the two men and the woman left the shop for steak and red wine followed by French coffee on the West Bank.

As they sat there basking in their success, the men enjoyed the parade of exotic prostitutes that passed in high heels and fishnet stockings. They came from almost anywhere imaginable: France, Germany, Eastern Europe, Russia, America, but none were so bold as the Spanish. One tall, voluptuous Spaniard with wild purple hair sat right at their table and started talking to Paul. She spoke some French and almost no English but made it clear that she was available for a price. Her name was Maria and she obviously knew what she was worth. Paul tried to bargain with her but she was firm in her demands. He told her she was not worth that much, which earned him a torrent of Spanish invective. They watched her walk away, swinging her hips and Paul mused that perhaps he was wrong. Perhaps she would have been worth it. Katherine Sylvan snorted and Roger Forster shook his head grinning.

On the way back to the hotel they saw her again, leaning against a wall. Paul told his companions to keep walking, that he had business to take care of. His curiosity and his libido had overcome his frugal nature and he was now willing to pay her price. They spoke for a few minutes and then followed the others to the hotel.

Maria insisted on taking a shower first and Paul joined her in the shower. When they were finished he had to admit that she was worth every penny she had insisted on. It had been wilder than he expected, and she was probably the hottest woman he had ever had. She was so pleased with his assessment, she gave him another for free. Even though he knew better, he let her have another shower afterwards and never saw her leave. He was sound asleep.

The following day he woke to find that she had stolen his wallet on the way out.

The money and his English driver's license were gone but the wallet was turned in to the front desk. Paul Phillips cursed himself for a fool and shoved the billfold back in his pocket saying "No such thing as a free ride."

Katherine Sylvan was just returning from across the street. She had purchased three breakfasts to go at the all-night bistro. She grabbed Phillips by the arm and pulled him into the elevator. The two rejoined Roger Forster and sat down to breakfast. The other two got a good laugh out of Paul's misfortune but none of the three suspected the true story. As far as they could tell, he was slipping and had gotten cleaned out by a streetwalker. Since she had only gotten the money in his wallet and there were no credit cards, the whole event was written off. A telephone call to London took care of the driver's license. It wasn't in his real name anyway and it took him a moment to remember what nom de guerre was on the card. He had to look at his passport. That mirrored the name on the license.

Chapter Twelve
Payoff

"Anastasia, that was the most effective use of the world's oldest profession I have ever seen. How did you know she could do it?"

"My love, these women will do anything for the right price. I made sure the price was right for her and I made sure she would catch his eye. Also, I needed to make sure he did not suspect anything, being a tight-assed British prick. That is why I told her to overcharge him at first and walk away. She performed only half of what I said her to do. What I really wanted was his passport so he could not leave the country."

Gordon MacMaster was holding Piccadilly Paul Phillips' driver's license between his thumb and forefinger and flicking it with his middle finger. The name on the license was not his but the picture was unmistakable. "It would not have stopped him. Getting the number of the hotel room was more important."

The Argentine woman continued, "I saw him sitting there and knew it was he... him. If I thought he would not know me I would have done it myself and killed him, but he knew me as your woman. I knew I needed to act or lose him, so I did. It was good but not perfect."

"Darling, it was magnificent. I am so proud of you."

"Can we nominate her for the Nobel Prize later and figure out what they are doing in Paris first?" Kingston was edgy. "How did they know where we went?"

"I don't think they are after us," Anastasia said slowly. "They are professionals, yes?"

"Yes. A bit rusty perhaps, but professionals." The Scot already knew where this was going.

"Professionals don't sit on the Left Bank drinking coffee and buying whores when they are on the job."

"We were sitting on the Left Bank a couple days ago."

"And we are in Paris looking for people we want to kill? Though that one would be on my list if I had one."

"No, my love, we are not and, if I might mention, we are in disguise," MacMaster replied, enjoying the conversation.

"Drunken, cigar smoking priests."

"We are not renting women or molesting little boys, however."

"Humph. I am going to my room to shower. If you are not there 15 minutes after that I am going to sleep without you."

"Ah. His master's voice," quipped Terry.

"Tangiers, I'll relieve you in six hours; you relieve Terry in three. Terry, no buying whores. Terribly unprofessional." Gordon gave his Australian friend a grin and a broad wink and turned to follow his paramour to the hotel, just down the street from that housing the British agents.

Terry Kingston broke into a chuckle. Ahmed de Ketama el Bali maintained his stoic countenance.

"Are you uncomfortable, Ahmed?"

"Why do you ask this, Terry Kingston? It is not cold, although it is damp. It is not going to rain on us."

"No. I was referring to the disguise. I never saw an Arab priest before."

"I am generally indifferent to religion. What was written these thousands of years ago was appropriate for its time but not for now. For instance, when was the last time you saw someone wash someone else's feet? Yet they did it in your Bible all the time."

"I see."

"I ask you now if you think heaven is populated with virgins?"

"Uh… no, mate. That doesn't make much sense."

"We agree on this but there are others who will insist that this is the reward for long and loyal service and belief."

Terry took a long pull on his beer, reminding himself that he had promised it to be the last for the night. "It's the word 'belief' that binds men to religions of all kinds."

"Yes, belief. It is also the teaching of appropriate doctrine for the time and place. Egypt has a long history of religion. It was religion that caused the Egyptians to move mountains into the desert with no engines. Engineers today cannot fully explain how they built the pyramids, physically. It was faith."

"So… tell me about your faith."

"I have faith. That is all you need to know."

"Then tell me about your belief."

"My belief. It, He is something and everywhere. It is alien to man yet a part of him. I pray to this force for guidance and strength but never for material things. I do not like to name my belief, for to name it is to give it doctrine and it has no doctrine. It cares for no doctrine. It does not favor one group over another and it does not call for faith or sacrifice or donations. I believe I will sleep now and I believe I will wake in the morning. If I am mistaken, it will not be the first time nor will it be the last. Ah, perhaps it will be the last. But, I will not make the arrogant and overbearing mistake of thinking that there is an all powerful force that cares a heap of sand whether I was a good man or not. When the spark in my eye is gone and the worms eat my flesh, the only thing that matters is that I treated those still living with a fair hand that will cause them to mourn me if I would have wished it so while I lived."

"Just so, mate. Get some sleep and then get back here."

"Just so. Honor be upon you."

Terry Kingston watched his Moroccan associate walk out of the dimly lit bistro and found himself wondering what it was that he, himself, really had faith in. What did he really believe and why. The word 'honor' kept playing in his mind. It briefly amused him but then he thought of the Turk, Van, who was going to take care of his friend's family. He thought of the way Ahmed had refused to accept the dirty money, the proceeds from the arms delivery. His introspective condition was peppered with the thought that there is no honor among thieves.

"What is honor? What is it and why do I need or care? I have all I need and want and was already retired until Mack called. Why am I pursuing a dangerous and unprofitable task? Why not just disappear again? Mexico or Bolivia or Rio, no plague in South America. If there is a Hell then I am already doomed to it."

The piano player had stopped playing hours earlier but the place never really shut down. The waiter came around asking if there was something else and Terry asked for coffee and shut him up with a wad of Francs. His bible was in front of him and an open International Herald Tribune. Terry could read the Parisian newspapers in French but didn't want to bother when the same thing was printed in English the same day.

The news from the Middle East confirmed that the plague was spreading without check. The epicenter in Iran had been cordoned off, but cases were still cropping up as residents tried to escape the area. The places in Iraq and the former Iraq that had been spared previously were now infected. Baghdad was now showing signs of infection and panic was setting in. The various subgroups of Islam were blaming each other and the sectarian violence that had waned in previous years was erupting with a vengeance. There was still no cure on the horizon though money was pouring in from around the world in search of it.

"Honor. What honor is there in a life of murder. Blood money. Still, until now everybody I sent off deserved it. With a few exceptions they were all guilty of sins against humanity not just sins. Sin. Honor and sin. Interesting to think I could be an instrument of the Lord. Shit, I was comfortably retired. I knew something stank about this job and I never should have gotten in on it. I never could quit when I was ahead."

The hotel desk was open all night but the light coming through the doorway was through the half window on top. If the door were opened, the light would spill out to alert anyone watching for the event. The back door to the hotel opened into an alley. The mouth of the alley was in darkness, but Terry could see any headlights turning into it from his position inside the bistro. He could not be seen from the rooms in the hotel due to the canopy over the street-side tables.

Personally, he felt Anastasia Viuda was wrong. The presence of the English agents was too great a coincidence to be discounted. The very man who had recruited Gordon MacMaster in the first place had been sitting on the bank of the river having coffee. Not only was the British system to be admired for that but the agents at hand must not be underestimated again. He had been introduced and it made him a target. His avowed solution, seconded by the Moroccan, was to dispose of the British agents before disappearing. They were an immediate representation of the guilty parties. There was no moral dilemma in eliminating them.

Three hours passed as slowly as could be expected. The beer he had consumed had been passed through by then. Tired, he waited for Ahmed to relieve him, still fretting that they had not posted two people at a time. He could not watch the door and use the water closet simultaneously and the strong French coffee on top of the beer had his plumbing flowing.

Ahmed de Ketama el Bali had no such biological concerns. He drank one cup of tea while he sat and needed nothing to read. His granite-like pose would have caused some stares had there been anyone there in the middle of the night but there was not. The staff was making up the dough for the morning's croissants, cleaning the coffee pots and utensils and readying the business for the breakfast crowd.

The unusual priests who took turns at the end table tipped very well and needed little. If they had been French they could have been assumed to be policemen. Some of the staff was convinced they were Interpol.

Though the still dark man wore the robes of a priest, he did not read from the open bible in front of him. He seemed totally lost within himself for the three hours he sat there then got up and quietly left when he was relieved by the Scotsman.

The breakfast crowd was filtering in when the woman dressed in business attire joined the ostensibly Irish Father at the table. They spoke for a moment and he left.

Katherine Sylvan had never so much as seen a picture of Anastasia Viuda. There was no recognition that morning when she visited the bistro. Anastasia on the other hand had seen Katherine dining with Paul and Roger the day before. The Argentine had acted on what she thought, having only seen Paul twice in her life and that in a completely different setting.

Ahmed was in a different disguise an hour later when the British trio left the hotel. A flowered shirt and cheap stretchy pants marked him as a tourist. The white pork pie hat completed the illusion. Somehow the disguise added 20 years to his appearance without the use of makeup. A stooped posture and a cane hid his face, an unnecessary precaution since none of the British team had ever seen him.

It was easy to follow the three English assassins down the promenade that fronted the river. They did not act as though they were looking for anyone or were in any kind of a hurry. They did look behind themselves often, probably out of long-standing habit.

The trio went to an auto rental service and rented a 15-passenger van with windows all around the outside. The clerk was a young man who, while friendly, was not particularly enthusiastic.

An hour after they had left, the clerk was confronted by a tall, burly, bald man in a business suit. The newcomer started by counting out large bills on the counter and then asked the clerk if he had made this much money last week. The clerk was perplexed and did not answer right away, so the man counted a couple more bills.

The clerk was alone in the office since the manager had just left for breakfast. The manager did not spend much time there. He would be back in an hour, work an hour and then go for his two-hour lunch.

"Sir," the clerk asked in French, "do you wish to rent an auto?"

"No. I wish to find one that you rented an hour ago. It was a large Ford van."

"And may I ask what this is all about?"

"No, you may not. You will take this pile of Francs and punch in the GPS tracking number into your computer. I wish to know where the van is and what direction it is heading in."

"This is against policy. I cannot do this."

The large bald man counted out two more bills onto the counter and then casually laid a straight razor next to them. "We can do this to your benefit or we can do it the unpleasant way."

The clerk needed no further enticement. He slid the money off the counter and put it in his pocket then he proceeded to pull up the tracking plan for the van. The location was in script but a few clicks brought up a map of France with the auto as a red dot on the southeastern highway.

"Bon. I wish to give you twice as much money as I have already. Do you wish this as well?"

"Oui," the clerk replied cautiously.

"Then I need you to call this number once an hour and tell me where this van is. You must also call me immediately and tell me if the van has been returned here or anywhere else. Agreed?"

"Oui. I can do this."

"At closing time you will go to dinner and then return here to continue doing this thing for me, yes?"

"Oui."

"Good. Here's a few more Francs. Remember, this stack is yours if I know where this van goes all day. If it takes more than one day I will pay more. Do not split this with the manager and do not declare it on your taxes."

"Oui." The clerk was serious until he realized that it was supposed to be a joke, then he got a weak smile on his face.

"Oy, Mack. We're gonna miss our flight out." Terry was in the Paris hotel room wearing a priest's vestments. The black leather bags they had for clothing were packed. Terry Kingston was feeling exposed and missing his pistols. They did not have an acceptable means of transporting them overseas and had left them in London. The briefcase full of money taken from The Director's stronghold had gone to Paris on overnight mail disguised in foil lined coffee bags and was used to open 12 different bank accounts in various names and various banks. The law was such that cash deposits over a certain amount would be flagged by the tax examiner so the deposits were kept below that amount. The paperwork for these accounts was secreted in four safe deposit boxes. Each team member kept a key. Each of the accounts held enough for an emergency, enough for a couple of months in the very expensive city of Paris.

"Look 'ere, Tarrytown, we got something going on. I'm too curious an old goat to pass it off."

"Alright then, ya ol' goat, what is it?"

"Piccadilly Paul and his friends are going to Switzerland. They were not after us at all."

"Well. Good then. They don't want us and we don't want them so it's a mutually advantageous relationship, a win-win as they say in the States."

"Yes and no. I'm still not convinced they are not after us. If we lose sight of them now we will be watching our backs forever."

The Moroccan chimed in, "Are we to remain in Paris then when the devil is free in New York?"

"Tangiers. Eliminating this threat may seem an unnecessary risk to you but if they are not after us now, they will be later. These people are as responsible for the plague as we are or more so. They were in Athens brokering the transaction. Ask Tarrytown who got us the plane."

"Yes, it is so. They have compromised our honor. I merely ask why we wait. Will you be able to hold them down?"

"Yes. I am tracking their movements by proxy."

"How soon?"

"Hard to say. They may start back today but probably not. In any event, I won't leave Paris until I know what they are up to. I will feel much better if I can eliminate the possibility of their following us, forever."

Victor Rothchild was very glad to be free. He was lucky to ever be released after The Director was found to have been murdered. John Marshall vindicated him after a couple of days and MI6 had him released from local custody. Victor was also unsure of his immediate future. He had a modest sum set aside, enough for a frugal life style for a few years but he judged that the risks he had taken and the services he had performed for the Crown should be worth more than a senior's pension and a life of poverty.

He called the bank in Switzerland identifying himself as Hyperion Particka's secretary and asked if the vault box had been accessed. The bank would tell him nothing. Then he called the two numbers he did have, Paul's cell phone and Roger's pager. He got no response from either of them.

Victor Rothchild became very angry for a moment and then a chill entered his soul. He might be looking for dead men. Gordon MacMaster might have killed and buried all three of his partners. If he could kill The Director, he could have found the deputies easily. Victor took a chance and e-mailed Paul Phillips' address. There was no reply but the mail was transferred. That told him there was a chance the owner was alive and simply not taking calls right now for one reason or another. He was on a razor's edge as to whether he should stay in London and keep calling or try going to the mainland. Once on the mainland he would be looking for a needle in a haystack since he did not have the account numbers.

Part of Victor's anger and regret came from the fact that he had never taken advantage of the opportunities afforded him to steal over the years. He had the opportunity to take, for instance, the money he had returned to the account in the Credit Suisse recently. He was simply not very inventive and he knew if more than one man knew a secret, it was no longer a secret. There had been other opportunities, however, where he could have padded his nest and had not. He had simply never seen the assassination of The Director and his subsequent unemployment as a realistic situation. The Director was The Agency and once he was gone, the real retirement payoff would stop existing. Of course, Deputy Rothchild still had his job, a position that paid a pittance, and his pension which would pay less.

Victor felt very much like killing somebody but not just anybody, he felt like killing Gordon MacMaster. If he could have found him he would have gladly put a bullet in his brain. Once he saw the report on Gordon's death in the museum he was even further infuriated. He considered going to MI6 to try to determine what was going on. They knew Victor in a roundabout manner, after all, they were responsible for getting him released. They were also responsible for the report then, he reasoned. That meant he would get nowhere looking for Gordon MacMaster there.

He sat in his flat cleaning and oiling his guns and calling his associates from time to time. He was still getting no response. The lack of a plan or even the ability to make a plan was driving him mad. Then it struck him. In the absence of The Director, there was a plethora of electronic surveillance equipment sitting idle in the musty basement stronghold. It was off limits for a while; after all four bodies had been discovered down there along with a somewhat distressed Second Secretary tied to a chair. That director position had been created many years earlier and subsequently hidden and disavowed. It was questionable if the current administration even knew what transpired in that rat hole of an office. Victor was not the inventive type. If he had not been part of The Agency he might not even have believed it existed. But it did exist. It employed about 18 people on a sporadic basis and it was an invisible body wanting a head.

There was a multitude of printing shops in the financial district. Victor chose a small shop with an aging staff of well-respected men. His raised seal, diploma-type promotion was as authentic looking as could be expected. The scribbled signature of the head of MI6 would never be brought into question because The Agency, and consequently The Director, did not exist. In truth, the powers that be would more likely approve the subterfuge on the grounds of convenience for all involved.

In the back office of the internet café, the owner tried to tell him that the authorities had sealed the area. Nobody is to be allowed down there.

"Think again, old boy. I'm unsealing it. It is mine as of today. I'm the new Director."

The owner of the café squinted at the paper Victor

Rothchild held up before him and scratched his chin. "Will there be any change in circumstances applied to this change in personnel?" he asked, convinced but concerned for his cash cow.

"No. The circumstances remain as they were with the sole difference that I will emerge from the hole from time to time."

"Then I'll ring you down. Don't forget when you change the passwords and protocol to let me know."

"Of course, right away. I will also be disallowing any visitors for the first 30 days. I will subsequently provide you with a revised list of those with access. If anyone comes around hoping to join me down there, short of the head of MI6, the site is sealed by executive order and no one is going down there."

"Very well Mr. … Ah Mr. Director. You will not be joined by a soul until you authorize it."

Without further ado the new Director entered his subterranean lair.

The British were pretty much rubber stamped through the border between Switzerland and France. The rented van was peered into but none of the receipts and declarations of value that they had spent so much time acquiring were even asked for. They had the lost masterpieces and were on their way toward the payoff. A quickly organized and quiet private auction would turn the paintings into cash and they would disperse from there.

Roger was, by now, deeply in love with Katherine. His plans included her in everything and he consulted her on their future. Paul was less attached and planning to make an international affair of it. His first move upon gaining access to a large store of cash would be to book passage on a world wide cruise ship under an assumed name and disappear.

The trio had left all electronic devices at the hotel room

to ensure they could not be followed. They had left the batteries in to show location for the trackers but that only pinpointed the Paris hotel rooms they would never return to. They were feeling invisible and untraceable when they pulled into the dock behind the art dealer's office. The dock was a function of it having been a grocery store at some time in the past. The dock door opened and they moved the three paintings into the dark opening. They were confident they were alone.

The British agents spent no more than a few minutes with the art dealer. Enough time was taken for him to verify that the paintings were indeed the ones he had seen earlier and that they were, in fact, authentic. In four days the auction would take place and on the fifth day all three of them would be independently wealthy.

The conversation that ensued that evening was animated. Paul Phillips was all for including Victor in the proceeds. Katherine Sylvan was of another thought.

"Look, Victor did nothing for us. While we were securing the paintings and the broker, he was safe back in London eating steak and kidney pie. He has no way of tracking us and no idea what has transpired. After all, he wouldn't answer his phone. I say we cut his portion into three and keep it for ourselves. He may never forgive us for it, if he's still alive, but what is he going to do? The Director won't sanction actions against us and without his authorization Victor can't touch us. I say we forget about the past. We can become wealthy financiers with a low profile and live a life of comfort and serenity overseas until we die."

"It's still possible that Victor could expose the affair and tie up the proceeds in international court. We'd never see the money 'til kingdom come." Roger's argument was weak and even Paul could not defend it.

"That will never happen," Paul said. "If Victor's part in this is exposed he will be incarcerated and prosecuted. None of us can ever involve the government of any country, you know that. The offshore accounts do not acknowledge a freeze by the courts any more than the Swiss. Once the money is there, it is ours."

"So, it's agreed? We split the proceeds three ways and retire comfortably?" Katherine was smiling widely.

"Agreed," stated Roger firmly.

"No. I propose an alternate plan," said Paul, a nagging feeling of danger sprouting in his mind. "I propose we create an account with the money Victor would have taken and let it sit for five years collecting interest. If Victor does not show up in this length of time to claim it then we split the proceeds among us."

"We could set it up so it needs all three of us on hand to access it," Katherine Sylvan suggested, but that was not acceptable to either of the men.

"Look, dear, we may not all be here in five years. I suggest a timed account, a certificate of deposit or the like. If the money has not been accessed before maturity then it reverts to cash and is split into three accounts we create for just this reason. Yes?

"We've all been about long enough to know that a backup plan is needed. The Director may not sanction us but Victor may take a holiday just to find us. Or, The Director may take a personal interest and track us down. Paul was able to track down MacMaster by something as mundane as his shoe size in an internet catalog order. If we are to be safe we must think of everything."

"What's this about shoe size?" Katherine asked.

"Not many men wear a size 16 boot and not many shops sell them. Twenty years ago he would have needed them custom made but the internet changed a few things. I had surveillance flag all size 16 purchases and then backtrack looking for Irish, English or Scottish names. If he'd been smart he would have ordered the boots in an obviously

African name. We turned up a pile of them."

"So what was the story about the funds transfer?"

"Just cover and misdirection. I don't want everybody knowing everything. That would make me superfluous."

Chapter Thirteen
Auction

The arrangements for the private auction had been made. The only persons invited were those rich enough to bid and most were already aware of the Van Gogh self-portraits and the questionable past they held. Francois de LeMarque was happy with his recent acquisitions and had no idea of the blood that stained them.

The early summer sun was streaming in the window and the parade of people past the gallery was encouraging. Francois was thinking about going to Monaco and visiting some of the more upscale casinos when the door opened and a couple came in dressed in severe business attire. They both wore sunglasses that they kept on during the entire visit. They were also carrying a briefcase full of pound notes. They claimed to be representing an offshore client who was interested in investing in some high-end art, the kind that was paid for by cash. They were obviously not French though they spoke French. They had bad accents.

Coincidences happen and it was not the first time Francois had been approached in such a manner. If it had not been for the cash on hand he would have told them they were looking in the wrong place. As it was, a satisfyingly large down payment for his services was offered. Then a bundle of money was thrown on his desk. It convinced him he was dealing with genuine if somewhat unethical clientele. He began to explain that there was an opportunity in four days that required a private invitation. Then he stopped and insisted that a different bundle of money be used as a down payment. He would not accept the first bundle because of concerns that the couple was trying to buy art with counterfeit money as a laundering scheme. The male of the team was unconcerned as he pulled a different bundle out of the briefcase.

Using his powers of observation, honed by years as an art dealer, he noted that while the man's hair was black, the hair on his arms was blond. Also, the obviously Spanish woman was wearing a wig.

"Come back tomorrow. I will then tell you what we have and where. I am here every day and if there is a problem the down payment will be returned to you."

"Our client will be informed of this. He will be disappointed. I pray for the life of your children if you try to double-cross him. He lives his life by a certain set of principles and is an uncompromising man."

"There will be no trouble but a man in my position must be cautious." Francois de LeMarque then switched to English. "You may be MI6 or Generale de la Securite Exterieure or Interpol or CIA or the fucking French Foreign Legion. I need to be assured of your situation. So assure me."

"We will return tomorrow. Do not think too much, it will make your head hurt."

After the couple left, the art dealer made some phone calls. He was attempting to determine who had sent the newcomers to him. The third call was to a young dealer who despite his age had contacts all over the fine art community. His uncle had been in the business and had introduced him to all the upper-class collectors and purveyors of true art. This young man was very personable and while he still had a lot to learn about art, his network was well respected. The reply was that yes, representatives of Abu Nassir, an Egyptian, had been directed to him and he had directed them to Francois de LeMarque. The young man assured him he had contacted Abu Nassir personally and while he could not be there personally, the representatives were genuine.

Not fully convinced, Francois insisted on getting the telephone number of the prospective client. He verified that the number indeed reached an Egyptian man named Abu Nassir, in Cairo, and then called the number. He then took three bills from the middle of the stack and went down to the bank to have them verified as genuine. His expertise was a different sort of art. There was no problem with the bills; they were genuine British Pounds.

The clerk had been up all night tracking the van. It had returned to Paris but had not been checked back in. It was parked right down the street at nine o'clock when the bald man, now wearing a hat, returned to the office. He thanked the clerk for his attention and paid him handsomely. He then warned the clerk that if word of his interest reached anyone else that the repercussions would be biblical in scope. It was six months before the affair was even mentioned to anyone.

Victor had pinpointed the Paris hotel. He was no expert with the systems that were now his to command but he was computer literate enough to follow the programs. The satellite pictures were not very helpful in such a cluttered area. The cell phone that had been left in the hotel room was, however. All he had to do was call Paul Phillips' number and the tracker led him right to it. The fact that they had called him and hung up sealed their fates as moths in amber.

It was ironic that he was sitting in the very same chair Terry Kingston had sat in two days earlier. The newspaper that covered his face was in French and he was trying his best to read it. There was nothing about the impending art auction in the paper but he had known there would not be. That information was squeezed out of the schedules of the auctioneers for Sotheby's. Nobody was supposed to have access to that information but The Director had ways of finding out almost anything if it was on a networked computer. Automatic password deciphering and decryption programs were set up so the system would get in anywhere and find out anything given enough time. The system was not foolproof however. The sites with real invasion protection would detect such depredations and shut themselves off from his spying.

Paul had not paid for the van rental with a credit card, but the rules were such that the credit card number was required on all rentals in case the vehicle in question was not returned on time. The number was entered into the system and even though it was not used, the number set off an alarm in the system. The GPS tracking device led Victor to the hotel rooms the trio had rented after returning from Switzerland.

Sotheby's had no permanent auction facility in Paris but often held private auctions in various sections of the city. They understood the need for discretion and adding their name to the auction lent an air of legitimacy to the affair. In truth, there would be no record of the auction in Sotheby's books. The auctioneer was employed by them but was not on their payroll that night. He was listed as being on vacation in Paris and had been privately contracted. Sotheby's name was being used in the former grocery store without their knowledge or consent. They would never have authorized this one.

The bidders in attendance were, for the most part, not the actual men and women looking to purchase masterpieces with questionable ownership. The representatives did not bring the required cash with them either. The money was secured in banks worldwide and the representatives of the powerful collectors were only middlemen with authorization to purchase. Most were experts in the painting world who acknowledged each other with a nod and a wink. They all knew the inherent dangers involved and they all followed the unwritten code of silence that rang in the rarified air of such events.

The auction was to begin sharply at nine o'clock PM The large white van left the hotel at eight thirty. Victor

Rothchild was five minutes behind it, the tracker he had attached to the van showing him where it turned. While the auction was in progress he waited outside the building in his rented Mercedes. His anger was gone. He knew that emotion led to mistakes and he willed himself as cold as the Russian winter.

With the inside information gleaned by Terry Kingston and Anastasia Viuda, the other interested parties knew that the payoff was not to be until the next day. The cash was not present at the auction itself but would be delivered to Francois de LeMarque the following day. They knew that the three receiving parties would be there and were not willing to show up at the auction. They would take care of their business the following day. They did watch the front of the building for a while to make sure that there was an event taking place that night. They were in the front of the building while Victor was watching the white van parked in the back of the building.

The auction was over in less than an hour and the crowd inside dispersed. The five people who stepped out the back door were cautious but could not have seen the man watching them from down the street in a Mercedes. He was using a powerful set of field glasses and caught every movement they made. He knew that the kind of money those paintings would go for could not be secured in a purse or wallet and that cash was the only currency allowed for the purchase. He saw the envelope handed to the auctioneer and the handshake all around but he did not see the real payoff he was looking for. His hands started shaking and he willed them to stop. His former associates got into the van and drove off. The last man directed the armored car to the rear of the building and supervised the transport of three packages into it. At that point Victor was assured that payment would be forthcoming but not tonight.

None of the interested parties slept well that night with

the exception of Ahmed de Ketama el Bali who slept like a stone.

Guns are extremely difficult to come by in England unless one has the right contacts. Guns are a bit easier to acquire across mainland Europe, getting easier as you move east. Victor Rothchild's new position made it possible for him to get any sort of weapon, anywhere. The previous Director had set up caches of weapons across the world. Victor blessed him for that. The muffled Uzi he had in his gym bag came from one of those caches.

In order not to be seen, he waited until his screen told him that the van had arrived at the art gallery before he took up a position down the street. His palms were sweaty as he thought of the money that would soon be his and the retribution against his erstwhile accomplices. The armored transport truck that had transported the paintings was parked behind the building. He kept it in full sight.

He saw the first of the couriers pass through the intersection in front of him. A few agonizing minutes later the back door to the gallery opened and the art dealer appeared with an escort. The back door of the truck opened and a package was transferred through the art gallery. It was almost an hour before the door opened again and the second package was transferred. The third package took only 15 minutes after that.

"The third package has arrived." Anastasia was speaking into her cell phone from the roof of the apartment building on the corner. The phone had walkie-talkie capability but each number needed to be accessed separately.

It was going to be warm that day, too warm for the long, oversized leather coat she wore. The inside of the coat had pockets sewn into it.

"We have a problem." From blocks down the street

Terry and Ahmed had seen the Mercedes parked directly where they would have parked the BMW MacMaster had rented the day before. They also saw the man sitting in it but could not see his face. "We are not the only crew watching this transaction."

"How many?" Gordon MacMaster was in an old Bentley he had purchased two days earlier but had obviously not registered.

"I only see one but my line of sight is limited. Any closer and he'll see us."

"Let's wait. I need to know who is where and why. He may be a security measure or part of a team with the same objectives we have."

Anastasia had not heard the conversation because the phones transmitted directly to each other. "Rio, stand down," was all she heard, so she slipped behind the edge of the roof.

A very tense 10 minutes ensued while everybody watched. Finally the back door opened, and without hesitation the female and one of the males exited with a pair of large briefcases and jumped into the back of the armored truck, slamming the doors behind them. The other male, Roger Forster jumped into the front seat of the van. Both vehicles began moving. The Mercedes followed them.

"Tangiers, follow them. If they go to a bank we will be out of luck for the money." Gordon quickly changed numbers from the short list. "Rio, get down here. There has been a glitch."

Anastasia slid down the stairs as fast as she was able and dove into the Bentley as it was pulling up.

MacMaster drove while Anastasia spoke into the phone. "Where do they go?"

"It looks like the hotel."

"Watch behind you. Does any follow?" Anastasia's voice was trembling.

"No. It seems as though that Mercedes is the only one

following but us."

"We meet you at hotel. Okay?"

When Gordon pulled down the street from the hotel, the armored truck was pulling away on the other side. He turned quickly and kissed Anastasia, holding the back of her head. "That man is Victor Rothchild," he whispered in her ear. He has an auto in that bag. Close your eyes most of the way and watch where he goes."

"He went into the hotel."

"Shite. I'm not walking into an auto. We'll have to surprise them… from behind. Tell them to hold their positions. Merde, I wish I had a gun."

In the hotel room Roger announced his intention to take a piss. Piccadilly Paul Phillips never even saw it coming. As he bent to open the first of the cases Katherine pulled a machete from under the pillows of the other bed, spun around and chopped his neck to the spine. He fell to the floor screaming and flopping around as the blood flew all over the room. A second chop silenced him as it cut through his throat. Roger charged out of the bathroom with his member still out and spewing urine. He ran directly into the point of the blade which slid between his ribs and tented the back of his suit as it slid out the back. The look in his eyes as he stared at his lover was pathetic.

"Sorry, darling. It's nothing personal but this money's mine," she said sweetly.

He opened his mouth and tried to speak but nothing came out. Paul stopped flopping on the floor.

"I really did like you and you're not a bad fuck for a white guy."

Roger Forster let go of the machete that was cutting his hand in half and reached for her throat. She dodged around his grasping hands and he slipped on the blood. She let go of the machete and reached into her waistband. The knife was probably not necessary but she used it anyway, slitting her lover's throat and ending their last dance.

Congratulating herself on a job well done, Katherine Sylvan stripped to the skin and placed her clothing over her victim's faces. Then she took the blankets off the bed and covered the pooling blood on the floor as far as the door. She took the two briefcases with her into the shower and cleaned the blood off them and herself. Then she opened the cases, thinking to transfer the money into one of them. There was not enough room in one and she ended up with two full cases of cash.

Inside the closet was a fresh set of clothes and shoes. She changed into them quickly, put her hair in a wet ponytail and stepped through the door ready to begin her life of luxury. Outside the door she barely had time to open her mouth before Victor Rothchild opened up on her. The bullets stitched their way up her leg and torso, throwing her against and through the doorway.

Victor expected to see Paul Phillips and Roger Forster inside and almost shot one of the corpses on the floor before he realized they were already dead. He tossed the Uzi onto the bed, peeled off the driving gloves he was wearing and grabbed the briefcases that were once again covered with blood.

"Down the stairs, not the elevator," Victor muttered to himself as he headed for the stairwell. He dashed through the lobby wishing he had left the motor running. He tore open the back door of the Mercedes and tossed the dripping cases into it before slamming it shut. Then he ran around to the other side, opened the driver's door and was half inside when the Bentley took off his leg and the car door. He tried to scream and was unsuccessful. Within seconds he was unconscious. Within minutes he was dead.

Gordon MacMaster grabbed the bloody briefcases from the back seat of the Mercedes, left the Bentley where it was and stepped into the BMW that pulled up next to him. In this car were already two men and a woman with their shirts pulled up over their faces.

By the time the French Police arrived on the scene, the BMW was halfway to the airport. The passengers worked quickly, transferring the money from the briefcases into the inside pockets of their coats. They double-checked to make sure there was nothing in their pockets that would trip the metal detectors at the airport. Even their belt buckles were discarded. Their fake passports would get them through the screening process but the events of the past few days concerned them. They did not want to be pointed out.

"Well, it'll be a long time before I can show my face in Paris again." Gordon's face was tight and his eyes moved to watch all around them.

"I'm not welcome in Sydney anymore said Terry Kingston. Los Angeles either, though I think they caught that bloke."

"Which?"

"You know, that kiwi, uh, Kragon, Jerry Kragon. He killed a senator or congressman or some such. He was the one that shot that secretary, Prometheus Chamberlain's secretary. Anyway, I think they got him.

"Maybe. I think I shot the slippery bastard myself. If it's the same man. Looked a lot like you." Gordon's brow furrowed as he remembered the incident.

"We need to split up, right from the parking lot. Take different flights to different destinations. Then we can get back together, later. My face is the only one they will be looking for and probably not for some time. Ahmed, park in the long-term lot. We call each other Monday, noon, Greenwich Mean Time. If there is trouble in the terminal, we do not know each other. Get the first flights out."

The airport was packed with tourists and businessmen. Gordon cursed himself for changing out of the Catholic

Priest disguise too early. There was no chance of making it through the terminal in an expeditious manner but, although it went slowly, all four managed to get flights out. Waiting for the planes to board was agonizing. All four wore long coats packed with money but carried no luggage that would be x-rayed. The gendarmes were concerned with bombs and weapons and made a show of checking Ahmed carefully. They were not looking for money though and passed him through.

Gordon MacMaster took the first flight leaving the continent. It took him to Madagascar. The itinerary was to Georgetown, South Africa but Gordon took a different flight out, back to Madrid. From Madrid, he bought a ticket to Philadelphia, Pennsylvania with a stop off in Newark, New Jersey. He never got on the local flight out, however; he took a train into New York City.

Anastasia Viuda was more confident of her anonymity and waited four hours for a plane to Lisbon. From Lisbon she took a tour in a bus full of American and English retirees. The tour took a couple of days and gave her a chance to relax and reflect. Upon returning to Lisbon, she got a ticket directly to Miami. In Miami she booked a last minute cruise to the Western Caribbean, stopping in Grand Cayman where she set up an account with a generous return on investment. After the cruise, a direct flight to New York was no problem.

Ahmed de Ketama el Bali took a flight to Cairo planning on paying a thank you visit to Abu Nassir. He stayed there for a week as a guest waiting to see if there was anyone who wanted to talk to Nassir about the auction. He already had a bank account in Cairo and deposited a large sum of money in it. Ahmed had no qualms about accepting money from the sale of stolen art or the assassination of British agents. Nobody contacted his host in a week and he took a plane to Toronto from there. From Toronto, the Moroccan took a bus to Niagara Falls and walked across the bridge. He bought a used car cheap and left the expired plates on it as he drove across the state, deserting it in Albany and taking a train into the city.

Terry Kingston got the flight directly to New Providence Island in the Bahamas, then took the ferry to Paradise Island where he spent two days gambling heavily and losing a bit of money. It was not much considering what he had. He hooked up with a Swedish woman on vacation and spent a couple of days enjoying her company as well. Then he opened the account that was his intention originally, took the remaining cash and with a sigh of regret bought a flight to New York City.

Chapter Fourteen
Petroleo

The best way to follow anyone in New York City is in a taxi cab. There are so many cabs and they all look the same that you can never be sure who is behind you. When there is a Hindu driving behind you with a turban on his head it makes it a little easier to distinguish one from another, but if he takes off his turban and puts on a baseball cap, how would you know?

James Scott, the president of The Hercules Investment Corporation and Finance Bank had no idea the cab that pulled away from his house as he pulled in his gated driveway was the same one that had followed him as he left the parking garage. He had never needed to check for people following him before and did not bother doing so.

When the bank president was kidnapped from the side of the road two days later, he was taken early in the morning along his normal route to work. He had a flat tire on his new car and had already called the roadside service. What he did not know was that the flatbed that pulled aside and backed up to his vehicle was not the roadside service he had called. The two-man crew were dressed in garage grays and acted perfectly professional. They told him he had no spare in his trunk and he knew no different. The president did not know that there is never a two man crew on a flatbed wrecker and it is against the law for him to ride on the back of the truck in his vehicle. When the truck pulled off the main road and onto an alley, it was too late for learning lessons. He was a captured man.

New York City is a small place in terms of actual mileage. In terms of humanity it is huge and as complex as history. A man can hide or be hidden forever in New York City. Inside the slums, nobody sees anything unless they are paid to see it, and nobody knows anything unless there is reason to know it.

The apartment was expensive for what it was because there is no cheap accommodation in New York. It was not what Scott was accustomed to. He had made his fortune backing ventures that were not the mainstream 'Wall Street Stock Market' type. He moved money for those who could not move it themselves. He took a percentage of payments that nobody wanted to advertise. He had dealings with men that public figures would not work with and corporate figures could not afford to be seen with. He washed money that was covered with blood and cleaned money that had been buried in cocaine. He backed ships full of young women bound for the sweatshops of Chinatown and trucks full of men bound for the bean fields of California. James Scott had made a good living doing what he did, but it had caught up to him that day in early summer. He vomited on his silk suit after being punched in the stomach in an expensive but run-down apartment in a bad neighborhood of the city.

The financier had no idea who the men were who had kidnapped him. He assumed they would hold him for ransom. After a couple of hours they took his blindfold off and explained that he was directly responsible for the plague in the Middle East. Of course he knew nothing of this. He protested his innocence and denied all involvement. His captors told him outright that they did not want money and they were not going to kill him outright as long as he cooperated with them. If he did not cooperate then… the big one shrugged his shoulders and the smaller one opened the door to the bedroom. In the bedroom was a man in the black leather mask of a torturer and the flowing white robes of an Arabian Sheik. He pushed a small table on wheels into the room with a collection of stainless steel devices designed to inflict agony. The torturer took a stone and some oil and began to sharpen some of his tools. When he felt that a particular tool was sufficiently honed he would test it on a piece of Mr. Scott's clothing. The man said nothing during this process and the others had left the room.

Scott began to cry and thrash around, trying to free himself from the chair that he was tied to with large wire ties. His captor spun once, his robes billowing out around him and the cleaver he was sharpening spun around with him, stopping a hair's breadth from Scott's eyes. It quieted him down immediately. His face went white and he began to shake. He was having a significant emotional event and was about to pass out from the stress.

The two men returned from the other room with a laptop computer. One of them was smoking; the other had a cup of something in his hand.

"We need to know where the money for this transaction came from. If we do not learn this in the next 5 minutes, our friend here will begin by cutting off one of your ears. This will be the least painful thing he will do and he will not stop until you have given us the information we need or you die. If you die, we will move on to the next member of the board of directors until we have the information we need and you will have died needlessly. Have I made myself clear?" Gordon MacMaster's southwestern accent was flawless and was complimented by the large black cowboy hat covering his shaved head. Texas would have been Scott's first call, perhaps Arkansas as a second guess.

The transaction in question was on the screen. It was a large amount of money transferred to a department of the British Secret Service. There was no address of origination, nothing but an account number that identified it as an account in The Hercules Investment Corporation and Finance Bank. "You will identify who owns this account and you will provide us with an address. We will decide then if there is sufficient culpability on your part to warrant your death."

"Please, we have nothing to do with how the money is

spent after we transfer it. You're trying to blame the weapon for the war. You need to look downstream at those who spent the money to determine what was done with it. You cannot blame me for what other men do with their money."

"Look here, Jimmy. If we wanted to get wanked off, we'd go find some filly to wank us off. I told you what we want and you're gonna get it for us or you'll end up eating your own body parts. Am I making myself clear, son?" The words did not fit with the accent but Scott was too distressed to notice or care.

"I can't chase a transaction back without being in the bank itself. The system won't let me. Take me to the bank and I'll get you the information. I promise no funny stuff. I won't call the police. I will just walk in and get you the information and we can walk right back out again."

The huge man in the cowboy hat nodded to the executioner and the silent man with the leather hood stepped forward and selected a hook shaped blade with its sharp edge on the inside. He took a another step forward and with a smooth motion, cut off the bank president's ear.

The bank president let out a howl, not so much from the pain but from the knowledge of what was going on. The slice itself had barely stung, the blade was so sharp, but the blood running down his face and onto his silk suit horrified him. It was almost as though he considered it a dream and thought he would wake up. The blood gushing down his neck disallowed this fantasy.

The executioner showed his victim the organ, then took the ear and stuffed it into the man's mouth, choking his screams. He held it there while the third of the men wiped some of the blood off the side of the captive's face and covered his mouth with duct tape.

There was no clock within sight so Scott had no idea how long the men left him alone after feeding him his own ear but it was long enough for him to become very nauseous.

It was a good thing he did not vomit as he may have drowned in it.

When they returned to him, James Scott was more than willing to give them whatever they wanted. The man in the leather mask was not with them.

"This had better be good information. The next body part is a little less public, but don't worry, you won't bleed to death. The Monster is very good at what he does." The man who spoke was the only one who had spoken all the time they were in contact. He was a large man but was beginning to look enormous. The accent was still difficult to pin down but definitely southwestern. The executioner entered the room then with a propane blow torch and a kitchen spatula and with a flourish he lit the torch and began to heat up the spatula.

Scott told the man on the laptop computer how to chase down the account number in a specific way. It was encoded and needed a password to access the owner's name, make transactions or check the records. He gave him the account number as tears ran down his face. He kept spitting to try to rid his mouth of the taste and he could barely speak as he developed a serious stutter.

The account history was brief but descriptive. The bank had made a small fortune handling the account. The initial deposits were all from one account, officially belonging to Petroleo Corporation. The withdrawals were in large amounts, the first three were transfers to Waxmark Biopharmaceuticals Corporation in Russia, and the fourth was to the British account where Victor Rothchild and Katherine Sylvan had accessed it. There was still a substantial amount of money in the account. That money was immediately transferred to a different account, in Grand Cayman.

"I give you everything I have," blubbered James Scott, "You can have all that money, keep my car, anything. Just let me go. I won't tell anybody who you are. I don't even know who you are. You had ski masks on. Your hands were black. Please, let me go." He fell apart completely and started crying like a baby.

"We have almost everything we need already. There will be more but we need to discover where to get it. We need to know who, at Petroleo, is responsible for the program that left us where we are. We need to know who authorized this abomination and why. The persons withdrawing this money are already dead. Now, we want those depositing it." The huge man's accent did not match his syntax quite right, as if he were used to talking to people in a foreign language.

"I don't know. I need to get back to the bank for that." Scott was wailing. "Please, just let me go and I will get everything you need."

"Leave him for now. We need to make some inquiries."

James Scott stared at his captors as they left and he almost passed out a minute later when a woman entered the room in a bikini, covered with sun tan oil. Her head and face were covered with a long scarf wound around it so she could see but he could not see her face. Her eyes had a glowing violet color, not remotely natural. She took a pan of water and cotton gauze, cleaned and bandaged the side of his head where his ear had been. She was an incredible specimen of a woman, even without a face. Tall and slim, voluptuous and slathered with oil her presence aroused the president despite his situation. She never spoke a word while she was attending to him. She gave him a couple of pain killers and a drink of water for which he was incredibly grateful and then left him feeling very sorry for himself and praying for the first time in years.

Bob Hoerfinger had worked at Petroleo Corporation for three years. He was good at playing the corporate game and had found a mid-level manager who would pull him up the ladder with him. Bob was in accounting and was the first to point out irregularities on someone else's books. He spent his entire career making other people's mistakes or deliberate prevarications into their eternal regrets. He had no conscience when it came to ferreting out misuse of corporate funds. One of the reasons he was so dedicated to the path he had chosen was that he was not paid on the same scale so many of the long-term employees were. He was a relative newcomer and had been hired at the reduced wage that had come into effect after Petroleo had consolidated its hold on the world's oil distribution network. He worked for people he considered much less professional, dedicated and talented than he, and who made a lot more money. As a consequence of his actions, he was careful to keep his own records impeccable. There were those at Petroleo who would have had his cods on a plate if he got sloppy.

It did not take Gordon MacMaster long to figure out where the employees of the downtown Petroleo Corporation offices drank, and it does not take long to strike up conversations with people when you are buying the drinks. People love to talk about themselves and people they hate so it did not take long to figure out who drank on a regular basis in the Oil Barrel.

The Oil Barrel was a large enough place to gain some anonymity and small enough that you would not lose your date for long. They served beers from all over the world and all the popular brands of liquor. The bartenders and waitresses were young and beautiful but not very good at mixing drinks nor did they last long on the job. The patrons covered a range of ages and styles but the drinks were expensive so as to keep out the riff-raff.

New York City is cosmopolitan enough that people are not as impressed with foreign accents as they might be in the Midwest. People do appreciate when others are willing to throw around a little money though and the cash was flowing well on Friday night.

Terry Kingston and Gordon MacMaster were playing the role of wealthy foreigners here for a look at some real estate investments in the Poconos. They were drinking and dancing, buying drinks for the bar and throwing money around. Anastasia Viuda was there as a single woman who was looking for a good time. All three found someone to be with that night: Terry found a secretary to a vice president, Gordon found a transportation manager and Anastasia found Bob Hoerfinger. Bob pronounced his name with a soft gee so it came out Herfinjer. He had been subjected to jokes about his name his whole life and had all but changed it on several occasions.

Terry Kingston slept with the secretary who was happy to cook him breakfast in the morning. Gordon MacMaster put the Transportation Manager into a cab with his phone number in her pocket. Anastasia Viuda had Bob Hoerfinger so worked up she knew better than to be alone with him. He was drunk and aroused and would probably have raped her, or at least tried to. She left while he was in the bathroom but he found her name and phone number on a napkin under his drink; Maria Alejandros.

Anastasia was not surprised when Bob called her the next day and invited her out to dinner. She declined, saying she had to work the night shift for the next few days, but she would meet him at the Oil Barrel for lunch on Monday if he wanted. He was more than willing.

James Scott was spending a lot of time in a chair. From time to time they let him out of the chair and into the bedroom to sleep. He never saw the woman's face, nor did he see the face of the man who had cut off his ear but he memorized the face of the huge man in the cowboy hat. The other man had not returned to the apartment for two days. Scott was afforded the television but had to be contented with the news channel. This was a deliberate maneuver in that he got to see the devastation that the plague had wrought on Iraq and now, Iran. It had not moved across the desert to Syria or Jordan but was creeping southward toward Saudi Arabia. None of the Muslims would approach the dead for fear of contracting the disease. The Red Cross and several other disaster relief programs had shipped in earth moving equipment and were burying the dead in mass graves. It looked like a scene out of the Nazi death camps as piles of bodies where pushed in front of bulldozers and into the pits. Mosul and Kirkuk were devastated. Irbil, a city of more than half a million residents, was a charnel pit. The virus may have passed through, but the piles of bodies left behind were more than could be dealt with, even with bulldozers. The new government ordered the city set on fire and burned. Accelerants were dropped from helicopters to speed the destruction. Northern Baghdad was being cordoned off from the southern half of the city to stop the epidemic but it was having limited success. By the time some one exhibited symptoms, they could have infected dozens of people, and the women were covered head to toe with traditional garments so the symptoms were not even identifiable until they started staggering and falling down.

James Scott was sickened and revolted by the scenes and, despite the fact that he had made his living brokering shady deals, remorseful that he had been a factor in the distribution of the plague. It was true that he had not known anything about the plan, that he was simply the financial conduit but he could not help but feel guilty. Then came two stories he had not expected to see. First was the story that he had robbed the bank he worked for. He had transferred a huge sum of money to his personal account in Grand Cayman and disappeared the same day. There was a side bar on how he had called for a tow truck but the car was not there when the truck arrived. It was dismissed after the initial story and not commented on again. The second story he had not expected to see announced the death of the man who was holding him captive. According to the news, he had died two weeks earlier trying to bomb the London Museum of Natural History. A short and attractive blonde member of the bomb squad was shown with the briefcase bomb they had brought into the museum. She told the story about how she had been walking her dog and the dog indicated that there was a bomb in the case. The two men were killed as the bomb squad attempted to apprehend them. The story was aired only once and never mentioned again.

Michael Galliardo was a very happy man. As the number one sycophant of the lead man in Petroleo, he had the world by the balls. He made a great wage, got to travel the world and had lots of time off in New York City. He knew, as the mouthpiece for Albert Epstein, he was vulnerable but he had never had a major problem. He knew he was a potential target for a kidnapping and that nothing would be paid for his ransom. He was cautious but not cautious enough: he had been robbed at gunpoint twice, had his apartment broken into once and had a woman steal his wallet from the table beside his bed. None of the thefts had cost him much but he was now in the habit of carrying pistols when he left the apartment and had an arsenal locked in a gun safe in his living room. He did not, however, stop walking around the city at night.

Michael was in the habit of acquiring and discarding girlfriends, assistants and roommates regularly. Currently he was between women and was on the prowl. He had set his sights recently on the Vice President Arthur Emmerich's secretary, Suzanne LaLonde. He did not know that Suzanne had found some company recently.

Suzanne's company was driving her crazy. He was over six foot tall and Australian. He was more than a good listener;

he wanted to know everything about her, her job and everybody in her life. He was incredibly strong and sexy, with a set of scars that testified to a life of adventure. He was tanned and had just dyed his hair back to blond. They did not sit around talking all the time. He took her to see everything: movies, plays, carnivals, restaurants, night clubs and shooting clubs. In the two weeks they had been together, she had fallen madly in love with him and was dreading the day he would leave her. She felt it almost inevitable that he would leave. With all the money he had, he was entrenched in a different social stratum than she and he was a foreign investor.

In the past two weeks, Gordon MacMaster had been out with Margaret Calley a couple of times but she did not have the access he needed. She worked in the scheduling and delivery department and though she was a manager, she did not have access to the upper echelon. Her card would not allow her to enter the upper floors where the real decision makers were. Margaret initially had some reservations since she had seen Gordon, whom she knew as Jerry, get out of a cab with a tall brunette who had also been drinking in the Oil Barrel that night.

Bob Hoerfinger was beside himself. Anastasia Viuda was the cause of his distress. She would take him to within inches and then change her mind and leave him all jacked up. He needed her so badly he was sure his head was going to explode. She had kept asking him about the people he had discovered and exposed. Then she started asking about James Scott who had robbed the Hercules Bank and disappeared. Bob had nothing to do with that until she pushed it. She insisted that he look into it, what if there was a link to Petroleo, and that he could make himself a hero by exposing it. After their third date, he had started investigating it and found the large transfer to the bank that had been pilfered. He did not have the full story but she told him she worked at

The Hercules Investment Corporation and Finance Bank and showed him the printout of the transfers into James Scott's personal account. Then she told him that he needed to go to the press with it.

"But wait, first we must determine all the people and factors involved. Bob, we need to figure out who authorized the transfer to see if there was a conspiracy; we need to see if anyone else is benefiting. I'll get a printout of all the transfers out and where they went, you get me a printout of all the transfers in from Petroleo and who authorized them. Then we'll be famous and we'll be together forever." That was her hook and it would not have worked with an older or more experienced man, but Bob was entranced and thinking with the wrong head.

"Mack, I fear I must need to sleep with this pendejo to set the hook. I will never sleep with another man for desire. I need to whore myself for a job before, before I meet you, but if it costs me your love then all the money in the bank makes it worth nothing."

"Anastasia, I have never doubted you." He put his hand behind her head and kissed her long and slow. "I have not done another woman since we met and will not willingly but if it is a requirement to finish a job, I will. There is no other woman for me but you, however. I do not know where this adventure will end but if we are both alive at the end then it will be you and I. If it becomes necessary, then do it as part of the job. If it were necessary I would sleep with Margaret for the job. She is mine for the asking. But I do not, out of respect. Not respect for her but for you."

"Sleep with her and I will kill her."

"If that is what you need to do then I will not only allow you to kill her, I will watch. But this is not what needs to be done. She is not who needs to die. What needs to be done is to kill those who set us up for dishonor."

The following night Anastasia Viuda met Bob Hoerfinger in the Oil Barrel. He had the printout listing of who had authorized the transfer. The transfer had required three signatures. President Durham, Vice President Arthur Emmerich, and Economic Advisor Albert Epstein had all authorized the transfer. When Anastasia saw that, it was all she needed. She memorized the names, noting with pleasure that the vice president's secretary had already allowed Terry to move in. She gave Bob a long sensuous kiss and ordered another gin and tonic. When Bob went to the bathroom, she took the printout and disappeared again.

Gordon called Suzanne LaLonde's apartment. Terry Kingston answered the phone. Suzanne was at work at this hour. Terry was just getting out of bed.

"Okay, Romeo. You got the prize."

"Sure did, mate. This one's a keepah."

"But not for you."

"I'm not so sure. Yeah, she's American and still young, but she's smart and efficient, loyal and dependable, I think."

"I don't want to hear about your love life, Terry. You may change your mind when I tell you who the job turned out to be."

"Life goes on, mate."

"Arthur Emmerich is on the list. President of Petroleo, Danny Durham and Albert Epstein."

"Gotcha. Look, I think this might be easy, but if we don't do it undercover or simultaneously then it gets a lot worse. If we could kiss the three of them in a board meeting or something it would be the easiest."

"Meet me at the Golden Dragon. We'll get some mu shu pork and talk about it."

"Sure, mate. The Golden Dragon."

Terry and Gordon met down the street from the Golden Dragon. They never did enter that august establishment but watched it for a while and watched the streets outside. They did not detect anybody watching the place.

New York is the best place to follow someone, especially during rush hour. It is also an easy place to lose a tail if one is detected. Dodging into an alley will bring anyone following into range, and the crowds of New York have made an art of not seeing what they think someone else might have seen.

Once they determined that there was nobody after them, they slipped into a small family place, an Italian restaurant run by a pair of fat old women and a wiry old man. They ordered fettuccini and beef carpaccio with a gallon of red wine. Then they ordered some spicy sausages in red sauce.

Once they had eaten, they started considering the different ways they could make their marks pay for what they had done.

"It's always the same. You can crash anybody but I'd like to get out alive. These are some of the most powerful men in the world. They move in bulletproof comfort and carry the fates of nations in their briefcases." Terry's lightly freckled face was red with the spices and wine. "If we do this, we need to do it from afar and then vanish like smoke or we'll never get out of Manhattan."

"Terry, who are you talking to?"

"I'm sorry. You told me things like that 10 years ago."

"The difference is, that back then I told you that it didn't matter what a man did or did not do. I told you that if it ever became personal then your career was over because your life would be over. Following that advice has kept us both alive. Now we are on the verge of becoming old men. Our former employers have written us off or tried to bury us. We are on a job for personal reasons and you are talking about taking the secretary of a mark into your confidence."

"Hey, Mack, you're starting to sound like some melancholy old bastard crying in your beer. What's this all about?"

"I told you. I'm feeling like the end is near and I don't know where to go from here."

"What the 'ell mate? I never seen you like this. You got a hell of a woman, a Swiss bank account, a final job for the good of mankind, to pay back some of that guilt that crops up once in a while, and the British have released you by publishing news of your death. You got the world by the tail and all of a sudden you don't know what's next?" Terry took a long drink of wine, wiped his lips and grinned. "You're sitting in Manhattan eating raw flesh and you don't know where you're going? I'm not gonna marry the little twat; I'm just having fun. I get lonely from time to time and need a little company. We can't all troll the Argentine Secret Service for a lassie to play with. So get out of your piss pot and let's take care of business. Or call it off and slip out like smoke.

"Yeah, I had second thoughts about it. Something is telling me we got no business here. Retirement was boring but it was safe and real. This could turn into a blood bath an' drown us both. Part of me wants to say piss on it and part of me wants to take down the whole building. If ya surf the reef, respect the sharks."

Gordon grabbed the gallon of wine and took a huge pull off it, grinning with the blood red fluid running down his face. "By god you're right. I must be getting old. We have a real challenge in front of us and I'm pissing like a woman. Let's talk business. Your new woman is secretary to the Vice President?"

"Well, she's temporary, but most of them are these days. They need to prove themselves for a year or so and then they get hired, maybe. Sometimes they sleep with the boss to get the job; it usually doesn't work but women always think it will. Anyway, she has been there for nine months, doesn't sleep with the boss and will probably get the full time job if her boss survives. She doesn't like 'im much. I'm sure something 'appened but she won't say."

"He won't survive this one. What can she do for us?"

"She can get us into his office and she can get us his address and the layout of his house. She can get us invited to his parties and introduce us to the cream of the crop."

"Just what we need. Petroleo headquarters is going to have a lot of security."

"Tons. Cameras trained on card activated doors, guards at check points. The bloody building is 54 stories tall. Some of the upper crust live on the top floors I think."

"Hmm. Do you have access to Arthur Emmerich's office or do you have to steal her key card?"

"During normal business hours any employee can get to Suzanne's office. Emmerich's office is a ring-through from there. Off hours, though, Emmerich or above are the only ones with access. It's a pretty tight system but nothing we can't get past."

The waiter showed to see if there was anything further. Both men looked at the wine bottle and decided that coffee was more in order.

"Danny Durham, the president, seems a bit less accessible. I didn't get much from Margaret Calley on him. She's a typical mid-level manager. I think micromanager is the term. She has a real thing about being in charge and knowing where everything is all the time. I guess that's why she's got the job she has. I didn't get too involved with her. She doesn't have keycard access to the upper floors though I don't know why not."

"You ever worry about doing a job with your woman before?" Terry asked slowly.

"What?"

"I'm thinking you spent you whole life alone and in charge of the situation, now you got a woman to protect and she's on the job with you. You wouldn't be the first man to fall apart over a woman." Terry was saying one thing but it was clear that his concern was something else.

"I'm far from falling apart," Gordon said. He was trying to work through what was going on.

"Mack, you taught me all this stuff so long ago. Don't forget the lessons. Take Beatrice Ward for instance. The Warden. She and I have met socially and professionally but never let the lines cross 'til just now. I get together with her once a year or so and we'll spend a week or two together, socially, then I'll go back to what I'm up to and she'll do what she does. Hot as a pistol in the sack, cold as a fish on the job. I never expect to see her again. We crossed the line and we can never go back. It's gotta be that way."

"Enough. I'm seeing it. A pistol on the plate, a fish in the dish. You used her for the museum switch and now you can't trust her. That's obvious, but you have something else on your mind. You're considering settling down with this secretary. You almost said as much."

"No, that's not what I said. True, though, I'm still human. Not much of a romantic but I recognize a good woman." Terry was half smiling.

They finished their coffees, paid the bill and left a good tip, then headed out the door.

A couple of blocks away they stopped in a bar for a game of pool and more liquor. They scanned the street on the way in and watched the few people who entered after them. They were alone, as they had expected, but complacency was a luxury they could not afford.

It started to rain as they left the bar, the fat wet drops nailing the dust to the street and then carrying it off like ants on a mulch pile. The two stepped into a deserted bus shelter and sat down. A police car screamed by with its sirens blaring. It reminded them that they were in a foreign country on illegal business and they could be detained without warning. They looked at each other and laughed. New York City is the best place in the world to be anonymous.

"Well then, old man," Gordon started, "should we send them an exploding box of Girl Scout Cookies?"

"A poisoned pie? A spring-loaded briefcase blade?"

"A hive of bees? A wolverine in a box? Exploding Cuban Cigar?"

Terry became very serious. "I'd like to give him the plague he authorized."

"Terry, you've hit on it. All three of them deserve to die of the very thing that they unleashed. Oh.... Terry Kingston, you've hit on it. That's just what we're going to do."

"I don't follow. I'm 'alf drunk but..."

"No, I don't have it to give them. But they don't know that."

"Why on Earth are you getting all fancy on me? Let's just kill 'em and be done wiv it."

"They can't tell us what we need to know if they are dead."

Chapter Fifteen
Retribution

Ahmed de Ketama el Bali was sick to death of watching the one-eared bank president. Anastasia was a much more agreeable figure when she was around, but she and Gordon had begun spending nights elsewhere.

James Scott deserved to die for his role in the planting of the plague, but so did every one else familiar with it who instead did nothing. It did not appear he had known what the money was for. The team did not really want to kill the banker but they could not let him go, even after they had ruined his credibility.

For two weeks Ahmed had been tying and untying the man while wearing the torturer's mask. Terry Kingston had been cavorting with a young woman and Gordon had been dating one woman while sleeping with his own woman. Ahmed did not agree with that sort of promiscuity but had nothing to say if others practiced sins of the flesh. He was however, bored. New York City has something for everyone and he wanted to taste a little of the life the city was so rich with.

Then Terry and Gordon showed up together and changed the outlook. They knew the three men responsible, were here, in New York. Rich, powerful men who manipulated the world with their money and power and thirsted to join the elite ranks that included Mao Tse Tung, Josef Stalin, Adolph Hitler and Pol Pot; world class genocidal murderers whose personal agendas included none of the spark of human decency.

Now Ahmed was ready to go. His granite exterior was beginning to crack. As far as he was concerned, he would force his way into Danny Durham's residence and carve him up with a cleaver. It took a little convincing for him to see the benefit of a different course of action.

"We must get them simultaneously and we must get them alive. To warn any of the three would be to lose him to the wind and therefore lose the edge." Gordon's demeanor had taken on an intensity that glowed out of his face. "The President and Vice President get dropped off in front of the building by limos in the morning, when they are both in town at the same time. This Economic Advisor, it seems, lives in the penthouse of the building. I think he is much more than some sort of consultant. His authorization would not even belong on the transfer with the President's, otherwise. If we can get him first, in the middle of the night, we can summon the other two into our web.

"Terry, go to work with Suzanne in the morning. Make some excuse to meet her boss and figure out how to get into the penthouse. Find out when all three men will be in the building at the same time. I will be visiting the scheduling offices to see if anything comes up of value. Ahmed, I need you to play a game. You will be a nephew of the Sheik of Somebody here under your own initiative to negotiate an arrangement for oil because your family is dying of the plague. Can you handle that?"

"I go to work now." Ahmed just needed a direction to follow. He had been inactive for too long and wanted to do something besides watching a one-eared man tied to a chair.

The havoc in Iraq made the subterfuge almost too easy. The air conditioning in the lobby was frigid, to the point where the receptionist was wearing a coat. Ahmed was expected, but not by the President. He spoke with the Head of International Relations, but true to his disguise, he was rude and intractable. "I did not come here to speak with an underling. I am putting myself at risk in being here. I am here for business, not International Relations. If I want relations, I have 13 wives. They will bear relations for me. I will return tomorrow and I will see the President or I will go to a competitor. Yes, you still have some competitors. You do not have the entire market yet. Have I made myself clear?"

Ahmed de Ketama el Bali stormed out of the building in a lather. If he had not been so careful in choosing his nom de guerre, he would not have been allowed a second interview. He was, however, two days later in conference with the President of Petroleo. One of his greatest concerns was that he would be seen coming in and out of the building. He covered his face in all but the most private of areas. It was of the utmost importance that he not be seen because he is not in charge yet, and he did not wish to be seen as the one who organized the extermination of the rest of his family. Many had already been killed by the plague, but there were others with rights of primogeniture and he was adamant that they would not be getting the inheritance.

"Is there an alternate route out of here; a discreet exit for one who does not wish to be seen?"

The President was jocular and effusive. He smelled a coup on the horizon and fully intended to exploit the obvious inexperience of this young man. "Please, Sheik, accept the hospitality of Petroleo while we negotiate. We have a penthouse for guests of notoriety whereby we can supply all that could be desired. Whatever it is, we can have it for you. Women, drugs, anything. Whatever you need."

"I would like some roast lamb and a warmer climate."

"Of course. We have a full exercise room upstairs and a steam room. It is almost always empty. We have one full time resident of the penthouse but he uses the steam in the morning."

It was more than could have been expected. He was not only in the building; he was being offered the penthouse accommodations. The penthouse with one of the men he was aching to kill. He could almost taste the blood.

As he sat in the steam room he examined its architecture. The walls were stainless steel on the outside and polished teak wood on the inside. It had one window that looked bulletproof it was so thick and a stainless steel door that opened outward into a tiled hallway with a shower on one end and a dressing room on the other.

Ahmed made himself very comfortable in the penthouse suite. The lamb was quite good, though cooked in the Greek way. The view from the windows was quite appealing. The short, young brunette who cleared the dishes was dressed in a French maid's outfit and the offer was obvious but not blatant. Ahmed did not respond and she left for the day saying she would be back with his breakfast in the morning. Not trusting his hosts not to bug the room, Ahmed acted just as he would be expected to. He went to bed and went to sleep.

In the morning, breakfast appeared as promised but Ahmed wanted none of it. He got into the steam room and stayed there until Albert Epstein joined him.

"Oh, I am sorry, forgive me, I did not know there would be someone in here."

"You must be Sheik Rahman il Kirkuk."

"Indeed I am."

"I am a chief advisor to the President. I had actually hoped to meet with you."

"Ah. Well then, fortune shines upon us," Ahmed replied.

"It does. I have consulted with the president and some of our mid-east experts. They tell me that your claim to the oil north of the Kirkuk oil fields may be contested."

"It may be, but not for long. I have supporters in the area who are willing to lay down their lives for me. The current administration is doing nothing about the plague and the traditional views are no longer appropriate. We must move into the world, not hide from it."

"I agree. What about the sanctions imposed on oil from this area?" Epstein asked.

"Hah. Sanctions are like tying yourself off when you need to piss. It works for a little while but increases your need until you can no longer stand the pressure and must relieve it. I welcome sanctions since it drives the price of oil up without exhausting our reserves. You must understand, however, that it will be some time before I can be sure I have the only operating power in this area. No one is entering and none can leave because of this plague."

"Of course. A terrible thing. Terrible."

"I have decided that I like negotiating this way, in the steam. You must join me and the President after lunch. I will exercise, and then we will eat, then into the steam to negotiate. Is anyone else necessary? No? Then it will be the three of us."

Despite his expectations, not one room in any of the penthouses was bugged. Extortion or blackmail at that corporate level would leave you with lungs full of Hudson River water. Albert Epstein had not missed the scars on Ahmed's body though. Two were unmistakably bullet wounds, one was a knife cut down one arm and there was a six inch gash on his throat where someone had tried to open it up.

Ahmed did just as he said he would; he exercised. Epstein called some contacts in the Middle East. He was not sure that Sheik Rahman il Kirkuk should be covered with scars. Before his contacts had gotten back with him, lunch was served and then, as expected, they were joined by Danny Durham, president of Petroleo and all thee got in the steam.

Vasilii Ivanov Scarkovich did not understand what had happened. James Scott had robbed the Hercules Bank and disappeared according to the American news service. Examining the numbers and revisiting the circumstances refuted the report as absurd. Had Scott wanted to rob the bank and disappear, he was in a position to steal a lot more.

While the theft had been substantial, it was by no means close to the amount he had access to several months earlier. In fact it was paltry compared to the amount of money he made regularly from his contacts around the world.

"Stephan, call the Jew in New York City. Epstein. Find out what really happened to this James Scott. If our interests have been compromised, we may have to purge the system."

"Tell the cooks I'm ready for lunch in 15 minutes and I'll want a woman in about an hour. The Vietnamese woman."

"Check on the shipment from Bulgaria to Germany, and make sure the woman brings a cigar with her."

Terry Kingston had been more interested than ever about the daily workings of the upper echelon. As Max Preston he listened, fascinated, to the story of the Iraqi Prince who had showed up and been assigned the #3 penthouse. He listened to the secrets of how the penthouse had its own maids and cooks and there was even a selection of women on call for the guests.

"Hah! Are any of them as beautiful as you?"

"Well…"

"No. They're not." He picked her up and threw her over his shoulder and carried her to the bedroom. His performance was as long and exhausting as he could physically make it. He needed to make sure he could make her believe what he said next.

"I love you, Suzanne LaLonde. I never want to be without you. Will you marry me?"

"Oh, my God," she heaved. "We just met. I'm not sure…"

"Shhh. Think about it tonight. You can introduce me as your fiancé in the morning, at work."

"Ohhhh, Max, I…"

Terry did not allow her to speak further but smothered

her mouth with kisses and then they made love again, Terry telling her again and again how much he loved her.

In the morning he went to work with her as he had promised. This was actually the first time he had been in the building. She was bouncing like a schoolgirl on prom night. His temporary pass was paper and did not allow access anywhere, but Suzanne's pass was relatively comprehensive. She took him to the secretaries' break room on the 40th floor and introduced him as "Max my fiancé." He caused a stir like a celebrity. Then she took him to her post in an anteroom outside the Vice President's office. She showed him her desk and ushered him into the Vice President's office. This was where things started to get interesting.

The knife was carbon fiber so it had gone through the metal detectors without a peep. It did not have an edge and never would but it was not designed as a slashing weapon. It was a stabbing point with a triangular blade for strength. The blade was in a forearm sheath.

The Vice President reached out his hand to congratulate "Max" and did not even know what happened next. His hand was behind his back, his face was on the desk and there was a very sharp point pressed into his temple. "One move, mate, and I'll stick this piece in one side and out the other," said his new acquaintance.

"Max!" Suzanne screamed. "What the hell are you doing?"

"Calm down, baby. I love you and this is the point where you make a choice. It's him or me. You go with me or you stay here a slave to this murdering pig."

Suzanne LaLonde backed up into a corner of the office with her mouth hanging open. The suddenness of the attack and the savage ferocity exhibited by her new fiancé struck her like a physical blow to the chest. She reached the corner and sat down on the floor, her mouth opening and closing like a fish.

"Suzanne, call the powuff." Arthur Emmerich's plea ended prematurely as Terry slammed his face onto the desk.

"Suzanne, my love, stand up and come here." Terry's voice brooked no argument and to her own surprise she did what he asked. "Now kiss me." She looked at her boss and back at her man a couple of times apiece and a tear rolled down her cheek. She leaned forward and kissed him full on the lips.

"Good girl. Now, what we are going to do is take the duct tape out of me coat pocket and tear me off a foot long."

When she had done as he asked, she started getting a smile on her face. "All right girl, tear me off about a meter."

Arthur Emmerich began to groan loudly as Terry Kingston bound his hands behind his back. Suzanne LaLonde started grinning and slapped the shorter length over his mouth. Terry could see from the smile on her face that he had nothing to worry about as far as she was concerned.

"Suzanne LaLonde, I love you beyond measure."

"Max, I have to tell you and I need it to be now."

"What love?"

"This man raped me about four months ago, right on this desk. I got a raise and an extra week vacation out of it but I never got hired and I need you to know that. If you think that makes me a whore then I'll understand."

Terry looked at her quivering lower lip and then at the duct taped Emmerich. "What should we do about that?"

"If you don't want me any more then…"

"Be silent. I said I love you. Does that mean in 10 minutes I don't love you? I feel about you the way no other woman has made me feel and this man hurt you. I want to know what we should do about that."

Suzanne was bouncing again. She went out to her desk in the outer office and got a nail file. She took the point of the nail file and stabbed her former employer in the cheek of the pants. The stab drew a spot of blood and when his head came up off the desk, Terry slammed it back down.

Suzanne tore the back of Emmerich's pants open and pulled down his boxer shorts. He started to cry and whine through the duct tape.

"Don't worry, baby, it won't last long and I'll make sure you get what its worth," she said, obviously repeating something she had heard before. "I know you want it any way. I can tell by the way you look at me."

The Vice President of Petroleo had never found himself in this position before. For decades now, he was able to get what he wanted and pay for what he had to take. He had never had it taken from him and did not like it much. His body was racked with sobs that had no way to get out.

Suzanne LaLonde went to a cabinet in the office and picked out a square bottle of Mexican Mescal, the kind with two worms in the bottom of the bottle. She took a healthy pull off the bottle, swallowed half of it and spit out the other half. Then she took the open bottle and stuck the neck between the exposed cheeks of the Vice President's bottom and shoved it in.

Emmerich's head and half his body came up off the desk. Terry punched him three times to make sure he did not try to get free and Suzanne took off her high heels and kicked the square bottle that was hanging from his ass.

It was still a half hour until lunch time. Suzanne opened the door to her office. She had her shoes back on and had composed herself in her private bathroom. She was beginning to lament giving up such a nice office, but one look at Terry's grinning face erased any regrets. Terry was actually carrying the VP in a rolled up carpet. The roll was secured with duct tape and the ends were folded over.

The elevator to the penthouses was exclusive and Emmerich was one of the few who had access to it. Fortunately it did not require his palm print or Terry would have had to do something differently. The man's badge opened the elevator and the couple with their cargo stepped aboard.

At the penthouse, they stepped out of the elevator. The hallway ran in two directions, on one side was the kitchen and housekeeping staff, on the other was the living areas. Terry strode forward to the door to suite three. Suzanne opened the door with the badge and they stepped inside. Terry threw the carpet on the floor and looked around for the resident. Behind him the door closed, seemingly of its own accord. Behind the door, dressed in a towel, was Ahmed de Ketama el Bali with a meat carving knife in each hand.

"Have you taken a job moving furniture?" Ahmed asked, looking at Terry but watching Suzanne LaLonde.

"Yes, my friend, furniture."

"Bring it in here."

Terry groaned as he picked the body in the carpet back off the floor and followed Ahmed to the steam room. The door was propped closed with a hardwood curtain rod. Inside, wrapped in towels, were the President of Petroleo and his Chief Economic Advisor.

The Vice President was ignominiously dumped on the floor of the steam room. Terry advised the two men they had better let him out of the carpet or he would probably die. When they had released him from his captivity, Emmerich was unable to stand or sit and it was up to the President and his advisor to remove the remains of the broken liquor bottle from his ruined rectum.

Suzanne LaLonde and Terry Kingston did not make it back to the elevator before stepping into one of the other suites for a mad round of sex. She was sitting on top of him pounding his chest with her fists and screaming in orgasm.

It took a shower and some makeup to get Suzanne looking professional again. They took the elevator back down about an hour before lunch. They went out on the street and walked a couple of blocks to a doughnut and muffin place where they each had a cup of coffee and Terry made a phone call.

"I gotta know. What the heck is going on? Max, I love you to death but I gotta know," Suzanne said. She had his face in her hands and was looking him in the eye.

"Terry, Terry Kingston."

"What? You never even told me your real name?"

"Suzanne, please keep you voice down. In my line of work it is not wise to reveal yourself too quickly."

"What is that, exactly? Your line of work." She removed her hands from his face.

"I do the things other people are unwilling or unable to do."

"You kill people, don't you?" she said in a choking whisper.

"Shh. Too many people." He put a finger to her lips.

"Well, you better start leveling with me. After all, I don't think I can get another job as a secretary after shoving a tequila bottle up my boss' ass."

"Come on. We gotta go." Terry paid for the coffee and they left. They walked to the end of the block, she keeping a little distance between them, and stood on the corner.

"Why are you getting so shy all of a sudden?" she asked.

"Discretion is the name of this game. We cannot go telling everybody what we do and who we are. I'm already compromised. They got me on camera and that ends my career for good. I'll be on the run forever."

"Who are you? Unless "we" is somebody I don't know. Again, you kill people don't you?"

"I have."

"Are you going to kill me?"

"Suzie, my love, I can't kill you."

"If I had tried to call the cops, would you have killed me then?" her eyes pinched as the tears welled up.

216

"I…Yes."

"So I mean nothing to you?" she looked at the ground.

"You don't understand. You mean everything to me. I've known you for two weeks and I want to be with you forever. I won't lie to you, I've been with a lot of women in a lot of different towns but you are different. I would have mourned you for the rest of my life if I had been forced to kill you. But, if you had chosen the job and him over me, it would have been over."

"Can you teach me what's going on, and who you are? I mean, I thought I knew but …"

"Not right now, but I think you already have the basics. We are a set of sociopaths, trained in different countries and taught different sets of values. We work together because we cannot live with regular people." He was leaning forward and talking low and slow in her ear. "We use men and women to get what we want, but we cannot be with those who are not like us. We cannot do an eight-hour-a-day job. The boss wants to abuse us and doesn't survive the week and then we are in hiding. You are one of us, I see it in you. If you want to go, pretend it never happened, disappear, you can. You will find someone else if you escape the police dragnet and will live your boring and pedantic life in obscurity but… the truth is, you will never forget shoving that mescal bottle up the boss's ass. I've ruined you for life." As he said that, he placed his lips on her neck and kissed her long and slow. He could feel her shaking with the power of her feelings.

"Why don't you two get a motel?" The voice was low and powerful with the unexpected force of a sudden air horn from behind you on the expressway.

"Mack, you monster." Terry grinned.

"I saw you. I saw you the night I met Max, uhh… Terry, right?"

Gordon raised his eyebrows but Terry brushed it off. "We got all three of them together in a steam bath. It's perfect."

"A steam bath? I love it. Nothing better."

"Are you going to introduce us?"

"Suzanne LaLonde, Glasgow."

"Glasgow?" she asked, self consciously.

"Call me Mack."

"Okay then, Mack. I think you should know that I'm in this one, whatever this one is. This is my man and I'm not going anywhere without him. I know what you are; sociopaths who work together because you can't work with others. I'm in for the long run now. I'm unemployed because of Max. I'm going to call him Max and you need to count me in."

"Well, that's very forward of you."

"Mack, you haven't seen forward yet. Have you got a pass?"

"Yes, but we need a distraction. She's moving into place now."

They moved back to the Petroleo building, Suzanne and Terry arm in arm. Gordon MacMaster waited until Anastasia Viuda had the security guards full attention and swiped himself in as Margaret Calley. Suzanne used her own pass, wiping Margaret's face from the screen and then rang Terry through as he flashed the guard his temporary day pass. Anastasia was adamant that she was here to see her boyfriend and that he was to be contacted. She would meet him where he worked, but she needed to see him today. The guard insisted that she was wasting her breath and she should be talking to the receptionist but he did not tell her too quickly. He was enjoying the enchanting fragrance she was wearing. He had always fallen for redheads and her accent was almost as sensual as her lips. She did not speak a good English and got agitated when she was not allowed to simply walk in. She began swearing at the guard in Spanish and he asked her to leave. This caused her to become even more agitated and the security guard grabbed his microphone from his lapel and called for support. The backup was not necessary though since the emotional woman turned and stalked to the door, still spewing invective. Her spike heels were all but striking sparks from the marble floor as she strode from the building.

In the penthouse, things were getting hot. The housekeeping staff had been given the rest of the week off with pay. The cooks however were cooking sumptuous gourmet meals for a group with gargantuan appetites. The staff only got to see their Arab guest, though they delivered a feast for 10 men. Then they got the rest of the day off, with pay, at the order of the Sheik.

Terry, Gordon and Ahmed enjoyed their meals with gusto. Gordon drank Scotch and Terry had a splash of some really good bourbon.

"Well, we really mucked ourselves up this time." Terry knew it was the end of their careers.

"Hardly. We secured a good payoff from this mess."

"Aye, a good payoff but they got us on camera. That makes it messy. We would have been better off sniping the bastards."

"A job well done is worth the extra time. We are the right tool for the job and nobody else was going to do it. In an hour, we'll have all the information we need and we can get out of here." Then they went to the steam room.

It is in the nature of a steam room to both relax and invigorate a person when taken in smaller time frames. The men in the penthouse steam room had already been in there for three hours. Three hours in a steam room will dehydrate a man to the point of cramping and possible heat shock. These men were reaching their limit and had decided to rush anyone who opened the door. The sheer size of the man who did open the door almost caused them second thoughts. He was wearing a gas mask and a pair of rubber gloves up to his elbows. He had a bottle of water for each of them but before he could toss it to them they rushed him. He said nothing from inside the gas mask, just swung twice. They were lucky the water was in plastic bottles as it knocked them down without splitting their skulls. Arthur Emmerich was too damaged to have participated in the action.

As the men rose from the floor, they saw their oversized captor reach around the door and grab a clear plastic bag. It only took Albert Epstein a fraction of a second to realize that he held a vacuum-packed bag of bullets and a knife.

The knife came down into the plastic of the bag and giving it a little wrench tore a larger hole.

Albert Epstein screamed and ran toward the door with his breath bated and his head held low. He had no hope of getting past the human wall that filled the entire doorway, but in his panicked situation he was willing to try anything. His hair was grabbed and a knee caught him in the chin. He flew backward onto the wooden bench while the man in the gas mask threw the bullets to the floor and slammed the door behind him, blocking it with the curtain rod.

Chapter Sixteen
Redemption

Michael Galliardo usually called before entering the penthouse suite inhabited by his sole benefactor. Today he was expected at two PM, so the number did not get called. The elevator had a strange smell in it, a perfume that he recognized but could not place, and he found himself thinking about females. Another couple of hours and the work day would be over. He hoped Albert would not keep him long as there was happy hour to be had and pussy to be plundered.

The elevator door opened and Michael stepped out. Something did not feel quite right, immediately. He stood in the hall and sniffed the air. The mixed aroma of cooking and tobacco was not what was unsettling him. It was the lack of commotion from the kitchen. The kitchen was usually a hotbed of activity and the sounds of pans and plates were silent today. The kitchen was empty of life, in fact. Where the staff had gone was a mystery to the assistant.

The door to Albert Epstein's permanent residence was seldom locked but it was today. When he had used his key, something he rarely needed, he stepped silently into the suite. He saw the bed was rumpled, something Albert would never have allowed. He saw Albert's lunch on the dining room table, untouched.

Michael Galliardo reached inside his suit coat and unsnapped the catch on his shoulder holster. He had been Albert Epstein's chauffer, bodyguard, advisor and procurement agent. He had seen what the smell of money did to people and was prepared to exterminate anyone he determined not to belong in the upper reaches of the Petroleo building. He knew there was a Middle Eastern visitor, but there had been no report of anyone else.

Once he had determined that the suite was empty, he

headed for the exercise room. Someone had been in there recently because there was sweat on the bench back of the leg press and wet towels on the floor. The staff usually cleaned up such detritus immediately. The boiler for the steam room was running as well though Albert never took steam in the afternoon or evening. Epstein was an organized man and his exercise was always in the morning and the steam came afterward.

There was no sound of falling water coming from the shower room so Michael slipped through that door as quietly as he could. The floors were wet and there were more wet towels. He could still hear the sound of the boiler, even though it was on the floor below. He looked down the aisle where the steam room was and the first thing he saw was the hardwood curtain rod leaning against the door. He did not hear anyone from the steam room or the locker room but caution grabbed hold of him. He was determined to be the hero of the scene but he would not sacrifice himself at the same time. Dead heroes are still dead.

Unseen, Michael Galliardo slipped back through the shower and the exercise room and into Albert's apartment. In the study, there was a red phone connected directly with security. He grabbed the receiver and listened as it rang at the other end.

"This is Michael Galliardo. I am in Albert Epstein's penthouse. Something is wrong here. I want security up here now, and call the police as well."

Seven years earlier, Petroleo Corporation had downsized its security force. It had permanently laid off all its long-term, pistol packing guards and hired a security firm. The security guards are no longer armed and have no loyalty to Petroleo. Given the wages they make as rent-a-cops, it is surprising they have loyalty to anyone.

In the beginning, there were drills for the guards to practice and training for situations that might require more than escorting a drunk off the property. The training fell off after a while and the drills disappeared after new personnel moved through. It was a good job for college students who needed something they could earn money with while they were studying. When a job opened, they had a hard time filling it because of the drug test requirements. Eighty percent of the applicants failed the test. Raises were nonexistent and students finished college or dropped out and quit.

The staff was less than enthusiastic about going into the penthouse at any point. They had heard the rumors of what went on and who might be in the penthouse. One overzealous employee had been fired for responding to a call from that red phone in the study. There had been no one on the other end but the guard could hear some scuffling so he went to the suite and burst in with his can of pepper spray. Albert Epstein had a French maid bent over the desk and was nailing her from behind. She had knocked the receiver off the cradle and caused the stir. The young and ambitious guard no longer worked there or anywhere else for a while. Eventually he moved to the Midwest since he was effectively blacklisted in New York. The story had been retold so many times that security was unwilling to even step foot in the penthouse.

The security staff assembled at the lobby elevator for a quick conference. The Sergeant was making a slightly better wage than his twelve subordinates and had a bit more enthusiasm than they did. He carried a 50,000-volt stun gun. It was against policy and insurance rules but it was ignored by authority. The Sergeant was about 35 years old and with a medium build that spoke of an active lifestyle. He crowded into the elevator and four guards followed. The others took the other elevators.

Reaching the top accessible floor from this elevator, they grouped around the penthouse elevator. They had not counted on one of the top brass' secretaries being on the wrong side.

The call went in. "Max, my love, something is wrong. Security is converging on the elevator."

"Thank you, my dear. We will take care of it. Please evacuate the building." Closing his cell phone, Terry said in a quiet voice, "We have company. We need to secure the area."

Terry crept to the kitchen and housekeeping area after bracing the elevator door open, but found no one. Ahmed went to the locker room and shower area, but found no evidence of an intrusion. Gordon investigated the other suites, keeping his ears open. It was the sound of a hammer being drawn back that alerted him to his present company. The sound came from behind him and most men would have frozen in place at the sound. MacMaster did not freeze. He spun to the side and crouched, pulling in the wooden curtain rod and lashing out with it, point first. He missed Michael Galliardo, but he also spoiled the shot he might have taken.

Michael recovered and was pointing the gun toward his huge opponent when the rod flashed sideways with tremendous control and knocked the gun aside again, numbing Michael's wrist as well. Before he could recover this time, Gordon swung a wide arcing blow. The fist flew in with more speed and force than could be expected, the thumb was sticking straight out and leading the way. The thumb pounded into the spot between Galliardo's ear and his jaw, releasing bursts of lightning behind his eyes. Before he got his sight and equilibrium back, a massive fist crashed into the end of his jaw and rang his bell. Gordon MacMaster was in possession of the pistol before its former owner hit the floor. No shot had been fired.

Stripping the Italian of his other weapons, which amounted to a stiletto and a razor, Gordon grabbed him by the belt and carried him bodily to the steam room where he joined his employers.

"Wait," wailed Albert Epstein. "I have the cure! You can make yourselves rich beyond your wildest dreams."

A cure was a new twist on the scene. The invaders had not considered there could have been a cure; they had hoped to discover the manufacturing source of the plague. This made the entire endeavor worth more than money or retribution. This would wash their hands of all the blood they had soaked them in. A cure would turn them from wanted men to world class celebrities overnight. They could never acknowledge the fame, but the sheer honor would be emotionally overwhelming.

Gordon MacMaster held his dehydrated captives at gunpoint and asked "Where is the cure, how do we get it, what is in it for you?"

"It's hidden in the building. I'm the only one who knows about it. I'm the only one who can get to it. I can take you to it. You are infected now. As soon as you opened this door, you infected yourself and you will die the same as we will. You need to take me to the cure, now."

"What about your friends?"

"Pure cover. I am the power here. Let them die, I need to live."

"Come on then." Albert left the confines of the steam room and Ahmed braced the door behind them, leaving the hapless President and Vice-President screaming and crying inside.

The Sergeant had finally decided that the elevator was not available and had decided to try the fire stairs. A security pass would allow access to the exclusive nadir of corporate indulgence even though the security team was treated as if they were insects. Four of the men were left waiting for the elevator; the remaining nine, five men and four women headed for the stairs. It did not take them long to walk up the four floors between their present location and the penthouses but the door was blocked when they got to the top. There was no procedure or authorization for breaking down doors. That venue was left for the New York City Police.

Danny Durham would have called the Chief of Police if he put in a call and it was not responded to immediately. Albert Epstein would have called the mayor. The 911 call from Petroleo Corporation that told of a phone call about something being wrong and access being blocked to the penthouses did not constitute a citywide emergency. It was in fact relegated to the list and responded to three or four hours later when the patrol officers got done with some of the more important calls.

Albert Epstein was well dressed. His suit was dry though his hair was a bit damp-looking when he stepped from the elevator with his three associates. The Sheik was standing close behind him and the other two were on either side. Albert insisted that he was just fine, knew nothing about any call for help and would fire anybody who went up to the penthouses. His assertion that the guards were to return to their posts was taken at face value by all but one. The one guard tried to press it further and acquired a lesson in paying attention to his superiors. Albert Epstein dressed him down in true capitalist fashion. History and gossip served to cement the command and the guards retreated in quick order. The three men and their captive then went to the other bank of elevators and down to the 43rd floor.

The 43rd floor was deserted. It was an unused floor due to corporate downsizing. The four men walked down the hall cool as cucumbers in the air conditioning. Ahmed de Ketama el Bali kept Michael Galliardo's pistol trained in the middle of Arthur Epstein's back, but hidden by the flowing robes he wore. They stopped before an office that required the highest level of security clearance to open. Inside, there was a spacious office that held no furniture, but did present them with a walk-in Wells Fargo vault.

"I need reassurance. I have the combination to this safe and the cure is inside. I need to know you will not shoot me after I get it for you."

"I guarantee we will shoot you if you don't."

"Then I will die quickly and you will die a slow agonizing death of the plague," sneered Albert.

Gordon MacMaster's smile was not intended to put his captive at ease. He pulled a tool from his pocket and asked if Albert recognized it. It was a straight razor with elaborate gold filigree on the handle.

"Yes, that was Michael's razor."

"Did you see what my associate did to your Vice President?"

A visible shudder raced down Epstein's spine. "Yes, I saw."

"My associate is an amateur. I have managed to keep a man alive for a week in the kind of pain that makes him beg for death."

"You don't have a week," Albert replied haughtily. "You probably don't have an hour. If you leave now, you might be able to make it out. When they catch you, you may get assault charges if we use the cure. Murder charges if we do not."

"You are going to talk to me about murder charges. You requisitioned and caused the plague that is killing millions in the Middle East. You have a cure for the disease and you kept it to yourself and you want to talk about charges. You degenerate sack of vomit. Open the safe or I begin by cutting off your toes, then your ears."

"I don't think so. I think you need me more than I need you, now."

Gordon had listened to enough of this arrogant swine and wanted no more of it. "Hold him," was all he said. Terry and Ahmed grabbed him and he pulled off a shoe. When Albert started struggling Ahmed bashed him in the forehead with the butt of the pistol. Gordon moved like a surgeon and cut off three toes without catching the razor in the bone. The razor was so sharp there was almost no pain. There was an awful lot of blood though.

Albert Epstein looked down at his foot and the realization dawned on him that he was not in the position of power he thought he was. He was dealing with desperate men and he had no experience with people that routinely cut off other men's body parts. He opened his mouth and found it full of cloth. Ahmed was not going to allow him to scream, even though that was not his intention.

Terry Kingston grabbed his captive's ear and growled, "Let me cut the ears off."

Epstein tried to talk through the cloth. He was not screaming or struggling so Gordon pulled it from his mouth. "I will open the safe. Please, do not cut me again." He hobbled over to the Wells Fargo and rolled the dial, slammed the handle and slowly pulled open the door. Inside there were half a dozen stainless steel containers roughly the size of a coffee thermos.

He hobbled inside the safe and picked out one of the containers. Unscrewing the top revealed perhaps two dozen injectable plastic ampules inside, filled with a liquid. Albert pulled one out and pulled a plastic tip off it, then plunged it into his arm.

"Here, this is the cure. I have enough for a couple of hundred men. This is worth a fortune, millions. All three of you are infected, cure yourselves. There is more as well. It is hidden many, many miles away but there is enough to cure thousands."

"Hold him," was all the Scotsman said and his partners grabbed the hapless advisor again. They stuffed the sock in his mouth again. This time the razor was going for his ear. It was unnecessary to cut the ear off. The rag was pulled from his mouth and Albert could not give his captors the information fast enough. Terry wrote it down. Albert blurted out the address on Yahuda street in Jerusalem and told them about the Waxmark Biopharmaceuticals Corporation facility in the outskirts of Moscow where both the plague and the cure were manufactured. He was crying like a baby now. He had never been so helpless. Even held and gagged, he had thought there was still some form of leverage, but there was nothing. In the hands of these men he was nothing but a child with a secret.

Gordon gave him that smile again. This had worked out better than he could have anticipated. He calmly folded the razor and handed it to Ahmed de Ketama el Bali. "It is my pleasure to inform you that you never had the plague. Neither do we. Your assumption has done our job for us."

"You pig," Ahmed said. "You have unleashed a living hell on my people and expect me to save myself. I came here to find you specifically and to kill you. Have you anything to say?"

Albert's mouth opened but nothing would ever come out. Michael Galliardo's pistol was pressed to his temple. Terry spun out of the way and Albert's brains erupted from the other side of his head.

"It is a better death than he deserves, but we are pressed for time."

The pistol was placed in Albert's hand and his shoe was placed back on his damaged foot so a quick glance would see a suicide. It would not hold up to an autopsy but might buy them a critical minute. Five of the stainless steel containers were taken. The trio took the stairs to the 44th floor and took the elevator down to the 3rd floor from there. They split up, and each made their way to the street by a different path.

Back in the hotel where Gordon and Anastasia had been staying, Terry finally had to ask. He was too professional to ask during the job itself, but once they were out he needed to voice his concerns. "Are we getting sloppy, Mack? I didn't like leaving the witnesses. We never would have done that in the old days. You know, dead men tell no tales and all that."

"Terry, I did that for a reason. Here in America they need someone to target. A face to go with the name they love to hate. They will mourn a dead villain, but will vilify a live hero if they can find the slightest chink in his armor. We cannot play the hero or we will be just as quickly discredited, jailed and convicted, first by the press, then by the court. It doesn't help," Gordon continued with a smirk, "that we're as guilty as crows."

"But now we've got so much backlash we'll never be safe."

"Safe... Safe? We're not getting sloppy, Terry, we're getting old. When was it you started worrying about being safe? Ah. I get it. You went and fell for that blonde woman. What was it you asked me? You wouldn't be the first man to fall apart over a woman."

Suzanne LaLonde was still somewhat shell shocked. She had left the Petroleo building as directed. She had taken the elevator, and waved to the receptionist on the way out. Once she stepped through the doors, the enormity of her situation hit her. She did not feel safe going home nor did she think it advisable to visit any of her regular spots. She wandered about for a while feeling terrified and alone, then stopped into a self-proclaimed Irish pub and watched the news on the television while sipping a couple of beers.

"Oh, Suzie, what the fuck did you do this time?" she asked herself. "I wanted to do that for a long time, but now I'm stuck. No job. The police are gonna be after me. I don't even know if I'm ever going to see the sociopathic Australian again. Oh, Max. Why couldn't you have just been a regular guy, with a regular job and a house in the burbs somewhere?"

There were only a few men in the bar and no other women. One of the younger men came over and sat next to Suzanne, offering to buy her a drink.

"I have a drink."

"Well, let me buy your next one."

"Look, I'll buy my own damn drinks."

"Sorry, just trying to be sociable."

"I'm not in a very sociable mood right now."

"Fine. If you change your mind I'll be right over there." The man moved away and sat with a couple of friends at a booth. The inevitable jokes ensued from that quarter.

"That was a regular guy. He probably has a regular job and an apartment in the city somewhere. I could have hooked up with a regular guy somewhere down the line. I could hook up with one of them if I wanted. Suzie, face it, a regular guy was never what you wanted. You've been waiting for some kind of extraordinary man. Then, when you find one, he fucks your life up within two weeks and you'll probably never see him again." A tear rolled down her cheek and dropped onto the bar.

Another man, already sitting at the bar asked her what was wrong, and what he could do to make it better.

"You poor, bald bastard, you probably think about fucking sheep while raping your little sister. If I want something from you, I'll walk over there and beat it out of you. If I don't talk to you it's because you're not worth talking to. Now leave me alone." She bit her lip and wondered what came over her. The words rang in her ears; "The truth is you will never forget shoving that mescal bottle up the boss's ass. I've ruined you for life."

She bought herself another beer and took it to a booth in the back. Her phone rang a couple of times but she did not want to talk to the people calling. By the time her fiancé called, she was as drunk as a sailor on shore leave.

"Suzanne, my love, I hope you haven't gone home."

"Max, you called." The tears streamed down her cheeks in a mixture of fear and rage and relief.

"I told you, girl. You're mine now."

"Where are you?"

"We got out and we're in an apartment here in the city. I don't want you to come here and I don't want you to go home. Have you got any money?"

"God damn it, Max, I thought you had all kinds of money."

"Suzie, what's wrong?"

"What's wrong? I lost my job, I can't go home, I'm drunk, and now you want money. What the hell do you think is wrong?"

"Listen and listen carefully. I don't need money, you do. Do not use a credit card and do not go to a bank. Do you understand what I just said?"

"Max, what the hell are we going to do?"

"I need you to sober up. Tell me where you are and I'll come and get you."

She gave him the general location of the bar and the name, hung up the phone, and put her head down on the table and cried.

"Mack, I need to get her. She's gone and gotten herself drunk and I think she's losing it."

"Is she going to be a liability? If anybody slips today, we're done for."

"I've got her under control. She's not used to this sort of thing and probably feeling a bit stressed. I'll pick her up and bring her back here. A quick nap and some coffee should straighten her up."

"Make sure you keep her under control or else..." The sentence did not need to be finished.

Ahmed came out of the shower in the hotel room and Gordon went in. The regular network news was sketchy so Anastasia turned on Univision and got a more complete story. The Hispanic TV station had film footage of the three men who had been locked in the steam room being escorted from the building on stretchers. The female reporter on the scene was wearing too much makeup and too little clothing for the job, but the news coverage was more extensive. An hour later, the body of the Economic Advisor to the Petroleo Corporation was found, the victim of an apparent suicide. He had shot himself in front of an open vault where one stainless steel container was found. Univision actually showed the body, though briefly.

The container was taken into police custody as material evidence. The only prints lifted from it belonged to Albert Epstein, the victim. Inside the container was some unknown substance contained in injectable ampules.

The New York Times headline on Monday read "Mysterious Benefactor Leaves Cure to Plague". To paraphrase the article, somebody left a stainless steel cylinder with 25 doses of a cure for the 'Persian Plague' in the New York Times mailbox. It had taken a couple of days to verify. There was a letter with the gift, listing some devastating allegations against Petroleo Corporation. The address of the warehouse where thousands of doses of the cure were stored was included in the letter but not in the article. As soon as it was confirmed that the cylinder truly held a cure, a team of reporters was dispatched to Jerusalem. An investigation was launched by the US Government's Central Intelligence Agency that protected the Israeli portion of the cure from the inevitable mob activity by moving it to an undisclosed location.

On Wednesday, packages were delivered to research facilities: the University of Michigan Medical School in Ann Arbor, Johns Hopkins University in Baltimore, Maryland, Yale in Hartford, Connecticut and Stanford University in Stanford, California. Each one had the same explanation and directions. The cure for the plague was in them and the source of the donation was listed as The International Association of Fighters against Bioterrorism. The members were listed here as Jerry McMinster and Max Preston. The indictment against Petroleo Corporation was also included in the communiqué. There was no mention of the British role in the affair.

It was too late to claim hero status, but it was not too late to deny all knowledge of malfeasance. By the time the Petroleo Corporation President was released from the hospital, Israel had announced that it had discovered a source of the cure for the plague and was shipping its stockpile to Iraq. With the CIA's implicit assistance, the ampules were transferred to humanitarian aid agencies. Waxmark Biopharmaceuticals in Russia released a similar report. Its product had not gone through the clinical trials necessary for export so it was not yet deemed safe for human consumption, but that did not stop its export. The process would be hurried along, but the men and women at risk of infection did not have the time to wait. The profit would not be as extreme as might have been expected, but Waxmark Biopharmaceuticals was poised to make a fortune.

"So this whole thing was not about money?" Suzanne asked, sober now and enjoying her stay in the hotel. "I thought you were some kind of assassins for hire." It seemed to Terry that it was her romantic notion of the job.

"Well, yes and no. It all depends on whose perspective you're looking at it from. History will not record us as heroes. The price of gas will triple behind this little fiasco and the American public will be crying for blood. We will not be available for a public lynching but Danny Durham will be." Terry was grinning.

"No, what I mean is you weren't getting paid for this?"

"No, dear. We did this to rectify something that was so morally hideous, we could not let it pass. If we had not taken the job in the first place, we might not have been so sickened by it, but the filthy dogs used us to deliver it and then tried to snuff us out. We were filled with righteous indignation, as they say. In a life full of violence and sin, I…we got a chance to redeem ourselves."

"Then you are heroes."

"We are, and without you, we could not have done it."

Suzanne collapsed into Terry's arms. "Max, I love you so much. Wherever you are, I'll be there."

"Now we need to get out of this city," finished Gordon MacMaster.

Margaret Calley awoke on her bed in the apartment her ex-husband had paid for. It was late morning and she felt very sick. She tried to move but her hands and feet were tied. The night before was a blur. Events flowed back into her mind like slurry and she tried to connect them to reality.

Jerry McMinster had taken her to the theatre. They had seen some off-Broadway show about broken marriages. It was okay, but not top notch.

She shook her head and cleaned off her tongue on her teeth. What had happened? Why was she tied up?

Dinner. They had eaten dinner together at a nice restaurant, Beef and Brass or Steak and Scotch or something like that. Dinner was nice. He had been kissing her hands.

It wasn't a bar she knew. It was some Irish pub. They had been drinking Killians Red and shots of Old Lumberjack or something. She never blacked out but was having some trouble recalling how they had gotten home. Her home. She never brought men home, but Jerry was different. They had been going out for a couple of weeks and she was starting to think there was something he was not telling her about.

He had to have drugged her. She never slept past six and here it was almost noon. And she was tied up. Why in hell was she tied up? Had he raped her? She was much too willing to have required that. Maybe she changed her mind and got drunk and nasty.

"Well, shit. It had to be too good to be true." She would have liked to remember though.

She slung her legs off the bed and knocked the receiver off the phone where it lay on the bedside stand. She listened for a dial tone and when she found one she dialed 911 with her nose. The operator was cordial and Margaret explained what the situation was.

It did not take long before the New York City Police arrived on the scene. The door was locked so they had to smash a window to get in. They had a female officer with them who was adamant that they should take her to the hospital to have her checked for rape. Unlawful imprisonment was a serious enough charge, but rape went hand in hand with it and the two charges cemented the case together.

Margaret Calley was certain she hadn't been raped, just drugged and tied up, but in her diminished condition she did not argue with the officers much. She had been fully dressed when she awoke and had no bruises. The doctor confirmed that she had not been sexually active within the last week.

The police took her statement and put out an all points bulletin for Jerry McMinster. By the time they returned Margaret to her home, it was past dinner time. She called work to say she was ill and would not be in for a couple of days. She tried to eat but threw up so she went back to bed, sick and perplexed.

When the police rescued James Scott from the chair, he was so dehydrated he was just short of dead. It was days before his doctors would allow him to be interviewed, and he answered no questions until he had consulted with a bank of lawyers. He was never arrested for the suspect transfer of funds, but a slower and more inexorable movement was put in place, to try him along with the entire Boards of Directors of both the Hercules Bank and the Petroleo Corporation for crimes against humanity.

Chapter Seventeen
Direction

Temporary disguises were adopted to facilitate leaving New York City. A beat up red Chevy minivan was bought from a corner lot in New Jersey, and it was registered and insured in Gary McCormic's name. The team needed to move quickly. It would only be a matter of time before the fake American passports they had used to enter the country would be discovered and flagged, not by immigration, but possibly by the CIA or FBI. The commercial airports were not considered an immediate option since security was so tight.

Driving at night, obeying the speed limit and sticking to the busy interstates got them past the Mississippi River. Anastasia Viuda rented one motel room off Route 70 in Missouri. Ahmed de Ketama el Bali rented another. Everything was paid for in cash and names were never given. Any signature required was an indecipherable scrawl.

The national news was biased toward reporting the fugitives as vigilantes for justice. The network show America's Top Ten was not so generous. It ran pictures from the surveillance cameras, relatively clear pictures, better than the grainy, indecipherable black and white photos usually captured. It ran Suzanne LaLonde's driver's license photo. Three of the five members were so badly compromised they couldn't show their faces in public until changes were made. There were no pictures of Ahmed's face. It remained covered in all the camera shots. Gordon MacMaster was shown bald and shaven. Terry Kingston was blonde. While there was no doubt the police were looking for Anastasia Viuda, her picture made neither the news nor the most wanted shows. The segment ended with the inevitable "Let's get these terrorist scumbags off the streets and don't allow them to get out of the country."

Suzanne did not cry as Anastasia cut off her straight blonde hair and shaved her head. The red head wig that Anastasia had worn in New York had been replaced by a pageboy-cut black one. Suzanne was on her way to becoming a curly brunette.

"How could you tell?" Ahmed asked Terry Kingston.

"Tell what, mate?"

"That she would be worthy. That she would choose you over her life."

"I don't know what it is. Something in her eyes, something in her manner. The way she brushes off little things that worry other women. I don't know."

"If she had chosen otherwise?"

"Yes. I would have done what was necessary."

"She has no training. She will fold under pressure. You may need to do what is necessary regardless."

"Is that your professional opinion?"

"As a man."

"Let's hope she doesn't get put under pressure."

"Max, it is your turn," called Anastasia from the bathroom. Everyone had taken to addressing Terry as Max.

Terry was rather short on options since shaving his head did not change his appearance much. He allowed the women to dye his hair black and then shaved his arms. The weather was getting warm and long sleeved shirts would attract notice unless in full business attire.

Gordon MacMaster tied a handkerchief around his head and slipped on a jeans jacket with cutoff arms. The disguise was not perfect since there was no gang patch or colors and the denim wasn't worn or stained. It was an attempt to slide over to a different segment of American culture to divert attention but only made it halfway there. MacMaster's options were limited however by his size. He was not so huge as to stand out like a basketball player, but large enough that it was difficult to find clothes in his size on the rack. In the cheaper, one-stop-shopping stores the sizes ran small anyway so anything that was labeled 2Xlarge often still came up short and 3Xlarge was often nonexistent. The better shops had brand names whose sizes ran closer to true, but they were located in malls where he stood a much greater chance of being recognized.

It was often the day after a profile ran on America's Top Ten that the police were alerted. People relish the opportunity to say they had been the one who did this or did that. Gas station attendants and shopkeepers were the most dangerous segment of society for a man on the run, followed by waitresses and bartenders. Pizza delivery men ran high on the list also and take out food was necessary since most motels had no cooking facilities.

The money offered for Gordon and Terry's heads on a stick was extreme. It was a 'last job/retirement in luxury' amount. It prompted a lot of very competent chasers and bounty hunters to start searching, but the team had dropped off the face of the earth. The hunters who needed a steady income to survive stopped looking after a few weeks and went back to chasing bail jumpers. The real professionals had plenty of backup finances to continue their search.

The one resource others did not have that gave the British an edge was John Marshall. After being found bound to a chair and keeping four corpses company in The Director's subterranean lair, he was held without charges and without bail. They did not know what to do with him but they could not let him go. He was the only link they had to the team that had started the plague in Turkey, Iraq and Iran. He was the reason they had gone and he was the proof that they had come back. He was like an addiction they didn't really want but they needed.

The surveillance camera pictures from Petroleo were good enough for the British to pick out the pair immediately.

The names on the letter were added to the list of known aliases.

Despite his apparent willingness to help, John Marshall was not much deliberate assistance. It was his contention that the team referred to each other as Hamburg and Berlin and Troy and Sparta and Roma. They did not use names and they all looked about as ordinary as they could. All three Germans had blond hair and blue eyes. They had all been 5' 10". The Italian was shorter and had black hair. None of them had scars or tattoos. The only differences were that some made it through the adventure and some did not. Gordon MacMaster did not look ordinary of course, but Terry Kingston could have been any number of Australians; tall, blond and tanned with an Australian accent. The last thing John Marshall knew was that they were going to disappear into the Australian Outback. That was what he had been told and he had seen them buy the tickets.

The Service grilled him mercilessly until John Marshall forgot what he had said and had not said. He began to contradict himself on tape and change his story as memories of little incidents came back. He never gave up any names that the Service didn't already have and he tried not to disclose the safe house in Van.

When he was first taken from the basement he was so glad to be released from the chair that he was willing to tell them anything. He saw this as his final rescue and was certain that he had come home at last. Tears of joy and relief had run down his face. He had not expected to be treated like a returning hero or conquering general and he knew there were questions to answer, but he was not prepared for the reception he got.

One day after several hours of going over the same information over and over again, John Marshall had taken all he could stomach. "Hang on for just a moment. I have answered all these questions before, more than once. I wish to speak with my solicitor."

"You have no need for your attorney since we've charged you with nothing."

"I want legal advice. I am the victim here. I have done nothing and been charged with nothing yet I am incarcerated. I am the one who was kidnapped. I am the one who was forced to jump out of an airplane or be shot down. I was forced to dress like a woman and was very nearly killed by bandits. I barely got out of Turkey before the plague swept the country. I am the one who has been forced to hide like a thief and now I am denied my rights as British citizen. I am done answering questions until J. Howard Camden, Esquire walks through that door."

"All right. We'll get him for you. Now, let's go back to when…"

"No. We go back no where. I want my solicitor. You are violating my rights. You are holding me without charges and I want to leave. I will go downtown and find a pub and have a drink and if I feel randy, I will pick up a trollop and have my way with her, but I will not say another word to you or anyone else until I have been represented!" And true to his word he said not another word until his lawyer was on hand. His lawyer secured his release and escorted him personally to a hospital. A doctor looked at him, saw no physical wounds and sent him off, telling him to get some rest.

The English culpability for arranging the delivery had not been exposed. John Marshall had been warned in no uncertain terms that he was to keep his mouth shut. He would be well cared for and would continue to work for the government as long as there was no leakage of information. If he could not keep his mouth shut, then the Secret Service would shut it for him along with the rest of his family. Marshall understood without question. He had witnessed enough before he left Turkey to seal his lips forever.

MI6 would have been much happier to have Gordon

MacMaster and Terry Kingston silenced even more permanently but they were not about to send a squad to America to search for them. The fact that they had not implicated the British was enough to create an uneasy truce of sorts. If the pair ever returned to England, they would disappear without a sound, but if they held their tongues, the Service would not hunt them abroad for the murder of men who officially did not exist.

The discovery of a cure and the consequent humanitarian effort had been too little and too late. Twenty million people had died and more were dying each day but the epidemic's spread had been stopped and it was being forced back, albeit slowly. The main cure was still quarantine until death and then bulldozers came through three or four days later. Other diseases were beginning to crop up as well, as the swelling bodies were invaded by maggots and worms. There was so much death, the crews could not keep up with the bodies. Irbil, Mosul and Kirkuk had been burned already. Baghdad was thrashing itself to death like a rabid animal in its final death throes. The violence that followed the American invasion was horrible, but nothing compared to the nightmare of plague-ridden Baghdad. It was cut off from the world so no supplies were being delivered. Money lost its value as people began to barter for the things they really needed, then started killing and taking them instead. As many people were murdered as died of the plague. In one sense it made for an easier death though not all those who were shot died right away. Air conditioning was in short supply at the best of times. When news that air conditioning would prevent the plague circulated, the riots that ensued destroyed most of the air-conditioned places. The havens of cool air that remained where a temporary reprieve at best as the crew that manned the power plant sickened and died, and there was no one left to monitor and maintain the power grid.

The bridges in and out of the affected area were destroyed to keep anyone from driving out. This was a two-edged sword since it kept any humanitarian aid from getting in. People were shot by the thousands trying to run roadblocks or sneak around them. A week from infection, it was safe to handle the bodies, but there was no way to tell if someone had been exposed for the first two days, so it was safer to shoot them. The troops guarding the perimeter could not be blamed. Their orders coincided with their personal beliefs and fears. Shooting anyone from inside the infected area was the only course of action they could reasonably be expected to take.

The supply of the cure was limited and it turned into another debacle as humanitarian aid workers were murdered to obtain the ampules. The black market demand for the secret serum was overwhelming. The chaos was such that almost none of the warehouse-full of antivirus made it to those infected. Waxmark Biopharmaceuticals was pumping it out as fast as it could be created, but shipments disappeared, truck drivers became rich or got murdered. It became so dangerous to try to deliver within a 100 miles of the blockade that armored personnel carriers were needed and they seldom made their destination. Corrupt officials commandeered shipments and distributed them to populations that were not diseased. The misconception was that the cure was a vaccine that would prevent the plague. Truthfully, it was only effective in cases where the subject was already exposed but had not shown symptoms yet; a very small window of opportunity. A great deal of the medicine was wasted and even more was stockpiled by the rich. The carnage continued within the kill zone. Very few of those trapped within would survive.

Michael Galliardo was surprised to still be employed. His mentor was dead and the Board of Directors was being investigated pending indictment. The only thing that saved him was the address book with the passwords. He had access to all the people and information that Albert Epstein had used in the course of business. He knew it would not last long since the investigation would focus on who knew what and when and who authorized what. As his assistant, Michael had known it all but had authorized none of it. He might be guilty of conspiracy, but it would be difficult to prove. Petroleo had some of the world's best lawyers, but it was implicitly understood that a sacrificial lamb or two would be required to slake the public's need for blood.

"Vasilii Ivanov Scarkovich, good of you to take my call."

"Dangerous for me to take your call."

"Acknowledged. I think there are things we need to agree on."

"Acknowledged. Albert is deceased, yes? Our entire enterprise was compromised at its core. Your security was lax and it has backfired in your face, yes?"

"Hold on my friend…"

"Wait. You use the term 'friend' too loosely. To say I was your friend would mean I trust you. This is not so. I view you as a liability and only speak with you to allow you to redeem yourself in my eyes."

"Let's look at everything we have on the table before we go any further."

"Good. I assume you are not on a personal or corporate line."

"No. I am in a telephone booth in Manhattan."

"Good, but I am not convinced. We need to meet face to face to have this discussion. There is much to determine and there is little time."

"Where would you suggest? It is not so easy to visit overseas these days."

"You can drive to Canada, yes?"

"Yes, as long as I have not been indicted."

"We can meet in Niagara Falls. I have never visited there, but I am told it is lovely."

"I can be in Niagara Falls in about eight hours. Call me with the details and the time and I will be there."

"I will be looking forward to it. Is there a possibility that your financier um… this Mr. Scott, could join us there?"

"I doubt it. He is still in the hospital from his ordeal."

"Very well. I will be there as soon as it can be arranged."

"I'll be waiting for your call." Michael Galliardo hung up the phone, shut off the portable tape recorder and moved back to the bar. Something was bothering him, nagging at the back of his head but he did not know what it was.

James Scott was still plugged into a saline drip to counteract the effects of being without water for three days. The side of his head itched abominably under the bandage. He supposed he was lucky to be alive. He had no doubt that The Monster would have killed him without a second thought.

"Why did they spare me?" was the utmost thought in his mind. "It's not like they owed me anything. I cooperated with them but that means nothing. The things I have done in the name of money condemn me. The bank will be audited and I'll surely lose my position if not get imprisoned for it. Imprisoned for it. Once they start looking at who and when and where, I'm finished. There's no way around it. They already cancelled my access to any of the bank's funds and my funds in the bank. If they had known I had an offshore account, they would have raised a stink, but it turned out to be the best thing I ever did."

James Scott had no illusions about returning to the financial world. He would be a pariah, a leper. His only chance was to move and move quickly.

"The money in my offshore account is still there. If I can get to Grand Cayman, I can access that money and get away. I can't do it electronically without getting slammed, but if I can get out of the country, South America maybe, I can live well and be safe."

Michael Galliardo woke in the middle of the night with an ache in his head. He was hung over but that was not what hurt so bad. He went to the bathroom and relieved himself then went to his computer and logged in. He did a search for "James Scott" and was brought to the latest headlines involving him. The New York Times had not reported on his rescue yet. Michael knew he had been found because one of the bank president's lawyers had called him, but the press had yet to be alerted. That was what he had caught on the telephone the day before, and why his head hurt this morning. How had Vasilii known that Jimmy was still in New York and alive?

"I'm not in the business of finding people outside New York. I mean I deal with Jersey, Philadelphia, Albany, Utica from time to time, but past there I got no contacts." Joe Barrancotta was young to be a Capo. He had shown promise early and moved up the ranks easily since he was able to think as well as act. They called him The Barracuda on the street.

"Joe, I need your expertise. The press is all over me. I won't get out of the hospital for a week. I don't think they left, I think they're still here in New York. I want them found and I want them killed in horrible ways."

"I'm sorry, I don't perform that sort of service. Goodbye." The phone line went dead.

Arthur Emmerich hung up the phone. Joe Barrancotta had never let him down before and never accepted anything on the telephone. They never met in person after their first encounter knowing that discretion and deniability were necessary. Arthur's lawyers would take care of the details, negotiate the fee and pay the principle.

If the perpetrators of the Petroleo nightmare were in the tri-state area, they were dead men.

"I don't mean to be a doubting Thomas, but..."

"Tomasina."

"What was that, dear?"

"You are a woman, Suzanne. You cannot be a Thomas, I cannot be Thomas. You must be Tomasina."

"Thank you, Anastasia. As I was saying, what are we doing in the middle of nowhere, Missouri? Shouldn't we be trying to leave the country?"

They had been in their hotel rooms for two days with Ahmed going to the various stores to pick up supplies. The couples took full advantage of their time alone together, but there was only so much of that a couple can do.

"Look at those who would find us. Where would they look? If I look for someone who is trying to leave the country I must look in the airports and sea ports and at the border. Yes?"

"Yes, but..."

"The last place to look is in the middle of the country, yes? So that is where we are."

"But we can't stay here forever."

"Trust him, Tomasina. He will get us out of this country."

From that day forward, the new member of the team, Susanne LaLonde was called Tomasina.

Michael Galliardo was standing on Goat Island, that little spit of land jutting out between the two sides of Niagara Falls. The roar of the falls was in his ears and the vibrating power of the cataclysm filled his bones. Suddenly, there was a bear behind him. He sensed the bear rather than seeing it, but he knew that the bear spoke Russian and it was hungry for his flesh. He felt himself hoisted in the air and flung into Niagara Gorge. He fell faster and faster toward the churning maelstrom of the river. As with most dreams, he woke before he hit the water. Sweaty and gasping he stared into the darkness, terrified of his impending fate.

After he had calmed down some, Michael lit up a cigarette. He watched the smoke curling in the air and the red coal burning away the tobacco. When it got close to the filter, he turned it over to tamp it out and got a tightness in his throat. He couldn't breathe properly. He tried to swallow and couldn't do that either. He began to panic as his chest became tight and his hands trembled. He shook his head, opened his mouth and willed his throat to open. It finally did and he sat there gasping through his mouth. The vision of Niagara Falls was still in his mind and he could taste Lake Erie in the back of his throat.

Michael Galliardo got out of bed and got dressed. He threw a couple of suits and shirts into a suitcase and headed out the door. He would miss the feeling of power he had momentarily enjoyed, but he would not miss the money. He knew where the money was.

"Prevarication is the key to survival. Even as you move to the left, you say I'm going to move to the right and mean it. That's why you make a reservation in Virginia Beach, giving them your credit card number, but never step foot in Virginia. It will only work once, after that they know enough not to jump at the herring."

"Herring?" Suzanne had never heard the term.

"Yes, the red herring. Pay attention. If you access the internet, do it from a public machine, in a library or do it wireless. Do not e-mail anyone since that leaves an address, a hard line address that can be traced. Do not order anything online for the same reason. If you find something online you want, get an address and use a money order. A check will draw them to you; a credit card will draw them to you. For any other purchase, use cash.

"Your credit is something you will need to learn to live without. That is not so bad since it also eliminates the bills. Your past life is a complete wash, scrubbed clean, unless they find you. If they find you it all turns to a dung sandwich."

"Yummy."

"It's a thing you'll never want to taste, and a taste you'll never forget," Terry said grimly. "Pay attention. If you have a credit card at the start of the run, use it to send the hounds in the other direction. Use the telephone to order things sent to different locations but not, of course, where you are. Never use a land line for this. Never use a disposable phone within a hundred miles of where you bought it. Pay attention to the rules; they usually say you must call from your regular land line to activate the phone. This can be traced as easily as any other number so be aware of where you are in relation to where the phone was activated. Never use a phone with a GPS device in it. Petroleo had your phone number and could use it to track you. That's why we had to throw it in the river. Our phones were all activated in New York and no one has the numbers so they are safe to use, depending on who you call. It takes very specialized equipment to track a call and most people don't have access to that, but you must be careful anyway.

"Here's an even tougher one. If you have an accent, lose it and adopt a different one. It doesn't have to be perfect, but it should be credible. Not all of us can do that." Terry Kingston coughed and took a deep breath. "Nothing stands out so much as a foreign accent. If you're on the road and need something, stick to the bigger gas stations or preferably truck stops. They see a thousand different people every day at truck stops and seldom see the same people twice. If they do, they don't recognize them. But even there, a foreign accent sticks out. A New York accent in California is nothing in a truck stop, but a British accent turns heads everywhere in the country." Clearing his throat, Terry turned his head, cocked one eye and said "Well, darlin' I was jes passin' through and thought I'd like a steak. Didn' know I'd like the service better than the food."

Suzanne LaLonde broke out in long and genuine laughter. "You sound like Elvis!"

"Well, thank ya, thank ya very much. Yer a wonderful audience. Jes wait 'til ya hear Mack. He's up next."

"I'd remember that accent."

"Perhaps, but it doesn't stick out like an Australian one does it?"

"No, I guess not."

"Work on your accent a little."

"Uh, you bet, pilgrim. We got a lotta miles to drive this herd."

It was Terry's turn to fall into a laughing fit.

"Stephan, I want to know who paid to have the Petroleo affair exposed. Nobody does anything for nothing, especially in America. Get the hackers to break into whatever database they need to and find out who paid these men to do this."

"Yes, sir."

"I want you to contact Danny Durham, President of Petroleo. Let me know when you have him on the phone. Call The Director as well. No, cancel that. If he contacts me, put the call through but do not call him. He has been silent for weeks. I suspect his intentions."

Waxmark Biopharmaceuticals was making money hand over fist, but not the way it should have. Vasilii Ivanov Scarkovich knew that the trail would eventually lead back to him, but he had covered his tracks well and it would be a long time before his name was exposed, unless he was pointed out by those who knew the specifics of his involvement. Most of his dealings had been with Albert Epstein, a man famous for holding his tongue, but there were others involved that were not, perhaps, so closed mouthed. Michael Galliardo would be taken care of within days, but his disappearance could not precede finalization of plans by much or the strained relations he had with Petroleo would fall apart.

The call went through but Mr. Durham was unavailable. He would, in fact, never be available.

Vasilii checked Petroleo stock online. It was still in free fall. He squinted and stroked his long Romanoff mustache. A few more minutes passed, and he put in a limit order for 100,000 shares. In a matter of hours, that order had been completed and the stock price was still falling. Vasilii smiled and put in several more orders of decreasing price and increasing numbers. Petroleo was too huge to collapse, but not immune to takeover. Confidence had been lost in the corporation when it was reported that there was a correlation between Petroleo and the Middle Eastern plague but whatever happened, the oil was still there, the pumps were still sucking it out of the ground and the cars and trucks were still burning it up. Panic selling would cost investors huge sums of money but shrewd investing at this point would reap a fortune after the panic was over. Petroleo stock would become a phoenix, rising from its own ashes and burning brightly.

A grin split Vasilii Ivanov Scarkovich's face. Waxmark Biopharmaceuticals stock was soaring as well. It was already ten times the price he had paid for it. He sat and watched it rise until there was a minor downward dip, and then he sold every share he had. His holdings were so substantial that it caused a minor run on the market and the majority of investors took their profits. The following day the stock was sure to rise again. There was no doubt about it since it was the only reliable source of the cure. Vasilii put in a market order at the very end of the trading day and picked up about half of what he had sold. It was the middle of the night in Moscow when trading stopped in New York, so the Russian took a final shot of vodka and went to bed. The following afternoon he watched as the stock skyrocketed again.

The gamblers' code is to quit while you're ahead. Most gamblers do not follow the code and so never come out ahead. Vasilii Ivanov Scarkovich knew when to quit. Halfway through the trading day, as the Waxmark Biopharmaceuticals stock was going wild once again, he sold every share he owned. He never looked back.

Three of the limit orders for Petroleo stock went through and the price stabilized. It was at a 20-year low but Vasilii owned a 150 million shares. It may take some time for the furor to die down and the stock to regain its value, but it would happen.

In an emergency session of the Board of Directors of Petroleo Corporation, Arthur Emmerich and Danny Durham were both given votes of no confidence and ousted from their positions. Arthur was still in the hospital and was voted out in absentia. The Board knew who the real driving force was. With his death, there was a huge vacuum that needed to be filled and they were scrambling to fill the void. Durham and Emmerich were the ones indicated in the letter to the New York Times and so they were sacrificed. It was a bit of a knee-jerk reaction, but the Board was in damage control mode and those two had made themselves targets. They knew nothing about the judicial relief valve that Arthur Emmerich had created for himself. In fact, nobody but Arthur did.

Danny Durham had not managed his finances with the same care that Arthur Emmerich had. He had no offshore account. His money was tied up in Petroleo stock and that had become all but worthless overnight. He had a mansion he could not pay for and staff he could not pay. He had a fleet of classic cars that had not been paid off. He had a trophy wife that brought in no money and three children in Ivy League universities that cost more a semester than most men make in a year. His life insurance policy did not pay on a suicide, but accidental death would reap them the benefits. It did not come as a great surprise, to those familiar with his situation, when President Daniel Durham drove his 1971 Mustang into a bridge abutment at 120 miles an hour.

Chapter Eighteen
Dispersion

"I am at peace. I have fulfilled my debt."

"Aye, and in so doing have acted as an inspiration to me."

"Gordon MacMaster, we acted together on this. All our lives were on the line and not for blood money. I feel redeemed."

"Honor is upon you Ahmed de Ketama el Bali. History will sing songs of your honor, and cleansed of all past doings, your soul will rest in your heaven."

"I am now a liability. Your American television has put out the call for three men and two women. If we remain together, we will be seen and reported. While I am a benefit to you in that I have not been seen, I am a liability."

"We are a diverse group. Heads turn if we walk down the street together."

"Precisely. You still lead, but if I may be so bold as to suggest, we should no longer be seen together. My payoff is banked at home. I wish to leave."

"Aye, I have no quarrel with that. If the fates are kind, we will never meet again. I will always think of you with fond memories."

"Honor be upon you, my Scottish friend."

"Honor is upon you, my Moroccan ally."

"It's time we moved on anyway," Terry added. "We've got no cover out here. Nearer a city we can say we're in town for a convention or some such. Out here there's nothing to justify our presence. What do you say, Saint Louis or Kansas City?"

"Saint Louis. There's nothing on the other side of Kansas City except Kansas. I can't imagine wanting to go to Kansas unless we were hunting tornadoes. Besides, the further west we go the more likely we are to run into immigration roadblocks and spot checks. Texas is peppered with them. We may have passports but our pictures don't really correspond with our present images and for all we know the agent could be watching America's Top Ten as we pull up."

"True. The further west we go the closer we are to California. Not sure but that they would still like to have a wee chat with us out there. Saint Louis will work as well as any other."

"Anastasia, what made you do this?"

"Please, call me Anna or Annie. What is it you mean by this?"

"Well, it is so unusual for a woman to be, you know, doing this."

"Tomasina, we do not all end up being what we wanted to be."

"What did you want to be?"

"It's not important and I don't think I will talk about this."

"Oh. I'm sorry. I should have thought that... it would be too..."

"Forget it. Let's join the men. I wish I could take a swim."

After going back to the rooms from poolside, they learned that they would be going back toward Saint Louis to drop Ahmed off at the airport.

"I have a thought. It may be total bullshit or it may be the wrong thing to do, but if we are going back to Saint Louis, why not use a red herring?"

Gordon sat back in his chair and looked at Suzanne in a very different way.

"I have four credit cards in my name. They will be useless after the next time I use them but if we use them backward, starting in Saint Louis and moving west we can convince whoever is watching that we are headed to Kansas City, when we are really moving the other way."

"Who have you been talking to, girl?" Gordon chuckled.

"Well, I started thinking about the red herring thing after Max threw my cell phone in the river. I started thinking it would have been better if I left it in the bathroom of a river boat casino."

"Nice try, but the casinos are all permanently docked. Still, you got the idea. Max, old boy, you were right. She's a quick study."

Anastasia stepped over to her man protectively. The glare on her face only lasted a second but Suzanne LaLonde did not miss the implication. Gordon MacMaster was off limits on pain of death. Anastasia Viuda should have known that there was no interest on either party's part, but Suzie thought Anastasia might have some issues.

"Ah, no riverboat casinos. Okay. I was thinking it would take more than one vehicle. We book a reservation at a hotel in Kansas City then spread out along the interstate back to Saint Louis. We would make purchases at predetermined times using each of the four credit cards, making it look like we were moving toward Kansas City intending to spend the night in a hotel with a reservation."

Terry Kingston lit an Old Gold and asked, "Why would you use a hole card when the rest of the deck has yet to be dealt?"

"I thought it sounded like a good idea."

"Oh, it does. But at present there is nobody I know of that has the slightest idea where we are. If I'm wrong, correct me, but if we haven't broken it, let's not fix it. At present, as far as anyone knows, we could be from Maine to California. To narrow it down in the name of misdirection is defeating the purpose.

"So, Mack, who's taking the man to the airport," he

said in a sudden change of subject.

"We'll figure that out when we have a time and an itinerary. We need to get out of this town, though. Outstayed our welcome."

Checking out went smoothly and both renters pointedly asked about locations to the west. There was no reason to believe that there was anyone coming to ask, but sometimes it pays to hedge your bets.

They were unusually quiet on their way back to the city each trapped by their own thoughts.

Ahmed and Anastasia each rented balcony rooms in a nationwide chain hotel, then called the airport looking for outgoing flights.

The redeye out of Saint Louis, stopping in Atlanta, left Ahmed with a four-hour layover, another layover in Berlin and final stop in Cairo. He would stay there for a couple of days before going home. It was as good as could be expected, and the stop in Cairo was an unexpected bonus. He was more than welcome there.

Terry Kingston was sitting on a hotel chair on the balcony, smoking a cigar. The pool was lit up below but no one was swimming.

Suzanne LaLonde visited Anastasia in the other room. "Annie. I want to make sure we understand each other. I do not want your man and will not sleep with him if he asks or ever make a pass at him. Max is my man and I don't want anyone else. I just wanted to say that, so we could both understand."

"Why do you say this? Has he said anything to you?" The Argentine's eyes narrowed suspiciously.

"No. He doesn't say much to anybody."

"This is good. I thought maybe he said something."

"No."

"Good. You have your man and I have mine."
Something about the way she said it conveyed an inherent

distrust, despite what she had said.

Suzanne wondered if there was something in the past that she should know about. She left the room and pulled the other chair out of the room to sit by Terry.

"Max, is there something I should know about Annie?"

"What is you mean, dear?"

"I don't know. I get the feeling she thinks I'm after Mack. I'm just thinking maybe I don't want her pissed off at me for something I didn't do."

"You got that right. But let's look at it objectively. What do you have?"

"Well, I had a nice little apar..."

"Not had, sweetheart, have," Terry cut her off.

"Uh... I guess I've got nothing, now. Nothing but you."

"Proper. Now, how many times in your life have you found yourself in that situation?"

"Well, once or twice."

"Really? Tell me about them."

"When I first graduated from college, I was out on my own with no job and no way to pay the bills."

"But you had bills. That means you were paying for something. A flat, heat and water, maybe cable television. Yes?"

"I'm beginning to see where this is going."

"Right then. When you find yourself changing everything in a day, it's nice to hold on to what you can. You spend two or three years doing something, somewhere, say you're a librarian in Pot Luck, Illinois. Suddenly you need to leave in a day and take one bag of things with you. You need clothes, maybe a snack for the trip, but you'd be taking one of your favorite books, too. Wouldn't you?"

"I understand."

"There are very few things you can count on in this world. You have to be ready for this kind of life."

Suddenly the precariousness of her situation came home. She was wanted in connection with a murder. She had no money of her own. She couldn't leave the country without a passport and she didn't have an alias. Her existence was tied to a man she had known for a couple of weeks who might dump her at any minute and run off to God knows where. He was even capable of killing her before he left. The thrilling adventure she had embarked upon was colliding with reality and it came up short. Her heart began pounding and genuine fear gripped her. "Max, you ruined me for life and now I've ruined my life. Where does it go from here?"

"No worries. We need to get you some paperwork and slip off to some quiet town where nobody knows us." Terry took a final puff on his cigar and laid the butt on the railing.

Suzanne picked up the chair she was sitting on and took it back into the room. She sat back down on the chair, put her head on the writing desk and began to cry.

Michael Galliardo was born and raised in New York City. He had been around the world a couple of times, but it was always with a round-trip ticket. As tough and self sufficient as he was, leaving the country for good was scary. Leaving New York was scary enough to him that he hesitated a couple of days. He justified this by working hard at consolidating personal affairs as well as corporate business.

After the emergency meeting of the Board of Directors was finished with its vote of no confidence, he saw he had waited too long and bought tickets to Grand Cayman that day. The tickets were not good for that day but the day after. In the back of his mind, he knew he would be returning to the States if not to New York. He couldn't see himself retiring to some beach community and drinking margaritas for the rest of his life. He was too young and vibrant.

The trip to Grand Cayman was boring with a short layover in Miami. For the first time in his life he had gone on a one-way trip with no plan past the acquisition of capital. He had the numbers; he just didn't know how much money was in Epstein's account, or if the password had been changed since he observed it. He didn't know if Albert Epstein had noticed him scoping out the numbers. Michael had very good credit so he could arrange a flight back to New York if his plan didn't pan out.

Bull Bradley had been a bouncer in a bar in Amarillo when he was young. He picked up his nickname by picking up a man and bodily running him through a wall. It wasn't a sheetrock wall; it was time-hardened oak planking. The drunken patron ended up missing a couple of days of work due to hospitalization. Bull had been born Barney Bradley so he was in desperate need of a nickname anyway.

Lawrence Terwilliger never let anyone call him Larry; he just wasn't a Larry kind of guy. Thin and very self contained, he constantly smoked little cigars through a cigarette holder. He seldom opened the windows of his cramped little house and had everything, even his groceries, delivered. Lawrence Terwilliger was a hacker of extraordinary skill. He spent all his time with his computers. The only physical contact he had with another human was the once-a-week visit by Mistress Antoinette.

Lawrence and Bull Bradley were in business together by dint of the fact that the former could find almost anybody and the latter, with his team, could bring them in. It was a mutually beneficial alliance though neither of the men liked the other.

The reclusive Mr. Terwilliger lived outside Denver, Colorado and Mr. Bradley had a place halfway between Dallas and Houston.

The cell phone that rang was always on charge. It was the business phone. Mrs. Bradley answered it in the kitchen and called to her husband.

"Well, bring it here, bitch. An' bring me a beer," came the bellow from the living room where Bull was in his underwear watching professional wrestling on television.

Mrs. Bradley unplugged the phone and took it to him. She did not say another word. If he punched her in her other eye, they would both be swelled shut and she wouldn't be able to see.

Bull muted the television and put on his most civilized demeanor. "What ya got, Lawrence?"

It was distasteful to Lawrence Terwilliger to even speak with Bull Bradley, but their alliance was so financially beneficial that among his contacts, Bull was the first to get the call. "I think I have something on the Petroleo murder."

"Great. Have you contacted the guys with the cash?"

"Pay attention, Mr. Bradley. This is a dead or alive proposition, which means they don't want them alive. I contacted the payers two days ago to cement the terms and conditions. This one pays enough to keep you in Lone Star for years."

"Hah, you don't know how much I can drink."

"Regardless of your gustatory capabilities, this job will set us up if we can pull it off."

"We'll get 'em. Just tell me where they are and send me the pictures.

"The pictures are on their way. Make sure your fax is on. Now I cannot promise that we have them. They have been quite discreet and are obviously professional."

"Waddaya mean."

"Have you ever reviewed this case? They walked into the headquarters of the most powerful corporation on Earth, tied up the President and killed the number one finance man. Then they walked out again, like ghosts, with the cure to the Persian Plague. Could you do that?" After a few seconds of silence, the hacker continued. "Right. Now I have a list of names that came into the country within a couple of weeks of the incident. Most of them are easy enough to discount. European vacations, Indians coming over to study, refugees from Africa, international entrepreneurs. Some of them are a little harder to track. I weeded out the students and vacationers and narrowed the list down."

"I don't give a shit how you found them. Just tell me where they are, I'll go get 'em."

"It's a little more complicated than that; allow me to continue. We have a Max Preston who entered this country with an American Passport from the Bahamas. He flew to the Bahamas from Paris, but there is no record of his leaving the country to go there. Also, his Social Security number never recorded him as paying taxes, anywhere. This is one of the men who pulled this job. Any questions?"

Bull Bradley just growled into the phone. It was so small it disappeared in his hand as if trying to hide from his face.

"Next is Gary McCormic. He lives in some flyspeck in the mountains, right here in Colorado. He has a credit card that he seldom uses, a pickup truck that is up for registration but is not in his driveway..."

"How do you know?"

"I can look at his house. I can see when he's sleeping, I know when he's awake."

"Yeah, yeah. Yer fuckin' Santa Claus. Get on with it."

"Mr. McCormic made a mistake and reentered the country using that name after a long, undocumented trip abroad. The Immigration people will never catch that but I did. He came back into the country in New Jersey and never got a flight back to Colorado. Then, a couple of weeks later, he buys a red Chevy van in New Jersey and registers it under that name. I guarantee he's our man. He is undoubtedly also this Jerry McMinster of the International Association of Fighters against Bioterrorism."

"Sounds like bullshit to me."

"I assure you, my brobdignagian associate, this is our man. People act in predictable ways, they move in predictable circles. Some are unable to change the cycle they have created for themselves until it kills them. When people do unusual and unpredictable things, it is because they have motives that are ancillary to their obvious lifestyle or they are insane. Our quarry is not insane."

"I wish you'd speak English. I know they're not crazy. Jes' tell me where to find the bastards and I'll bring 'em in.

"I'm getting to that. I have no access to the police interrogation of this tall woman who was asking for her boyfriend, if they indeed questioned her. She left without talking to the receptionist who would have gotten him for her. She was cover for these men who snuck in while she was yelling at the security guard. She is an accomplice of theirs and unless I miss my guess, her name is Anastasia Viuda. The owner of record of Gary McCormic's address is Anastasia Viuda."

"Mexican, huh? We got a picture of her too?"

"Of course, I'll send it along with the rest. The man in the turban is a complete mystery. He came in as an Iraqi Sheik but I am sure that is not genuine. I have nothing on him so we'll need to play that by ear."

"The last member of this team is a mystery as well but for a different reason. Suzanne LaLonde, no middle name. Born in New York City, twenty-seven years old. She did average in Community College, worked her way up as a temp in Petroleo after working as a temp for Dow Chemical, AT&T, Comcast, something called The Archive Press and Chrysler after the split from Mercedes but before the merger with Fiat. She's always been a secretary, never been arrested, has no traffic tickets because she has hardly ever driven a car. You'll see the picture. I got her information from her online resume. I'll send you a copy. She has no passport, never left the country. Her phone records have no international calls.

She doesn't fit the profile. She's just a sweet blonde who could have come from the Midwest if she hadn't been born in Manhattan. I think she was probably coerced in some way into this affair. I expect the authorities to find her body in the Hudson River."

"Okay. So I listened to all this crap and you still haven't told me what I need," Bradley snorted. "Where the fuck are they?"

"I don't know."

"Are they going to Mexico?"

"I cannot be sure."

"Then why did you call me? What am I supposed to do?"

"I've given you the preliminaries so you can sober up for a couple of days, gather your crew and be ready when I find them. They have made mistakes and will make more. Nobody can hide in America any more. Not when I'm looking for them. I will find them and then it will be your job to get them."

"All right, send me what you got. We'll be ready to roll when you give me something real."

Michael Galliardo flew into Owen Roberts International Airport as the sun was going down. The banks were closed for the night so he took a hotel room and walked to the Hard Rock Café. He had been here before and knew he could walk all the way around the city in a couple of hours. The night air was comfortable enough but the summer sun could bake a man in his suit. The food was good at the café, though everything was expensive in Georgetown. Michael bought drinks for the ladies and danced. He was disappointed when none of them wanted to go back to the hotel with him. They spurned him with "You not in Jamaica, white man."

Waking early, he took a walk on the beach, enjoying the surf and sand. It was so different from New York, he didn't know what to think. He had been in a hurry for so long that doing nothing bothered him. When the bank opened, he walked in with an empty student-sized backpack and explained to one of the officers that he wanted to drain a specific account and that he wanted it in American funds.

When the officer looked into the records she told him that would not be possible. His heart was in his teeth when he asked why not.

"I do not think we have that much on hand in American funds. We can perhaps provide you with a $1,000,000, but the rest will need to be in check form."

It was a credit to his self-control that he was able to keep his face in check as he said, "In that case, let's make it simple and give me $500,000 in cash and cut me a check for the rest."

"Very well, it would be my pleasure."

The amount of the check was staggering.

Michael left the bank with heartfelt thanks and hailed a cab. The cab took him to the Cayman National Bank where he deposited the check in a new account. The cab took him back to the hotel where he stashed some of the money in the hotel safe, some in his room, and he went back to the Hard Rock Café. Today it was filled with passengers from a tour ship who were more than happy to drink on his dime and he corralled one of them to join him in his hotel room for a little while.

After his company had left, Michael Galliardo began to feel panicked. He had not imagined how much money would actually be in that account. All Albert Epstein's onshore accounts had been frozen upon his death but the offshore accounts were subject, not to the owner's identity, but to the access numbers. While his head was swimming with an ecstasy of true financial gain he also feared there were others with real claims to the money that would be looking for it. He also thought about his dream. If the Russian found him, he was going to die. He was only lucky that big bald son-of-a-bitch didn't kill him back in the penthouse. He flirted with putting a bounty on the bald one's head but that would require making himself available. He did not want to be available, he wanted to disappear.

The hat hurt the left side of James Scott's head where he used to have an ear. He was wearing it for the sake of discretion. The bulky bandages left more to the imagination than the scabbed over wound. The doctors knew it was too late to attempt a transplant. After the wound healed, they may consider some sort of reconstructive surgery. Jimmy did not expect to stay long enough to give them the chance.

As soon as he could get released from the hospital, James Scott was on a plane to Georgetown, Grand Cayman. His account had been full enough to allow for a life of luxury in a third-world country. Once he was gone, flight from prosecution was the least of his worries. Though he had been cleared of the embezzlement charges, he knew he would be required to return the money that had been transferred to his account. That would leave him with a couple of year's salary and no prospects. He had counted himself a rich man before this episode but he was rich as so many in America are; credit rich and cash poor.

He had a wife who had married him for money and stayed with him for the same reason. She had visited him once in the hospital. His two daughters were grown and off on their own. Neither of them had visited. His home was half paid for and his wife had put that on the market as soon as he was reported missing. She was actually the stronger of the two when it came to the marriage; she was in it for the money. The sale of the house would leave her set up for a while. She would have no problem finding herself another sugar daddy since she had taken very good care of herself.

The plane touched down in the full light of the

Caribbean sun and James was actually grateful for the hat. He tried to buy some sunglasses but the bandage that covered his lack of an ear made it too difficult to wear them. The air conditioning in the airport was pleasant but as soon as he left its cold embrace, he was struck by the full force of the southern sun. A cab took him to the hotel and he checked in using his own name and a credit card. He had stopped carrying cash years ago.

James Scott had no luggage to speak of, just a briefcase and that was as empty as his future in New York. He took the briefcase to the Cayman National Bank and told them he wanted to empty his account. His numbers were all correct but when the account was accessed, it was found to be almost as empty as his briefcase. Half the money had been transferred to an account in the Bahamas; the other half had gone to Switzerland. Overnight, the wealthy President of the Hercules Bank and Investment Company was virtually destitute.

Arthur Emmerich was not allowed to leave the hospital for a week after he was admitted. He had a ruptured colon and required surgery and observation.

Arthur had been born to privilege the way none of his associates were. His family had made its money in bootlegging and political graft as well as oil and electricity. Arthur was not to be ruined by a quick turn of fate and exposure did not bother him. Being voted out of office at Petroleo was a black eye but it was not a death sentence.

It was Arthur Emmerich's money that was initially offered for the capture of Gordon, Terry, Suzanne and their accomplices. Arthur's associates at Petroleo had been forced to vote him out but they knew him as old money and a competent administrator, if somewhat flawed. They were willing to funnel some of Petroleo's less traceable funds to him to expand the offer. It was his contacts and their support that made the bounty so large and attractive.

Since Arthur was already independently wealthy, he was not terribly concerned with finances. He had invested in Petroleo stock and would have lost a bundle if he was forced to sell his holdings but he could afford to hold onto them until they regained some of their value. His greatest concern was the potential legal repercussions involved, but he had set himself up to counter that as well.

In truth, he was in no shape to travel far and the thought of the medical facilities overseas was more than he could bear. If legal proceedings were initiated against him, he would consider making a move to Western Europe but until that happened, he would concentrate on healing and finding those who had damaged him. His greatest venom was concentrated on Suzanne LaLonde since he considered her a traitor. He had been having his way with women for years and had seldom been taken to task for it. None of them had ever hospitalized him before.

Max Preston was next on his list. He didn't know if Preston was his real name or not. It was not that it mattered. He could call himself King of Prussia if he wanted. Arthur wanted him dead. The third identifiable member of the team was Jerry McMinster. It turned out that he had been dating Margaret Calley, the Transportation Director. Margaret had taken a couple of days off after being tied up and drugged by her new love interest. She had not mentioned it for a couple of days after that, but it eventually got through the New York City Police paperwork and the connection was made. The pictures were shown to Margaret and the fact that it was her badge that he used to gain access to the building was brought to light. She was released from service immediately but there were no charges filed.

America's Top Ten ran a revision the week after its first highly accusatory broadcast. They tempered their tone somewhat this time with new information about the cure for the plague and the potential involvement of Petroleo in the original infection. They ran the pictures again but still left Anastasia's footage off the air.

The tabloids had jumped on the bandwagon with remarkable restraint given that their stock in trade is to shock and offend. The headlines ran more along the lines of "Jerry McMinster was Sent by God to End the Persian Plague" or "Fighters Against Bioterrorism Linked to al-Qaida."

Once the story of Margaret Calley was released, they were all over her for a story. Margaret was a reserved person and the pressure for an interview was intense. She refused to give them an interview the first week and the stories ran as "I was Inseminated by the Devil" and "Pregnant with a Bioterrorist Baby."

The talk shows also courted Ms. Calley and their offers were more attractive. Talk radio was taking opposing viewpoints from across the country and the debate began to take fire on the air. There were internet polls to ask what America thought. As usual, the polls gave insufficient answers to choose from, but the consensus of opinion was that the Fighters Against Bioterrorism were heroes.

Chapter Nineteen
Staging

A rented post office box was a good enough address for all the mail this group would be receiving. The cell phones were adequate for communications as long as they didn't call anyone who was hunting them. Board games and cable television were onerous but sufficed to keep them mildly entertained. Suzanne LaLonde liked reading romance novels. Gordon MacMaster bought the newspapers from the honor boxes every day. Anastasia Viuda scoured the internet for news, dissecting every story and getting help with words she did not understand. She went to the post office box every couple of days to check for a package.

In Saint Louis, they moved into a couple of suites in an extended-stay hotel. These had kitchens, a welcome relief from fast food. All four of them were feeling the lack of exercise.

Without further grist for the mill, the tabloids went back to reporting who was in rehab and who was sleeping with whom. Petroleo Corporation continued to make the news, but mention of the alleged homicide stopped rather sharply. Of course the plague was always big news, and since there was no oil flowing from Iraq, the price had risen sharply but began to drop slowly once the cure was released.

Without proof of the allegations against Petroleo Corporation, their stock regained some of its value. Waxmark Biopharmaceuticals was forced by international pressure to release its process for creating the antivirus and drug companies worldwide geared up to begin producing it. Waxmark's stock stabilized.

"Gordon, my love, I must ask after this is all here. Why did you not tell of the real source of the plague?"

"Annie, in truth, it would have done no good and much evil. The only men on the planet that know how to make the cure are those who created the virus. If they were exposed as the monsters they are, then no one would be making the cure and the plague would still be there. They will be exposed; it just takes some time. What I feared was that the facility would be bombed and the cure lost. People get overly emotional and given a target they often kill their best friend."

"So, given this, what is to be done with these demons?"

"I think the vengeance of the Lord will be upon them. It just takes a little time."

"And now we?"

"What are you asking, love?"

"We cannot stay here much longer. Are you sure your associates in Prague will deliver? We are on all the news."

"It won't last much longer. What we need to watch for is the FBI. They will not forget so quickly. The American public has an attention span of a couple of weeks, months if the press keeps pushing, but you know how the Federal Services are. I'm rather certain Her Majesty's Secret Service would find a nice dark hole for us."

"I do not feel safe."

"In six months, we could tour the White House and nobody would notice."

Despite his jocular attitude, Gordon MacMaster insisted no one leave the hotel but Anastasia.

"So you went out with him five times?"

"That's right, Marty."

"And the fifth time, he tied you up and raped you?"

"No. He never raped me. Except for drugging me and tying me up, he acted like a perfect gentleman."

The studio audience for the Marty Williams show roared with laughter.

"So, if he didn't rape you, why did he tie you up? Why didn't he just leave you there drugged?"

"I can't be sure, but I think he wanted some proof it had been him. That he had been the one in the pictures. That he was the one who went into Petroleo and got the cure for the Islamic Plague."

"We generally call it the Persian Plague."

"Whatever works. He wanted my access card and he got it. He didn't want me. He took me out to dinner, to movies and plays. I think he's gay because he was so cool, but he didn't hit on me. Then the last time we went out, he started moving in close and whispering in my ear, suggesting we go back to my place, and then he drugged me," She finished sourly.

"Wow, that's quite a story. We'll have more on this one-sided romance after this." The television switched to an advertisement for a skin care product and Anastasia muted it.

"It is true, then. He did not sleep with her."

"Why would he have?" Suzanne was sitting on the bed next to her. Gordon was in the kitchen chopping up lettuce for a salad. Terry was showering in the next suite.

"Men do things for reasons women do not know. Sometimes the job calls for intimacy. I would not hold it against him. I might hold it against her but she knew nothing."

Suzanne passed her hand over her bald scalp and in a revealing moment looked into Anastasia's eyes. They locked gazes for a few seconds then broke away, each embarrassed for the other, neither wanting to get any closer than they needed to, despite an obvious mutual attraction.

When the commercials were over there was little more to be gleaned from Margaret Calley. Marty Williams ran the picture of Gordon MacMaster that had been released to the press. "This is the man," Marty continued "that drugged this beautiful woman and tied her up so he could get access to the cure for the Persian Plague that was reportedly being held at the Petroleo headquarters. She was the Transportation

Manager for the world headquarters, a position, I should add, she no longer holds. He is also wanted in connection with the death of the Chief Financial Officer for the corporation. Now we have the security guard who found the body of Albert Epstein, who says it might not have been a murder."

The security guard who had found the body came on stage and talked about finding the body with the pistol in its hand. He was certainly no expert in forensic science but he gave his observations and his opinion that Albert Epstein may have been overcome with guilt and killed himself on the spot. The gun that killed him had belonged to Epstein's assistant who had been released from the steam room. Michael Galliardo had told the police that the gun had been taken from him by Jerry McMinster but Michael had disappeared. He had gotten out of the hospital, stayed in New York for four days and then hopped a flight to Grand Cayman. He was not currently available to testify further.

"I just want to point out that the entire security staff has been fired for incompetence in this matter so anything they say should be looked at in that light. Next we have a man who was arrested for driving his motorcycle drunk and naked. Yes, naked through the streets of Scranton, Pennsylvania. He says he was beaten by his wife and ran off naked to keep her from killing him. After this."

Anastasia shut off the television and said. "He probably deserved it."

Gordon entered from the kitchen with a salad and some blackened chicken breasts.

"We're still news."

"Yes, love, I heard."

"It does not make good sense but there was a transfer of funds from Hercules Bank to separate accounts in the Bahamas and Switzerland. This money came from the private account of James Scott, the same account that the money was transferred to while he was missing. It does not appear that anyone was actually paying these people, other than Scott. It looks like they went rogue."

"Thank you, Stephan. Perhaps it would be best if we called Mr. Scott."

"He has gone to Grand Cayman. I am sure it was to clear the account in question. He has been there for two weeks."

"Who owns the accounts the money was transferred to?"

"We cannot access any names, just numbers. I feel sure the accounts belong to the men in question."

"Yes, no doubt. Has this Roman, Michael Galliardo been taken care of?"

"He too is in Grand Cayman. We have not been able to ascertain why. Perhaps he and James Scott are in business together. They are not in the same hotel. Galliardo is staying in a five-star hotel, under his own name."

"I see. They are both liabilities. I want a man sent to decommission them."

"Certainly."

"Is there anything new on Emmerich?"

"No, sir. He stays in New York recovering from injuries. His reward for the men stands. Would you like him decommissioned as well?"

"Not yet. I may still have a use for him and if his money finds our rogue agents then it will be more than worth leaving him alive for a while. Is he granting interviews?"

"No, sir, not even to the FBI. They will need to subpoena him, I think."

"He has not been arrested then?"

"No, they see him as a victim."

Vasilii Ivanov Scarkovich snorted with disdain. "A victim. That works well for us."

Michael Galliardo was unsure of his next move. He took a drink and looked at the dejected man sitting next to him. James Scott had never looked so old.

Michael had been walking on the beachfront road still exultant and confused about what to do. He had been attempting to plan between bouts of deep drunkenness and chasing women. He had never really considered leaving New York for good. It had everything he needed. Everything anyone needed. He did not have many friends though and his acquaintances would turn cold over his associations. He did, however, have a passel of money and he was still young. He was wrapped in his own thoughts and did not see the man with the small bandage on his head until he was addressed.

"Hello, Michael."

Almost jumping out of his skin, Michael turned and saw the ex-President of the Hercules Bank standing beside him. This was the last thing he had expected and was momentarily speechless. He looked around, frantically, expecting to see other men accompanying his decrepit erstwhile ally. There was nobody else evident.

Michael took another drink. His head was swimming and he needed time to think over the ramifications of having Jimmy here, with him. The bar was almost empty. The passengers on the cruise ship that had docked this morning had not begun to disembark.

"They cleared my account."

"The bank?"

"No, the bastards that left me tied to that chair."

"So... what are you telling me?"

"I can't go back to New York and I don't have any money."

"Wow. I wish I could help.

James Scott's eyes narrowed. He was no fool regardless of the fact that he had been robbed blind. "What are you doing here?"

"I needed to get away and think for a while."

"So you came here. I'm skeptical. You came here to get money. That's the only reason you could have. If you're not on a cruise ship, and you're not, you're here to get money. Help me out."

"I don't know what you're talking about."

"Don't try to bullshit me, Michael. When you need to think, you have a cottage in Vermont. Those sons-of-bitches screwed us both. You had a good position and a promising career. I was set up nicely until they came and uh… set me up in a different way. I'm broke and I need some money. Help me out. After all, you were the one who came to me with the money. Epstein stayed in his ivory tower pulling the strings but you were the face I saw. As far as I know the entire affair was your idea. If I were to talk to the Feds…" There was no need to finish his statement.

"You're talking out your ass, Jimmy. I'm already out of the country. I got a couple thousand dollars but I'm not set up either. I'm on the run."

"Bullshit. You wouldn't be here for a couple thousand. You got access to Epstein's money! That makes you as guilty as he was, and fuckin' rich. There isn't a place in the world you can go where they won't find you if I start talking."

"You aren't going to say anything to anyone. You'd implicate yourself."

James Scott knew then that he had his associate in a corner. He also knew he was right about the money. His banker's mind started to click.

"They'd give me immunity if I handed them the man responsible for the plague. We both know that. I want a $1,000,000 and I'll disappear."

"I can't access that kind of money. I don't have it."

"Bullshit. Let's go to the bank right now. One million and you'll never see me again."

Michael Galliardo knew that $1,000,000 would only be

the beginning. Despite his appearance, James Scott was an accomplished criminal. He was simply smarter than most criminals.

"I don't have that kind of money."

"What do you have?"

"I can give you $10,000 if you come to my hotel room with me."

"Fuck you. A $100,000."

"Let's have another drink."

"I don't want another drink. I need money and you're going to give it to me or you're going to end up facing the World Court on charges of Crimes Against Humanity, if you live that long."

"What do you mean?"

"If Islam gets a hold of you first, I don't know what they'll do." With his hole card played, James Scott tried to look as ruthless as he was. Michael Galliardo was not used to playing with the sort of money in this pot. He would flinch or he would fold.

The two stared into each other's eyes for a long minute, then Michael said "Let's go."

"Now we're talking."

"Gordon, we must go. We must go now."

Anastasia seldom called him Gordon unless there was a serious situation at hand. "What happened?" he asked.

"Ai, I got the package from Prague but as I pull out of the parking, this fool runs into me. I could not get away, the cars they were..." She punched her hands together in front of her. "Tight together. He pushed me into another, a truck. I could not get away."

"Are you injured?"

"No. He hit me hard but he hit me in the back, on the side. The auto will drive but it is damaged but the police were there. They took the numbers, your name, the registration.

They got our address in Colorado. They got the license plate. My driver's license says Maria Alejandros, they know that name in New York and this van is registered to Gary McCormic. We need to go; we need to leave the van and go."

"You pack up here and I'll go next door."

Next door was the adjacent suite. Terry and Suzanne were both naked and covered with sweat. He had obviously interrupted something intimate but carnal pleasure was secondary to escape.

A quick wipe down of the most often used surfaces was done with glass cleaner and paper towels. They wore latex gloves for the task. When the gloves were bought, they made sure they were not the powdered kind. In their haste they could not be sure they had gotten all the fingerprints, but they did their best with the time that was at hand.

They threw everything they had into their suitcases and cleaned the refrigerators into a garbage bag.

The door on the far end of the building was in direct view of the hallway but unless someone came around the counter, it could not be seen from the check-in desk.

They pulled out slowly. Anastasia was driving, the rest were hiding as best they could in the back of the van.

They pulled onto Lackland Road in Westport, turned south onto Ashby and then west onto Page Avenue. I270 rings the outside of Saint Louis, and they felt a bit better merging into the rush hour traffic regardless of the fact they were in an old red minivan with the panels caved in on the driver's side. They headed south to Route 64 and into the heart of the city. Gordon MacMaster jumped out at a stoplight and Anastasia parked the van in a grocery store parking lot off Grand Avenue.

They felt more than a little out of place since they were virtually the only white faces in the parking lot. They took their time sorting through the garbage bag full of food that had been in the refrigerator, wiped down what was left and tossed it in the store's dumpster.

Feeling already compromised, the three went into the store itself looking for things they could take with them such as canned food granola bars and ramen noodles.

It took a couple of hours, but a cell phone rang and Gordon gave the address of a retail superstore for them to meet him. They drove the 10 blocks to the location and parked the red minivan in the lot of a restaurant that bordered the superstore. Anastasia went into the restaurant and ordered some take-out food. While she waited for the order, the other two went into the larger parking lot and into a full-sized work van. It had no windows on the sides and the rear windows were covered on the inside with wire grating.

"Not a bad size, eh?"

"No, Mack. Not bad. No seats in the back though."

"I thought of that. Come into the store and we'll take care of that. Here, get these items and I'll get some others."

Terry picked up four folding lawn chairs, a pack of conduit brackets, some sheet metal screws, screwdriver bits and a rechargeable drill.

Gordon bought a 12-volt cooler, some lunch meat, cheese, mayonnaise, mustard, four loaves of bread and a small power inverter.

The cashiers were bored and indifferent. They didn't even look their customers in the face.

Done with their shopping, the men returned to the van, started it up and pulled into the restaurant parking lot, behind the ruptured minivan. It started and followed them out into traffic. The neighborhood the minivan was deserted in, with the keys in it, was guaranteed to make the vehicle disappear within a couple of days, maybe a couple of hours.

"Terry, we need to stop calling you Max. That name is compromised. From now on you're Frank, Frank Candle. My friends in Prague have done a bang-up job." Gordon pulled an American passport and a birth certificate with a raised seal out of a cardboard box. The passport had Terry Kingston's face on it, his hair dyed black. The name was Frank Candle. Suzanne LaLonde, with dark brown hair, became Roxanne Trieste. Anastasia Viuda with her short black wig on was now Marisol Torres. Finally Gordon MacMaster became Brian Farnsworth.

The rechargeable drill was plugged into the power inverter at the cigarette lighter. A hundred miles later, they stopped in a rest stop on Interstate 55 and secured the lawn chairs to the bed of the van with conduit braces and sheet metal screws. That done, they plugged the cooler in and tossed the remaining perishables into it.

"Mack… I mean, uh… Brian, if I had known we were buying this cooler I would have kept the groceries we had."

"Don't worry about it, Marisol. I didn't know myself until I found this work van. The cooler wouldn't have fit in a car."

"Brian, do you think we should split up? Maybe we could escape easier as two couples than as four wanted felons. Now that we have ID, we could even go our separate ways." It seemed Suzanne was picking up the life naturally.

"We will need to split up, Roxy, but not yet. I think we got away clean, but I can't be sure."

Suzanne stuck her tongue between her lips as if tasting her new name. Roxanne had quickly become Roxy and though she thought it made her sound like a stripper, she knew she had no choice but to use the name.

Bull Bradley took the call the same day the accident occurred. Lawrence Terwilliger had one system dedicated to tracking the plate number, VIN and name of the owner of a certain red minivan. The flag went up as soon as the numbers were entered into the system.

"They are in Saint Louis. There was an accident. Gary McCormic still owns the van. Maria Alejandros was driving it.

She has a commercial driver's license, oddly enough. She used to drive a semi out of Salt Lake City. Unless I miss my guess, she is also is Anastasia Viuda. That is not her real name either but it's all we have."

"How do you know it's not her name?"

"Viuda means widow. It's not a name held by any Hispanic family I could find. I don't think a man would hold that name anyway."

"Widow? Okay. What else do we have?"

"The accident occurred as she was pulling out of a strip mall. Somebody knows something there. There is little reason for her to be in that parking lot. She was getting doughnuts, checking a mailbox or buying furniture. There is a restaurant there; she may have been eating, or she was getting her hair done. Her driver's license lists an apartment number in Salt Lake City, but I'm sure she's never lived there. I'm faxing you the accident report, with the other two vehicles and the owners' addresses. I expect there is something to be gleaned from them as well. Take this phone with you and I will call if anything else comes up. A red Chevy minivan with the side caved in and New Jersey plates should stick out even in Saint Louis. I'll be on the satellites looking for it. If I find it, we're in the money. If not, we'll have to press the witnesses."

"Why can't the Feds track this stuff?"

"They could if I worked for them. They have the whole country to watch, though. I'm focused on these men. Now I have work to do. You need to get moving."

Lawrence Terwilliger set down the receiver and fitted a filtered cigar into his cigarette holder.

A few phone calls and 45 minutes later Bull Bradley, Fred Pardoe, Bill Barry and Roger Rennick were in two Suburbans heading toward the Interstate.

Lawrence began searching the area where the minivan had been involved in an accident. It was a quarter to two and the traffic was just about to explode into rush hour.

"Where would you be, where would I be? A motel? No, too exposed. A long-term hotel." He took a puff on the cigarette and looked up extended stay hotels in Saint Louis. The majority of them were clustered around the west side of the city, north of Interstate 64, and east of Interstate 270. The map showed their general locations. He zoomed in and it showed their exact locations. Feeding the locations into the satellite vision system, he painstakingly examined each parking lot. The third lot he examined had a red minivan but it was not damaged as best he could tell. The fifth one had a red Chevy minivan with the side caved in. "Bingo," he said and reached for his cell phone. The van began to move and he dropped the phone in his haste to tag it. Once tagged, the system would follow it and he could watch it almost wherever it went. He retrieved the phone from the floor and dialed the number.

Bull Bradley was not driving; Fred Pardoe was behind the wheel. They were just getting on I45 toward Dallas. "Whatcha got, Lawrence?"

"The van is on the move. I'm tracking it. We have them now; they're in my sights. It's pay dirt as long as you do you job."

"I always do my job. Keep us on the right track and we'll bring 'em home."

Two and a half hours later, they got another call. Lawrence had caught the vehicle transfer. "This one isn't registered. It's a full-sized van, not a minivan. It had a logo on it at one time but that is spray painted over. It's a Chevy, gray or blue. It's hard to tell which. They are moving both vehicles together but I suspect they will be leaving the minivan somewhere. They are heading east. Where are you now?"

"We're a 150 miles north of where we were last time you talked to us. You got anything in that system to move us any faster?"

"No, unfortunately. I may be able to slow them down a

little but that would entail pulling another group into the mix. I can't have the police stop them or we lose our edge. You know what that means, no Lone Star for you."

"I been sober for a week. I been waiting on you."

"Just keep driving toward Saint Louis. I'll make sure you get to them; you make sure you get them."

"Roger that, Cap'n."

"I'll call in an hour."

Lawrence called an hour later to the minute. "They have indeed left their previous conveyance and are proceeding east on Interstate 55."

"Can't go east on 55, Lawrence. I55 goes north to Chicago."

"I can see that, Bull. I'm doing my part. You take care of yours'."

"Yeah. I tell you what, I'm gonna take a nap so I can drive later. Call me in four hours."

"Very well. Remember, this is dead or alive."

"That's easy for you to say. I prefer to bring my cows in still kickin' and let somebody else do the butcherin'."

Chapter Twenty
Lights

Michael Galliardo wished he had a gun. He'd get this little weasel into a nice quiet place and put one in his head. He couldn't do it in his hotel room, but there must be some deserted area suited to the task. Michael was not a murderer by nature and had never taken a life before. He had carried guns for a long time but never had to use them until recently. If he could be sure Jimmy Scott would take the payoff and not come back for more, he would simply pay him off, but extortionists were never satisfied with the initial payment. They would always come back for more.

James Scott wished he had a gun. Finding firearms in Grand Cayman was no easy task. The island produced nothing of its own. It imported everything and it did not import firearms. There was no hunting on the island so even shotguns were almost impossible to find. His mind was racing with possible scenarios. Killing Michael was not a realistic option unless he could get off the island before the body was found. Killing the goose that laid the golden egg did not fit his plans but if it became necessary he would have it done. This was something he had always contracted out before. He had been responsible for a few deaths over the years but they were all professional. Jimmy never did the wet work himself.

The sun beat down furiously, making the pair feel like they were in a foundry. The sweat that ran down their backs was more than just the heat though. They had reached another life altering point and the next hour would determine what the rest of their lives looked like.

The air conditioning in the high-class hotel was a welcome relief, bathing them in cool, dry currents. Neither of them said a word until they reached the room then Jimmy spoke softly. "This hotel is $800 a day. If you had come for a short payoff, you would not have checked in here. You pulled a jackpot."

"I managed to get a 150,000 bucks and I'm willing to share it with you. We'll split it right down the middle, but that's all there is. I'll be alright for a couple of months then I'm broke. I guarantee it."

Scott considered it for a second and then nodded his head. "All right. We split it down the middle and part friends. I think it would be a good idea to stay in touch. To keep each other updated on any indictments or subpoenas. It's not that I ever intend to testify, but I would like to know what's going on.

Michael opened the briefcase and separated the money into two piles. Neither of the men dared to turn their back on the other. The final bundle of cash was split in two and Michael looked Jimmy in the eye. "I will not put up with you coming back to me asking for more money. If you try to extort more money from me, I will take extreme measures. Do we understand each other?"

"Michael, I wouldn't do that. I just need a little grubstake to set myself up in a different business."

"Yeah, what sort of business did you have in mind?"

"I have friends back in the states that can set me up in some of their enterprises. This will be enough to get me established."

"Where were you thinking of going? New York is out of the question, now. You must realize that. I considered it but I can't go back there either." Galliardo watched as Scott picked up the cash.

"Boston, Washington, Atlanta. One of the major cities presents opportunities for an entrepreneur. I'll be all right. What were you thinking of doing?"

"Los Angeles. I know a man with a strip club there. He will let me take care of it for a modest sum and I'll be set up. Not like I was, but I'll survive."

Both men knew the other was lying to him but they were both consummate liars. Neither of them flinched, blinked or fidgeted.

As soon as James Scott entered the elevator, Michael Galliardo took the stairs. He watched through the window as Jimmy exited the hotel into the furnace heat of the tropical sun, then he slipped out after him. Michael was no expert on human nature but he could recognize the seedier segment of society. He was staying out of sight of his quarry and keeping an eye out for a likely candidate. Finally he saw one, a tall, beefy island native in ragged clothes. He was leaning against the stone railing that ran down the length of the road, smoking a cigarette.

"If you follow that man and find out where he is staying, I will pay you $500. If you get me the case he is carrying, I will pay you $5,000. Meet me in the Hard Rock Café."

"Ya, mon," was all the man said. He headed after the former bank president like a hunting dog.

Michael watched Daniel Terifon, his new island employee, until he was out of sight, then returned to the hotel. He packed his luggage and the remaining cash into his suitcase and called a cab for the airport. Seventy-five thousand dollars was a large sum of money for most people, but it was peanuts compared to the windfall he had just acquired. The setup was by no means foolproof but given the fact that the island's main industries were banking and tourism, it stood a good chance of ending the situation. Offering the native a large sum of money for the briefcase almost guaranteed that that he would never see the money again. More importantly, that he would never see James Scott again.

The airport was a disappointment. There were no flights to Mexico. Most of the planes were on their way to America. Flights to Europe all stopped in America first.

There was a flight to the Bahamas, however. It left in an hour and Michael Galliardo was on it.

Daniel Terifon followed the man in the business suit to a lower class hotel. It was not a dump by any means but it did not represent the upper class lodging available on the island. He watched as the man entered a 2nd floor room and noted the number. Terifon was not an affluent man. He made a sporadic living selling things to the tourists, doing tattoos, dealing drugs when he could get them and whatever means otherwise came his way. Five hundred dollars was not that much money in the Cayman Islands but $5,000 was a good payoff. More importantly, whatever was in that case was worth more than $5,000 or he would never have been offered such an amount.

The Hard Rock Café was half full of tourists but Daniel did not see the man who had offered him money for information. He could not have known the man was about to leave the island. Down the street was the house of a friend; one who had joined him in several sordid adventures. They had never gone so far as to kill someone before and Daniel steeled himself for the possibility they may have to. He hoped not since a quick snatch would work better without the repercussions. His Jamaican-raised friend Molee was all for breaking into the man's hotel room. Daniel scolded him for acting without thinking.

"This is how we do it, Molee. Keep some loose rags around our face like the PLO. We keep them around our necks until it is time and then put them up over our faces. You run at the man and pow! Knock him down wit' yer clothesline." Daniel slapped his left bicep. "Then, when he falls down we just take the case."

"Is dat simple, mon?"

"Yes, that simple."

"Den we do it, mon."

"Good."

"I man sure it not locked on him wrist?"

"The man didn't say so and I can't find dat man right now. He said he meet me in 'ard Rock. Maybe he mean later. I don't know wha's in that case but is not chicken feed."

"What if is just papers? He got some paperwork worth five t'ousan to him but nott'in to you?"

"I-man-I willing to take dat chance."

"Okay, mon. When we do dis ting?"

"We need to watch dis hotel room. If him come out without the case we go in and get it. If him come out wit' it, we steal it there. You gotta good point. Do you still have dem bolt cutters?"

"Ya, mon. I got dem loose pants an' hide em inside. The case on a chain we go snip snip." Molee's grin was infectious as usual. Daniel could never justify that Jamaica, whose economy was in the toilet and had been for years, had the happiest people. The formula didn't make sense to him.

They watched the hotel from down the street, taking turns, moving around. They did not want to alarm the guests or staff. Most of all they did not want the police to notice. A small town with a lot of banks necessitated a large, quickly mobile police force. The police in Georgetown knew every permanent resident of the town and knew their business. If the pair was spotted hanging around a hotel then whatever happened at that hotel would be blamed on them.

Inside the hotel room, James Scott was feeling abused. Seventy-five thousand dollars was chicken feed compared to the funds he was used to dealing with. It would keep him for a while on one of the less affluent islands and might even serve to set him up in a business of some sort, but it was nowhere near what he was used to. The authorities would be looking for him in New York. They might not have followed the money trail yet but they would. He had no idea that the trail ended at London. As far as he knew, the electronic transactions would be incriminating enough to land him in prison for the rest of his life. Worse than that, if the families of plague victims were to be set on his tail, he would be tortured to death.

He made up his mind that Santa Domingo would be the best destination for the time being. He started to call the airport and had a revelation. If he were to charter a boat to take him there he would have effectively disappeared. Examining a complimentary map of the island convinced James that the best bet for a discreet boat would be on the north side of the island by Rum Point, in Little Sound. He called for a taxi as the sun went down.

"Frank, we're going to need to pull over somewhere. I need some… feminine things. We need to stop at a drug store or a grocery store."

"Awright, luv. I'll take the next exit and see what we got." Gordon was driving and Terry was trying to sleep in the passenger seat. "Here we go. Looks like there's a Whale Mart down this way. Go down West Market Street and there's a motel next door."

"That'll work just fine. Ann… Uh, Marisol, would you like to go in with me?"

"Yes, I will go with you. I need some razors."

Gordon parked the van and left the engine running while they watched the ladies walk across the parking lot. Neither said a word until the ambulatory pair had disappeared from sight.

"Northern border, into Canada?" Terry asked.

"Aye. The way I see it, we can pass through Wisconsin then west to Minnesota or east through Michigan. There canna be many livin' up that way."

"By that token we might be standin' out. Sometimes bettah' lost in a crowd. This van don't really make it either. Seems like vans went out with the hippies. All the stylish fugitives use motor homes."

"Too big, can't maneuver in something that size."

"Only fooling, mate. I was thinking though, some inflatable mattresses might be a good idea and maybe some sleeping bags. I'm getting deathly sick of trying to sleep in a chair."

"Yeah. I like the idea. They probably sell 'em here. They sell everything else."

Terry scratched the blonde stubble on his chin thoughtfully. "I'll bet they have what we need, but if you look over there we have a sports store. The quality will be more acceptable there. Better to spend a couple extra pounds and get what we need than to go cheap and waste our money. I need to check the laws here but I don't think we can purchase weapons without a background check here. I feel stark naked without me pistols."

"Yer right, this time. We'll stop in there in the morning. Take a room here for the night. Did'ja notice where it is we are?"

"Normal. Normal, Illinois."

"Is that really the name?"

"Actually, Normal, Illinois is a couple of miles down the road. I think this is Bloominville or Bloominton or something close to that."

"All's good then. Normal."

A few more minutes and the ladies returned to the van. They went right next door to the motel and rented two rooms for the night. An hour later, all four of them were sleeping.

Morning came around with a heavy belt of fog. It was so thick the 82nd Airborne could have been waiting for them and hidden in it. It was chilly as well. Gordon and Anastasia took the van across the Whale Mart parking lot to the sports outlet. They were forced to wait a couple of minutes for the doors to be unlocked.

Inside, the couple picked up four sleeping bags, two air

mattresses, a 12-volt air pump and a foot pump. Sixteen pairs of wool socks joined the cart, four insulated shirts, four sets of long underwear, stocking caps, gloves, flares and an axe. The law in Illinois was such that guns could not be purchased without an instant background check and a waiting period so they eschewed the weapons temporarily.

"Looks like you're going camping. Going north are ya'?"

"Into the Dakotas," Gordon told the pimply, young cashier, with his best Southwest accent. "A little fly fishing an' some hunting. My uncle owns a ranch up there, pretty much on the north-south border. Needs some coyotes dusted off."

"Have you got a first aid kit?"

"That's a very good suggestion, young man. Marisol, could you grab a first aid kit for us?"

"Very good. I hope we won't need it but better safe than sorry."

"Ya know, I've got a perfect coyote gun right over here. If ya think ya need an extra, for the lady. A high velocity .223 with a scope. It's got almost no recoil, it's light as they come, got a carbon fiber stock. Dead nuts accurate."

"No, sir, I don't think so."

"Well, if you think you'll change your mind, I'll have one just like this for sale at the gun show tonight, at the armory. It's my personal weapon; I'm selling it real cheap. Of course I'll still need to do a background check but you won't need to wait to pick it up from the gun show." The clerk winked and started ringing up the sale.

With the camping items paid for and stowed, the pair went back across the parking lot to the motel.

"Frank, my love, how are we to move across the border without registering this vehicle?"

"We can't. We'll need to do that before we hit the border, but none of us live in this state so we cannot register it here. We can get a permit to move it but I don't think they honor that at the border.

"Marisol, get on the internet and research the gun laws for us. Unless I miss my guess, we can get guns in the northern states without too much trouble."

Anastasia was on the job immediately. "We should have gone somewhere else. Illinois does not hand out guns the way some of them will. We are sitting like ducks when we could have been armed."

"We could always rob a gun store," Suzanne said cheerfully.

"Way too high profile, luv." Terry was looking askance at his paramour. "The fires of 'ell come down when a gun store gets robbed. Much easier to pick one up where its legal to pack it in me pocket."

"Here. Indiana has no check at gun shows for personals... personal transfers," Anastasia reported.

"Used guns. Usually old, collector's items. Not really what I'm looking for. Hmm, I'm out of cigars."

"Let's go over to Whale Mart. We can get some cigars and some chocolate. I want some chocolate."

"Awright, luv. Let's walk." Terry and Suzanne left the room arm in arm and headed across the parking lot to the megastore.

Bull Bradley was driving when the phone rang. Fred Pardoe was sleeping in the middle row of seats. The rear row of seats was a custom job with rings set into the frame for handcuffs so it was not very comfortable.

"What's up, Law-rence."

"There's no need to be rude, Mr. Bradley."

"Yeah, sorry. What we got?"

"The subjects spent the night in the Bloomington-Normal area. They haven't left town yet. How close are you?"

"We're an hour south of Normal now. If they start to

move, give me a call. Otherwise I'll need to know where they are."

"We have Interstates 55, 74 and 39 intersecting right there. As soon as I know where they are going, I'll call."

"No, Lawrence. I want to know where they are right now."

"They're at the Whale Mart on Market Street, right off exit 137. They spent the night in the motel next door and they're shopping this morning.

"Good. That means they don't know we're on 'em. Keep up the good work. We're goin' ta town."

An hour later Fred called Colorado again. "They still there, Mr. Terwilliger?"

"Is this Mr. Pardoe?"

"Yeah."

"It seems they have returned to the motel. I cannot tell what rooms they rented because of the overhang and the fog. It does not look as though there are any back doors to the rooms, however. If you are unnoticed on the way in, it should be a simple extraction. The parking lot runs the length of the motel in the front, and there is access from the Whale Mart parking lot. You can block both sides of the parking lot so they can't drive out. You'll see the van. It's an old Chevrolet with no side windows or doors. It has a logo of some sort painted over with a spray can. Remember, these are professionals. They are undoubtedly armed. Surprise is your best weapon."

Bull grabbed the cell phone. "You did your part of the job, Lawrence. Don't tell us how to do ours."

"Four crème filled, four crullers, four maple glazed and four apple fritters. Oh!"

"Something wrong, miss?"

"Uh… no. Nothing wrong. Let me have four large cups of black coffee as well."

"Coming up."

Suzanne LaLonde put the doughnut box under her arm and carried the cardboard tray with the four cups of coffee back across the street but not toward the rooms they had rented. From the doughnut shop on the far side of the road she had seen something that disturbed her. Two Suburbans had entered the motel parking lot, one from each end. The front seats each held men that looked as though they belonged somewhere else and while one blocked the exit to the parking lot, the other parked right behind the van. Gordon had not parked the van in front of the rooms they had rented, it was parked four rooms down, eight parking spots.

Suzanne walked diagonally toward the paint store next to the motel, keeping an eye on the newcomers. Something was not right and it bothered her immensely. Three men stayed in their vehicles while the driver of the vehicle that was blocking the van got out. He was a large man dressed all in denim with his jeans stuffed into his knee-length boots.

Bull took the pictures of his quarry into the office and showed them to the check-in clerk. "These people are wanted for murder. I'm a licensed bounty hunter and I need to know what rooms they're in."

The clerk was happy to supply him with the information. This was the most exciting thing that had happened to him in years. He was quick to explain that the four did not look exactly like that but he was talking to Bull's back, Bull was already walking out the door.

The back doors of the Suburbans opened. Fred Pardoe slipped around the back of one with a ram. It was actually a cement filled post pounder. Pardoe was dressed all in black, with a black cowboy hat and a string tie. Bill Barry held the other ram. Where Fred was six foot, Bill was short and built like a brick. He had a full beard and was dressed in camouflage; his shirt had the arms cut off, combat boots covered his feet. Roger Rennick was in between, about 5' 10". He wore no shirt, just a leather vest and blue jeans. Tattoos covered both arms and his chest. Bull and Roger carried shotguns, Bill and Fred both had Smith and Wesson revolvers in shoulder holsters. They looked every bit as efficient as they were.

As quiet as ghosts, they took up positions on either side of the motel room doors. On Bull's finger signals they swung the rams and the doors burst open. The barrels of the shotguns were the first thing inside the doorways followed by screaming bounty hunters. Both men and a woman were in one of the rooms, the other room was empty. The occupants were caught flat-footed, peering into the screen of a laptop computer.

"Face down! Face down on the floor! Hands behind your backs! Nobody move! Let me see your hands! You, in the bathroom! Come out with your hands up!" All four men crowded into the occupied room yelling contradictory commands. Their quarry stood stock still with their hands in the air. "Quiet! Quiet! All three of you, lie on the bed with your hands behind your backs. Where's the other one?"

"There is no other one, mate. You got us."

"Shut up. There's another one; a blonde woman. Where is she?"

"We left her behind."

"You killed her, didn't you? You scum bucket!"

"We left her in Saint Louis."

"Shut up! Fred, cuff 'em. Bill, check the van."

"I'm telling you we left her in Saint Louis." Terry was the last to get handcuffed. Nobody noticed the paperclip between Gordon MacMaster's fingers.

Bill slipped out the door and around to the back of the van. He could not see through the windows because of the cloth draped over the grating on the inside. He opened the door carefully as far as he could. He couldn't open it all the way because of the vehicle parked behind it. First he stuck his pistol in, then his head. There was no one in the van. When he pulled his head back out he didn't have time to yell before he got a face full of lacquer thinner from a plastic squirt bottle. His finger tightened on the trigger and the bullet blew a large hole in the side of the van and shattered a window in the office. Then he collapsed as an unopened gallon of paint crashed down on his skull.

Two faces appeared in the motel room window and an arm holding a pistol snaked out the door followed by half a face. They could not see what had happened, but Fred spotted Bill's camouflage shirt on the ground behind the van.

"Come out with your hands up or I'm gonna shoot this woman," yelled Bull.

The only reply that came from the vicinity of the van was the smoke that suddenly billowed from the window of the Suburban.

"Shit! She torched my truck! I'm gonna kill that bitch."

Fred dropped to the ground looking for feet underneath the van. "She's not behind it. She must be in the van."

Bull smashed the window with the barrel of his shotgun and unloaded into the side of the van. Nothing happened. He fired again. Sirens began to sound in the distance.

"You three, on your feet, NOW!" Before the handcuffed trio had an opportunity to react, the glass in the rear of the room shattered and Roger Rennick screamed and collapsed, his hip was shattered by a .45 slug. The back wall of the room exploded as Bull and Fred returned fire with their shotguns. When they had all but destroyed the wall, Bull strode over and cursed again. They had hit nothing but wall. The field behind the motel was empty except for the chrome-plated Smith and Wesson lying just outside.

"She dropped the gun and ran around the side of the building. Get 'er." Bull turned around to see Fred running out the door to the left. He started following and stopped suddenly as the Milky Way suddenly blossomed behind his eyes. Gordon MacMaster had jimmied one side of the cuffs and planted the other side in the middle of Bull's forehead. By the time he could see straight, he was handcuffed himself.

At the end of the building, Fred had his knee in the middle of Suzanne's back and was trying to get her other wrist into the handcuffs. The butt end of the shotgun disabused him of that fantasy.

When the police pulled into the parking lot, they found a van filled with bullet holes, one Suburban burning like a torch and four bounty hunters in a sad state of disrepair. They blocked off the street but were forced to back off and wait as the fire reached the ordnance in the truck. Fred was able to get Bill Barry away from the burning vehicle before the boxes of shells caught fire and ruptured the fuel tank. Once the gas tank was compromised, the vehicle exploded. First the fumes went off like a bomb and then the liquid ignited everything around it. The fire spread to the sleeping bags in the van through the open back door, and the fire department, warned off by the police, let both vehicles burn.

The Illinois State Police were apprised of the fact that there was a stolen Suburban with Texas plates exiting the area. They assured the local constabulary they would be on it as soon as it entered one of the interstates.

"I told ya she had it, mate."

"Incredible. Suzie, we're in yer debt."

"Let's worry about this thing later," Anastasia said, biting her words off sharply. "We need to get rid of this truck."

Suzanne LaLonde sat in the back with Anastasia, her mouth hanging open and a glazed look in her eyes.

"Roxanne. Roxanne Trieste… Suzanne."

"Uh, yes uh, Ann, uh, Marisol… I'm sorry…"

"Do you think you can straighten up to take the handcuff keys and to free my hands?"

"Oh, of course." Taking the keys Gordon was holding out, she fumbled around with them until Anastasia was free then leaned over the front seat and freed Terry's hands as well.

"Quite a rush. Eh?"

"You have no idea. I never shot anyone before. Before today I hardly ever held a gun. I dropped it, you know. When I shot him, it jumped so bad I dropped it. It wasn't like the target pistols at the rod and gun club."

"Yeah. A .45 is no gun for a sheila. Kicks like a mule. We need to get you some practice, that's all."

"We need to get under cover," Gordon broke in. "Whoever's tracking us is using satellites. That crew came from Texas and pulled right in on us. That means we're still under surveillance."

"Take a left, Brian."

"State 150. This'll take us right back to the interstate. We won't make it 10 miles down the road."

"No. Right down here is Trucker's Lane. I saw it on the way in. On the right. Aye. Now, pull in one of these truck stops. Everybody out, stay undercover as much as ye can. Go inside and out the back way. Separate. Marisol, pick out a truck in the back and get the driver to open up. You know what to do then."

"You're betting the bank on a long shot, Frank." Anastasia had a grin on her face however. She knew exactly what to do. "Drop me off on the back row. Roxanne, come with me. I talk, you just standing with me and looking pretty."

Gordon MacMaster drove the Suburban around to the auto fuel aisle after dropping the girls off in the back. He and

Terry got out and went inside separately, Gordon stopped to buy a roll of aluminum foil as Terry exited at the truckers' entrance and walked into the back. They were 30 feet apart when they saw the headlights flash on a Peterbilt. They climbed inside and saw the driver handcuffed on the lower bunk. He was a small, wiry man with long hair and a beard. He had the most confused look on his face. Before they left Gordon climbed out on the catwalk and covered the Qualcomm antenna with several layers of aluminum foil. The yellow light for no signal showed on the console.

With Anastasia behind the wheel, they pulled back out.

Chapter Twenty-One
Launch

"'Ere 'im comin'"

"Ya, mon. 'Im gonna getta cab."

"We gotta get it afore 'im downstair." Molee started running. He was halfway up the stairs when Jimmy Scott was halfway down. His bare arm came out and as if it had been choreographed and rehearsed, Jimmy went head over heels.

Daniel Terifon was right behind Molee and gleefully grabbed the suitcase from Scott. "'Old 'im down," he said.

Since Jimmy was head down and face up on a set of stone steps he was easy to control.

Terifon unzipped the suitcase and a stack of American bills fell out. "Thar she blows," he said, stuffed the wad back into the suitcase and headed down the steps.

"'Ey, mon. Where you goin'?"

"I-man-I got it all. I-man gots to take care of dat man."

"Gots to do it all. Bombachek. Lie still, blood clot." Molee punched James Scott in the nose, once, hard. The results were predictable and Molee got up and ran after his partner in crime.

A well-dressed man got out of the taxi that had been waiting at the curb. Without a word he walked up to the bleeding wreck still trying to get on his feet. He grabbed the man's hair, pulled back his head and cut his throat with a straight razor. Without haste he waited until the gushing of the blood subsided a bit before releasing his victim and stepping around the crimson pool as best he could.

The following day Daniel Terifon and Molee were arrested for capital murder. As evidence, Daniel still had Jimmy Scott's suitcase full of money.

"I thought, sir, you would be interested in knowing that the President of the Hercules Bank and Investment

Corporation was found dead in Grand Cayman. Two locals have been arrested in connection with it. The prosecutors say they have an airtight case."

"Very good, Stephan. This Roman, Galliardo, was not retained in this?"

"No, sir. By the time the body was found, Michael Galliardo was already on a flight to the Bahamas."

"I assume he has been followed?"

"Yes, sir. I have no doubt he will be liquidated by the same agent within days."

"And the team that exposed the cure?"

"They are still hidden. As far as we know, they are still in America but they have not surfaced. They have not accessed the accounts in Switzerland and Bahamas. We may need to wait until they do this. They cannot remain hidden forever. If I might, it has been put forth to me that they may be the same team that delivered the plague."

"I don't think so. I don't think that team made it out of the Middle East. Has The Director called?"

"No, sir."

"Get him on the line."

"Yes, sir."

"Do we have men in place to monitor the account in Switzerland?"

"Yes, sir."

"Keep me apprised of any changes in status."

"Listen to me very carefully, driver. We do not want your load and we will not harm you. Is that clear?" The huge man with the stocking cap spoke slowly.

"Fuck you."

"No, sir. You are not getting the point. I will repeat myself. We do not care to take whatever you are hauling. It is yours to deliver, though it may be a little late. We also have no need to harm you. Have I expressed myself well enough for you?"

"You talk shit while I'm chained to my bunk. Let me free and we'll see who gets hurt."

"Marisol, you picked a live wire this time. I may need to kill him if he doesn't calm down."

"I'm sorry, I just wanted to drive this Peterbilt 13-speed. He happened to be here, with it."

"If we need to kill him, let me do it," Suzanne spoke up.

"I'm not sure we need to yet."

"I'll let you make that decision. But if he must die, I want to do it."

The driver had nothing more to say. When faced with a man he was all brass and machismo, but his entire attitude changed when faced with a petite young woman asking outright for his blood. He did not notice the huge grin on the lips of the tall brunette woman behind the wheel.

The citizen's band radio was useful for locating open weigh stations and finding speed traps, but there was less and less traffic as they headed northwest. Gordon alternated the driving task with Anastasia, two hours on and two off. The driver was left on the upper bunk, still locked to the handle. They pulled into a Love's Truck Stop once for some take-out from the restaurant and a gallon of oil. By that time, the driver had lost some of his spunk.

While Suzanne and Terry were getting food, Gordon tried talking to the driver again. "Now that you've calmed down a bit p'raps we can talk. I'm willing to pay you for the use of the truck. I have nothing against you except that you're rude. We have no plans to keep your load or to injure you and we will return the truck when we are done. I think $1,000 should be sufficient."

"Why didn't you say so? I would've taken care of you if you put it that way."

"I'm sorry but we cannot trust you. When we are

finished with the truck, we'll leave it and you at a truck stop
with the money. If you give us trouble between now and
then, I will let the lady practice her carving skills on you. She's
developed quite a taste for blood lately and I fear she won't
do it quickly."

"I gotta piss."

Gordon emptied the dregs of a quart bottle of orange
juice out the window and handed it to him. "That's the best
you'll get for now. We won't need the truck much longer."

Bull Bradley and Fred Pardoe were released from the
hospital at more or less the same time. Roger Rennick
required a much longer stay and would likely never walk the
same again. William Barry had a serious concussion and
severe damage to his eyes. It would be at least three days
before he could leave and quite a bit longer before he could
drive. The police had been satisfied with their credentials but
had issued them a number of tickets for firing weapons in
residential areas and reckless endangerment. Lawrence had
paid their fines by wire, and they had been released as long as
they committed to leaving town and not returning.

As they exited from the emergency room, they were
confronted by half a dozen swarthy men in very expensive
suits.

"Excuse me, sir," began the smallest of them, "I
believe we have a mutual interest in seeing certain individuals
brought to justice."

"You're shittin' me right?"

"No. I am as serious as a high tide."

"Get out o' my way. I got things ta do."

The two large men flanking the spokesman put their
hands inside their jackets. "I think," he continued "it would
be in your best interest to give us the time of day. We have
come a long way to take care of this little problem and our
employer is a generous man, but intractable in the face of

opposition."

"Where the fuck did you come from, asshole? I bet you're a Yankee."

"I am indeed a Yankee as you so colorfully put it. I am also a Guido, a Wop, a Guinea and a Dago. Or I am a Greaser if you prefer," He spoke slowly enunciating every syllable and becoming more and more serious. "I have also been called much worse, none of which I am eager to demonstrate. Now, for a man walking out of the Emergency Room, you have a very abrasive attitude. Perhaps you are disappointed they did not keep you longer. Perhaps you would like my less patient associates to give you reason to go back through those doors, though I cannot guarantee you will walk through them." The last three words were spoken as if they were each a sentence in themselves.

Bull took a second look at the men confronting him and decided he would choose the better part of valor. He needed a ride anyway.

A pair of men in a rented Hummer watched them as they walked into the parking garage, and then followed the 2 Cadillac limousines that pulled out shortly afterward.

While they were riding to the hotel, Bull's cell phone rang. He answered it "Hello, Mom," but it was taken from his hand at gunpoint.

"Mr. Bradley, I tracked Roger Rennick's SUV. It was deserted at the Petroleo station near the Interstate. I did not catch what vehicle they left in. The Suburban has been impounded... Mr. Bradley?"

"No, Mom, this is not Mr. Bradley. It is one of his new partners. Whatever services you have been providing for him you are now sharing with me as well. I assure you that remuneration in accordance with your services will be forthcoming."

"I see. Is Mr. Bradley still available for consultation?"

"I assure you we have no animosity toward your

somewhat crude associate and he will be released forthwith assuming he is of some assistance to us."

"I see. It seems we find ourselves in a forced alliance."

"I would prefer to think of it as an unanticipated collusion."

"Very well. I must say it is gratifying to work with an educated man for a change. While Mr. Bradley is usually extremely efficient at his chosen venue, his conversation often leaves something to be desired."

"I concur. It is my sincere desire that we will be able to work together amicably."

"What name should I address you by?"

"Just call me Sergio. I can call you Mom if you like."

"No, please address me as Lawrence. The Suburban in question is at the impound lot on Springfield Road in Bloomington. I don't know what good that information is to you. It was deserted at the Petroleo station on Trucker's Way, right off State Road 150, exit 137."

"It seems our alliance is to be beneficial to both of us. If you would be so kind as to call us with any further developments, we would appreciate it. I give you back to your former associate."

"Hey. Yeah, we got shanghaied. No, these guys look like real pros, I figure New York Mafia. I'll call ya back."

The spokesman turned to the driver and told him to turn around and head toward the entrance to the Interstate. They had not made it to the hotel.

At the Petroleo station, the limo pulled into the auto island and the short, dapper leader of the group went into the store and flashed a badge at them. "ATF agent Hicks. I need to ask you about the Chevy truck you had towed out of here a little while ago. Did you see any of the people who got out of that truck?"

"No, sir. I think Charlotte did."

"Is Charlotte still here?"

"Yes, sir. Just a minute. Charlotte! Get out here!"

A few seconds later, a tall heavy brunette came out of the back office.

"Charlotte? I need to ask you some questions about the people who were in the Chevy truck that was towed out of here. Can we go in the office?"

"Sure."

"You won't get in any trouble?"

"I'm the manager."

"Good. What do you know about the people who were in that truck?"

"First of all, Mister...?"

"Hicks, Agent Hicks."

"First of all, Agent Hicks, you can call a Suburban an SUV or a pickup but a truck has at least 10 wheels and pulls a trailer. I'd expect an ATF agent to know that."

"I hope you'll forgive me, Charlotte, I'm used to speaking with citizens who don't know that. Yes, it wasn't a truck, it was a Suburban."

"Okay. I don't know how many people were in that Suburban. The only one I saw was a big man who stopped on his way through to buy some tinfoil and walked out the back door. The truckers' door."

"Tinfoil. That's all he bought?"

"Yeah. That's all he bought."

"Do you have cameras, tapes of the last few hours?"

"Sure. Would you like to review them?"

"Yes, I would."

"Then go get a police officer or a real ATF agent or someone with the authority to request that. You are none of the above."

"I beg your pardon?"

"Oh, come on. You pull up in a limousine, wearing a thousand dollar silk suit and try to say you're with the ATF. Give me a break."

"You're very astute."

"Shit. A blind man could smell that you're not a fed."

"Actually, I'm with the Benjamins," he said reaching into his inside breast pocket and pulling out a billfold. He counted out five $100 bills, which Charlotte stuffed into her brassiere before leaving the office and closing the door behind her.

A couple of minutes later the manager returned with six videotapes. "Three cameras, six hours apiece. Don't bother with these three. Start with this one, it's the auto islands. There's a time stamp in the lower right corner so you get a time for when they pulled in. That way you can get a feel for what they pulled out in. I'll bring you a cup of coffee if you want and get some to your driver as well. If you need anything else just call."

Two hours later, the man exited the office with a sheet of notes and one question. "What did this man want the tinfoil for?"

"Who did you say you were with, sweetheart?"

This time there was no question. Sergio already had another Benjamin in the palm of his hand. It didn't see the light of day going between his hand and her bra.

"He wanted to mask the antenna for the Qualcomm and GPS. Covering the antenna prevents the company from knowing where the truck is. If he is late delivering the load, the company checks his location. If the antenna is masked, they can't find it. Some of the companies have antennas on their trailers as well. If they are not masked, they can track the truck that way, they just can't communicate."

"Thank you. It has been worth my time. Perhaps we could get another round of coffee now?"

"Help yourself. It's on the house."

Back in the limo, there were some calls to be made. The truck that pulled out with the fugitives in it was a distinctive Peterbilt. It had a lot of chrome pieces on it such as the flame-shaped exhaust stack, shrouds and a grill guard shaped like teeth. The trailer was light blue. There was only one company in the business that consistently painted its trailers light blue; Noah's Transport. The video was not good enough to pull off the license plate number but the truck itself was numbered 448597.

Noah's trucks were registered out of Oklahoma. The nearest terminals were Indianapolis, Indiana to the east and Des Moines, Iowa to the west. There was no terminal in Chicago though there probably should have been, given the volume of freight going through Chicago.

It took a long time for someone to answer the phone at the Indianapolis terminal, but a secretary finally answered.

"Hello," said Sergio. "One of your trucks was involved in a little accident. It's no big deal but I wanted to talk to the driver and he took off. All he did was bend the plastic on my fairing. Actually, he broke it away from the metal section. I'll need it replaced, but I wanted to talk to the driver to give him the opportunity to make it right without the insurance company getting involved."

"I'll transfer you to claims," said the obviously bored secretary

"No, please. Let me speak with dispatch."

"Okay."

The line went dead for a moment, then, "Larry."

"Hello, Larry. One of your trucks was involved in a little accident. It's no big deal but I wanted to talk to the driver and he took off. All he did was bend the plastic on my fairing. I'll need it replaced but I wanted to talk to the driver to give him the opportunity to make it right without involving the insurance people."

"What's the number of the truck?" came the sleepy reply.

"448597. He was in Bloomington, Illinois this morning."

"Give me a second. Okay, I'm sending him a message."

"Is there any way you can give me his phone number?"

"I'm sorry, I can't do that," replied dispatch, "but I can send him your number."

"All right, please do that, but don't be surprised if you can't get in touch with him. I saw him putting foil on his antenna."

"Oh. Okay. Thank you. Is there anything else I can do for you?"

"Yes, what is the trailer number he is hauling?"

"I'm sorry, I can't give you that information."

"You have it; you simply won't impart it to me?"

"That's correct. Is there anything else I can do for you?"

"No, I don't think so," Sergio finished, frustrated but not surprised.

Dialing another number got him through to Lawrence Terwilliger.

"Sergio?"

"Yes, Lawrence. I need to find a truck they have commandeered. It's a Noah's Transport truck, number 448597. I don't have a trailer number. Also, I think his antenna is blocked."

"Let me see what I can do for you. I'll call you back."

Twenty minutes later Sergio's phone rang. "I'm going to need you to call this number." Lawrence gave him the number. "They will probably not answer the phone, but it does not matter. I can pinpoint it when it goes to voice mail. Keep the connection open for as long as you can and I will get you a general position, a place for you to head toward."

As predicted, nobody answered the call and it went to voice mail. Sergio began to hum the Star Spangled Banner into the receiver aware that some phones will stop recording if there is a moment of dead air. He kept the connection open as long as it would stay active, then hung up.

"Sergio?"

"Yes."

"They are heading north out of Des Moines, Iowa. If they stay on Interstate 35, they will be in Minnesota in an hour, in Minneapolis in two-and-a-half. There is no possible way for you to catch them unless I have some of my Northern associates slow them down considerably. This may be no simple trick as they have proven themselves to be resourceful. We got lucky with the cell phone, this time. I imagine they have turned it off now to prevent us from playing that game again. I need to keep trying the trailer GPS. There may still be a way."

"I take it, then, that you have associates in the Minneapolis area that could potentially assist us in our present endeavor."

"Yes. Allow me to access their services and I will call you back when I know something concrete."

"Stephan, why am I not speaking with The Director right now?"

"I cannot say, sir. We have never been put on hold for an extended period of time before. It is his usual operating pattern to return our call the same day or early in the morning the following day. It has been two days since I put out the call and nothing has come back. No message, nothing. In fact, it has been about six weeks since we heard anything from our British associate. Would you like me to try again?"

"No. If he has changed operating patterns, there is a reason for it. He will call or he will not. He took too much risk to create this war chest. He will not desert it without good reason. Has there been anything from America?"

"No, sir. We are tapped into a variety of networks but nothing has surfaced."

"Tell them to keep on it. I want these assassins located and liquidated before the American authorities get a chance to question them. They have potentially damaging information we cannot afford to have disseminated.

"Have that new Indian woman cleaned up and sent to my chambers. I do not wish to be disturbed for two hours."

"Yes, sir."

Exactly two hours later, Stephan knocked on his employer's chamber door.

"Come in."

"Sir, we have news that the team we are interested in has been located in America. They managed to slip the American bounty hunters that were sent to capture them. They hospitalized two of the four. The FBI is on the job but all they have is the last known location: Bloomington, Illinois."

"How old is this information?"

"About four hours old."

"Good. Is there an airport near there?"

"Yes. There is an airport in Bloomington. Well, close to there. It is actually in the city of Normal."

"This is the name of the city, Normal?"

"Yes, sir."

"Four hours ago. This is good; they cannot be further than 400 kilometers away."

"Yes, sir, but our information does not tell us what direction."

"Does this airport accept international flights?"

"No, sir, it is too small."

"Then why did you mention it? What is your feeling? They were in New York City and now they are halfway across the country. Will they continue west?"

"No, sir. I think they will go south to Florida, hoping to get to Bahamas, or north to Canada. One of the bank accounts is in Bahamas. However, if they wanted to go to Florida, they would not have gone across the country; they would have gone south on one of the Interstates. They may have wanted to hide for a while but it would have been in Tennessee or Georgia. I think they are going to Canada."

"Why not stay in the United States?"

"They are being hunted in America. The bounty hunters almost got them today. I do not know how they located them, but they must have some extremely sophisticated assistance. The FBI does not know where they are but the bounty hunters did. They need to escape. Originally, I would have expected Mexico but there may have been a problem in that regard. I think the woman they have with them would have a problem getting across the border. Chicago is a large city. They may try to hide there for a while. I'm surprised they did not separate. It seems the team is still together, though."

"I want four men flying to Chicago today."

"Yes, sir."

"Do we have anyone in Chicago now?"

"Yes, sir, we have some American associates in Peoria, Illinois. I took the liberty of mobilizing them already. There are others in Chicago who could be mobilized until our people get there."

"Good. Call them. Have them track the bounty hunters. Under no circumstances do I expect to see these people taken alive. Is there any news from Bahamas?"

"No, sir."

"No matter. Keep me up to date if anything new comes in and have them prepare me a salad for lunch. All this meat is binding me up."

Five people makes for a very crowded cab. There is barely room for two on a bunk. By the end of their long day, the team needed a place to stop. Just south of the Minnesota border on Interstate 35 North, there is a rest stop. Gordon slid the truck into one of the parking spots. The ladies visited the washroom first. The men followed suit, freeing the driver so he could relieve himself. He did not attempt to get away or alert any of the other drivers parked there. That may have been due to the large chrome-plated Smith and Wesson Gordon had liberated on the way out of the motel.

"That's a proper attitude. I did not wish to have to bury you in the woods. Accept this as a token of my appreciation." Gordon held out a colorful bill.

"What the... What do I look like a currency exchange?"

"It's a British hundred pound note. It's worth a couple hundred dollars in exchange at any bank."

"I knew there was something wrong with the way you talk. I been all over this country and I can't place your accent. That's 'cause it's fake. You're English trying to fake Texas."

"It does no harm for you to know but I must warn you, there are people who want us dead, and so we are willing, individually and as a group, to take whatever steps are necessary, including killing strangers to keep from meeting these people."

"What did you do?"

"I imagine you saw the news about the cure for the plague?"

"You're full of shit!"

"No. We invaded Petroleo's World Headquarters and stole the cure from their vault."

"Take off your hat. Holy shit. Holy shit. It is you. I saw your picture on TV. Son-of-a-bitch, why didn't you say so? You're my fuckin' heroes. If I knew that, I would've driven you myself. Take this thing back, you don't need to pay me for this. It's my pleasure. What the fuck. Half the truckers in America would kiss you. Of course the other half wanna kill you."

The look on Gordon's face was befuddled.

"We been cryin' over the price o' diesel forever. Petroleo got it locked in and they're doin' us dirty for years.

Now your little piece jacked the price up even more, but it hurt the bastards. Damn. I wish I was there. You're my hero.

"Well, I appreciate that, but I insist on paying you for the service."

"Okay. I'll take it, but I'll never cash it in. Hey, can you sign it for me?"

"Sign it?"

"Yeah. You guys are like movie stars. Sign it with that felt tip."

"Capital. Remember we needed to be careful. There is no telling what sort of reception we will receive." Gordon was more uncomfortable with this reception than he had been with the outright aggression.

"Well ya got no problems here. Holy shit. You're celebrities. Like fuckin' movie stars."

"We're also wanted fugitives with a price on our heads."

"They ain't gonna find ya here. I'll be dipped in dog shit. Hey, you guys need another gun?"

"Max here could use a pistol. He doesn't feel right without one."

"The overhead on the driver's side. Reach around, the holster's velcro'd to the wall. I was waiting till I could get it and shoot the bunch of ya, but shit, this changes everything." Inside the cubbyhole was an HK Tactical. "She's a 40-caliber German beauty. Fiber reinforced frame. She holds 12 and 1 in the chamber. I had 'em stiffen up the action a little so it won't go off from banging around in the truck."

"Is this gun legally yours?"

"Sure, it was, but I just sold it to you for a dollar. So now it's yours."

"Well thank you. Please, call me Jerry, this is Max. Marisol and Suzanne."

"I'm Ralph."

"I think I speak for all of us when I say 'I'm pleased to

meet you, Ralph.'"

"You tell me where you want to go and I'll drive ya there."

"Where was the load supposed to go?"

"I was supposed to be in Chicago sometime after midnight. Ya wanna go ta Chicago? I can jump on 90 just north of here and be in Chicago right on time. This is a drop and hook so I'll just hook an empty and go. I'll call the office and tell 'em I'm takin' my 34-hour reset. With that much time, I can get you anywhere. I'll need ta fuel up though."

"That sounds like a plan. We didn't want to get you in trouble either but we had to get out of Normal."

"Hell, normal's one thing you ain't."

"We need to get a change of clothes before too long as well. We were forced to leave everything behind."

"You got no clothes in that bag?"

"No. That's not clothing."

"Well, the little warrior woman can wear my clothes. Suzanne, right? I got some clothes that'll fit her. The rest of you are shit outta luck. We can stop at a mall and pick up some stuff cheap if ya want. Get anything ya need in Chi-town. State Road 59 is nothing but stores."

"What are we waiting for?"

"Yee-haaa. Let's rock-n-roll." Ralph jumped into the driver's chair, adjusted his seat and mirrors and slid the transmission into gear. "Wait'll I tell the wife about this!"

Terry, Gordon and Anastasia all lay down in the back. Suzanne stayed in the passenger seat with the loaded German pistol in her purse. Both she and Ralph knew she was not going to shoot him while he was driving, but she felt better with it on hand. It would not have mattered any way since 45 minutes later the steady hum of the diesel engine had lulled her into a sense of security. Fifteen minutes after that she was sleeping like a baby.

Chapter Twenty-Two
Redline

Lawrence had phoned his contacts in Saint Paul and mobilized them. They were posted on the overpasses south of Minneapolis with binoculars, certain in the knowledge that the Noah's truck was coming their way. If their quarry had not been alerted, there was no other logical way for them to go. The Minnesota contingent would be disappointed.

One system was set to pick up Ralph Wingert's cell phone. One system was set to pick up his truck's Qualcomm. He had not been able to find the truck on his imaging system though he had tried for some time. The time they should have entered Minneapolis came and went and they were not spotted. Midnight came and went and they still were not seen. At two AM, the system set to Ralph's cell phone rang, waking Lawrence from where he had dozed in his chair. Ralph had called his home terminal to report that he had delivered his Chicago load and was out of hours for the week. He was going to take a 34-hour reset before picking up another load. He intended to stay at the I55 Truck Stop in Joliet, Illinois for the reset. Yes, he knew his Qualcomm was down, that's why he was calling. Lawrence did not intercept the conversation, just the location.

Hanging up the cell phone velcro'd to the dash, Ralph looked over at the woman sleeping in the passenger seat. He was feeling pretty damn slick. He had dropped the full load and located an empty trailer without waking any of his passengers. He did not expect to be able to hook the empty trailer without waking somebody up.

Gordon MacMaster woke when the fifth wheel slid under the empty. He tried not to wake Anastasia when he got up, but she awoke anyway. He pulled back the curtain as he was putting on his shirt and saw Ralph getting back into the cab after hooking up the empty.

"Morning, Ralph. Godawful. I used to stay awake for three days on end wiv' two hours sleep. I'm fallin' off the deep end now. How long?"

"Oh, you slept about four hours. I told you I was gonna take care of you."

"Right you are, but I couldn't have known I wouldn't wake up in chains."

"Gotta trust somebody sometime."

"Hah. It usually doesn't pay."

"Well, you got lucky this time. Look, we got a day and a half or two days before the company will even get suspicious. I could use a little nap but I'm gonna get us out of Metro Chicago first. Not that I don't trust your driving but I know where I am and you just woke up."

"We are on Harlem Avenue. Heading south." Anastasia's rich voice was half drowned by the engine as Ralph pulled away from the stop light. "The Tri-State Tollway breaks off here somewhere."

"Damn, woman, you really did drive truck. 'The Tri-State Tollway breaks off here somewhere.'" Ralph laughed. "I'm getting on 55 South before we hit the Tollway anyway, but that was a good call. There's a mall right off 55 at Lincoln. We can park there 'til they open in the morning or we can go to the I55 truck stop but at this time of night I doubt we can get a spot."

Gordon all but picked Suzanne up and shoved her into the top bunk. She only half woke as he did so.

"You did mention getting some clothes; is that still a priority?"

"I'm not sure it was a priority then."

"Well, that's the only reason I suggested the mall. I do need to fuel up though. I'll either need to use the Qualcomm or call the terminal. That is, unless you wanna pay for a couple tank fulls. That's about 900, or a thousand bucks."

"Well, I don't have that much in coin of the realm. I

need to get to a bank to exchange some currency."

"I won't pretend I understood what you just said, but I do understand a bank. They got one outside the mall. I55 is right here. No traffic this time of night. Sit back and relax. I got it all in control."

"Sergio."

"Sergio, they did not stay on I35. They turned off at some point and went to Chicago. Where are you now?"

"I am just north of Chicago on I94, heading north. We are passing a town named Gurnee. We are on a toll road."

"A toll road. Of course. I should have thought of that myself. Most of those trucks are equipped with transponders that allow them to weigh on the fly and pay tolls without stopping. It's all toll roads in the Chicago area. We will hoist them by their own petard. Turn around and go south if you would. I will get back with you in a moment."

Sergio told the man driving that he was to turn around and head south, then he called the other limousine to get their status. They were about thirty miles north of Des Moines. He instructed them to turn around as well but decided between the two that it was more expeditious to run down State Road 20 to I380 through Cedar Rapids. Sergio was adamant that they should stop on I80 before the split at Moline. His justification was that if the limo was going down I80 east while their objective was on I80 west they would miss each other. If the limo was on I80 and the truck came down I88 they would miss each other. After consulting the map, the driver determined he would pull off and park on a westbound entrance ramp the way the truckers do.

The phone rang as soon as he hung up. "Sergio. That truck is not on a toll road right now but I will know it as soon as it is. At four o'clock in the morning precisely, I want you to call the number I gave you before. I pinpointed him from the cell phone an hour ago and if he left it on, I'll do it again.

At this juncture it might be a good idea to let Bull Bradley have his reign. If I had more than one vehicle on the road, it would expedite our objective."

"I regret that I cannot accede to your request at this time. Your associate with the knee-high boots is constrained to remain where he is until I can be assured of the completion of my assignment."

At four o'clock precisely, Sergio rang the cell phone number he had called earlier. If it had been turned off, it would have gone directly to voice mail but it rang several times first. Once the time for a message had elapsed, Sergio called Lawrence Terwilliger's number again.

"Sergio, you are quite close now. The signal only moved 40 miles so they must have shut down somewhere."

"You cannot do better than that?"

"I regret that unless I can find the truck visually, I cannot provide you with an exact location. It does appear they are in Joliet, but there are a lot of other trucks in Joliet as well, many of them are Noah's Transport trucks. I cannot zoom in close enough to see the antenna or the numbers but if you see one with tinfoil on the antenna directly behind and above the cab, I think that will be our man."

"Very well, we will continue looking. Have you any suggestions?"

"There is a large truck stop near the confluence of I55 and I80. There's three Noah's Transport trucks in the parking lot that I can see, but all three have a signal. I would begin by looking there. I cannot tell if there is more than that until the sun comes up. After sunrise I can probably spot them, but not in the dark."

"Ralph, did you turn your cell phone back on?"

"Yessir. I had to. We're set for a day and a half now."

"Please turn it back off."

"What? How could anybody be looking for my cell

phone? They don't know you're with me."

"I don't know who knows what. I'd prefer to be safe than sorry. If we send any kind of a signal, I'd like it to be one we sent deliberately," Gordon insisted.

"Okay. I'll turn it off but I think you're being paranoid."

"It's a possibility, however stranger things have happened. Don't park in the mall parking lot. I feel exposed."

"Okay. I'll go north a little bit and park in a plaza."

"Can we park behind a plaza?"

"Sure. It's nice and dark behind the JCMax plaza. I'll pull in the dock if there's a door."

"That's a toad in the hole."

"Right, I guess."

As it turned out there was an empty door, so Ralph backed the truck into it. It would make a perfect disguise until the employees showed up in the morning. By the time the stores opened, five hours later, Ralph had pulled his truck back out of the dock and into the mall parking lot next to a branch of the Charisma Bank.

Gordon went into the bank to exchange some pound notes for greenbacks. Two days stubble on his face and a stocking cap along with the sleeveless jacket made him look somewhat like an indigent. He had not considered that the look would not go well with foreign currency and it might raise questions. As it was, they only allowed him to convert $500 because they couldn't check the British bills for authenticity. He was gently informed that there was a currency exchange at the airport and he should use its services upon arrival. He thanked the teller and left quickly.

"I'm afraid I did not take it into consideration. We may need to visit several banks or visit a real currency exchange before we can get any quantity of American currency."

"I'll tell you what. I'll drop the trailer on the backside of the mall and we can bobtail downtown. Or do you want to buy some clothes first?"

"Not here. Too many people in the mall. The bank is bad enough. The more people who see us the greater chance some bloody housewife is going to say 'Hey, I know that man!'"

"Boy, you sure are paranoid!" said Ralph.

"I need to be."

"Let me go in the bank, then. You know I'm not going to leave my truck behind."

"Let me consider this. Do you have a padlock?"

"Sure, an Enforcer Lock, but there's nothing in the trailer to steal."

"Let me see it. Oh, serious!"

"All the truckers have 'em. You can't get these at Whale Mart though. Gotta go through the terminal."

"Perfect. Lock it up."

"Sure. I tell you what, I got some people I want to meet you."

"I can't afford to meet anybody."

"Okay. But they sure would like to meet you."

Stephan was obviously feeling very slick. "The men from Peoria have called, sir. The bounty hunters have been picked up in a limousine. It looks as though they have a bearing. Our associates tagged the limo while it was at a gas station and have followed the signal to Chicago. They do not know why, but it turned around north of Chicago and headed back south again. The tracker they used has a limited range so we cannot pick it up by satellite, but our associates are right behind it. Our Chicago contingent has rendezvoused by telephone with these men and are waiting to act if need be." Stephan smoothed his collar.

"How soon will our men be in Chicago?"

"Their flight is expected to land in two hours."

"That soon?"

"Yes, sir. They flew out of Los Angeles."

"Good. Now why do the bounty hunters use a limousine?"

"That is unclear. Our contacts tell us that it looks as though the limo belongs to another group of hunters. It makes no sense to hunt from a limo but it seems as though that is what they are doing."

"Very well. Is there any way we can get a satellite image of the limousine if we have its address?"

"I have the crew working on that now. If they stop moving long enough to get a fix on them, we will get an image."

"If they get a feed, have them send the image to the television in my office."

"Yes, sir."

"One other thing, Stephan. The men from Poria, what manner of men are they?"

"Peoria, sir. They are licensed Private Investigators."

"And the men from Chicago?"

"A street gang called the Black Vikings. They are well connected and have proved to be ruthless. They have been alerted but not yet mobilized."

"Mobilize the street gang. You should have known to do that already. The investigators from Peoria might balk at liquidating the targets, but the Vikings sound more amenable to suggestion. I do not need to remind you that I do not want this crew taken alive."

"Yes, sir."

"Lawrence?"

"Sergio, have you found them?"

"I'm afraid they are not at the truck stop."

"That's what I was afraid of. The signal did come from that general area, however. I am still working on it. If you call the number again, I may get something."

Sergio called the number, but there was no response. The cell phone had been turned off.

"Sergio, we need to determine why they went to Chicago. They were heading to Minneapolis and then suddenly changed course and I think the driver delivered his load. Yes. That load was delivered. They may have changed vehicles on the interstate but that doesn't explain why the cell phone is turned off. We need to find that truck. If the four targets are not in that truck, then the driver knows where they are. This is assuming they allowed him to live. I must assume this to be so since the load was delivered. The targets would not have done that."

"So where do we look? Wait, let me back up momentarily. Does whoever is driving this truck know we are chasing them?"

"They know they are being chased but I cannot tell if they know we are so close. Do you have enough people with you to take five professionals?"

"I believe so. Beside myself I have two men of my own and two bounty hunters from Texas. Aside from their abrasive personalities, they seem to be professional enough. They do not, however, seem to have the spine to do what needs to be done."

"And that is?"

"Not a broadcast subject. Mr. Bradley tells us you can locate anyone. He calls you Santa Claus. So please find me that truck, Santa."

"I'll find it. Please put Mr. Bradley on if you would."

"Bull, are you all right?" It was unusual for Lawrence to address him as Bull and even more out of character to show any empathy.

"Yeah. They're treating us okay. I could use a beer and the cops got our guns, but we're okay."

"Good. I need you to start thinking. I know your brain rolls once you jump-start it. Why did they go to Chicago?"

"The driver delivered his load, right?"

"Yes. His load is listed as delivered."

"But he never called the cops, right?"

"I've located no such report."

"Then the truck driver has come over to their side or they delivered the load for him."

"Yes, but why? They would not have delivered his load for him."

"Have you watched any television lately? Petroleo got a shitload of bad press," Bull elaborated. "They had a cure for the plague and these guys jacked it out of 'em. We're talking about a trucker, someone sensitive to the price of oil. So... when the price of oil hit the roof because of the plague and Petroleo had the cure but didn't release it... how does that make people feel? How does that make truckers feel? They pump diesel two and three hundred gallons at a pop. It's their heaviest investment. So these guys might be shining lights to some of the truckers."

"Now I see. Thank you for that well reasoned and astutely put theory. You do surprise me from time to time. So, given that they have the good will of the diesel driving community, they could be anywhere by now."

"Yep. We need to find this truck driver and find out where they went."

"We are back where we started. We need to find this truck driver."

Once the Black Vikings were mobilized, their network connections expanded through the Chicago area. There was nowhere to hide in that area. It was a soldier of the Latin Kings who spotted the truck bobtailing north on State Road 59 between Naperville and Aurora. He called the local Prince and the Prince called Viking clubhouse. The calls went out from there.

First one then another, late '70s Oldsmobiles with tall

chrome wheels converged on the truck as it moved north.

"Lock your door, will you? I think we might be in for some trouble."

"Blimey, mate, what're you talking of?" Terry locked his door immediately, though he didn't recognize the danger.

"We got gang members all around us."

"What? In these old cars?"

"Yep. Once they stopped making Oldsmobiles, all the black gangs started buying 'em up. That model was the best selling car in America in 1978; the Cutlass Supreme. So they got lots to choose from and they're not real classics like the Camaros and Mustangs, so they can get 'em pretty cheap. I can't outrun the bastards, but if they try to stop me, I can fuck 'em up. They ain't too fuckin' smart but I think they know that."

"Let's just change direction," Gordon said from the bunk. "Get off this street and get away from them."

"Will do, boss." Ralph pulled the right hand turn without a turn signal and drifted through the tollbooth onto Interstate 88. The Oldsmobiles followed him. More pulled on at the next entrance. They were waiting on the shoulder as they went by.

"Yep. They're after us."

"How did they find us?"

"Dunno. That's not the real question. What do we do now? That's the question. They won't try to stop us on the expressway, I don't think, but we can't drive forever. I told you I needed to fuel up."

"How far can we drive?"

"Fifty, maybe seventy-five miles."

"So we can't outlast the wogs either."

"I've got an idea." Ralph grabbed the microphone of his CB radio and started broadcasting. "Break one nine, this is the Noah's bobtail heading east on 88 at the Naperville Road exit. I need some company. I got a bunch of four-wheel gang members trying to take me down."

The response was immediate. "Whad'ya do, driver?"

"I got Jerry and Max in the cab with me, y'know, the guys that hit Pertroleo? I think there's a price on their heads and these boys think they're gonna collect."

A chorus of disbelievers replied.

"Listen up, listen up. I got the men responsible for hittin' Pertroleo and bringin' the price of fuel down. They need help and I'm helping them. We got a dozen pimped out gang wagons around us and I'm gonna have ta start rammin' the bastards. I need some help. Max is sitting in the passenger seat, come alongside and you'll see 'im."

Interstate 88 is three lanes in each direction this close to the city. Ralph slowed down to about 50 miles-per-hour in the right-hand lane. The cars on his left side slowed down and the traffic began to back up behind them. At the Interstate 355 entrance, a truck pulled in front of them. He got on the CB "Break for the JB truck just pulled on 88 east from 355. This is the Noah's bobtail on yer back door."

"Go ahead, driver."

"I got a problem with these pimped out gang wagons. I got two men in this cab they want and I'll be damned if I'll give 'em up."

"How can I help, Noah?"

"I need some help making some space."

"Is that all? Yeah, we can do that. Johnny Reb, you catch that?"

"Pulling in behind ya'. Break fer Sister Sidewinder, that you comin' down the hammer lane?"

"Sure is, Johnny."

"Let's see if we can make some room here. These four wheelers are givin' Brother Noah a hard time. I think we oughta slow 'em down a little."

The truckers started pushing the gang cars around like

chessmen. More trucks joined the game and surrounded the Noah's truck. Moving over and slowing down, they cleared a path in front and blocked the traffic behind. Even the shoulder got blocked. Ralph had a clear lane and took it.

"Sergio, I have them. They just got on the I88 Tollway. Get on I55 North and stay on the phone. I'll let you know where they turn off." Lawrence was sounding bleary but excited.

The limousine was back on the interstate in no time, heading northeast.

"I've got the truck tagged. It dropped its trailer off somewhere, but it is the right truck. I knew they had to get on a toll road somewhere. Okay, they passed their first exit. Something is going on. They have an escort. They are still on I88. Something is happening though. There are cars waiting for them at the next exit. I don't know who they are but they're boxing the truck in. They may have paid a group for protection. I have you tagged as well. Keep going. We have them in our sights now.

"Something else is going on. I can't tell if… Yes, there are other trucks joining the group."

The line went dead for a little while, so Sergio set the speaker and set down the phone. When Lawrence's voice came back on, his tone had changed. "The trucks have formed a rolling barricade, slowing down the traffic. It looks as though they have trapped the previous escort behind them. They have slowed down the traffic behind them but the truck is still moving at speed and it has an escort. Not cars now, trucks. I may need to concede that Mr. Bradley was correct. I don't know exactly what happened but if I were to take a guess, I would say a rescue maneuver."

Bull spoke up at that point. "Truckers have gotten a bad rap for a long time, but there are a lot of good people out there behind the wheel."

"Yes, Mr. Bradley, and any time you ostracize a segment of society, that segment will band together into its own subgroup and develop its own subculture. Sociology 101. Please contain your respect and admiration and assist us in completing this assignment."

"Sure thing, Lawrence. It'll make good conversation for your next dinner party."

"Gotta say, mate, that was bloody smooth."

"That's the name of the game, Max. Smooth."

"I thought I needed to start shootin' but no such thing."

"Well, I hate to burst your bubble, but we're not out of this yet. We got gangs on us an' we're heading in the wrong direction. If we turn around, we lose our assistance."

"Worse than that, we're being tracked from the sky," Gordon interjected. "It's been fun Ralph, but I'm afraid we need to find an alternate means of transportation.

"Well, that ain't gonna be that tough, but goddamn it, you never did tell me where you wanted ta go."

Back on the CB, Ralph put out the broadcast that he needed someone to take a couple of VIP travelers. If anyone wanted to volunteer, the best place to facilitate the transfer would be at one of the overhead islands since they had no access from the surface roads. The overhead islands are a recent addition to the Chicago toll roads but they act as fueling stations with businesses built on what amounts to foot bridges over the expressways. There are no islands on I88, but there are some on I294.

"Ralph, I need to thank you for all you've done. We cannot afford a protracted adieu but be assured you have our lasting appreciation."

"It's been a pleasure and an honor. Now, when I pull off on this island, the two ladies can get to the other side. There is a Furio Logistics truck on the other side. Carla will get you out of the area. Carla's a good woman 'though she might talk yer ear off. The four of you can hook up later."

Gordon MacMaster grabbed his woman's hair and planted his mouth on hers. She kissed him back so strongly that he fell backward on the bunk.

"Sorry, guys, no time for that now." Ralph smirked, then he grabbed the microphone and thanked each of the trucks accompanying him individually before pulling onto the short steep exit ramp to the island.

Suzanne and Anastasia got out and went into the glass-walled overhead island.

"It doesn't matter now, they are already tracking us. We can pull the tinfoil if you want to get some fuel."

"No, no, no, it doesn't work that way. It shows up when and where I fuel. I'll get a guaranteed log violation for being here and we'd have to wait for them to authorize it."

"Pump in a 100 gallons, I'll pay for it."

Terry stood by the gasoline pumps as if he was with one of the cars. Gordon stood near the payment booth still wearing the sleeveless denim. Ralph pumped the diesel.

"Annie, Mary, whatever you want me to call you today, I need to visit the ladies room before I go any further." Suzanne had a pained expression on her face.

"Yes. I go to see if the truck is there. I should use the room as well." Anastasia walked over to the coffee counter and stood in line while staring out the other side of the island as surreptitiously as possible. When she reached the counter she purchased a small cup of coffee. She turned to look again and saw a truck pull away from in front of the Furio Logistics truck being fueled by a large woman dressed as a man. Anastasia walked into the bathroom where Suzanne was washing her hands. After they had both availed themselves of the facilities, Anastasia mapped out what she expected. She was nervous because the arrangements had been made over the CB. Anyone could be listening in. While it was true that few people had citizens band radios in their personal vehicles any more, it still represented a possibility.

Suzanne LaLonde stepped through the glass doors of the comfort stop with a cup of coffee in her left hand. Her purse was unsnapped and hanging from her left shoulder. Her right hand was under her left arm.

Anastasia Viuda walked through the same glass doors and directly toward the Furio Logistics truck where the driver was just finishing the fueling process.

Suzanne was not attracted to women ordinarily but she found herself fascinated by the grace of her accomplice. Anastasia walked across that lot like a hunting cat leaving a carcass; top of the food chain... untouchable. She walked up to the driver and smiled. The woman's mouth hung open with the same expression Suzanne had seen on so many drunken college boys and horny old corporate drones. Her reaction to that expression was usually "Shit, here we go again." This time she fought hard to swallow her grin.

"Crap, I'm watching the wrong thing," she thought. "I'm supposed to be watching for street gangs, cops, feds, Asshole Texans, and everybody else and here I am watching this woman."

Anastasia got in the passenger side of the cab and the driver got in the near side. She started up the truck and was about to put it in gear when Anastasia stopped her. Catching Suzanne's eye, she motioned her to join them. Quite consciously Suzanne stalked across the parking lot in emulation of her associate. She kept her eye trained on the driver and saw the open-mouthed stare again. The smile on Ms. LaLonde's face was genuine.

Chapter Twenty-Three
Chicago

"Shall we move along before we attract unwanted company?" Terry asked.

Gordon MacMaster was watching the entrance ramp closely, his hand inside his denim vest. He saw several vehicles that looked very much like the ones that had been shadowing them cruising north at high speed.

"Something is not running a straight line," said the Scotsman. "Those cars looked very much like the ones that were following us. If they had been tracking us by satellite, they would have known we were here but they did not. It's time for a little sleight of hand, so to speak. We need to get off the expressways and find a quiet spot to park, away from the regular public. I don't see much of that around here though."

"Jerry, the gangs are all over this city. Chances are they'll spot us before we clear the metro area." Ralph did not sound very confident.

"Is there any hope of making the next exit and hiding long enough to get this chrome off the truck?"

"We can try. Roxanne took the HK with her, right?"

"I had to let them have something. I still have this Smith and Wesson hand cannon but I'm short on rounds."

"Short on... Where the... I've got it. We can park behind a business I know. It's muddy back there but if we're buying, we can stay all day. They just changed the laws a coupl'a years back. Didn't use ta be able ta buy guns in Chicago."

At the next exit, they turned off into a busy retail section, then turned onto First Avenue. Half a mile down First, Ralph pulled behind a business that advertised guns and cigars. Terry shook his head and commented, "Only in America."

Terry went around to the front door and pushed the buzzer to be allowed entrance. Inside was a veritable smorgasbord of tobacco and firepower. He purchased a half dozen Churchill-sized cigars, two boxes of shells and a speed loader for the revolver. When he stepped out of the door, he felt naked and exposed, completely vulnerable. He walked around to the back and found Ralph with a pneumatic wrench attached to one of the truck's air lines. Both the chrome pieces from the exhaust were already off. He helped Ralph pull the hood forward to get to the brackets for the chrome teeth on the inside of the grill and looked around for his partner. Try as he might, he could not see him. There was a decrepit brick wall running behind the narrow dirt alley and a dumpster halfway down the building. Gordon was behind or in the dumpster, Terry was sure of it. The building itself had one barred window above the dumpster and a heavily-barred door between there and the corner.

Ralph finished removing the decorative teeth and put the chrome pieces inside the cab.

"Stephan. Stephan!"
"Yes, sir," came back through the intercom.
"You've slept long enough, you slug. Get out of bed."
"Yes, sir."
"I need to know the status of our targets."
"Give me a moment, sir."
"Tell the cooks 'eggs Florentine' and I want my coffee strong this morning. I am going to shower and I expect the report and my breakfast when I'm done.
"Yes, sir."
The shower was long and hot. A pretty little French girl toweled him off but he eschewed her other, more personal, services. His breakfast was served on a silver tea set with coffee, hot and black. Uncharacteristically, Vasilii called for a glass of orange juice as well.

"Stephan, report."

"Well, sir, our man in the Bahamas reports that he is having trouble finding his target. Michael Galliardo has found a warren to crawl into or has managed to leave the islands surreptitiously. He has not used his credit cards nor has he accessed the considerable fortune he deposited in the Cayman National Bank. He undoubtedly had some cash when he hopped islands but life is not cheap in the Bahamas. He will surface before long if he is still there and he will be liquidated at that point. It has been weeks since he flew there. He is certain to become comfortable soon and once he is, then we have him.

"The French are having a problem tooling up for the process. Their labor unions are objecting to extended shifts. The Germans will be on line within days. They will have a shipment to transport within a week. The Americans are right behind them, perhaps two days behind. They will be producing the cure as fast as they can.

"We are still shipping as fast as we can produce and will continue to do so. The bioengineers predict this plague will run its course by the end of the year if the current levels of containment are maintained. They say there will not be a living thing left alive within the plague zone."

Vasilii did not see the shudder which wracked Stephan's frame as he continued to report.

"In America, the Black Vikings found the truck but could not stop it. It escaped them an hour ago. Our men have reached the airport and are clearing customs now. The Investigators from Peoria are still following the limousine, which has started moving again. They have access to something we do not, I think. They started moving almost as soon as the Vikings reported that the truck had been sighted."

"So where is the truck, now?"

"They are not sure of its exact location, but it will never

make it out of Chicago. My personal feeling is that they will not last the day."

"I did not ask for your personal feeling. I do not pay you for your personal feelings. Get back in touch with the investigators. Tell them we will pay them an additional $100,000 apiece for these four individuals. And Stephan, make sure you stress alive or dead."

"Yes, sir, I can do that, sir, but I think I should point out that if they see financial gain they will possibly attempt to cut out the Chicago contingent. This may not be the most efficient method of operation."

"Those stupid blackamores had them and lost them, correct?"

"Yes, sir, but they were able to find them. They did not spend time following some limousine back and forth."

"Stephan, you are beginning to annoy me. Carry out your orders as given."

"Yes, sir." Stephan exited the chamber and made the phone call.

"Sergio?"

"Yes, Lawrence?"

"Take your next right. The truck has come to rest about half a mile down that road. You should be able to see it after you turn the corner."

"Take a right," he instructed the driver. "What side of the road?"

"It looks like the right side."

"I do not see it."

"Nevertheless it is down there. You just passed it."

"Stop. Right here. Back up." The limo stopped.

"Can't back up. Too many cars back there." The driver said.

"Then open the trunk."

The driver popped the trunk lid.

"Drive around the block and pick us up here. You two, out."

The four men exited the back of the limousine. Sergio and his associate went to the trunk and pulled two AK47s out then closed the lid.

Sergio turned to the two Texans and told them, "I give you your lives. If I ever see you again, I will shoot you without question."

Bull Bradley and Fred Pardoe looked at each other then turned and walked away, fuming silently.

The two Italians walked down the front of the Guns and Cigars building and turned into the small parking lot. The truck was not there. They walked through the parking lot and into the dirty area behind the building. There was the truck. The smaller of the two motioned his subordinate to open the door. As he moved forward, silent on the dirt, he heard the click of a hammer being drawn back, above and behind him.

"Drop the weapons," came from the same direction, galvanizing both men into action.

Sergio turned and ran back around the corner. His hapless subordinate turned his rifle around, searching for a target. He never got a round off.

The revolver exploded fire and lead from its business end. The gangster's skull also exploded as the round flattened and separated on one side and blew out the other like a water balloon.

Gordon MacMaster dropped flat onto the rooftop as a burst of bullets from Sergio's automatic strafed where he had been standing. By the time Gordon got a look into the parking lot, the expensive silk suit was rounding the building on the other side of the lot. He did not have enough time to get off the roof before Terry was racing across the same lot with the dead man's weapon in his hands. He stopped, aimed and then pointed at the sky, turned and ran to the back of the building.

By the time Terry reached the truck, Gordon was off the roof, and Ralph was in the driver's seat. The engine had never been shut off. Gordon was in the back and Terry was halfway through the door when the clutch was released. Dirt flew under the truck from the tandems as the tractor roared backward, and then flew behind them as Ralph jammed it into fourth gear. He barely slowed at the sidewalk, just enough to make sure he didn't broadside a Toyota and then they roared out onto the street. There was no gunfire from behind.

Two blocks down they passed a pair of very angry bounty hunters standing on the corner.

"Where the devil did they come from?" Terry asked.

"They were in the limo but they were not there by their own volition unless I miss my guess. The one that got away almost shot them from what I saw."

"That was slick. I thought you were in the dumpster."

"Always take the high ground when it's available. Ralph, we've got a problem. I don't know how they got a bead on this truck but it's being tracked. We need to get a different mode of transport. I don't know if they can see us so we need to get under cover."

"Sha... Sha... SHIT! You shot that... that guy. You blew his fuckin' brains all over the side of my goddamn truck." Ralph was shaking in a somewhat delayed reaction.

"Better he than you."

"But you shot him. Right in the head."

"Did you see him coming?" Terry broke in.

"Well, yeah, I caught him in the mirror. Hang on, sharp right. I saw him coming up behind."

"What did you think he was going to do with his weapon?"

"Fuck, I don't know, I thought he was FBI."

"Perhaps if they had been your Federal Bureau of Interrogation they might have arrested us but the FBI does not use Russian weapons. Second, they do not drive around in limousines. Third, they do not wear silk suits. We are in Chicago and their limo had New York plates on it. If you see it again, speak up, please."

"He looked like FBI to me."

"No, he was no federale. Given a list I'd say New York Mafia. They look a little silly outside New York in the limo and the silk suits. Way too cliché; they stick out like a pecker in a convent."

"I'm really sorry, gunshots kind of fuck me up. Tell me what to do. I can't keep driving around this city." Ralph was looking really bad; shaking and white he was sweating and his breath had a gurgle to it.

"We need to get undercover. I'll buy the truck from you but we need to dump it. It's no longer safe to drive."

"How ya gonna do that?"

"I think our primary concern is to be alive when the sun comes up tomorrow. We need to hide. We need to find a building that we can hide this truck in."

"Gary."

"Yes."

"No, Gary not Jerry. Gary, Indiana. We'll need to hit a toll road to get there but we can get off before the toll road starts in Indiana. The EZPass will click when we leave Illinois but it won't click again. It'll look like we took I94 into Michigan. I don't know if that'll help, but once we get to Gary, there's all kinds of train yards and abandoned steel mills. There's a terminal there too. I can drop the truck and just leave. I'll go back in a week and pick it up. Wait a minute, here's I290. I can get us there without hittin' the toll road after all. Hang on," he coughed as he cut off a Mitsubishi.

"This truck will not be safe to drive. Probably ever after. Terry, got any US bills?"

"Not much. A couple thousand. I thought I'd be gone long before this."

"Aye. Well, we need a different vehicle again. So let's have what you've got and drop me at an auto lot somewhere."

"I know a spot. Wait till we get across the border."

"What border?"

"Indiana border of course."

"Oh, right. Of course."

"Lawrence?"

"Sergio?"

"We ran into a little trouble."

"I assumed that when I saw the truck beginning to move again."

"I parted company with your southwestern associates. I assume they will be contacting you soon. I took the liberty of retaining this cell phone, however."

"Yes, they have contacted me already."

"I assume we still have an arrangement? Your former associates are now without transportation or firepower. They are dead in the water. If you wish to work with me, we can still finish this assignment."

"Very well. They dodged back and forth randomly but have just pulled onto I290 east. This is two miles ahead on your present heading."

"Good. I will call you back in five minutes."

Sergio hung up and called the number of the other limo. They were cruising across the state at a frightening rate. They had planned on turning off onto I55, but changed plans again as they headed east instead.

"I'm sorry to report that there has been a problem, Sir."

"What sort of problem, Stephan?"

"Well, sir, it seems the men in the limousine, the men from New York, dropped off the Texas bounty hunters and went after the truck themselves. One of them got his head removed. The limo is still trailing the truck, but the two bounty hunters are now in the company of the Private Investigators we retained from Peoria."

"Are they still following the limo?"

"Yes, sir, but as I predicted we offered them the generous bounty and they ceased to communicate with the Black Vikings."

"The Vikings have proven themselves to be useless. If by some chance they find the truck and acquire the target then we will pay them. If they do not they will get nothing. Tactfully communicate my disappointment to them, will you?"

"Yes, sir."

"Are we in Indiana already?"

"Yes, Boss. Gary's right up here. East Chicago, Hammond, Gary, the whole area took a hit when the steel industry went overseas. Then everybody was surprised when the steel from overseas was shit."

"What will your song be?" Terry Kingston was thinking aloud.

"What?"

"I knew a German man fond of asking 'What will your song be?' His way of saying if you don't do it right, no one will remember you even lived. Or they'll be cursing your name, I think. History sees only heroes and villains. What will your song be?"

"Whatever. I'll be taking a couple of real sharp turns under these bridges. There's a building of sorts over here. It's half demolished but they cleaned up the debris and left the other half standing. Somebody ran over the fence years ago but it was never repaired."

The building had brick walls and a steel roof. There was no insulation or inside walls, nothing but the bare Ibeams. It had been some sort of foundry or rolling plant. They would have had to vent the heat in the dead of winter from the look of it. The inside of the ceiling was blackened.

The truck fit inside. It would have fit inside with a trailer and another three could have parked next to it.

Terry got out without a word and walked to the other side of the far wall. Behind him was a fence and new growth trees twining their way through the wire. To the right of the building sat an empty lot paved with cinders and chunks of blacktop. It was sprouting some weeds but nothing much else until the fence between the sidewalk and the lot. It looked as though the lot got quite a bit of traffic. Terry walked a short way down the back of the building and urinated. It was obvious that the path had been created by people doing just that. The far side of the building was too close to the fence. The trees had sprouted up so there was no way through. Terry walked back around to the truck and told Ralph that there was no vantage point, that they would need to put some distance between themselves and the truck.

Ralph sighed deeply, handed Terry the nylon bag with the AK47 in it, locked up the truck and rested his hand on the fender for a second before the two of them walked away.

Under the bridges there was some cover. It was even deeper down the railroad tracks. There were spots where it looked as though children or homeless people had built little shelters. One spot had a good view of the building the truck was in, though they could not see the truck.

Terry turned on his cell phone and made sure it still had a charge. They had been leaving them off but plugging them in for a recharge when they had the opportunity.

The first vehicle to pull into the lot was a Cadillac Escalade with some black guys in the front seat. It pulled in close to the truck and the driver made a quick phone call. Then the SUV pulled out and was gone. The Cadillac limousine drove past the place twice before its occupants spotted the truck in the old shell of a building. They pulled in slowly, blocking the truck's exit but they did not exit the vehicle immediately. The tinted windows did not allow visual access to the interior.

The Hummer was less discreet in its entrance. It squealed around the corner and pounded over the curb grinding to a halt on the cinder-covered surface of the lot. Two private investigators from Peoria jumped out of the front seats with pistols in their hands. Bull Bradley and Fred Pardoe got out of the back seat with shotguns. There was little coordination with this new group. They were yelling contradictory commands at each other. Clearly there was no accepted leader and they were vying for the title among each other.

The second New York limousine that pulled into the lot made the same grand entrance the Hummer had. The difference was that the Italians who got out of the limousine were quieter, more restrained and much more professional looking. While the men with the shotguns were yelling at them to get back into the vehicle or suffer the consequences, the two men who got out quietly went to the trunk and got out their AK47s. The driver stayed in the limo.

The Mexican Standoff got even tenser when the two men in the first limo got out. The driver had a pistol in his hand; the passenger had an AK47. The men continued to yell at each other for a minute, neither group willing to concede an inch. Then Bull Bradley walked up to the driver's side window of the Peterbilt and smashed it out with the barrel of his shotgun. He got up on the step and unlocked the door then he stepped back, opened it and stepped inside. A moment later he showed his face again with the news that there was nobody in the truck. He reached over and opened the passenger side door.

The two groups might have found common ground and reached a consensus of opinion, except for the two carloads of black men that showed up at this point, alerted by the men in the Escalade. These men did not stop to ask the time of day; they simply opened fire on the men already in attendance. The fired-upon men, quite naturally, fired back.

The Oldsmobiles full of gang members screamed into the lot with their windows open. One pulled right along the side of the second limo, the other pulled left, behind the first one. Two men slithered out of each car while the four facing the building simply opened up directly from the windows. The first burst of rounds cut down one of the standing Italian men and the driver of the second limo. The return fire from the Italians killed both the driver and the passenger in the car that had pulled to the right. The two firing from the other Olds found themselves in direct line with two Texans holding shotguns. The devastation wreaked upon them would make them all but impossible to identify visually. Their faces were destroyed by the buckshot.

Everybody dove for cover but cover was hard to find. Two more Italians went down in the rain of bullets, but only one of them was hit by fire from the gang bangers; the other was shot by one of the private investigators. Unfortunately for the investigator, he had chosen to carry a 9mm pistol rather than something with a heftier load. As the gangster went down, he shot both of the investigators with most of a clip from his automatic. Neither of them ever got off the ground.

Sergio lay on the ground behind one of the limos and deftly strafed the ground under the jacked-up Oldsmobile in front of it. The shells all but cut the feet off the men using the car for cover. When they collapsed, he finished them.

Two remained cowering behind the other Olds. They were hiding in line with the axles so there was no easy shot. Sergio turned on the two men with shotguns hiding, now, behind the dormant semi. He cut Fred Pardoe down in a spray of blood and turned back to the gang members. He was a millisecond too slow and the slugs from a Glock perforated his chest on both sides. The air went out of his lungs and he lay gasping for breath that would never come.

A quarter mile down the railroad tracks, Ralph Wingert was doing his best to crawl underneath a pylon. Terry Kingston on the other hand was standing tall and grinning like a baboon. He had his own AK47, but he was outside the immediate kill zone. The shooting went on for only seconds and stopped abruptly. Terry took the safety off and set the rifle on full automatic. He could not understand what the men were saying, but they were obviously yelling at each other.

"Yo, Bloods, you don't get shit for shooting me. Everybody was here to get Max and Jerry and Suzie. They not here. The engine's still warm but the targets are gone," Bull Bradley was bellowing.

"Lyin' motherfucka. Tha's the truck; one'a these crackah's is pay dirt. Maybe is you."

"No. It's not me and it's not any of these Wops either. I'm here trying to make a buck but the sons-a-bitches blinded my cousin, shot my brother and ran off with my fuckin' truck. I'm hunting the bastards, just like you."

The sirens began to wail, not far away.

"We gotta go." The two men opened the doors to the cutlass. The driver pulled the dead man out of the driver's seat, but being a two-door, he didn't even attempt to take the man out of the back seat. The men jumped into the Olds and screamed into the street in reverse but ran into the vertical I-beam across the road in their hurry. The I-beam had a concrete barrel around the bottom and the bumper rode up on the barrel. When the driver put it back into drive, the drive wheel was off the ground. The engine was roaring and the axle was spinning but the auto was not moving. Swearing a blue streak, the driver jumped out of the bullet-riddled car. He didn't make it 50 feet before the blue and white police car ran up on him. He turned and fired straight through the windshield. The officer lost control. His foot went to the floor and he ran his attacker down. His partner jumped out of the passenger seat before the car crashed into the fence of the blood-soaked lot. As the officer stood up, the remaining gang member shot him three times.

The back bumpers on late seventies General Motors cars had the distinction of being attached by a large rubber block with no bolts running through it. This attempt at creating a better safety device led to the back bumpers falling off as the rubber dry rotted. The back bumper of the Olds hung up on the concrete was no exception. It supported the car for a few seconds but predictably tore off quickly. When the car fell, it was still in drive and the drive wheel ran over the standing gang banger's foot. He screamed and fell to the ground.

Bull Bradley was the final man moving in the lot. He dropped the shotgun, opting for the greater range and firepower of one of the AK47s lying next to a Cadillac. He moved around the torn fence and pointed it at the man lying on the sidewalk. "Freeze Asshole!" did not produce the requested effect.

The black man raised his pistol and fired in one motion, catching Bull in the abdomen. With a roar, the bounty hunter opened up and almost cut the man in half before collapsing.

Three more police cars roared up simultaneously and the officers leaped out screaming and pointing their guns. They did not see the two men hiding down the railroad tracks. They did not see them slipping further into the undergrowth and through a hole in the fence where the neighborhood kids had created a shortcut at the end of a dead-end road.

Terry Kingston left the rifle behind in the undergrowth. It gave him that naked feeling again. He was practically carrying Ralph until they got to the fence. Then he turned to him and hissed, "You are alive. Nobody has shot you. If you get yourself together and walk like a man down this street, you will survive. If you collapse right here, I will break your spine and leave your carcass for the dogs."

"I... uh... wow. Yes. I can walk. Let's go."

"If we get stopped, I will do the talking. Pretend you are drunk."

"Okay. I can do that."

Terry flipped open his cell phone and called Gordon MacMaster. He was mildly surprised that the call went through.

"Bloody 'ell, mate, you'll not believe what just went down."

"Where are you?"

"Are you mobile, mate?"

"Just finishing it up now."

"Okay. We need to get out of this neighborhood in a real hurry, but we're on foot. We're on Industrial Ave. 'eading north." Ralph grabbed Terry's arm and turned him around. "Oy, I guess we're 'eading south."

Ralph pointed to the end of the street where the Shaft Transportation sign indicated a company terminal.

"Meet us at the south end of Industrial Avenue, a Shaft Trucking lot." Terry closed the phone and picked up a brisk pace down the sidewalk.

Chapter Twenty-Four
Vasilii

"Stephan, come in here!"

"Good morning, sir."

"There had better be some good news this morning. Your track record is wearing thin. My little sister could have taken care of this situation by now."

"Undoubtedly, sir."

"I want eggs benedict this morning. I want three of those spicy little sausages. I want that coffee from Kenya, the light roast."

"Yes, sir."

"Have you taken care of that problem in Bahamas?"

"There is no word from the Caribbean."

"Have you taken care of the problem in Chicago?"

"That should have been taken care of last night. The investigators called and said they would have it taken care of, but they have not called back."

"What of the men you sent?"

"They are in the Four Seasons awaiting orders."

"And The Director; has he called back?"

"No, sir. We have heard nothing from The Director."

"So, you are telling me you don't know what is going on?"

"Without communication from our men, I am blind."

"Blind? You are a stupid, obsequious, little shit. Get away from me, and do not return until you know something."

"Yes, sir."

"Wait. I want you to arrange another shipment of our little disease. This time we simply mail an infected package to Iran. Your idea of having the British set up the deal sounded good to begin with, but turned into such a mess. Then you couldn't clean it up."

"Sir, are you sure you want to do this? If the package

gets halted on the way, it will be traced back to this area, if not to the company itself. We will need to mail it from elsewhere. You have made a fortune from it already and it has not been traced to you. It has not been traced to Waxmark. We are selling every dram of cure we can produce at usurious prices and there is no end in sight."

"Are you questioning my judgment?"

"No, sir."

"Then simply do as I ask and keep your mouth shut. You are right about the mail though. Mail it from elsewhere."

"Yes, sir."

"After breakfast, I want a woman. Have you gotten me any new women?"

"Yes, sir. A twelve-year-old Cambodian girl came in last night. I think she is a virgin."

"Fine. At least you're good for something."

Stephan left Vasilii's chambers in a somewhat foul humor.

While in Grand Cayman, Michael Galliardo had been careless and drunken. He had celebrated his good fortune with abandon but he was not stupid about it. The package from the hotel's safe would provide him with enough cash for a long time if he were judicious with it. The one thing that had slapped him in the face was James Scott simply walking up to him on the beach. James was no undercover agent or secret spy; he was no assassin. If he had been, Michael Galliardo would be in a pine box already.

Michael developed a healthy paranoia. He did not begin imagining unreasonable things such as famous people plotting his demise, but he did decide that his previous persona was something that needed to be set aside for a while. He did not rent a suite in one of the five-star hotels but went for a lower-end room. He hung up his suit and bought homemade clothes from the locals. He bought a number of head rags to cover his black hair and stopped shaving. The roads and beaches were too hot for bare feet but cheap sandals protected his soles. His physical appearance was easily changed by this swapping of accoutrements, but his attitude was much more challenging to adjust. Bahamas attitude was something that soaked every rock of the island and Michael attempted to soak it into himself. He bought a fishing pole and spent long days fishing from the shore for nothing in particular. He started hanging out with the locals, doing his best not to demonstrate how wealthy he was. He went so far as to soil his new clothes and not wash them for days. He would buy cheap rum and marijuana to share with the beach vendors and fishermen, immersing himself in the culture. He started calling himself Jamma. Developing a "No Problem" attitude was difficult, though. He had been born and bred in New York and battled his way into a respected position there. The hard driving atmosphere had developed a drive in him that was like the daily rush hour. Now he was trying not to be any such thing. He wanted to be a non-entity, a beach bum, unnoticed. He wanted to wait out the daily press, watch everybody else and do nothing himself.

Arthur Emmerich was anticipating good news today. He had not been getting much good news for the past couple of months. It had been his worst year since he was in Junior High and got caught with his head between the Music Teacher's legs, making her sing. He had never lived that down. It wouldn't have been so bad if she was a young thing, but she was past her prime and overweight as well. A couple of years afterward it had become a badge of honor, but it haunted him until tenth grade.

Arthur shook his head. Memories from that day and age should have been suppressed decades ago. He had expected Joe Barrancotta to call the night before, but there had been no such call. The Barracuda's crew had gone to the

Midwest as a sort of personal favor. Yes, the money was an incentive, but the New York Families did not like invading other territories without good reason. The Chicago Families could be every bit as vicious and uncompromising as their twentieth century bootlegging forebears, but were more discreet. They had been placated with promises of a piece of the action without having to take any action themselves.

The news came not in the form of a telephone call, but as a national broadcast on all the networks and news channels. There had been a huge gun battle where an officer had been killed along with at least a dozen other men. Details were sketchy as the police and the FBI attempted to determine who had been killed and why. It was tentatively labeled as a turf war but further reports would be released as information was gathered from the survivors.

Arthur knew things had just gone from bad to worse. He called his attorneys and had them send over a junior member to field calls and deflect the inevitable members of the press. Once it became public knowledge that the men had fought over the bounty, there would be questions he was not ready to answer. He thanked God he had the foresight to make that recording.

Suzanne LaLonde and Anastasia Viuda had managed to pull out of Chicago cleanly. Their new friend was very solicitous, claiming that she was doing so because she knew how difficult it was for women to escape a bad situation. It may have been because she was an open lesbian, or she may have been a lesbian because of bad situations she had been subjected to herself. In any case, she was not shy about it.

Bernice Roskoff had been driving her own truck cross country for 15 years and was well known along the I80/I90 corridor. Her handle was "Suicide Sally" which had nothing to do with her attitude, other than her willingness to take anything anywhere. It was a joke among many of the male drivers who knew her that it would be suicide to try anything with her as it was well known she carried a big gun.

Suicide Sally was as jovial as could be hoped for. She regaled her passengers with stories of burning out her brakes, jackknifing the truck on the ice in the Texas panhandle, driving through flooded roads in Mississippi and riots in Los Angeles. She told them stories with wildly humorous twists about the men she had duped and dumped half naked on the road. She told them of spending a week in Northern Canada when her fuel gelled and the truck stalled.

The truck, while running for Furio Logistics, was owned by Bernice Roskoff. It was a simple matter for her to find a load going south after delivering her present load. Anastasia did not ask to drive the truck, but she did swap stories about life on the road, enough to convince Bernice that she knew how to drive.

They drove Interstate 90 northwest out of Chicago and into Wisconsin. She was hauling paper towels and toilet paper to the Whale Mart Distribution Center in Fargo, North Dakota. On the way there, she called her Driver Manager at the dispatch center and asked about getting a load heading south. It turned out the Distribution center had a load of spring water and soda pop heading south, but it would not be ready until the following day. The passengers stayed behind the curtain while the trailer was unloaded, then they drove to a local hotel where Bernice rented a room with two king-sized beds.

Bernice dropped the trailer temporarily and went to get some supplies, leaving her new friends sitting on the beds in the room.

"Annie, we should get another room."

"Call me Marisol Torres, please. I remember you are Roxanne Trieste."

"Sorry. Marisol, do you think we should get a different room?"

"If you want, you can. I have no problem staying in this room."

"But you know she's a dyke. Even if I did swing that way, it's the wrong time of the month for me."

"If it looks like you should go somewhere, take a shower."

"You mean…"

"I mean nothing. There is no telling what might happen."

"What about uhh…"

"Brian?"

"Brian."

"He has no problem with this."

"But, I… I wouldn't do that to Frank."

"Right. Frank."

"He doesn't mind?"

"Roxanne, my man is secure with me. I will never sleep with another man unless I have to. I will never sleep with another man because I want to. A woman is no threat to him. A woman cannot give me what he gives me. He knows this. If I go with a woman he has no… hate for her. I will not share him with her. That is not right."

"Well then, what would you think if he went with a man?"

"He can do this thing. I do not think he will, but if he wanted to, he can. But he will not share me with another man. This thing I will not do."

"No. I don't think he would be interested." The pair caught each others' eye and held the gaze for a moment.

Anastasia uncoiled herself from the bed and stepped over to Suzanne. She pushed off the cap and wig, put her hands on both sides of Suzanne's stubbled head and kissed her full on the lips. "You and I can love each other some time, but if my man ever touches you, I will need to kill you both."

Suzanne sat without a word, reviewing what she had just heard, and breathing hard.

Bernice returned with whisky and soda; they got some ice from the machine in the hall and proceeded to get riotously drunk. All three passed out before midnight, still wearing their clothes.

"This piece of junk might have a few hundred miles left in it." Gordon was pulling out of the Shaft Trucking terminal in an old Chrysler. Terry Kingston was in the back seat and Ralph Wingert was in the front. "I bought it from a good looking young woman who looked down on her luck. We need to get out of town before we drop Ralph off."

"Bloody 'ell right, mate. It was half an hour after we parked the truck an' we had 'em all over us like crocodiles. I've not seen blood like that since Kazakhstan."

"How many?"

"There must have been twenty men all trying to kill each other. We had two limos, a Hummer and two of those things that were following us in Chicago."

"Cutlasses?"

"Tha's right. They all showed up one after another and then the Cutlasses showed up and everybody started shooting. The bronze showed up an' they got shot too. It's a really bad show and I want out of here in a hurry. We really planted a bad seed this time."

"We need to cook up a story for Ralph. He can't go back there and they'll be lookin' for 'im everywhere."

"Hell, I can handle myself," Ralph said. "I'll tell them you had me handcuffed in the back and I escaped. Put the cuffs on one arm and leave the other side free. I need a little practice getting them off me with a wire or something so when they ask to see it, I can do it."

"Problem is we left the cuffs in the truck."

"Oh. Well something along those lines. You're not

going to kill me too, are you?" the short driver asked with a half-smile.

"No, Ralph, we're not going to kill you." Gordon had a face of stone as he said this and it did not completely convince Ralph.

"We need to stay off the interstates. Keep moving until we can find a place to hide. Ralph, as much as we love you, we'll be dropping you off somewhere. It might not be the friendliest place. I hope this radio works."

The radio did work and the news was all about the massacre in Gary, Indiana. There was no attempt to correlate it with any of the three men; no official statements had been released. They took back roads and stopped in restaurants to eat. The sun went down as they hit Indianapolis on 35 south. Taking turns and driving the speed limit they drove all night. The old Chrysler kept on chugging away.

Suzanne was the first to awaken and get in the shower. She woke Anastasia who also took a shower. When Bernice had gotten into the shower, they called a cab to take them to the airport. They both wore hats and sunglasses. They left a note saying they would be back in 2 hours, but they never intended to return.

Security at the Hector International Airport in Fargo was not as discriminating as some of the larger cities and Suzanne had left the pistol behind. They had no luggage and their two forms of ID got them through the gate.

They flew to O'Hare but did not need to leave the terminal. They bought running pants and sweatshirts that proclaimed they were from Chicago then discarded the clothing they had been wearing. The next flight left an hour later and took them to Houston, Texas. They changed clothes again in Houston, opting for the same sort of identifying clothing. Anastasia told Suzanne to keep her mouth shut because the blonde could not manage a Texas accent to save her life.

They finally left the airport in Galveston and caught the shuttle bus to the cruise liner. Their cabins were waiting for them.

"This is the finest way I know to travel," Anastasia said.

"I've never taken a cruise before, Marisol."

"Wait until you see the ship. It's the finest way to travel there is."

"I wish they could have given me a different name. Roxanne Trieste sounds like such a ho."

"I'll call you Tomasina. If we get approached by any of the men on this ship, we are traveling together romantically. I do not want to throw some horny man over the rail because he does not understand English. It embarrasses them."

Suzanne LaLonde found that so amusing she laughed out loud and could not stop smiling every time she looked at her partner's face. She also found that Anastasia was right, there was no finer way to travel than on a cruise liner. They bought clothing at the commissary and at different ports of call, getting some luggage to carry it in. They bought coffee in Jamaica and jewelry in Haiti. The real surprise for Suzanne was when Anastasia went to the bank in Grand Cayman and withdrew a large bag of cash. There was no question when they got back on the ship. This sort of thing was not as unusual as might be expected.

Morning came around and Terry was driving. They had covered the entire length of Indiana and through Kentucky. There was a Noah's Transport terminal in Nashville, Tennessee.

"Okay, Ralph. I cannot express how helpful you have been, but this is as far as you go. There is one last thing I need for you to help us with. I need you to exchange some cash for us."

"Here in Nashville?"

"Yes. The laws are such that you cannot exchange too much foreign currency at a time. The taxman starts to get suspicious, so we need to be discreet. I need American cash and I intend to pay you for your services. You will rent a safety deposit box and that is where the bulk of the cash will be held; it will be in British pounds. This is very important; you cannot trade large sums of foreign currency at one time. If you get antsy and start playing with the money, the men who want us dead will hunt you down and torture you for information. Am I saying this clearly enough?"

"Yes. I can have the money, but I can't spend it."

"Not immediately and never at one time. You have been invaluable to us and I would not care to see you killed for it. In the UK, the law says 10,000 pounds will get your name sent to the National Criminal Intelligence Service. I think in the US it is $5000 in cash and the Internal Revenue Service gets your name. Now the immediate reason for these laws is the drug trade and as a trucker you might be immediately suspect. Am I correct?"

"Yeah, it might be a real concern."

"It is a real concern. A man can do what he wants but if he doesn't pay attention, he'll suffer. I'm guilty as any other. Here I've been carrying around all this foreign cash when I could have left it in an account and transferred money into a US account. Sometimes, though, cash is the only way to go. Do you have a preferred bank?"

"I've got a better idea. Take me to the YMCA."

"Where is it?" Terry wanted to know.

"I don't know, we'll need to look in a phone book. The YMCA will rent you a locker by the year if you are a member. The payment can be done automatically from your bank account."

Gordon looked him in the eye and said "Do not link your bank account to anything you don't want investigated, especially right now. The FBI will be into your business like a tapeworm. Don't make it easy on them. I like the YMCA idea. Not likely anyone will be trying to steal your towels and underwear but pay for it in cash."

"*Papi*, you called. You are safe?" Anastasia's relief made her drop her customary guard.

"Safe enough for today. Chicago turned into a rough churn. I'll be tossing this phone out or at least pulling the power. Where are you?"

"At sea."

"Miami?"

"Texas."

"Corpus Christi?"

"Galveston."

"Lisbon?"

"Oh, Si."

"Okay." Gordon hung up the phone and pulled the battery.

"What do you think, mate?" Terry asked. He was feeling better after a shower and a shave. He had re-dyed his hair black and shaved his face and arms.

"About him?"

"In the old days we would've killed 'im."

"I concur. We both got old and soft, yes?"

"Yes."

"Do you think he will wait?"

"I cannot say. I would have been happier just killing him." Terry looked grim and would have done the job immediately if Gordon had instructed him to.

"We didn't need to and he probably won't last a month after we're gone. If he does, he'll be a valuable asset."

"We never would have let 'im live in the old days, and I don't think I'll ever need him as an asset."

"I don't want to talk about it. I didn't want this job in

the first place and it turned into such a bollux."

"I only took the job because it was you asking. I was already retired. Regardless of which, it's time to split off."

"We hit the makeup shop first."

"Right-o, I need a beard."

"Both of us. I think I'll put on an eye patch this time."

"I'll be wearing sunglasses. Let's do this now. You have no idea how quickly the men came onto that truck. I had time to take a piss and that was about it. I don't know if they are on this one and I don't think they will be looking here for it but I do not want to be surprised again."

"No. We drive to the makeup shop and split up from there. A taxi to the airport and leave the country."

"What about the Russians? We never addressed those bastards." Grim would be an understatement when describing Terry's expression now.

"I have an idea that the worldwide production of the cure is well under way now. I am too tired and drawn to even consider another run at it. A letter to president Aahmed il Anahtirik will probably be all that is needed to shut down the Waxmark facilities. I'm going back into retirement."

"Sterling. Let's get out of here. We have other things pending."

The disguises worked perfectly. Gordon got a flight to Madrid and made his way by train to Lisbon. Terry got a flight to Barcelona and took a tour bus to Gibraltar where he deserted the tour and went back to Malaga. Suzanne LaLonde expected to be Roxanne Trieste forever and expected to be happier than she had ever been, living with her retired Australian in Spain. Anastasia Viuda was waiting in Lisbon when Gordon got there.

"Stephan, is the doctor here yet?"

"No. I never called him."

"What do you mean you never called him? I told you to

call him an hour ago. You imbecile, I feel like I'm dying."

"Yes, you are."

"What?"

"I've poisoned you."

"What?"

"Have you lost all faculties? I said I poisoned you. I have set myself up as your legal heir and executor and I have poisoned you. Before the end of the day, I will have burned this luxurious mansion, and I will be running your filthy empire from elsewhere."

"But... why?" Vasilii Ivanov Scarkovich crawled to the edge of the bed and vomited on the floor.

"Because you are the vilest, most disgusting creature I can imagine. My soul has been poisoned as surely as your body, and I will burn in whatever hell awaits me. You will meet me there. You will be there before me. I did not send the package you instructed for me to send. You have murdered too many already, and I could not let you live another day. The plague we sent to Iraq has run its course and left almost nothing alive in its wake. A blasted wasteland covered with the bones of the dead."

Vasilii tried to rise from his bed and fell on the floor clutching his chest. He was dying and he knew it. His assistant and number one confidant stood over him and watched him die. His last vision as the grey mantle of death enfolded him was Stephan spitting in his eye.

~~~